BLOOD VINE

AMBER BELLDENE

OMNIFIC PUBLISHING
DALLAS

Omnific Publishing
10000 North Central Expressway, Dallas, TX 75231
www.omnificpublishing.com

First Omnific eBook edition, January 2013
First Omnific trade paperback edition, January 2013

The characters and events in this book are fictitious.
Any similarity to real persons, living or dead,
is coincidental and not intended by the author.

Library of Congress Cataloguing-in-Publication Data

Belldene, Amber.
   Blood Vine / Amber Belldene – 1st ed.
   ISBN: 978-1-623420-04-8
   1. Romance — Fiction. 2. Paranormal — Romance.
   3. Vampires — Romance. 4. Vampire Hunter — Romance. I. Title

10 9 8 7 6 5 4 3 2 1

Cover Design by Micha Stone and Amy Brokaw
Interior Book Design by Coreen Montagna

Printed in the United States of America

For my mother, who is my constant inspiration

CHAPTER 1

The Hunter crouched close to the ground. As lights came on inside the house, a wall of windows gave him a perfect view of two figures. His breath hitched. The males were tall by human standards and they stood in what appeared to be a dining room. The dark-haired one was Andre Marasović. The blond must be the son. After nearly two centuries, his people had finally found the vampires. He wanted to laugh aloud, but that would be certain death.

He hid behind the trunk of a thick tree on the edge of the vineyard. An inky, moonless sky left him in complete darkness, but he didn't dare approach. He was there only to confirm. He took his phone out of his pocket and, careful not to let its light be seen, typed a message: "Marasović and son are here." As soon as he pressed send, his deeply bred instincts told him to attack, but alone, he was no match for the powerful creatures.

The wind shifted abruptly, and his stomach sank. He squeezed his eyes shut and whispered a silent prayer. *Please, don't let them smell me.*

When he opened his eyes, both figures faced him through the window. The vampires exchanged words and sprinted toward the door. Seconds later, another door slammed. The Hunter ran into the vineyard at full speed. Vines lashed his face as he hurled himself forward, hoping he had enough of a head start to reach his car. Shoes scuffed the dry earth in front and behind him. They had surrounded him with impossible speed.

Like a firecracker going off in his brain, he knew he was going to die.

To die on the Hunt was the greatest honor, though it offered little solace at the moment. That smug son of a bitch Ethan had been right—he shouldn't have come alone. Blood pounded in his ears. Would they make him watch while they ripped out his entrails?

One of the vampires called out to him from the darkness. "Hunter, don't they teach you to stand downwind?"

Words pressed against the lump in his throat.

"Too bad for you," the other said.

Then they were on him. One pushed him to the ground and placed a knee into his back. Dirt and dust filled his mouth, choking him, and he spit, trying to get the grit out. A hand gripped his shoulder and flipped him.

He looked up into the eyes of his target.

"It will have to be gory," said Andre Marasović. "If we do not make an example of him, they will think they've won."

"Can't have that," the son said.

"Kill him first. Then we will make our example."

Surprise was the last emotion to flutter through the Hunter's heart—a vampire had shown him mercy.

CHAPTER 2

Zoey Porter's feet were freezing as she stood on the polished concrete floor of Ethan's kitchen. Wearing only his dress shirt, she poured a cup of coffee and hoped the strong brew would warm her from the inside out. She tiptoed to the boxy white leather sofa, trying not to wake him. As she set her mug on the glass coffee table, her arm brushed against its metal frame and she shivered. The damn thing was even colder than the floor. She'd been in airports more comfortable than his stark, modern living room.

Her gray wool coat was draped over the back of the couch and she pulled it over her legs.

What the hell she was doing there? She'd sworn off Ethan a hundred times. Spending another night with him made her feel like a skipping record.

She had an early brief at the office, and then she could be on the road by ten a.m. If she hurried back to her place—

The sound of the water running in Ethan's bathroom warned her he was awake. When he appeared in the doorway, he ran his eyes over her and something like possessiveness flashed in them. Her hands closed over the fine cotton of his shirt, drawing the collar together. She should have gotten back into her own things, even if it meant squeezing into the snug blouse and slacks she'd worn yesterday.

Ethan wore black silk pajama bottoms that slid over his muscular thighs and revealed a growing erection. She did love his swimmer's shoulders and the way his square jaw made him look like an all-American athlete, but it was time to go. Too quickly, he was beside her on the couch. He kissed her temple, but didn't stop there. Her heart sped up a little as he licked her lips apart and cupped her breast.

That was how it always happened. Every night that Ethan invited her over, the heat of his body tempted her away from the empty bed waiting for her at home. But each time she woke up next to him, she would gladly give back every pleasure to be alone in her own apartment instead. And, if things went wrong between them, it could jeopardize her job, which was pretty much the only thing she cared about.

At least she had that new account waiting for her in Sonoma County. She was looking forward to it—the perfect chance to bury herself in work and escape Ethan at the same time.

"I need to go home and pack for my trip."

His broad-shouldered embrace pinned her against the couch, and she tensed as he kissed her earlobe.

"Ethan, I'm serious. I have to go. I should have packed last night."

"One of the advantages of sleeping with your boss is that he doesn't mind if you're late." He nuzzled her neck. "You're sexy when you're all business."

"Nice try." She made certain her tone invited no argument as she pushed his shoulders away. "And, Ethan, I'm always all business." She stood and headed to his bedroom to pull on day-old panties and wrinkled clothes. As soon as she was dressed, she left his high rise and headed back to her neighborhood.

Wisps of fog drifted down her street, and she shivered against the cold ocean wind. A classic summer day in San Francisco. A lonely leaf blew into the otherwise swept-clean entryway of her Victorian apartment building, which opened onto her steep stairway. Inside, she set down her purse and briefcase, kicked off her pumps, and picked up the mail. Shoes in one hand and junk mail in the other, she climbed upstairs with heavy legs. She could really use another two hours of sleep. At the top, she sorted through clothing and furniture catalogs.

A square green envelope dropped to the floor. Postmark: Nevada. Aunt Pearl. Eyes misting, she put the card down on her kitchen table, pressing it with her palm. She didn't need to open it. It would be Snoopy on his doghouse, and inside it would say, "Best wishes on your birthday." Every year since Michael had died it was the only birthday greeting she got. It was touching in a somewhere-a-stranger-remembers-me kind of way.

After a shower, she stood before the mirror on her closet door, wrapped in her towel, and looked closely at her face. Thirty-one, and it showed in the laugh lines at the edges of her eyes, from all the laughing she didn't do, and the tiny creases around her mouth.

She didn't mind. They were a badge of honor.

I've survived. Four years alone, and no more visits to the hospital, to boot.

If those signs of age and an ill-advised affair were the worst she had to show, then she was going to kick thirty-one's ass.

In the apartment below, the radio played some dance music. Her toe tapped to the beat.

She unwrapped her black wool skirt from its dry cleaner's plastic and slipped it on. The lining felt cool against her thighs, and she rubbed her legs together to enjoy the satin's softness as she peered into the closet. Running her finger over blouses in various shades of white, ivory, and gray, she picked one that looked crisp and professional, but comfortable enough for a car ride. As she pulled out the shirt, she stuck to her daily ritual and squeezed her eyes shut. She was always careful not to look behind the curtain of hanging clothes, to where the skeletons hid in her closet.

Finally, she held up two pairs of shoes. The pumps were better for kicking ass. But she was going to a winery, so the kitten heels were probably more practical. Plus, they were red and it was her birthday. So what if she wasn't having a party? Slipping them on, she clicked them together like Dorothy and headed for the door.

Zoey's secretary, Justine, handed her the Kaštel Estate Winery file and then poured her a cup of coffee. After a sip, Zoey said, "Thank you. I desperately need a second cup this morning."

Justine pulled her funky pink-striped reading glasses off and looked Zoey over with an odd smile. "I have a confession."

Zoey peered over her mug. They weren't friendly enough for confessions. "What's that?"

"I saw you leave with the big boss last night." Justine's grin was mischievous.

Zoey had been sure she and Ethan were the last ones in the office. She forced a smile. "You did?"

"Why are you sneaking around? He's nothing to be ashamed of."

"Because." Zoey set her mug down firmly. "It's no one's business but mine."

The clueless girl winked. "No prob, you can totally trust me."

The hairs raised on Zoey's neck, and she smoothed them down. It was nothing personal to Justine—she didn't really trust anyone. Armed with her coffee, she headed for the door, but Justine touched her shoulder.

"Have an awesome trip. A week in wine country sounds dreamy. Enjoy it."

Zoey nodded. It was a challenging project. Of course she would enjoy it. And she would kick its ass, just like she would kick thirty-one's.

She met Ethan and Lucas in the conference room. Ethan looked almost as good in his suit as he had out of it. Forcing herself to glance away, she took in Lucas's dark jeans and gray sweater. She never got used to how different the brothers were. Lucas was lean, carrying himself with a powerful feline grace, which was enhanced by his cat-like yellow eyes. They were the only feature he shared with Ethan. Lucas had told her once that their eye color was a Welsh trait, but she'd never seen irises like theirs, Welsh or otherwise.

At the moment, Lucas's eyes were bloodshot and too round. His fingers drummed against his thigh as he ran the other hand through his light brown hair. Too much coffee?

Ethan gestured for them to sit at one end of the long conference table. Once she was seated, she smoothed her skirt, waiting for him to begin. He liked to run meetings himself. His golden eyes rested on her a moment before he spoke.

"I want Lucas to fill you in before you leave for the Kaštel Estate. He can answer any questions you may have."

"I'm all ears," she said.

Lucas took a deep sip of his coffee and began. "I was in a tasting room a few weeks ago when I met the assistant winemaker for Kaštel Estate. His name is Pedro Torres."

A rare smile appeared on his face.

Ethan cleared his throat.

Lucas's lips pinched into a line before he continued. "He told me that Andre Maras acquired a large vineyard adjacent to their estate about ten years ago. He grafted some of his Croatian Zinfandel onto those vines and he's been nurturing them ever since. He plans to increase their production by thousands of cases and they hired us to oversee their re-branding."

"Let me guess. They want to maintain their high-end reputation while selling bargain bottles?" she asked. "That's not an easy thing to accomplish."

"Actually, that's not his goal," Ethan said. "I spoke to Maras by phone last week. He believes the wine is exceptional. He wants our help forging an entirely new brand around its unique characteristics."

"I read that in the file. But is there something unique about his wine?"

Lucas looked at Ethan before he answered. "I don't know. I haven't tasted it."

She gripped her file in irritation. Was there something they weren't telling her? "Well, it sounds simple enough. If the wine is really special, I'm sure we can give Maras what he's looking for."

"I'm not so sure," Ethan said. "Maras's expectations may be unreasonable."

She straightened her spine. He didn't usually anticipate failure. "Ethan, it's me. I'll succeed."

He held her gaze and nodded. "I have every confidence in you."

That was more like it. She always thrilled at the way they worked together seamlessly. If only it extended to his bedroom...she squeezed her thighs together at the memory of him. Oh, he could go through the motions perfectly, but there was no real connection.

Which was what she wanted.

Still, Ethan left her cold. Colder. She stood. "I'd like to get on the road."

Both men rose from their seats, and Lucas ducked out of the room. Ethan drew a little closer to her, but the glass walls of the conference room were her protection. He wouldn't want to be seen touching an employee.

"Don't let Maras get to you," he said.

Her skin broke out in goose bumps. It was definitely time to end things between them. She'd do it as soon as she came back from the job.

Glancing at the door, she said, "See you in a week."

To put distance between them, she hurried into the hallway and down the stairs into the parking garage. Excited to begin the project, she raced through the city streets, but just across the bridge, she had to screech to a stop. All her rushing was in vain. As far as she could see, orange traffic barrels blocked off an entire lane of the northbound highway. Oh well, it gave her time to think. Rolling her head from side to side, she stretched her neck, inhaled deeply, and settled comfortably into the car seat.

A car horn blasted in her ear. Next to her, the driver of a beat up green Honda spat out words that could only be spelled with four letters.

Poor guy, he obviously hadn't learned to cope with stressful situations. He just needed some simple breathing exercises, maybe a mantra or a visualization, and like her, he wouldn't get so wound up. She took a few deep breaths on his behalf and wished she could share some of her calm with him. There had been a time in her life when she felt that kind of stress and anxiety, but it was long behind her.

As she crossed into Sonoma County, the sun, perpetually hidden by fog in San Francisco, shone brightly through her moon roof. She was hot and her skirt stuck to her legs. Her armpits were getting damp too, so she cranked up the air conditioner. Great way to make a first impression. Perhaps she would keep her jacket on no matter how hot it was in Sonoma.

CHAPTER 3

Leaning over the sink, Andre Maras scraped his razor down his cheek. Gray flecks had appeared amongst his black stubble. He rinsed them into the basin, checked the mirror, and frowned at the unfamiliar image. He so rarely bothered with his reflection anymore that it was a shock. The silver hair glinting at his temples showed just how weak he had become. He finally looked the way he felt—tired and old.

Nearly two centuries had passed since the Hunters had run him out of Croatia. His health had remained stable, but clearly the wasting disease was progressing more quickly. It was only a matter of time before he shriveled up and died like a frail old human.

Stepping back from the mirror, he appraised his body. Biceps narrower, ribs jutting under his pectorals, quadriceps leaner. He turned, craning to see his glutes—hollow. He used to have an ass like a bull. He was not yet gaunt, but he had lost bulk, for certain. If he were not so bloody big to begin with, he would be skin and bones. Soon he would require sleep. And eventually, he would never wake up.

All around America, his old friends from the homeland were surely asking themselves the same question. By the gods of his father, he missed them, missed the old times. How many of them had already succumbed to the disease?

Maybe, just maybe, he could help them.

But he could not quite muster enough hope to believe it.

After dressing, he found his adopted son in the wine cellar.

"You look glum," Kos said, passing him a glass of wine. "This might cheer you up."

Andre recognized its earthy scent, the first vintage made with grapes from their new vineyards. As he swirled it in the glass, the acid-sweet aroma enveloped him. He took a sip.

"It's even better than it was four weeks ago," Kos said.

The liquid coated his tongue, causing him to pucker. The sugars hit his taste buds, and all the flavors came together harmoniously. He spit into the bucket resting on a nearby barrel. "It is better. The currant, the spice, the herbs—all the flavors are there now."

Kos took a sip. "I don't remember the texture being so dense. Was it really this thick on the tongue? It's like syrup; it's just like—"

"It was always like this. As thick as blood. I never thought I would taste it again." He needed the good news. Again, hope tried to rear its head, daring him to embrace it. Was it truly the same wine? And would it help?

Kos stared into his wine glass, probably wondering the same thing.

"Should we try it?" Andre asked.

"I really don't want to spend the day vomiting." Kos sniffed his wine, flicking his eyes over Andre's thinning body. "But I'm willing to risk it if you are."

To Andre, it was worth a day of painful dry heaving to know for certain. "Let's do it."

"Shall I take a picture, or something? To remember…if it works, I mean."

"Good God, no. Let's just get it over with," Andre replied, raising his glass. His only nod to sentiment was to add the traditional vampire toast. "To the homeland."

Kos lifted his in reply.

The wine was cool and watery. Clenching, his throat revolted. But he fought back the urge to gag. It was the first time in ages he had swallowed something besides blood.

Minutes passed, and when Kos spoke, Andre guessed he was trying to fill the silence.

"What do you think the chances are it will cure us?"

"Hell, I don't know." Andre pinched the bridge of his nose and closed his fatigued eyes for a second. "Nothing short of moving back to that Hunter-infested country will cure us, but maybe this will help. Anything is better than this slow death."

"I'll drink to that." Kos took another sip.

Was he as weak as Andre? Kos's eyes, the same blue-gray as his mother's, were sunk too deeply in his head. The bones of his shoulders were sharp under his button-down shirt. If he weren't so fair-haired, he would probably see gray on his temples too.

"You were a vampire for such a short time before the Hunters came," Andre said. "Do you even remember how strong the wine made us?"

"I remember, but I took it for granted. I was still growing stronger then. Every day I hoped I would fly."

The words were a lead weight in Andre's empty gut. He would give anything he had to take Kos back to Croatia, so he could attain his full strength and eventually fly.

"And," Kos said in a playful tone, "I was feeding more often than was strictly necessary." He flashed the smile all the Šoltan housemaids had loved. It had ensured he was always well fed.

Andre couldn't help but laugh at Kos's attempt to lighten the mood.

All at once, a warm energy built in his gut. It wasn't just the heat of his belly laugh. It was like being sated by blood, but better. Pure well-being radiated through his body like a small sun, just as it had in the old days, when he drank the wine of his homeland.

When the shock faded, Andre made his way to his office, checking barrels and the seals on wine bottles lining the brick wall of the cellar. Kos followed him in stunned silence. Andre sat down at his desk just as Lena knocked on the slightly ajar door and slipped in, giving him her toothy, eager-to-please smile. In spite of her undeniable beauty, he shied away.

"You wanted to feed?" she asked.

"Yes, thank you. Come over here."

She flushed pink at his command, and he tensed, annoyed.

He sat down in a large armchair and patted his knee. "Sit down."

She obeyed, leaning her back against his chest. Brushing her hair off her neck, he smelled her—clean and young and healthy. He hated being so close to her. Her body was shapely, but he did not want her. Not like that, anyway. A few sips of wine had done little to satisfy his hunger, and he needed her blood.

He tried to be friendly. "Were you picking lemons today?"

In the corner of Andre's vision, Kos turned away to examine a bookshelf.

Lena squirmed on his lap and sighed. "Yes, can you really smell them on me?"

"I can. What are you cooking with thyme and oregano?"

"A tomato sauce. Pedro brought me a flat of heirloom tomatoes from the farmers' market."

"Sounds delicious," he said, though he could not recall what food tasted like. Lightly, he caressed the pulse in her neck with his thumb. "Are you ready?"

She nodded.

His tongue touched the sharp points of his canine teeth. Saliva pooled in anticipation of a meal, and he sank his fangs into the tender flesh of her neck. She wriggled again and sighed with pleasure. Hot and salty, her blood tasted as it should. It filled him and began to pulse through his veins, relieving the gnawing ache of hunger. But it would not last long.

In spite of the beautiful woman, and the delicious blood, dark thoughts overtook him—feeding always reminded him that his exile was slowly killing him.

As he took another long swallow from Lena's vein, her hips began to rock a slow rhythm. She straddled one of his thighs, rubbing herself against him. Soon, Andre smelled the musk of her arousal and knew Kos would too.

It was so damn annoying that she always got turned on. He wished he could flip a switch and turn her right back off, wished he could just feed without making her want him. But that was how feeding worked. Sex and blood went hand in hand, at least for a normal vampire, one who was not broken, like him.

With one last draw on her neck, he retracted his fangs and licked the puncture wounds closed. He stilled her rocking with a firm grip on her hips.

Lena made a whimpering complaint.

"Thank you, Lena," he said. "I depend on your generosity."

She stood and crossed her arms. "It's my pleasure." Her pretty features settled into a pout.

Silly girl. He did not feel sorry for her. Straightening her clothes, she hurried out through the office door. He glanced at Kos and, as he expected, saw his son's eyes dilated with desire.

"You really pissed her off that time," Kos said. "I'm sure you got her hopes up, with all the talk of cooking."

Andre rolled his eyes. "I've told you before, if you want her, she's yours."

"Your castoffs aren't tempting." Kos sat down in the armchair across from Andre.

"If you say so."

"And more importantly, I don't think she'd take me. She wants you."

"I can't give her what she wants."

"Still, she expected all the intimacies when she accepted this position. Feeding from her without sex is cruel, although I know it's not your intention to hurt her."

What could he say? He just grunted. Kos always assumed the best of him. And he was right that Andre did not intend to hurt her. He just didn't want her.

He leaned his head against the high back of his armchair. No, he hadn't wanted a woman since his last visit to San Francisco more than a year ago. He used to frequent the bars where he could find a woman who did not want him to be kind or gentle. On a vinyl covered stool under a dim light, he would order a bourbon, and smell the sweet amber liquid as the women approached him. What they saw when they looked at him was a mystery, but they always approached. He was not picky—just looking for a woman whose eyes were as empty as he felt, and he would leave with the first one he saw every single time.

Andre would never use Lena or the other women in his household that way. It was his responsibility to protect them and provide for them. Throw sex in the mix and he would quickly feel like he had a handful of wives and all the accompanying annoyances. But even without sex, Lena was becoming a thorn in his side, and he would have to do something about her soon.

Thudding footsteps in the cellar distracted Andre from his frustrating thoughts. Those were Pedro's solid, human feet pounding the stone floor.

The man pushed the door open without formality and began speaking. "The woman from Bennett PR will be here any minute. Her secretary just called."

The spy. She would be on Andre's doorstep soon. He glanced around his shadowy cave of an office. It was where he felt safest. "Greet her out front and bring her here."

"Really?" Kos asked. "We could meet upstairs, in the daylight. Why did you bother installing the sun blocks if you spend all your time down here?"

"No. Here."

"No problem, boss. Do you want me to show her your coffins too?" Pedro asked.

His brilliant aquamarine eyes had that insubordinate glimmer, and Andre snorted in reply. There were no damn coffins, and he knew it.

With a smug grin, Pedro left to welcome their visitor.

Kos leaned forward over his knees, his voice quiet, although they were alone. "Do you plan to tell Pedro the whole story soon?"

"Soon," Andre replied. Kos's worried frown reflected Andre's own remorse. They had dragged Pedro into something larger than he understood. The smart-ass Spaniard had a way with grapes, and he had become like family since taking the job as Andre's assistant winemaker. He deserved to know the truth.

"I want to go on the record one last time to say this is a bad idea," Kos said. "Bringing her here is practically inviting the Hunters to be houseguests."

A wave of fatigue washed over Andre. Lena's blood was not strong enough to energize him for long. He slumped in the chair and kicked his feet up on the coffee table. "She's not a real Hunter," he said. "Their women are only for breeding."

"That makes me feel so much better." Kos leaned back and crossed his arms.

"We'll never reach the others without a public relations expert." In hindsight, his idea that all the Croatian vampires go into deep hiding had been a tremendous mistake. Now, he had no way to find them with this possible cure. "I owe it to them, Kos."

"So we need help, but it doesn't have to be from our enemy."

"Having her here affords us some protection. They won't set fire to a house with their own inside."

"Are you sure? They don't seem to mind slaughtering women and children."

No, he wasn't sure. He rubbed his eyes. "Kos, we can't flee. We drank the Šoltan vintage today. We drank. What if it makes us stronger?"

"But we agreed—never again, after what happened on Šolta," Kos said.

Squeezing his eyes shut, he saw kind old Magda, and that sweet maid, whom Kos had especially liked, beaten, used, and discarded on the front lawn. The blood curdled in Andre's stomach. No, he could not let that happen again. He tried to shrug out the knots in his shoulders. The whole damn world was resting on them, and he felt every pound.

"We will not let that happen again. But we need to see what they know first," he said. "And maybe Bel can help us. Do you know how to reach him?" It was a sad state of affairs that Andre had no idea how to find his younger son.

"Yes," Kos said. "He's got a satellite phone now. I'll call him. But promise me this—if we're in danger, we pack the whole household and we go. We forget about the wine."

His eyes flicked to the door. Outside, barrel after oak barrel of Croatian Zinfandel aged. To him, the possibility of a cure was the most important thing in the world. Almost. "Yes, you are right. We will not let anything happen to the household, Pedro included."

"If we have to go, it will be all right," Kos said, a little too fervently. "We've planned for this. There's plenty of money and a host of new identities. It won't be like the last time we ran."

In spite of his attempt at reassurance, they both knew that all those barrels of the Šoltan vintage in the cellar made it exactly like last time. Andre's gut knotted. They would lose all connection to their homeland once again. They would have to start all over…if they had the strength.

"Kos, you've done good work preparing for this scenario. Thank you."

Surprise registered on Kos's face for just an instant, and it saddened Andre. He should praise his son more. Kos had grown into a fine man over the last century, and his wise planning and investments had turned the estate's modest profits into a substantial fortune.

CHAPTER 4

Pedro backtracked through the dim, damp cellar on his way to greet the lady from Bennett PR. At the front door, he paused with a clammy hand on the knob. Like the entrance of a medieval castle, the huge door was rounded at its top and made of rough wooden planks. He puffed up, standing straight like a knight in Andre's service. Ms. Porter was on the other side, bringing some mysterious Bennett-related trouble. No matter how much he liked Lucas Bennett, his loyalty was with Andre.

Swinging open the door, he stepped into the bright, late-morning sun. The wet chill of the cellar burned off his skin in seconds, heating him to the bone. Or was it the thought of Lucas?

When he scanned the drive, there was no sign of the Porter woman.

She was probably friends with his yellow-eyed hottie. He'd only seen him that one time — strolling into the tasting room while Pedro manned the counter. His whisky-colored eyes were intriguing, so Pedro made a show of scanning his lean, powerful body.

Lucas returned the look, and the flirtation began. "How long have you worked here?"

"Oh, I don't. Just helping today. I'm the assistant winemaker."

Dark brows arched over golden eyes. "Really? Well, you make amazing wine. It's a favorite of mine."

A sincere compliment or a come-on? Pedro didn't care. It made him warm all over. "Thanks. What do you do?"

"I work in public relations. My brother has a firm."

That was good luck—Andre had a sudden need for PR help. "Have any wineries as clients?"

"A few. Why?"

He slid a legal pad across the bar, and tapped it with a pencil. "We need some PR. Give me the details, and I'll pass them along to the winemaker." With Lucas standing nearby, Pedro called Andre. "Hey, boss. I've got a lead for you."

"What do you mean?"

"Call Ethan Bennett at Bennett Public Relations. They might be a good fit for your branding project."

"Really?" The old guy sounded almost hopeful. "Give me the number. I'll call right now."

Pedro read it off.

When he ended the call, he found Lucas watching him.

Lucas tipped the last taste of his wine down his throat, his Adam's apple bobbing before he said, "Did you study winemaking in California?"

"No, in Argentina. I went to university there."

Lucas winked. *"Me encanta Buenos Aires."*

This guy made Pedro's head spin and his knees weak, like he'd downed a whole bottle of wine himself. *"Si? Yo tambien. Verdad, es un ciudad muy spectacular."* He poured a little more wine into the man's glass, brushing his fingers where they held the stem.

They shared their favorite spots in Argentina's capital, restaurants and gay bars, even museums.

"Well, I guess I should head back to the city," Lucas said.

Pedro reached across the counter and grabbed his wrist. "Not yet. I don't get down to San Francisco nearly often enough for me to let you walk away." When Lucas didn't pull back, Pedro dragged him into the office. In one motion, Lucas closed the door and pushed him against it. Lucas's kiss was hungry as he pushed his tongue deep in Pedro's mouth. Pedro's hands explored his muscled back. Lucas grew hard against his abdomen and pushed into him.

A bell jingled as the door to the tasting room opened and what sounded like a group of tourists milled in. Pedro tensed, and Lucas broke the kiss.

"Y'all open?" someone called out.

Pedro stifled his irritation at the interruption and cracked the office door. "Just a minute." Then he placed a more gentle kiss on Lucas's mouth. "Wait?"

Lucas shook his head. "I wish, but I've got to get back to the city."

Later that evening, when Pedro greeted Andre and Kos, they both bared their fangs and made a frightening, hissing growl. Pedro had never been scared of them before, but in that moment he nearly pissed himself.

"Who have you been with?" Andre shouted the question.

Pedro crossed his arms. "Excuse me?"

"You smell...like...someone," Kos said.

His slow, reasonable tone relaxed Pedro, and he grinned in spite of Andre's hostility. "I met a guy."

"Clearly," Andre said. "I can smell that he did not fuck you, but his scent is all over you. Who is he?"

"Jesus, you can smell when I've had sex? That is too—"

"Yes," Andre said. "We can smell things you cannot even imagine."

Pedro looked at Kos, who nodded, confirming the words.

"Now get to the point," Andre said.

"I met a man in the tasting—"

"I knew it," Kos said. "They found us."

Andre shook his head at Kos almost imperceptibly, but Pedro caught the gesture. What was going on?

"Tell us about him," said Andre.

"Nice guy. Hot. Unusual yellow eyes." Again the father and son exchanged glances. "I called you about his brother...Ethan Bennett."

"*Davo,*" Andre said.

Uh oh. He only used that ancient half-Latin, half-Slavic curse on the devil when he was really pissed.

Kos remained quiet, clearly concerned about whatever it was they were hiding.

"Did you call him?" Pedro asked.

"Worse. I hired him. He's sending his vice president in a few weeks."

"Call him back," Kos said. "Cancel."

In the silence that followed, Pedro could hear Andre's teeth grinding, which was saying something, since he didn't have vampire super hearing.

Finally, Andre said, "No, this is for the best."

Pedro had waited for Andre to say more. Nothing. Man, he'd wanted to know what they weren't telling him, but vampires had their secrets.

Pedro squinted into the morning sun, waiting for the PR lady to arrive. He still didn't know Andre's secrets, but without a doubt, it was best not to pursue Lucas, even if he didn't know why. His loyalty was with the Maras family no matter what.

As he expected, Ethan found Lucas waiting in his office.

"I just spoke to Stephen," Lucas said.

Ethan's eyelid twitched. It was irksome that Lucas insisted on calling their father by his first name—a useless rebellion. "What did Father say?"

"He wanted an update. He's got a small army ready to assault Kaštel at any moment. He's trigger happy, but I reminded him that Maras may lead us to the other vampires first."

"We can hope. Though, I'm sure they are exercising extreme caution after Owen showed up. Then you leave your scent all over that winemaker Torres. That was too sloppy, Lucas." He kept his tone neutral, but Lucas flinched anyway. Opening his desk, Ethan took out his gold handled dagger with the sun emblem on its hilt. He spun it on the desk, point down like a spinning top.

"You're right, it was sloppy. No doubt it put them on alert. But by sending in Zoey, we knew they would catch our scent eventually."

Ethan nodded. After a good long spin, the dagger toppled with a clunk. "As I said, I remain hopeful that she can gather information that will lead us to the other Croatian vampires." He picked up the dagger again.

"Do you think they will smell that she's sleeping with you?"

The dagger fumbled from his fingers, and for a moment it seemed it would crash onto the carpet. But he caught it. "I don't think it matters. Either way, if she smells like us, they won't trust her. They might even run. With Zoey there, we'll know if they are planning to flee. Any sign of flight, and we call in Father's soldiers."

Lucas leaned over the desk and dropped his voice to a whisper. "Do you think Maras will hurt her?"

Ethan polished the golden dagger against his knee. "I think he will do what they always do—try to seduce her, feed from her, and enslave her in his household."

Lucas leaned in another inch and his whisper became shrill. "So you're okay with Zoey becoming a vampire slave?"

The dagger glinted nicely when Ethan held it up to the light. "It won't happen. There's no way he could seduce her. Zoey's not the type to be wooed or used. She's as cold as ice." He liked her ice. It made her shiny and flawless like his golden blade.

"Zoey? She's a little reserved, but friendly enough once you get to know her."

It was fun to toy with Lucas. "She puts on a good show, but she's damaged."

Lucas sat back and crossed his arms. "Zoey? No she's not."

Ethan set the dagger down in front of him. "Trust me. I think it's because of what happened with her husband."

Lucas raised his eyebrows. "Zoey was married?"

"Yes. Several years ago."

"So she's divorced?"

This time he spun the dagger flat on his desk, like a compass. "No. He died in an accident."

"That's awful. What happened?"

"It's really not my place to tell you," he replied, as if Zoey had confided him. He wished she had, but perhaps that would come in time.

Lifting his eyes from the dagger resting on the desk, he caught Lucas watching him.

"Well, I hope she's safe up there," his brother said.

"She'll be fine. Zoey's always fine."

Careful to avoid smudges, he picked the gleaming blade up between his fingertips and set it into its velvet-lined case.

Between two low hills, Zoey caught a glimpse of the beautiful house nestled among the vineyards. Even from the front drive, the Kaštel Estate Winery was enchanting. Textured white stucco walls reached upward to the roof of Spanish tile. It was a picturesque Mediterranean villa, well suited to a family who'd emigrated from an island in the Adriatic Sea.

As soon as the entire house came into view, its large windows and old-fashioned door called to her invitingly. The white house and orderly flowerbeds were immaculate, but somehow it still looked lived-in, and she couldn't wait to see inside. She imagined walking up the front steps and putting her very own key in the lock. For the first time since she could remember, she wished she had a home, not just a place to sleep and store her things.

Thankfully, the troublesome feeling passed. But during her flight of fancy the car had come to a dead stop in the middle of the drive. Embarrassed, she scanned the façade for witnesses to her idiotic gaping.

In the circular drive, a stocky man waited for her to pull up. Dark brown hair draped across his brow and hung over his ears. She drove forward, rolled down her window, and extended her hand.

"I'm Zoey Porter."

"Pedro Torres." He shook her hand.

"Oh, yes, Lucas mentioned you," Zoey said.

His eyes crinkled at the edges, and Zoey couldn't help but grin as the dots connected. She'd been right. There was something different in Lucas's smile when he talked about Pedro.

"Pull in right over there, and I'll help you with your bags."

As she walked with Pedro through the front door, he handed her bag to a pretty blond woman wearing a kitchen apron. Was she a housekeeper of some sort? How old fashioned.

"I'll take you down to Andre's office," Pedro said. "It's in the cellar."

As Zoey followed Pedro down the stone stairs, she was thankful for the cool, moist air. She could comfortably leave her jacket on and avoid revealing her damp armpits.

CHAPTER 5

Andre and Kos both stood when Pedro opened the office door for Zoey Porter. She smelled of Hunter, though not as strongly as Pedro had the day he met Lucas Bennett. Still, the smell was enough to draw out Andre's fangs. He suppressed his growl.

As he clenched his fists and his jaw, working to control his predatory reaction, he observed Zoey Porter's feet. She wore feminine, red shoes with low heels. Her shapely calves ended where her narrow black skirt began, covering trim but strong thighs. Her hips curved gently, and her waist looked narrow. He wished he could see her breasts better under her jacket, and the rare desire surprised him. Andre had another surprise waiting for him as his gaze finally reached her face. Her mouth gaped, and her brown eyes were wide with recognition.

It was her. The beauty he had met more than a year back, the very last time he had gone to San Francisco. No, they hadn't really met. She had appeared next him at the bar and said, "I noticed you're not actually drinking that whiskey. Recovering alcoholic?"

"Something like that," Andre said, while turning toward her.

She'd taken the glass from him and swallowed it in one gulp. "Damn. That was a nice bourbon. I should have sipped it." She laughed.

Andre laughed too. "Yes, it's very nice. I enjoy the way it smells."

Her gaze roamed over him, but he didn't bother with the same full body perusal. He had seen what he was looking for in her eyes.

They were almond shaped and very dark brown. Behind their lovely color was absolutely no emotion.

"Please, have a seat," he said. He extended his hand and began to say, "I'm—"

"No names."

Andre's lips had twitched into a smile; that was how he liked it too. She'd climbed onto a barstool and propped one foot on the rung of his. Her tight black pants revealed perfectly shaped legs. Not that he really cared, he would probably only pull them down over her hips far enough to bend her over a table somewhere and take her from behind. He got hard thinking about it.

They sat quietly without looking at each other for several long minutes, and he indulged his fantasy a little longer. Her ass would be peachy soft, and she would clench around him, all hot and wet.

When the fantasy got too heated, he forced himself back into the present moment. It was oddly quiet. Normally, the women tried to talk him into leaving with promises like, "You can do anything you want to me, baby."

Finally, their eyes met. Had he thought hers were empty? Now they were full of something he couldn't name—a spark of recognition. Suddenly, her eyes said she knew things about him she could not possibly know. He did not want to be known like that. He looked at the scratched wooden surface of the bar.

She stood up and walked away.

"Wait," he said, and grabbed her arm roughly.

She did not flinch. "I'm leaving," she said. "This feels…" She waved her hand back and forth between them a few times. "Whatever this is, it's too much. I don't like it." She walked away in a hurry, heels clicking briskly on the floor.

Stunned, he watched her round, gorgeous ass until she went out the door. Once he got over the shock of the sudden connection and then separation, he was well and truly relieved she had the sense to leave when his own sense had abandoned him. Although, her good sense made her even more intriguing. A lot of women—hell, a lot of people—couldn't have walked away from a kindred spirit like that. Even if what they held in common was a desolate numbness.

Since that night, Andre could not shake off the memory of her. Sex had been a chore since his wife's death, and his wasting disease had diminished his lust for decades. But meeting her caused him to think about sex more frequently than he had in years, and it did not take much to trigger the fantasy of bending her over a table and driving into her.

No more trips to San Francisco; in spite of his desire, it was better to stay home. The wash of pleasure and pain that had come over him when she looked at him like she knew him — it had made him want to crawl in a hole and hide, and it had made him want to knock on every door in the city in search of her.

It took Zoey two seconds flat to realize that Andre Maras was the man who'd been haunting her dreams for more than a year. Had Ethan planned this?

Impossible — she'd never told him about her encounter with the stranger.

That night, she'd hoped for a few hours of invigorating distraction. She had walked into the barely lit club and immediately noticed a man seated on a stool, his broad back bent over the bar. The angle of his spine and the curve of his shoulders captivated her. What could burden a man like that? She leaned against a sticky wall by the entrance and watched him sit as still as a lion about to pounce. But he never did, even when a few attractive women approached. So she sat next to him. When their gazes met, his speckled green eyes bored right into the hollow place inside her.

She'd never regretted walking away, even if he appeared in her dreams almost every night.

In his office, he looked very much like he had in the bar. He'd worn an untucked, casual button-down shirt over dark jeans and black European-looking boots. He had a European accent to match, although he'd only spoken twenty words. Today he wore gray slacks and a crisp white shirt instead.

God, he was big — six feet four or five and stacked with the muscles of a warrior, the kind a man built with manual labor, not at the gym. His dark hair was clipped close to his head, but she could tell it would have a tight curl if he let it get longer. Just a sprinkling of gray showed at his temples. A prominent aquiline nose sat between his hazel eyes, and his olive skin was radiant. Though there was nothing pretty about him, his features came together in untamed perfection. She wasn't in the habit of thinking men beautiful, but he was.

As he examined her from toe to head, the heat of a blush followed his gaze. When his eyes finally reached her face, they opened in surprise. The spark between them ignited again, and her breath rushed out of her body.

Fuck, she thought. This is was last thing she needed.

Pedro and the other man chuckled. Great. Apparently, she'd said it out loud. The heat crawled up her neck and bloomed on her cheeks.

"I'm getting the feeling you two have met?" said the blond man.

She struggled to regain her composure. "Only in passing. We weren't properly introduced." Stepping forward, she extended her hand to the blond. "Zoey Porter."

"Kosjenic Maras, but please, call me Kos." They shook hands. "And this is my father, Andre."

Father? They looked to be about the same age, maybe thirty or thirty-five. How could he have a son that old? Maybe he wasn't as young as he looked. She turned back to examine him, only to notice he remained completely stunned to see her. Somehow, as huge and gorgeous as he was, he seemed vulnerable as he stared.

"Ms. Porter, can I get you something to drink? Coffee or water?" Pedro asked, as if trying to make up for Andre's silence.

"A glass of water would be great."

He walked over to a wet bar and filled a glass for her. Zoey noticed a decanter of something honey colored, probably more bourbon for Andre to sniff. She wouldn't mind a few fingers of that instead.

As if he heard her thoughts, Andre finally spoke. "Pedro, pour Ms. Porter some bourbon. One for yourself too. Can't have her drinking alone."

It would be professional to demur. Too bad. "Thank you. Kos, you don't drink either?" Kos looked surprised she knew that about his father.

"I don't care for spirits," he replied. "I prefer wine."

Taking her glass from Pedro, she said to all three men, "Please call me Zoey."

Andre gestured for them to be seated at four overstuffed, dark brown, leather armchairs around a coffee table. She liked the old world style of the office; it was comforting. The walls were the same brick as the wine cellar she had come through. A few large oil paintings hung on them. They showed quaint Mediterranean villages and Zoey guessed the scenes were of his native Croatia. Woven rugs added color in warm hues. His desk was clearly an antique, as were the floor lamps and some clunky brass sconces on the walls.

He looked longingly at his desk. Did the big boy want some protection? Surely she wasn't that scary.

Then he began to speak, and the impression of vulnerability vanished. "I assume Ethan Bennett has explained to you our goals for re-branding the wine from our new vineyard?"

"Yes, he explained all he could. But honestly, I don't understand what you're aiming for. I have a lot of questions."

"Certainly. Would you like to start with them now?"

"Actually, I'd like to begin with a tour of the estate."

"Ah, yes, a logical place to start. Pedro, would you give Ms. Porter a tour? Show her anything she's interested in."

It was funny that he wouldn't call her Zoey, but it was downright strange he didn't want to show her around himself, since the project seemed important to him. Why? Her toes twitched in her birthday shoes. Curiosity always made her jumpy, and she wanted to know everything about him.

Pedro as tour guide suited her fine, though. It would give her a chance to wrap her mind around this unsettling coincidence, and put up some defenses quickly. It was clear what she had to do — channel the curiosity into the project, and then get the hell away from him. Otherwise, she might shove Andre Maras to the ground and act out all her fantasies, whether he liked it or not.

CHAPTER 6

Andre took a deep breath when the door closed behind her. Kos waited for a few more moments before he said, "What the hell?"

Andre shrugged. "We met once in a bar."

Kos stood up and began to pace. "A bar? So, did you fuck her and then never call?"

"No, I did not fuck her. Nothing happened. We hardly spoke." Andre tried to stay calm. Since the moment he had recognized Ms. Porter, his heart had been trying to race right out of his chest. Best to keep that reaction from Kos.

"When was this?"

Andre sighed, trying to calm his nerves. He hoped he sounded impatient, not frayed. "I don't know. More than a year ago."

"That long?" Kos stopped mid-stride. "You were practically paralyzed with shock when she walked in. I've never seen you speechless like that."

"I never expected to see her again." He wiped his hand down his clean-shaven face.

Kos waited for more of an explanation.

"And I've thought about her a few times in the last year."

"I'm guessing those thoughts were not G-rated."

No. They were also not few.

Kos returned to his chair. "Back when you didn't fuck Zoey Porter, did she smell like Hunter? Because that's a turn off for me."

"Hell no."

"Well, you didn't fuck her, but a Hunter sure did."

"What? I didn't smell that." Instantly, he lost all the calm he had gained and his heart thudded insistently.

"Well, I did, when she shook my hand. It must be Ethan, given Lucas is Pedro's type."

Andre ground his teeth. He remembered that, when they spoke on the phone, Ethan had sounded rather possessive of her.

"Do you think she knows what they are? What we are?" Kos asked.

"I don't think so." Again, he wiped his hand down his face.

"Then what the hell are they trying to accomplish sending her here?" Kos asked.

"My best guess? They must know we smelled them on Pedro and they want to know why we haven't run yet."

Kos crossed his arms tightly as if he were cold. "I keep asking myself the same question."

"If we've found the cure, it's not just for us. It will help our old friends and all the other refugees from Šolta. That's why Ms. Porter is here—to help us reach them."

"You're right. But still, I have a very bad feeling about this," Kos said as he stood up to leave. At the door, he said over his shoulder, "Best to feed often while she's here. You were looking very hungry as you watched her walk out." He closed the door before Andre could reply.

Kos was right, he did need to eat more often to keep up his waning strength. But none of the women in his household—Susan, Ally, and the simpering Lena—seemed nearly as appetizing as Zoey. His body had finally calmed down, but a sinking feeling in his gut replaced the initial shock. The spark between them could seriously complicate his plans.

CHAPTER 7

Once she settled into her room, Zoey changed into a cool linen dress and spent the afternoon with Pedro touring the estate. He told Zoey the house was a replica of the Maras family home on the Island of Šolta in the Adriatic Sea. It was full of antiques, but Pedro said they were not original to the home on Šolta. That home and all its furnishings had been destroyed in a fire.

"I have a lot of questions," Zoey said. "I looked at the winery's website, but it's…"

"Lousy?" Pedro asked.

She laughed. "I wasn't going to say that."

"But it's true — it's homegrown and out of date. That's why we need you."

She pitied the man that tried to resist his charm. "Where does the name Kaštel come from?"

"It's a shortened form of the Croatian name for the Zinfandel grape, Crljenak Kaštelanski," he replied, with impressive pronunciation. "Zinfandel originated on the Dalmatian Coast of Croatia. There's a legend that the Maras family were the first to cultivate it."

"A legend? That should definitely be on your website."

Lining the walls of the foyer, watercolors in vibrant shades captured the blues and greens of the Adriatic shore.

"According to Andre, the Maras family made wine there for centuries."

"I've been wondering about that. The Kaštel Estate was founded in the late nineteenth century, so there have been Maras winemakers here for more than a hundred years. Yet Kos and Andre both have accents, I assume Croatian ones. Were they born here or there?"

"I am not entirely clear on the family history. You'll have to ask Andre that one." He winked at her.

No doubt about it, he had evaded her question. Apparently, she would have to ask Andre herself. Suddenly, insects far larger than butterflies flapped their wings in her stomach. She couldn't remember the last time she had felt nervous, and she didn't like it.

When the sun was no longer overhead, Pedro led her outside into the vineyards.

"Does Kos live here?" Zoey asked.

"Yes, mostly. He also has a cabin out on the coast. He and Andre are close, but he escapes out there when they butt heads."

"Kos doesn't seem much younger than Andre. I was surprised when he introduced himself as Andre's son."

"I had the same reaction when I met them, but then I learned Andre is his step-father."

Did that mean Andre had been married to an older woman? "What about you? Do you live here?"

"I have a room here. It makes it easier during harvest time when I work twenty-four-seven. There's plenty of room and Andre is a generous host. Speaking of which, Lena is preparing dinner and she's an amazing cook. You met her when you arrived."

She must be the pretty blond woman who took my suitcase.

"Come down for a glass of wine around seven," Pedro said, "and we'll eat after that."

Seven was hours away. Her stomach growled, and she glanced at her watch.

Pedro must have noticed because he touched her arm, steering her toward a door in the back of the house shaded by a stand of trees. "Let's get you a snack to tide you over."

As she walked alongside Pedro, Andre appeared above them, behind French doors that opened on a balcony. They locked gazes, but his expression didn't change. What he was thinking? Was he pleased by this bizarre coincidence? Was he upset by her presence in his home, a far more intimate connection than the one-night stand they might have had? Or perhaps he didn't care one way or the other. Given the intensity of his stare, that seemed the least likely option.

The kitchen was abuzz with activity. A thin woman sat at the table, appearing mesmerized by a ledger. The blonde who'd taken her suitcase earlier shoved a chicken into the oven. A petite woman with short hair came in through the back door, heading for the sink.

The blonde backed into her.

"Sorry, Lena."

"It's okay." Blank-faced, Lena pushed her bangs off her forehead with an oven-mitted hand. She didn't sound like it was okay. Zoey took in her appearance. She possessed picture-perfect beauty, marred by her pinched eyes and a pressed-thin mouth—it was the kind of uptight look Zoey expected in the conference rooms of her clients, not in the kitchen of a wine country estate.

Pedro offered Zoey an apple. "This is Lena. She's an amazing cook."

Her blond head bowed curtly before she spun around to stir a bubbling pot on the stove.

"And this is Susan." Pedro's tanned hand gestured at the petite one. "She's the gardener."

Andre barreled into the room, the door swinging into the wall with a bang. He surveyed the room, not stopping at Zoey. He paused at Susan, and his chest sunk as he visibly exhaled. Zoey squeezed her eyes shut; she had no business looking at his chest.

"Susan, would you help me with something upstairs?"

"Sure, no problem. Let me get cleaned up. Meet you in a few minutes?"

"Thank you." Andre headed toward the door without another word.

Pedro barred his exit. "I invited Zoey to have a glass of wine with us before dinner, at seven. I thought I'd bring up a decanter of the Šoltan so she can taste it while we fill her in on the project."

"Yes, good idea. I'll be there."

Zoey must have blinked, because it seemed like he vanished into thin air.

"I'm going to do some work in my room." Zoey tossed her apple core in the trash can. "Thanks for the snack."

Upstairs, she opened the window to her room and a warm breeze blew in, carrying the scent of dry earth and heating her skin. She liked the heat. Outside, some of the hillsides were covered in golden grasses and others with green rows of leafy, trellised vines. Putting her hand on the windowsill, she could feel the tension in her shoulders ease. It was nice to be out of the city.

The spacious room had pale yellow walls, honey-colored oak floors, and big windows to let in the late-day sun — the kind of light just right for reading novels and making love in the afternoon. An intricately embroidered quilt in reds and oranges lay on the bed. Two woven wall hangings matched it. The folk art was probably Croatian, like the rest of the furniture in the house. She hugged her arms across her chest. The warm colors enveloped her in a feeling of well-being. Come to think of it, the whole house did.

She dropped into the desk chair, remembering another sunny house — the one bedroom cottage in the Mission District that she'd shared with Michael. She'd loved that scrubbed-clean dump, at first. It was so tiny that they called it the cocoon. Too bad she hadn't emerged from it a butterfly.

On the day she'd moved out, her hands had trembled as she zipped up her sweatshirt, locked the door, and put the key back into the mail slot. A McGuire Irish Movers' van was double parked on Capp Street. Her second-hand furniture was nestled tightly inside. Michael's parents had loaded his clothes and his books into their minivan. They wouldn't look at her; they hardly spoke. She shook his father's hot, dry hand, and never heard from them again. Across town, the movers carried everything up her new, narrow stairwell. They must have guessed something of her turmoil; they both enfolded her in sweaty bear hugs before they drove off.

Suddenly, her breath came short. Her fingers went cold. She opened her eyes to see the Kaštel Estate vineyards out the window.

Idiot. What was she thinking, dredging up all those off-limits memories? It must be the birthday. With careful, slow breaths, she forced them down.

Her eyes caught on her trusty laptop, sitting on the desk. Its shiny metallic case was an uninviting contrast to the rustic desk and the earthy swath of fabric above it on the wall. Still, it was her salvation — work.

She opened the winery's dinky website and poked around. The site was shockingly bare and tacky, with a mismatch of fonts and colors that made her eyes cross. Why wasn't there a picture of Andre, or even Kos or Pedro? That was a serious marketing mistake. Men that pretty could sell anything. She'd even buy a box of tampons with Andre's face on it. Her fingers went to her lips, suppressing the urge to smile. A man like him wouldn't find the compliment flattering.

Her phone buzzed in her purse. Ethan. Not now. She stilled the vibration and tossed it back into the oversized bag. Before she'd even set her purse down, the damn thing was ringing again. Bending over to rummage for the phone, a lock of her hair fell into her eyes. She blew it out of the way and tucked it behind her ear.

"What?" she said.

"Hello to you too."

"Sorry." Not really, but she should pretend. Still, it was all the apology she could be bothered with. She waited, wondering if he might say happy birthday. But he could only know that if he'd looked for it in her files, and she knew beyond a doubt he wouldn't have.

"What have you learned?" he asked.

Her scalp tingled. Could steam really come out of a person's ears? "Are you checking up on me?"

"No, of course not. I simply wanted to offer my support, and see if things were off to a good start."

Oh. He was just being nice. "More like a slow start. I've toured the estate, but I still don't have a feel for what Maras wants."

"I see. Well, let me know if I can help."

"Will do."

She hung up, knowing he wasn't finished with the call, but his voice rankled her in a way it hadn't before. It was definitely time to break it off with him.

She went back to work. The webpage about this history of the winery was begging for that photo of Andre. A green background would make his eyes shine. She leaned closer to the nearly blank page, trying to picture it. No, a headshot wouldn't suit his characteristic scowl. A candid would be better, shirtsleeves rolled up and holding a glass of wine to look through, or examining a bunch of grapes with Pedro. She would suggest that at dinner.

Her heart sped up a little—the excitement of inspiration, or was it seeing him again? She had no business getting fluttery about him. Work hard, kick ass, go home. That was her plan.

Standing, she shoved the chair behind her and started walking circles around the room. Movement always helped her to think. Ideas about the project took shape, cascading through her mind. She paced faster and faster. Maybe a wine label echoing the estate's architecture, and a Croatian-sounding name. That would be exotic—like him.

But why the new brand?

She came to a halt, her foot hovering over the floorboards. The puzzle pieces weren't lining up. Pedro must have neglected to tell her something important, and she couldn't be successful without knowing what it was. Getting answers was simply a matter of determining the right questions. And there were only two that occurred to her: What did Andre really want to accomplish with this project? And why wouldn't anyone just come right out and tell her?

CHAPTER 8

Andre could not get the image of Zoey out of his head. She had changed into a sundress—unfortunate that it was not the rainy dead of winter. From where he had gazed down on her earlier, that strappy slip of fabric had afforded him a better view of her breasts. They were the ideal size for her body, just big enough to fill his large hands. Her features were expressive and her smile engaging, even though it did not reach her eyes. Her dark brown hair was glossy and plaited in a thick braid. She was certainly beautiful, but there was something else that drew him to her—the spark, the mutual recognition. Every time he looked at her, he expected it to be gone. Every time he was wrong.

Worse, he already hungered again. She had only been there for a few hours and he smelled her throughout his house. Early in his exile, he had trained himself to ignore the constant hunger. But smelling Zoey made him think about sex, and thinking about sex made it impossible to forget his need for blood. He was newly aware of the ache in his starving muscles, the stinging fatigue of his eyes, and the sluggishness of his thoughts. He needed to feed, even if it would not satisfy for long.

Andre could hear Zoey pacing in her room. More often than not, he wished his ears were not so keen. She was not exactly stomping, but the sound thundered because every footstep brought to mind her sexy legs scissoring as she walked, her breasts bouncing slightly in her dress.

The rap of knuckles on his door told him Susan had arrived. He hadn't even heard her approach because he had been listening to Zoey's footsteps.

With Lena, he always avoided the bed. With Susan, he simply sat down and indicated she should join him.

"Ready?" he asked.

"Sure."

He leaned into Susan and licked her skin where he could see her pulse. Salt lingered on her skin where perspiration had dried. She smelled clean. Under his tongue, her pulse raced in anticipation. He opened his mouth wide and extended his fangs, penetrating her delicate skin. She sighed quietly and relaxed into him as he began to draw warm blood into his mouth. He could sense her arousal, but she made no attempt to turn the feeding into a sexual act.

Tingling energy spread through him as his belly filled with her blood. It tasted so good, he could almost forget her blood lacked something. Would Zoey taste so good? How would she react to his bite?

She had only been in his home for a few hours, but a year's worth of barely repressed desire for her had been uncoiling through his body since seeing her again. He imagined Zoey's neck, her body against him. Suddenly, a large portion of that blood headed straight to his cock, pressing along Susan's thigh.

"Honey, I know that's not for me, but I think you've had enough."

Davo. He coughed a little and swallowed the last mouthful. That was the last thing he should have let happen. Susan was his one safe meal. He sealed her wounds with his tongue. "Susan, I'm so sorry—"

"Andre, I saw the way you didn't look at the businesswoman in the kitchen. It's obvious to everyone."

"Really?"

She nodded. "I don't mind at all. However, Lena...she minds."

It was time to do something about her. "Susan, can I ask you a question?"

"Okay."

"Lena finds it very...frustrating when I feed from her. You, on the other hand, don't seem bothered. I can sense you enjoy it, but—"

"Really—you don't know?"

He scratched his chin. "Know what?"

"That I like girls. Ally and I have been together for years, since you first hired me."

"You're kidding."

"Andre, can't you smell her on me or something?"

She had a point. He clearly wasn't paying much attention to her, because as soon as he leaned in and sniffed, Ally's smell was so strong she could have been in the room.

"Feeding you is like foreplay. You get me all hot and bothered and Ally seals the deal."

Andre raised an eyebrow. They were two beautiful women and the image that flashed in his mind was tantalizing. He flashed a deliberately naughty grin. "Can I watch?"

"I'd slap you if I thought you were serious." She laughed and swatted at his arm. "But, Andre, even if I wasn't with Ally, I don't consider myself entitled to your affections. I think Lena's off the mark there." Susan stood, her face a little flushed.

Had he misled Lena? It had become commonplace for vampires to employ skilled labor and compensate them beyond their professional wage. Yet, Lena seemed to believe she had signed up for the old way of doing things. She must have read too many vampire novels.

Running her fingers through her short hair, Susan went on. "You need to feed from us and you certainly pay us well for our service. It's lucky for your kind it feels so good. Otherwise how would you survive?"

Andre scratched his chin. "Sheer force, I expect. But I prefer the power of persuasion."

"Well, off to find Ally." She winked at him.

He stood and kissed her cheek. "Thank you."

As soon as she left, Zoey's pacing feet became audible again. It was all he could do not to burst into her room and bend her over the bed. But worse, even full of Susan's blood, he still craved Zoey's, which meant it was neither hunger nor lust cranking him up.

Davo. The blood bond was the worst part of being a vampire.

Hell could freeze right over. He was determined to remain unbonded no matter what. He'd learned his lesson long ago, when Mila broke their bond and nearly ripped him apart. But he could satisfy his desire for Zoey without tasting her blood. He had been with thousands of women without biting. Why not her?

CHAPTER 9

Ethan Bennett passed through the stone columns of the North Gate onto the campus of the University of California in Berkeley. The directions said to veer right, but there were two paths. He approached a loitering adolescent.

"Excuse me, which way is Dwinelle Hall?"

The oily-haired kid only looked up for a second, the arrow of his finger pointing to the second path on Ethan's right. There were an astonishing number of students wearing blue and gold sweatshirts. Most human beings were sheep in need of a shepherd.

Inside Dwinelle Hall, Ethan found the History Department's receptionist. He lifted a metallic case and set it on her desk. "This is for Professor William Oliver. Please make sure that he receives it and that no one else opens it."

"Of course," she said, staring fixedly at the case.

She looked too fascinated for Ethan's liking. The nameplate on her desk revealed her to be one Gladys Browns. "Ms. Browns, Dr. Oliver assured me that inside this case is perhaps the most ancient and priceless historical object he has ever seen. I trust you'll treat it with suitable caution."

She reached forward quickly, but Ethan didn't let go of the case. He held her eyes with his gaze until she blinked in submission. Then he let go.

He had always been confident the plan would work, but with Zoey inside the Kaštel Estate it was finally coming together. Soaring with optimism, Ethan had made the snap decision to put the next steps in motion earlier that day. He contacted William Oliver for help translating a book he had stolen from his father's collection of artifacts. To Oliver, Ethan had described the illustrated text as a family heirloom written in what he thought was a form of Gaelic. Doubt poured out of the telephone as Oliver explained the impossibility of such a book existing. Ethan scanned a page and emailed it to the professor, who called him back immediately.

"I'd like to see the codex first hand." The doubt had disappeared from his voice.

"So it's unusual?" asked Ethan.

"I can't say for certain until I see it. However, what you sent me seems to be written in the ancient language Brittonic, which predates Gaelic by many centuries. It's clearly a Celtic language that I cannot otherwise place."

"And that's unusual?"

"Unprecedented, actually. There are no texts and very few artifacts with any Brittonic writing."

"Can you translate it?"

"I can try. Brittonic is related to the Continental Celtic spoken around the same time. That's where I'll start. I'd really love to see it."

"I'll bring it by your office this afternoon, then."

"Wonderful."

After dropping off the book, he retraced his steps to a café on the north side of campus where he met another academic from the History Department.

He had found an article online about Professor Orhan Ganis's research into a tribe from the mountains of eastern Turkey. Because it had vanished in the ancient past, scholars had long presumed the tribe had been conquered by its neighbors. On a new archaeological site, Ganis had found evidence that the tribe had uprooted suddenly and migrated elsewhere.

The article caught his eye because of the tribe's name: the Nalkh. It was a word often repeated in the four Hunter commandments. No part of the guttural language survived other than those rules, but all

Hunters knew what they meant: The children of the Sun must hate the Night, they must never feed the Night, they must never let the Night bring shame upon them, and finally, the children of the Sun must destroy the Night.

With his curiosity piqued by the familiar word, he looked closely at the photos of the Nalkh artifacts excavated by Ganis. Shards of pottery and even bronze jewelry revealed the same decorative motifs that adorned Hunter artifacts from all over the world. It couldn't possibly be a coincidence, but he wanted to be sure.

Inside the Middle Eastern café, the closely packed tables afforded no privacy. At the moment only one was occupied by a thin man with black strands of hair combed over his balding head. Leaning over a stack of papers, he scribbled with a red pen. The whirr of steam sounded from the espresso machine. If that noise persisted, he wouldn't need to worry about being overheard.

"Professor Ganis?" As he approached the man, he smelled his spiced cologne over the heavy scent of dark roasted coffee.

The man stood and extended his hand. "Hello. Mr. Hunter?"

Ethan attempted a warm smile. "Yes. Thank you so much for meeting me." Ganis's bony knuckles felt frail in Ethan's hand.

"If you have what you say you do, I am certainly very pleased to meet you." Ganis articulated each word, rendering his accent easy to understand. "Try the Turkish coffee. Best I've had outside Istanbul."

Ethan sat down and opened an envelope. Inside were pictures of the artifacts he had borrowed from his father. When he slipped them out, Ganis reached for them eagerly.

"Oh my, this is fascinating. Yes, these certainly look like Nalkh designs. They differ slightly from their neighbors' handicrafts. The sun imagery, for example, and the golden eyes."

Ganis looked up and inspected Ethan. It had been wise to wear brown colored contacts for the day's errands.

"You said in your email that these objects are heirlooms from your Welsh family?" Ganis asked.

"Yes. Is it possible the Nalkh migrated that far in several centuries?"

"To Britain? Well, yes, it's theoretically possible. But I can't imagine what would have made them do so. Normally a tribe would migrate for better resources, or to flee hostility. Certainly they could have settled somewhere in Europe between the Caucasus and Britain."

A plump woman brought a cup of coffee that Ethan had not ordered. "It is difficult to imagine what would have motivated them," Ethan said.

Ganis spoke more rapidly, bending over the table past his stack of papers. "Mr. Hunter, I'd love to see these artifacts in person. May I?"

Ethan found the man's enthusiasm amusing. "Of course. When would you be able to visit my home in San Francisco?" The flavor of cardamom surprised him when he sipped his coffee. It would come in handy for what he was about to do.

"Let me check my calendar." Ganis bent down to retrieve something from his briefcase.

With his attention away from the table, Ethan sprinkled a small envelope of white powder into Ganis's coffee.

When the man sat up, excitement lit up his face and he opened his calendar. "Would later this week work for you?"

"Yes, certainly, at your convenience." Anytime was convenient for Ethan since Ganis wouldn't live to keep the appointment.

As he walked back to his car, Ethan ticked off another mental box on his list. Those ancient secrets would give him enormous power among his fellow Hunters. But would they make him their leader?

CHAPTER 10

Inside the door of his apartment, Lucas Bennett slipped off his shoes, then his jacket.

For some reason, his own gold-handled sun dagger drew him from deep within its drawer. It was hidden away in a locked box because seeing it brought to mind disturbing memories of his Hunting Rites. Lucas unearthed the knife, knowing it would call to mind the sick ritual he had enacted as a fifteen-year-old boy.

Orange and gold autumn leaves had zoomed past the car windows as they traveled from their home in Boston to rural Vermont where a small vampire nest had been discovered under the cover of a dairy farm.

A young male vampire employed the farm workers as blood slaves. He wasn't especially strong, but even the weakest vampire could scent or hear a surprise attack. The Bennetts arrived just as a band of Hunters made use of their firepower. They blew a hole in the side of the farmhouse, exposing the vampire to the full light of dawn. The vampire's shrieks were so loud and grating that Lucas covered his ears, expecting to feel blood trickle from them.

As the car came to a stop, bile sloshed in his nervous stomach. The ritual execution of blood slaves was the duty of the initiates and Lucas hoped that once he made his kill and earned his golden sun dagger, he would finally feel like a Hunter.

When his father learned of the young man who confessed to being the vampire's lover, he searched out Lucas. To the gathered

Hunters and initiates, his father said, "This slave will die at the hand of my son Lucas."

No one objected.

His father forced Lucas to watch as the elder Hunters beat him, even though he possessed no useful information. The blood slave was scared senseless and grieving for his vampire master. Quickly, his face became an unrecognizable pulp of blood and bone. Steel-toed boots kicked him and the Hunters cursed him as a double abomination: a male blood slave used by a male vampire. Lucas couldn't help but pity him, though the slave was a fool for getting seduced by a parasite.

He knelt and bent over the battered man. After the damage of the beating, wasn't it merciful to kill him? Lucas closed his eyes, picturing the ancient illustrations of the ritual he'd been taught. In his mind, the image became sharp enough to guide him through each step. Reaching out, his hand trembled, and he gripped his blade more tightly to hide his nerves. First, he punctured the slave's wrists, then crossed his bleeding arms. Only two more steps, thank God. He pierced the largest arteries in the slave's neck and his thighs. His crimson blood flowed freely, pooling onto the industrial blue linoleum.

Just when Lucas was certain the man had died, he opened his eyes to look at his executioner. Bloody and swollen, his eyes sockets were surely shattered; the flesh of his eyelids was pulp. Lucas was amazed he could even lift them. But they widened and flashed with some kind of knowledge before closing for the last time.

Was he able to see Lucas's regret? He didn't want to kill the handsome man; he would have loved to talk to him, to ask him questions about sex and life. Maybe even to kiss him the way he had imagined kissing a man.

After the rite, Ethan came looking for him. They'd been matched with two girls from Florida who had driven for two days straight in order to arrive in time for the Hunt. The girls told Lucas about how Ethan had subdued a strong farmhand before performing his execution. They kept whispering to each other and staring at Ethan. The foursome walked away from the farmhouse into the trees, but when Lucas stopped under a red-leafed maple, the other three continued deeper into the shadowy privacy of the woods. He was immensely relieved they were content to leave him out of their fun. Another mystery from that terrible day: Had Ethan been doing him a favor by screwing both girls? Or had he been trying to humiliate Lucas in the same way his father had?

The dagger glinted in the light of the desk lamp. Though he had been hunting Marasović for more than a decade, he hadn't committed any violence against vampires or their households since his Hunting Rite. The ritual blade stayed safely in the drawer.

He'd been pleased to land the Hunter equivalent of a desk job when he and Ethan were dispatched to California in search of the ancient Andre Marasović. Lucas researched the oldest wineries, slowly narrowing down the possibilities. When he actually found Marasović, he rejoiced. Perhaps his father would finally see him as a man. Then he'd realized Marasović might lead them to the other Croatian refugees. To Stephen's chagrin, they'd changed their strategy to infiltrate the household before executing him.

Lucas was repulsed by vampires—it was simply in his blood. But if the Hunt succeeded, he would be responsible for the death of Marasović's human household. The haunting eyes of the handsome blood slave opened again in Lucas's mind. He must do something to try to save the humans, even if it meant going to the last place on earth that he belonged.

Low in the western sky, the glaring sunlight strobed through the trees lining the rural Sonoma County road. Lucas found the flashes disorienting, each slice of white light ratcheting up his shoulders closer to his ears. He longed to stretch out his tense muscles, but where he was going, he would get his ass kicked if anyone saw him do yoga.

He pulled into the dirt driveway. Dandelions had overgrown the lawn and the house was in disrepair, showing serious damage to its dingy white siding and with several windows covered by plywood—Hunter headquarters. If he wanted to save the humans in Marasović's household, he had to be on the front line.

Lucas walked into the front door and it took his eyes a moment to adjust to the low light. The house smelled like mildew and felt like a medieval warrior outpost. Hunter relics covered cheap wood paneling. Lucas shuddered to see the Bennett family tapestries among other families' heirlooms. Drawing close to one of the ancient weavings, Lucas saw Hunters slaying vampires and executing households in one gory image after another. Vampires were burning. Women and children were slaughtered by the Hunters with their ceremonial daggers. Dismembered bodies lay in pools of blood. The Hunters' eyes had been carefully embroidered with fine golden thread. The whoosh of a car passing on the highway caused him to notice the silence of the house. Where was everyone?

Lucas hadn't seen the tapestries in more than a decade. The predominantly blood-red weavings geared up his tension even more, and he rolled his neck, trying to relax his muscles. Lucas had wondered if some instinct would kick in once he was in the midst of the Hunt and turn him into a warrior. Apparently not. The slaughter of humans who served vampires still repulsed him. His hatred of vampires couldn't justify it. According to his father, that meant he didn't hate them enough.

Did Lucas want to hate more? The only other option was hard to swallow—total alienation from the clan. If he disavowed the Hunt, he would become the hunted. Bloody images before him revealed exactly what that would be like.

Deliberately turning both from the images and the questions they raised, Lucas explored the house. A pile of musty blankets in the corner showed the Hunters slept on the floor of the main room. The greasy brown carpeting made Lucas anticipate a night of longing for his bed. He settled down on the floor and waited for the Hunters to return.

It wasn't long before car doors slammed outside. He opened the door to find Stephen and Mick, his father's old friend, ambling toward the house. Mick had gotten thick around the middle since the last time Lucas had seen him. Rolling back a vinyl cover, they unloaded a cache of weapons from the bed of the spanking new black F-150. There were tanks of gasoline and crates of incendiary grenades, as well as guns. Lucas moved toward them nice and easy while his stomach did jumping jacks. Shit. He wanted his desk job back. In fact, he would rather be anywhere else.

"Send out the initiates to help with these boxes," Stephen said to Lucas without greeting.

"There's no one here."

"What? Where are they?" Stephen put a crate down at his feet.

"I don't know. I've been here since five and the house is empty. I assumed they were with you."

"Shit," Mick said. He took a sweaty ball cap off his head and curled its bill tightly.

"Where are they?" Lucas asked Mick this time.

"Must have gone to town."

"No, they didn't. Hell no. Not even initiates would be that stupid," Lucas said.

"Yes, initiates would be that stupid. They're bored. We called them here for a fight and now you are asking them to sit on their hands."

Lucas crossed his arms and held his tongue.

Mick jumped in. "It's not all thirty of them. The full-fledged Hunters and about half of the initiates went out to do training exercises. They're camping until tomorrow night."

"So eight or ten?"

"Ten."

"Well, ten yellow-eyed kids getting drunk in one of these small towns is sure as hell going to get some attention, even if a vampire doesn't catch their scent."

"You're right, Lucas. This is a serious problem." Stephen surprised him by agreeing. "The only solution is that we accelerate our plans. We can't wait out your strategy any longer."

"Zoey just got there. We haven't been waiting."

"The initiates have been arriving for a week. They're young and itching for action."

Lucas itched to go home, and an accusation leaped from his lips before he could stop it. "You jumped the gun by calling them in so early." He sounded like a whiny teenager even to his own ear.

"I've questioned your strategy all along, Lucas. Now it's time for you to give up." He gestured at the crates in the truck. "Mick and I have enough weapons and explosives here to take out the entire Estate. Call the girl out of there and we'll do it tomorrow when those animals are stuck inside."

Resentment flared in Lucas. Stephen would act without his consent in a heartbeat, but he didn't want to alienate Ethan, his favored son. Lucas planted his feet, put his hand on his hips and looked down on his father from several inches.

"No," he said. "I'm calling Ethan in. We don't attack yet. We need to see what Zoey can learn."

"I have a proposal," Mick said. "A compromise, even."

"Go on," Lucas replied.

"What if we take a member of the household captive? Watching an interrogation will give our initiates some satisfaction. And when we've gathered the information we need, at least one of them can complete his Rite."

Mick and Stephen exchange a furtive glance. Had they already discussed this, or was Lucas being paranoid? "Do you have someone in mind?" he asked.

"Since we set up headquarters last week," Mick answered, "we've had someone watching from a distance during the day. The gardener often goes outside without protection." He put his hat on, the bill curled like a horseshoe. "Also, there's one we assume is the cook because she goes grocery shopping every few days. Usually in the morning. That one looks like she walked off the cover of the *Sports Illustrated* Swimsuit Issue. She could be a lot fun for the boys." He elbowed Stephen in the side.

The jumping jacks began again in his gut. Soon, he would be party to murder, torture, and rape, all by virtue of his birth. Lucas slid his hands from his hips into his back pockets and sighed.

"Wait until Ethan arrives tomorrow. If he approves, I agree."

The three men turned when they heard the sound of two SUVs on the gravel drive—the initiates. Lucas could see Stephen's anger beginning to surface. As a kid, he had learned to spot the early signs of the man's rage and make himself scarce. His father's ears turned red, his fingers twitched on their way into fists, and his eyes bulged slightly. Knowing the kind of punishment Stephen Bennett could dream up, Lucas actually felt sorry for the dumbass kids.

"Remember to have them unload the truck before you punish them. I'm sure they'll be useless afterward." Lucas headed back into the house without waiting for a response.

Inside, he sat with his back against the wall and checked his email on his phone. None of the emails were urgent, but it provided an escape from the situation unfolding outside. The teenage boys started carrying boxes through the main room back to one of the bedrooms. When they were done unloading, his father ordered them to strip, but keep their belts in hand.

Great. The idea of sleeping on the floor of this shit hole was bad enough. Now he would be sharing it with ten kids who'd just had to flay their buddies' backsides with their own belts. Damn, he was really not cut out to be a Hunter.

CHAPTER 11

The view from the parlor at sunset stunned Zoey. A wall of French doors opened onto a narrow balcony and displayed a pink sky, flush against the verdant grapevines that trailed over gentle hills. The landscape was more than enough ornament for the room, and Zoey was glad Andre had left the ivory colored walls bare.

He sat with Pedro, and they both stood as she walked in.

"Where's Kos?" she asked.

"He had plans to meet a friend," Andre replied.

She had to look a long way up to meet his eyes.

Pedro poured wine into three glasses.

"I should admit I don't have much of a palate."

"Don't worry, we'll guide you," Pedro said. He handed her a glass.

As she lifted it to her nose, Andre watched her. "Hhhmm. It smells so earthy. It's very unusual."

"Yes, the grapes are from our family vines on Šolta, before they were burned," Andre said.

"A fire?" How tragic, to lose so much heritage.

Andre sipped his wine before he said, "Yes, that's why I—why my family came to the U.S."

"When was the fire?" Zoey asked.

"Eighteen forty-seven," Andre said. Her next question had formed on her lips when he added, "It is a very long story. Another time?"

"Sure."

"This wine was produced from the Šoltan vines planted when this estate was founded, and recently spliced onto the vines on my new land."

"But—" Zoey checked to be certain she understood "—it's the Zinfandel grape whose name I have no hope of saying in Croatian?"

"Yes, that one." Andre nodded. "The vineyards we acquired several years ago bear a startling similarity to our vineyards in Šolta and the resulting wine tastes just like the ones we used to make."

"Were you actually able to taste wines made by your family so long ago?"

He tilted his head. "Able to taste them? Oh, I see. Yes, I was fortunate enough to taste wine made from that vineyard."

Why did she feel like he was evading her question?

Pedro lifted the glass and swirled it. "She's been breathing for a while now."

"She?" asked Zoey.

"I let Andre decide the gender. It's his wine."

Andre let out a quiet snort. "You don't let me decide anything." Then he raised his glass and said, "*Živili.*"

"*Živili,*" Pedro said.

"Cheers?" Zoey asked.

Pedro nodded. "Pretty much."

She brought her glass to her mouth and glanced at Andre to find him watching. She lowered her lids and concentrated. When the wine hit her tongue, she opened them wide again.

She ran her tongue along the back of her teeth, searching out words for the astonishing mixture of flavors in her mouth. "It's as thick as blood…and it tastes like sunshine, raisins, and peppery licorice."

The flecks in his green eyes glittered. "Yes, Zoey, it does." For the first time, he didn't call her Ms. Porter. "Your palate is perfect."

He looked delighted with her. She glanced away, her head suddenly light, as if she hadn't eaten all day. Darting her eyes back to him, his face had gone neutral. She wanted the delight back.

"Let's go in to dinner," he said, snapping her out of the trance.

For an instant, it seemed like he would take her arm and she leaned in, aching for the touch. Then he backed off. His deer-in-headlights look returned, and he pointed the way into to the dining room instead. Zoey walked ahead of him quickly, hoping her face didn't show her disappointment.

What the hell was wrong with her? She wasn't a swooner. And besides, he was clearly trying to keep things professional. She should follow his cue.

With the same ivory walls and French doors, the dining room appealed to Zoey almost as much as the parlor. Savory garlic and thyme scented the air. They sat at the end of a large table. Zoey was across from Andre, which required her to look at him often. His lips quirked into a grin sometimes, but what would it be like to see his handsome face in a full-blown smile?

Lena served tender homemade pasta in tomato sauce, a crisp-skinned roast chicken, and lemon tarts for dessert. Zoey had rarely eaten a meal so delicious in San Francisco's best restaurants.

Andre leaned over the table and gestured with his big hands like a stereotypical Mediterranean man. He spoke animatedly about local winemakers and their wines, hardly touching his food. Zoey asked lots of questions. By the end, she understood much more about the wine market. Nostalgia explained why the wine mattered to Andre, but she still didn't understand why he wanted to rebrand it.

Pedro slipped out without a word, and she assumed he would be gone for just a moment. Andre continued discussing the technical side of winemaking. She could listen to him all night, with that accent that made him sound like a sexy bad guy in a James Bond movie. He knew everything about wine, but he wasn't a snob.

After half an hour alone with him she guessed, "Pedro's not coming back, is he?"

Andre touched his forehead and shook his head. "I think not."

"Why?"

"I suspect that he and Kos were amused to find that you and I had—" he paused "—crossed paths before. Either they think they are playing cupid, or being very funny."

"Oh." She blushed. "Well, then can I ask you a question?"

"Yes. But I retain the right not to answer." Something glinted in his eye.

She suddenly felt like she had a genie in a bottle and only one wish. She wondered about him, his family history, his age. What if she didn't ask the right one? He probably wouldn't answer something personal, so she stuck with the question she had intended.

"Why am I here? There's something about your goals for this project that you're not telling me. If I don't know what you're really after, I can't help you get it."

"You're right."

She waited a long time for him to go on, forcing herself not to look away as he watched her.

Lifting his glass, he emptied it in one deep swallow. "Evening is my favorite time to roam. If you're willing to walk with me, I will try to answer your question."

"I'd love to. Pedro only showed me the vineyards close to the house. It would feel good to stretch my legs more."

"Did you bring a pair of jeans and some sturdy shoes?"

"Yes. I'll go change."

Which jacket should he wear? Andre's favorite looked threadbare, and suddenly he cared. Disgusted with himself, he shook his head and pulled on a utilitarian sweatshirt. Was it a mistake to invite her on this walk? Perhaps, but it was too late to change his mind.

Zoey was already waiting in the kitchen. She looked him over brazenly.

It was only fair to give her the same gaze, up from her tennis shoes to her thick brown braid and back down. Her tight jeans fit snugly to her ankle. They would have seemed impractical, but he had peeled jeans like that off enough women to know they were very stretchy. She filled them out nicely. He could not abide a skinny woman. Of course, she probably thought her thighs were too big, but they were to his liking, and would surely look even better wrapped around his waist.

Davo. His jeans were suddenly too tight for his growing erection.

She had on a long-sleeved athletic top made of some synthetic material that no doubt wicked, resisted, and blocked all manner of things. He held the door open for her and took a long look at her ass as she walked through. Just as sweet as he remembered.

Side by side, they walked north into a vineyard. The bright moon was helpful—she would be able to see well and wouldn't notice his keen eyesight. Even to his ears, the night was quiet, and he remembered the similarly companionable silence the night they met.

How to answer her question about the project? If she was Ethan Bennett's spy, his revelations might put the household in danger. Or worse. If the Hunters learned of the power of the wine, more than one hundred years' work would be ash.

Unsure what to reveal, he began. "You asked about my goals for the wine…" The sound of her breaths, quick and shallow, meant she was working to keep up. He slowed his pace. "I mentioned that my family's home burned in the middle of the nineteenth century?"

"Yes," she replied. She walked a few steps ahead. Gravel and dry earth crunched under their feet.

"It was a terrible war. Do you know about the history of ethnic conflict in the Balkans?"

"Only that there is one."

"Yes, well. One—" he searched for the right word "—clan was intent on killing my whole clan."

In front of him, she stopped walking and spun to face him, her mouth slack. Good to know she found genocide upsetting.

A few long steps took him to her side and she fell into pace with him again. "My clan was so frightened that we disbanded and went into hiding. We have all changed our names and spread out across the United States. We don't know how to find one another—"

"But, if you can't find them—"

"That is why I need you. I want to use the wine to send them a message. I hope it will allow us to reconnect."

Before he even finished speaking, her head shook. "Andre, you're talking about five or six generations. Why is this so important to you, and how can you know it will matter to the other descendants of your clan?"

If he told her more, would he jeopardize everything? Their footsteps filled the silence until he spoke. "My clan values its traditions and ties to the homeland above all else. I am certain these traditions are alive with the other refugees. Winemaking is in our blood, and I have to believe they will remain on the lookout for a message." He had told them to, all those years ago. *Davo,* they better still be paying attention.

She stopped again and faced him, forcing him to a standstill. "If your homeland on Šolta is so important to you, why don't you return? Or for that matter, just reach out to them on the Internet."

"Neither of those is an option."

"Why?"

He raked an arc in the gravel with his toe. "You may think us paranoid, but we do not believe we would be safe, even after all these years. We cannot risk being found."

She scratched her head through hair that looked delightfully thick. "Really?"

He nodded.

"You all have something like collective post traumatic stress disorder."

"Perhaps. But, as the saying goes, just because we are paranoid does not mean they are not out to get us."

She laughed, but he didn't. "You're serious? It's hard to imagine what would frighten a man like you."

Instantly, her cheeks went pink in the moonlight and she took a hurried step. How far did that blush go down her chest? He followed her. Yes, she would find it hard to imagine many things about him.

They reached the top of a low hill. He pointed at the vineyards most recently added to his estate. "This is where I stood when I discovered that land is very similar to my homeland." A breeze rustled through shrubs and once again the scent of the soil and plants became a portal to another time and place. His eyelids closed of their own accord, and he remembered what it was like to be safe and strong.

When he opened them, she was looking out over the vines that snaked along the rolling hills. It was a chance to watch her unobserved. At dinner and now, he noticed that, whenever she was silent, she had an unnatural stillness about her. It unsettled him — she was simply too calm. He wanted to shake her, or kiss her, or do something to draw the life out of her.

She stirred, and pointed at a wooded area in the shallow valley below. "What's that?"

Leaning in to follow the line of her finger, he answered. "A small spring. It waters all those shrubs."

"Will you show me?"

His fingertips came to rest between her shoulders. She jerked at the touch, then pushed into it slightly. What did she think of seeing him again, and what did she think was going to happen out here alone in the night with him?

He guided her toward the spring. The path narrowed. Behind him, her footsteps were a slow beat on the gravelly path. Darkness thickened on the descent into the little valley.

The telltale sound of rolling rocks hit him before Zoey gasped. She'd slipped on the loose gravel about ten feet behind him. He raced to cover the distance, just barely catching her before she hit the ground. Silently cursing his weakness, he righted her and held her arm until she found her balance. Moving like a tortoise was a nasty reminder that he was wasting away.

Clinging to him, and shaking her head, she looked stunned to be on her feet—clearly her mind had already prepared her for impact.

"Are you all right?" he asked.

She gripped his shoulder and his forearm, digging into his flesh with dainty fingertips. She blinked. "Thank you. How did you catch me?"

"You are welcome. But, Zoey, are you hurt?"

"Fine. Fine." She shook her head as if trying to clear it.

"Come this way, the spring is just over here." He tugged her wrist gently, hoping to distract her from the questions she wanted to ask.

The spring was surrounded by small trees and shrubs, forming an arching cathedral overhead. He stooped under tree limbs to reach the source of the water. Behind him, she had to squeeze closer to fit into the small space. As she drew near, he noticed how far she had to tilt her chin to look him in the eye. He was used to being tall, but he had at least a foot on her. Even little Mila had been several inches taller than her.

Stepping onto a rock next to him, she bridged the difference in their heights. "Thank you for catching me."

"As I said, it was no problem. I am pleased that you are uninjured."

She pointed her finger into his chest. "Andre Maras…it's strange to know your name."

Was she flirting? "It is a little strange, Ms. Zoey Porter."

The hint of a smile played on her lips. Her warm palms came to rest high on his chest and her fingers curled around his shoulders, tugging him closer.

"I don't know if this is a good idea," he said.

"Me either." It was so sexy, the way she bit her lower lip. "But, this coincidence is hard to ignore. Don't you wonder…?" Her eyelids lowered when she looked at his mouth.

Davo. This was not good. He blurted out the first thing that came to mind. "I haven't kissed a woman in a long time."

Stepping off the rock, she pulled away, leaving him cold. "What? Like since the last time you picked someone up in a bar?"

"Please. I don't kiss women I meet in bars."

"But you were there to pick somebody up that night? I couldn't have misread that."

"Yes, of course. But not for kissing, just for…you know, a quick fuck."

Her lips parted in what could only be astonishment.

Double *davo.* He'd made it worse. Women were impossibly confusing. "Isn't that why you were there?"

She threw her shoulders back and lifted her chin, recovering quickly from whatever had surprised her. It seemed Ms. Porter didn't like to be at a loss.

"Sure," she said. "But I've never actually picked up someone in a bar. I expected kissing."

"Never?" That surprised him. She'd seemed so confident sitting next to him that night. Then again, she'd seemed confident in every situation he had seen her in today. Even admitting her inexperience picking up men, she seemed self-assured.

She shrugged. "That was my first, and last, attempt."

Oddly, pleasure surged in him at her admission. Next came possessiveness, which made no sense—she wasn't his and he didn't want her to be. "Why was it your last?"

Wind rustled the leaves overhead, and a beam of moonlight broke through, causing her eyes to sparkle. She looked down at the pool of gurgling spring water. "I was looking for a casual hook up. I guess you taught me a lesson about getting more than I bargained for."

If she only knew.

Oh hell, she was walking back toward him—slowly. "Andre, how old are you?"

He gulped down a dry swallow, as he watched the way her slow gait made her hips sway. He should put a stop to all this right now.

Instead, he said, "Older than you, Ms....Zoey. What are you, twenty-nine, thirty?"

Her eyes jerked to his. They were the saddest things he had ever seen. But her tone came out light. "I'm thirty-one. It would have been polite to low-ball your guess, you know."

Watching her move hypnotized him. "Why bother? I'm not interested in girls."

The confession must have inspired her, because she made her own. "It's totally unprofessional to say this. But, this feels the same, like that night…"

Blood pounded hot through his veins, making his brain throb, making it hard to think. She was right, and he needed to keep away from her because of it.

She took another step, and the clean womanly smell of her filled his nose. "I'm curious why you make me feel this way. No one…" She froze, mid-sentence, inches from him.

Walk away, just like she did. Walk. Away.

The brown of her eyes was like the richest Šoltan soil. He searched them for the thing that drew him. This time it looked like pure desire. He had been half-erect thinking about her all day—her look of wanting brought him fully to life.

This time he was no tortoise. Lightning fast, he pinned her back against a tree with his hips. Growling, he bent his head to hers and began a kiss nice and slow, to rein in his animal instincts. It would take all the restraint he had to keep from biting. He brushed his lips across hers and felt her body tense up like a bow.

A second later, her tongue probed at the seam of his lips. It seemed that Ms. Porter didn't want him slow and restrained. Another wave of desire hit him, hard. She forced his mouth open and swept past his teeth until she found his tongue. He cupped her ass and her hips began to rock.

There was no stopping now. He lifted her so that she could wrap her legs around him. She rubbed herself up and down his length with the roll of her hips. He sucked on her tongue, and the taste of his wine lingered in her mouth. Then he stilled her hips with his hands and thrust both his tongue and his hips in a rhythm that caused her to moan.

He lifted her shirt, trying to reach her breasts. Underneath, she had on a tank top with an elastic bra built in. She lifted her arms.

Struggling with all the layers, he said, "Damn it, I shouldn't have told you to take off that dress. I could have had it off you much faster."

"What's the hurry, Mr. Quick Fuck?"

Still focused on peeling off her layers, her tone made him smile. "Time for slow later, I want you now." He lifted her tank over her head, baring her breasts, and growled again. "Beautiful. You are so beautiful." Looking up to her face, her smile was exultant and his heart soared.

He slid her down his body so her feet were back on the ground and then he knelt in front of her. He lightly licked one of her nipples. When her soft, sweet skin pearled under his tongue he moved to the other. Then he began to suck her breast harder and ran his hand up her thigh, using his thumb to search for her clit through her jeans. She gasped when he found it and began rubbing quick circles as he drew on her breast with his insistent sucking.

It had been so long since he had kissed or touched a woman like this, since he had lost his mind to desire. Every thought vacated his mind, save ones of her body, of getting inside her.

With one tightly budded nipple in his mouth and his hand rubbing Zoey into a frenzy, a memory of his wife Mila assaulted him. He had loved to sink his fangs into the soft pink flesh around her nipple and suckle blood from her breast as he made love to her. The bite had driven Mila crazy with pleasure. He wanted Zoey writhing and crying out underneath him the way Mila used to.

Carried away with the image, his fangs extended in his mouth. He pulled away to regain his control.

"Don't stop. That feels incredible."

"Just give me a minute, beauty." He kept his hand between her legs, cupping her with firm pressure as he stood and nuzzled her neck. "You're making me lose control," he whispered in her ear, and she shivered. Her nipples budded even harder.

"Lucky you still have some, I—" She silenced herself so abruptly that her teeth clicked when her mouth closed.

She must have thought of him then, just like he had fantasized about her. His face spread into a smile so wide that, in the dark, he probably looked like the damn Cheshire cat.

Pulling away from him, she pressed her lips into a grim line. It was sweet the way she regretted admitting it, or maybe she was worried about their business relationship.

"Zoey, I've thought of you often since that night. I don't see why we can't work together and…" He leaned in to kiss her again, but jerked back abruptly. "*Davo.* Zoey, get dressed. Someone's coming."

She opened her mouth as if to protest.

He cut her off. "Now."

The graceful line of her back sloped to the ground as she looked for her tank top. She huffed. "I don't hear anything."

"You will in a minute." He recognized the voices of the approaching men and relaxed. He adjusted his pants, his erection pressing against his inseam uncomfortably, as Zoey reassembled her layers.

His sons stepped through the surrounding trees into the clearing. The addition of two more big bodies cramped the small space.

Bel offered her his hand, "Lobel Maras. People call me Bel. You must be the lovely Zoey Porter. Kos told me about you."

She scrutinized Bel. She was sharp. No doubt she noticed how much he resembled Andre, and that he looked to be the same age as both he and Kos, or would have, if they had not wasted so much.

"You're his son, too?"

Bel nodded.

She gazed up at Andre. "Oh for the love of God, how old are you?"

He tried to laugh off her question and stepped forward to offer Bel his hand. "Son, it's been a long time."

The greeting was too formal, but at least Bel returned his handshake. There was a time when he would not have.

"I'm sorry, that was rude of me," Zoey said, stepping forward. "Nice to meet you. Do you live here too?"

"No, I live in London. I'm here for a visit, just arrived —"

"Are you two out for a pleasant stroll?" Andre asked, although he already knew the answer.

"I'm afraid not," Kos replied. "There's trouble with some of the equipment. One of the vats is leaking. Pedro wants to put the wine into the barrels a little early, but he wanted to run it by you first."

It was a lie; the vats were all emptied months ago. There was some other kind of problem. Kos's eyes were gray with worry, but he would have come right out and said so if it was a four alarm fire.

"All right, we will come back right now," Andre said. "Zoey, I'm sorry to cut our walk short."

Bel snorted. "Yeah, you'll just have to finish your walk later."

Andre looked at Zoey. She colored pink in the moonlit. Why did Bel have to embarrass her? Kos had probably heard their heavy petting all the way from the house and told Bel what they were up to. He would smell her too — she was putting off an intoxicating mix of pheromones and aroused female that would make any male vampire swoon.

Andre gritted his teeth as, two by two, they marched out of the clearing. Whatever the emergency was, it had better be good.

And could it possibly be as much of a problem as his attraction to Zoey? It was the memory of Mila that had snapped him. He had nearly forgotten the pleasure of sex and blood together. His sudden recollection made it damned near impossible to remember why he and Zoey could not share that pleasure.

But the presence of his sons reminded him why: she worked for the Hunters, and more importantly, the moment he swallowed a warm mouthful of her blood, his heart would be lost to her. If Mila had taught him anything it was that love brought pain. He had hoped they could indulge their attraction and enjoy each other for a while. But he was glad his sons had brought him back to reality. He couldn't risk being close to her like that again.

Zoey turned on the tap and squeezed toothpaste onto her brush. She didn't believe for a minute that the emergency was equipment failure. The men were clearly hiding something. Their silence on the walk back to house confirmed it. What was the big secret? And how the hell did Kos and Bel even find them all the way out at the spring?

With a tight grip on her toothbrush, she took out her frustration on her teeth. Soon they would be very clean.

At least Andre had finally told her why he needed her expertise. Now she had the feeling they were keeping something else from her. Earlier in the day, the secret seemed almost like an oversight, but now it felt deliberate, and she resolved to figure out what it was.

The room was still hot, and when she pulled her nightgown out of her suitcase, her skin prickled from the heat. Sleeping in just her panties and tank top would be more comfortable. When she slid into the clean, crisp sheets, she enjoyed the feeling on her legs. It was never warm enough in her drafty apartment in San Francisco to sleep without cozy pajamas.

Maybe he would come to her later to finish what they had started near the spring. He had promised a repeat performance...

The muscles between Zoey's legs clenched at the thought of him climbing into bed over her. She wanted to unzip his pants and free that mighty erection; she wanted to see it. Moisture pooled between her legs for the second time that night.

Too worked up to fall asleep, she touched herself while remembering the way he had expertly teased her through her jeans. Damn it, she wanted him inside her. If only he had slipped his hands into her jeans and spread her with his fingers. She imagined him finding the right spot inside her, and she stifled a cry as she quickly came. Promptly, she fell asleep, only to dream about him again, just like she had night after night since they had met.

CHAPTER 12

Andre had been too preoccupied with questions to wish Zoey a proper goodnight. Why had Kos and Bel sought him out? Did they have news of the Hunters? In spite of his concerns, it had taken a healthy dose of restraint not to follow her peach of an ass up the stairs.

Grudgingly, he followed his sons into the parlor instead. Bel headed straight for the bar. Kos opened a French door and a rush of cool air filled the room. The fact they were settling in meant the emergency was no more than two alarms.

Upstairs, he could hear the sound of Zoey getting into the bed.

"What's the problem? Did you find—"

Zoey's breath quickened. His tongue stuck to the roof of his mouth.

"You can't blame her," Kos said with a grin. "You left her in quite a state." He lowered himself onto the sofa.

Suddenly exhausted, Andre rubbed his eyes with his thumb and forefinger, then wiped his hand down his face. "It wasn't my choice to leave her in that state. And of course I don't blame her. I just wish her a little more privacy." He tried not to imagine her fingers, slick from touching herself. He sat down across from Kos.

"I'm sure you'd do the same thing if vampires were capable of doing that," he said.

Although Bel couldn't have heard Zoey, he must have guessed what they were talking about because he choked, dribbling his drink down his chin. "Vampires can't do that? Jesus, and I thought you guys were missing out on the bourbon."

"No kidding," Kos answered. "I was barely twenty when he turned me. I bet if Andre had told me I couldn't jack off anymore, I'd have changed my mind."

Kos laughed and Bel joined him. In spite of his impatience to learn news of the Hunters, Andre laughed too. He liked seeing them together, acting like brothers. Just then, Zoey's stifled cry slid through the floorboards and a tremor of relief went through him. Was it because she had found her satisfaction or because asleep she would be less of a distraction?

On the heels of her gasp, the notes of a familiar tune drifted from her room. He pictured her, full lips pouted, humming herself to sleep. What was that melody? Happy Birthday? Odd lullaby.

Bel interrupted his thoughts by saying, "Poor thing. She seems to like you."

"Lots of them like him," Kos said. "What's different is that he likes her. I've haven't seen him like this since…"

Andre looked at his son. Did Kos even remember when he and Mila had been in love?

"Ever. I've never seen you like this."

Andre gritted his teeth and willed away his erection. "Can we please talk about the goddamn Hunters now?"

The front door creaked open and he looked toward it. Kos said, "I called Pedro before we came looking for you. I thought it was time to tell him the whole story."

"Good idea," Andre replied. But then Pedro strolled into the room with his usual springing step, and Andre faltered, dropping into a chair. The whole story would change his life.

Andre said, "Bel, pour Pedro a bourbon."

"I'll have a beer, thanks," Pedro said, winking to show Andre how much he enjoyed being contrary.

Bel brought him a cold bottle from a mini fridge; when he realized he needed an opener, he popped the cap off with his teeth.

"Ouch, man," Pedro said, taking the bottle and clinking it with Bel's glass. "So, what's up?"

"Pedro, please understand that I trust you completely. I simply hoped you would never need to know—"

"Save the warm fuzzy stuff and just tell me your deep, dark vampire secrets." Pedro slumped onto the sofa next to Kos.

Laughter burst from Bel, and Pedro turned to look at him more closely. "Oh, so you're the other brother?" He craned his neck to give Bel a once over. "He got all the good looks, huh, Kos?"

"Piss off," Kos said, though he showed his dimples and shook his head.

When Andre had hired Pedro, Kos was freaked out about him being gay. So Pedro constantly called Kos ugly, to let him know he wasn't interested. The onslaught of insults became so funny that it had put Kos at ease.

Bel didn't get the joke, but he accepted Pedro's compliment with a thumb pointing at his own chest. "That's me. The good looking one."

"So what's up?" Pedro asked.

Bel took the seat next to Andre and began the explanation. "Hunters. There are people called Hunters who kill vampires and all the members of the vampire's house—"

"Lucas and Ethan Bennett are Hunters," Kos said, cutting to the chase. "That's what we could smell after you—" he hesitated "—met Lucas."

After blurting out the news, they were silent while Pedro absorbed it. Eventually, Pedro sat up straight in his chair. "They're trying to kill you while pretending to do your PR?"

"They're trying to gather information about us," Andre said.

"Zoey's a spy?" Pedro asked.

With all the laughter drained from the room, the weight of Andre's burdens settled down on him again, making his wasting muscles ache. "Yes, but I don't think she knows it," he replied. "We've been waiting them out, trying to figure out what they know about us."

"But tonight, Bel and I were in Forestville for dinner," Kos said.

"He eats?" Pedro asked.

"I'm not a vampire," Bel said.

"But aren't you like—?"

"I'm a half—"

"Later!" Andre growled.

Kos complied. "I smelled several of them — maybe ten or twelve Hunters. They were in the pub where Bel wanted to eat."

Andre had to unclench his jaw to say, "*Davo*. Did you get a look at them?"

Kos shook his head. "I didn't want to risk it."

"No matter," Bel said, gazing at the ceiling. "A bunch of guys in a pub sounds like initiates. We should assume the Bennetts called them in. Stupid of them to go out in public where you could smell them."

Pedro spoke up. "Who are initiates?"

"They're the young ones — it's like a rite of passage for them to kill someone who lives in the household," Kos said. "Which, I'm afraid, includes you."

Pedro took the threat in stride, just like he had all those years ago when he walked in on Andre feeding. "Initiation? That's messed up, man. How old?"

"As young as thirteen, I've heard. If the initiates are here, it means they plan to attack us soon," Andre said. He shifted in a chair, trying to soothe his tired bones.

By the time they had explained the pertinent details, Pedro's face was drained of color. "Shit. They hate you all for being predators, but they're the ones who sound like the animals."

"That about sums it up," Bel said. "Andre, do you know how much you've been weakened since you left Croatia?"

Andre shook his head. "I haven't wanted to test myself."

"What about you, Kos?"

"I don't know either."

"Well, it's time to test what you're capable of. Let's go over to the workroom and you can try lifting heavy shit."

"Why are they getting weaker?" Pedro asked Bel, as they descended into the underground cellars.

"Because they were made vampires in Croatia," Bel said. "It's their homeland. Their blood ties them there. When they don't live there, they're weakened."

"Why don't they go back?"

"Forced exile is the Hunters' strategy. They always patrol places where they've driven out vampires. If they were unable to kill them, they know the wasting disease eventually will."

When Andre opened the door, the musty smell of wine barrels was heavy in the cool air of the cellar.

"What causes the disease?" Pedro asked.

"No one knows. It doesn't seem to be in the blood," Bel replied. "Even if Andre flew in people from Croatia today and fed from them, it wouldn't help. I've considered studying it, but I don't even know where to start."

"Study? Like vampire medical research?"

"It's a hobby of mine."

Andre snorted. "If by hobby, you mean a graduate degree from Cambridge and four decades later one from Oxford." He was damn proud of Bel, actually, but every time he attempted to say so, his tongue tied in knots. He no longer tried.

"If the wine is making them stronger, why not study that?"

"My thoughts exactly," Bel replied. "I've got an experiment in mind."

"There's something I don't understand — if you weren't suffering from the disease in Croatia, why did you drink wine?"

"It made us strong," Kos replied. "We still needed blood, but much less."

When they arrived in the winemaking facility, Bel put them through a rigorous fitness test. Andre and Kos lifted empty oak barrels and then barrels full of wine. He estimated they weighed roughly five hundred pounds each.

"Why do we even bother with the forklift?" Pedro asked.

Disheartened, Andre ignored the joke, stooping over the stainless steel worktable.

"It's more difficult than you thought?" Bel guessed.

"I'm a bit fatigued," Andre said.

They all looked at Kos. "You?"

"I feel like I just had my ass handed to me."

"Let's try shifting one of the vats," Bel said.

Together, they were able to move an empty stainless steel vat several feet to the side. They couldn't even budge the full one.

"But it weighs forty tons," Pedro said. "How could you possibly move it?"

In reply, Kos asked Andre, "Do you remember the time you pushed over Uta's grain silo? God, that was funny. She had to come to you to borrow grain to feed her household. She was so pissed."

"Of course I remember. It's not wise to forget if you've angered Uta," Andre said. "I will never forget the look on her face." A smile came to his own. What was Uta up to these days? How would a former tribal queen and freedom fighter against the Roman Empire pass her time in the twenty-first century? Christ, she was a handful.

"When was the last time you flew?" Bel asked.

"No way," Pedro said. "You can't be serious."

Andre ignored him.

"Nineteen forty-two. I was curious about the fortifications being constructed along the California coast to defend against a Japanese attack. I went out to see for myself."

"Have you tried since?"

"No."

Bel gestured to the door. "We have a little while until dawn. Let's see what you've got left."

Outside, Andre stepped forward while they formed a semicircle around him. He planted his feet firmly on the ground and did not allow himself to think twice. He bent his knees and pushed off his toes. Shooting up into the air, he landed on the gentle slope of the roof.

"*Madre de Dios,*" Pedro said.

Bel and Kos exchanged a worried glance. It made the sinking feeling in Andre's stomach worse. No one said a thing, which gave him time to wonder how long he had before he shriveled up like a raisin and keeled over in the manner of a decrepit human.

"What?"

"You heard him," Bel said. "In 1942 he flew up and down the coast inspecting military fortifications. Today he could only hop onto the roof."

"Oh. What about you, Kos? Can you fly?" Pedro asked.

"No. You have to be an old vampire before you are strong enough to fly. And I left the homeland very soon after turning. I will never fly." He said it too matter-of-factly, his way of hiding his feelings.

The gray light of dawn peeked over the horizon as they entered the house. Andre said to Bel, "It's clear we are significantly diminished. We can't fight them. What do you suggest we do?"

"I'd like to call in my soldiers," Bel said.

"Vampires?" Andre asked.

"Some, and others with unique talents. They could provide a measure of protection day and night. There are a dozen of them."

"Yes. Call them right away," Andre said. "Of course we'll pay your usual rates."

Bel flinched, and his shoulders sagged.

His son's mannerisms were too much like his own for Andre not to notice. Bel was in a position to help him, and Andre had stolen his thunder, not on purpose exactly, but on instinct. A part of Andre wanted to engage in their usual pissing contest and insist he didn't really need Bel, but it seemed wiser to give in. One of them had to start acting like an adult if things were going to change between them.

"Bel, I'm grateful for your help. We'd probably be packing our bags tomorrow without you here."

Bel nodded. "I also think you and Kos should start drinking the wine. As much as you can tolerate. Let's see how much strength it will give you."

Andre had been so focused on how to share his success with his brother and sister vampires that he hadn't considered how much he needed it himself. This time the praise came easier. "That's a good idea."

"I agree. I'll even enjoy taking this medicine," Kos said.

CHAPTER 13

Zoey let herself doze in bed much later than she would have at home. The yellow room invited the luxury in a way Zoey's bare white walls did not. The morning sun poured in through the windows she had left uncovered and warmed her on the bed, as did the memories of Andre. Her skin began to flush. She wondered what would happen when she saw him. Would it be awkward? Would he be affectionate with her? She didn't doubt his desire, but she couldn't guess how he would act on it.

She grew restless thinking of him, no longer enjoying the bed. After a quick shower, she pulled on cotton slacks and a white blouse.

As she stepped out of her room, Andre's door opened at the end of the hallway and Ally, the pretty bookkeeper, stepped out. She straightened her clothing, her skin flushed just like Zoey's had felt only minutes ago. There was only one thing she could have been doing in his room that would have left her looking that way. Zoey stared, mouth agape. Mr. Quick Fuck was at it again.

As Ally exited Andre's room, the man himself was revealed behind her in the doorway. When their gazes met, she turned toward the stairwell. Ally was several steps behind her, but her footsteps sounded on the hallway leading to the south wing of the house as Zoey continued on to the kitchen.

Her heart pounded, and she wanted to hide. What was this feeling? Embarrassment? Disappointment? Whatever it was, she didn't like it. But one thing was abundantly clear—she wasn't numb. She should give him credit for that. Andre Maras had stirred up plenty of forgotten feelings in her, even if they were unpleasant. Unlike the base physical responses Ethan elicited from her, these feelings twisted her nerves and churned her stomach.

She tried to rally her sense of dignity and walked into the kitchen. Some of the women who worked on the estate were seated around the table. Yesterday, Pedro had introduced her to the cook, a house-keeper, and the winery's administrative assistant. Now, it appeared that Lena was holding court.

The women turned toward her, and she had the strange feeling they had been talking about her. What could they possibly be say-ing? No one uttered a greeting or offered her a cup of coffee. They simply stared. Zoey set her jaw and walked toward the coffee maker to help herself.

She pulled a barstool up to the kitchen counter and sipped her coffee, trying to ignore the awkward quiet. She was halfway through her mug, and still no one spoke. Being the odd one out was perfectly fine—she preferred to keep her distance from people. Being the object of scorn—that was different. The fraught silence exacerbated the yucky, unnamable feeling in her stomach.

For some reason, it put Zoey at ease when Susan came into the kitchen. She quickly saw the household staff seated around the kitchen table.

"Shame on all of you," Susan whispered, loud and clear. At full volume Susan continued, "Lena, Andre just called me with a message for you. He wants me to take Zoey wine tasting today and asked that you prepare her a nice big breakfast. She's drinking, I'm driving."

Zoey was surprised to hear he had given the instructions. "I don't think that's a good idea."

"He said you'd resist. He wants you to go tasting to get a feel for the competitors. He gave me a list of six wineries, several wines each. Lay down a good base to soak up the alcohol. Lena, she'll need eggs and toast. Oh, you made fried potatoes," she said while lifting the lid off a pan. "Perfect. Fruit, Zoey? Lena's got beautiful berries in the fridge. And here's some sliced melon."

Stunned, Zoey sat down on her stool and sipped coffee as Susan piled her plate with impossible amounts of food.

After devouring all her eggs and some of her potatoes, her stomach revolted at the thought of another bite. Susan must have sensed that she was upset. She hovered nearby, like Zoey's personal cheering squad in the clean plate competition. When she crossed the finish line, Susan swept her up quickly and led her outside and into a new model Mercedes coupe.

"It's Andre's. The car is so tiny, I think he must have to fold himself in half to fit in it." Susan chuckled at her own joke.

Zoey didn't want to talk about him. "Hmmm."

"…and Rock Fall, their Zinfandel is supposed to be very good," Andre said into the phone. "That's six wineries. Plenty to fill a day. I'll call ahead and let them know you're coming."

Kos entered his bedroom as Andre wrapped up his instructions to Susan.

"Sounds good," she said.

"Susan, I can't thank you enough. I'm afraid I've seriously offended her."

"I'll smooth things over for you, don't worry. If she's in the kitchen now, I better go rescue her—Lena's got her claws out. Bye." She hung up before Andre could reply.

"Lena's claws?" Kos asked.

"Don't ask me." Andre set the phone down hard. He would finish getting dressed, go to his office, and order that new bottling machine.

"What was all that about?"

"Zoey saw Ally leave my room just now. She looked…" Andre stared into his closet.

"You're worried you hurt her feelings?" The bed squeaked as Kos sat down. "Damn, Andre, you've got it bad."

He pushed the worries over what shirt to wear out of his mind, closed his eyes, and blindly grabbed the first in reach—stripes. Fine.

"I've got it under control," he said, turning to look at his son.

Kos raised his eyebrows as if he intended to challenge the assertion. Andre bared a sliver of teeth. He had tamed his animal instincts to be nearly invisible and had taught Kos to do the same, but sometimes it was just easier to snarl than to speak.

"I'm sure you do." Kos backed down from the challenge with a hint of sarcasm, squinting at Andre. "I have to admit, I don't really understand the problem—just sleep with her."

Unbuttoning the shirt off the hanger gave him an excuse to look away from Kos. "I can't—I'd bite her."

"So bite her. I'm sure she'd like it. They always do."

Andre barked out his reply. "Kos, I just can't!"

A quick gasp told him Kos finally put the pieces together. "You think you'd bond with her?" His tone was so gentle it completely disarmed Andre.

He sat next to Kos on the bed. "Yes. I can't keep my hunger for her blood and my…desire…separate. She's the first woman I've really wanted since your mother—"

"How did it happen so fast?"

"I don't know. It was the same with Mila. Within a day of meeting her, I wanted her beyond all reason." And there had been the little blond boy she always had in tow, who was equally irresistible in his own way. It had been a bad match from the start, and he would have spared himself centuries of pain if only…

If he had resisted his desire for her, there would be no Bel, and Kos would have never become his son. He would not trade them for anything—at least now. In the worst of his torment, if he'd had the choice, he might have wished them out of existence. Squeezing his eyes shut, he stopped what-iffing. What a terrible father he was.

"But how do you know you'd bond with her?"

Andre tensed at the words, sitting up straight. "*Davo*. I should have explained this to you long ago." No one had given him the vampire birds and bees talk. He owed Kos better.

"Give yourself a break. You've explained. Many, many, times."

Andre wiped his brow.

"But how do you know for sure?" Kos continued. "Blood and sex always go together—"

Andre's voice came out a whisper. "Since your mother's death, I have been cured of that particular association. The constant torment of being ripped apart cell by cell will do that to you."

"I was scared the severed bond would kill you," Kos whispered back.

"Many times I wished it would."

Kos patted Andre's back sympathetically. "I know, Father. I know."

Andre suspected he wasn't done with his questions about Zoey, but it was time to change the subject. "What did you want anyway?"

"What?" Kos replied.

"Why did you come looking for me?"

"Oh, right. Just wanted to tell you Bel arranged things with his crew and went to stay at my place."

"Good, that sounds good. I'll be in my office all day if you need me."

When he woke up, Lucas surveyed the meager supplies in the dilapidated kitchen of Hunter headquarters. In a rotten mood from a night's sleep on the floor, he became more irritable when he found there was no coffee in the house. He called Ethan.

"They are eating oatmeal from envelopes for three meals a day up here. Bring me a goddamn cup of coffee."

"Hello, Lucas." Ethan laughed. "Thriving in your native environment are you? I'm only half an hour away. I'll stop now, looks like the last chance for a coffee. Funny how every ten-person town in Northern California has at least one espresso bar."

"Yeah, funny." Lucas knew he did not sound amused.

"See you soon."

Ethan pulled up in his sports car half an hour later with a large cup of coffee for his brother. The first sip of milky coffee tasted like heaven, and the caffeine fix it promised was a godsend. Instantly, Lucas relaxed, shedding the thick skin he'd been wearing. Just having Ethan there made him feel less alien among the Hunters.

The brothers walked back into the house together to the master bedroom, which Stephen had claimed as the command center. Mick and Stephen stood at a makeshift table they had assembled with shipping pallets. Both men shook hands with the new arrival, and Lucas stiffened at the friendly pat Stephen delivered to Ethan's shoulder.

Lucas turned to his brother. "The initiates are restless and looking for action, but I don't want to pull out Zoey and storm Kaštel

Estate with guns blazing. I'm still hoping she'll call us with some useful intel. Have you spoken to her?"

Ethan took out his phone and looked at the screen. "Only briefly, no news."

"So, I suggested to Lucas that we kidnap someone from Maras's household to keep the initiates occupied," Mick said. "We may get intel that way too."

"Who do you have in mind?" Ethan asked.

"Whoever we can get our hands on." Stephen answered Ethan's question, but he stared directly at Lucas. A shudder started at the base of Lucas's spine, causing his whole body to tense. It was the shudder of sympathetic pain, as if he had seen someone else get injured. Only then did the kidnapping victim become real to Lucas. Plan B was a real person, a woman with hopes and dreams, soon to be at the mercy of sick creeps like Stephen and Mick.

CHAPTER 14

At every winery, Susan simply flashed her Kaštel Estate business card and they received generous hospitality. The wine and the VIP treatment began to relax Zoey.

They wound down a narrow highway shaded by redwood trees until they arrived in Guerneville, where Susan bought them both an ice cream. At a table in the shade outside the ice cream shop, Zoey asked, "What was that all about in the kitchen this morning? I don't know how I have made all the staff hate me in less than twenty-four hours."

"Oh, relax. It's not everyone. It's just Lena. She can tell Andre likes you and she's jealous."

"Well, she has nothing to fear. I'm not interested in becoming a part of his harem." Zoey spooned a bite of strawberry ice cream into her mouth.

Susan licked her spoon clean. "What do you mean?"

"I saw that pretty bookkeeper leaving his room this morning. They obviously weren't going over the books."

Susan laughed.

Confused, Zoey tried to explain. "If Lena is jealous of me, I'm guessing Andre must be sleeping with several of them, maybe all…" She set her bowl down. "Wait, are you sleeping with him too?"

Susan wagged the spoon at Zoey like she was a naughty child. "No, I'm not. And neither is Ally. I know that's what it looked like to you, but I also know for certain that's not what happened." She scooped chocolate ice cream onto the spoon and swallowed it. "Ally is my girlfriend; she's not into guys."

Zoey felt her forehead crease with doubt.

"I'm serious. Andre has a medical condition, it's not my place to tell you more about it—you'll have to ask him. But, Ally helps him out with it sometimes. Most of the staff is trained to help him with his condition."

"Really? You're sure? She looked rather…ravished." Zoey stared into the empty ice cream cup, embarrassed she might have assumed incorrectly about Andre.

"Ravished? That's funny. Yes. I'm completely certain." Susan scraped the last bit of ice cream for her cup.

Zoey was almost convinced. "But then why would Lena be jealous of me?"

"She wants him for herself and she's mad that he wants you instead."

"I'm not sure he does."

"I am. I noticed the way he was looking at you and the way he was not looking at you yesterday in the kitchen." She glanced up, her look knowing.

Zoey tingled all over, her skin heating. Susan's words pleased her too much.

"And he asked me to take you out tasting today. He's not a jerk, but he's not exactly considerate either. You know, he called ahead to each of these wineries. I expect he called in some favors."

"Really?" The possibility made Zoey's heart flutter.

"So what about you?"

"What do you mean?" Zoey asked.

"Do you want him?"

Zoey tilted her head. "He's very attractive."

"That's not my question."

"I don't know. I thought I didn't want to be with anyone, but we have a connection that I haven't felt in a long time."

"When did you feel it before?"

"With my husband."

"Oh." That seemed to catch Susan off guard, and she stopped asking Zoey personal questions. "On to the next stop?"

"Sounds great," Zoey replied.

Ally and Pedro met them for dinner. It cleared up Zoey's last doubts about Ally and Andre to see her with Susan. From the way they leaned their heads into each other to the way they finished each other's sentences, it was obvious they were totally in love.

"Pedro, what's your opinion of Kaštel's current marketing strategy?"

"Strategy?" Pedro blew air from between his lips. "There is no strategy. Andre makes damn good wines. To the extent they sell, they sell themselves."

"But you advertise some. In magazines and online."

Ally leaned over the table and spoke in a stage whisper. "Don't tell that to Andre. You'll get us in trouble."

"What do you mean?"

"He forbids it." Pedro laughed. "Honest to God, Andre refuses to use the Internet."

"But I've seen the Kaštel Estate website."

"It's awful. Kos and I built it. Andre doesn't know." Pedro's laughter grew deeper.

"It's true." Ally giggled too. "I buried the costs in the accounting books."

Their laughter was contagious, but as Zoey joined in the mirth, the story seemed odd. Pedro made Andre sound like a grandpa and not a strapping hunk of a man that she wanted more than she ought to.

It was a rare warm evening and Pedro enjoyed the feeling of the air rushing past him in his open jeep. Pushing down the gas pedal, he hoped he didn't get pulled over for speeding. He turned on Miles Davis and the sultry blues horn solo led his thoughts straight to Lucas. Those golden eyes, hooded with desire, and that serious mouth turned hungry were proving hard to shake.

The wind moved over him like a lover's touch, caressing his arms and feathering through his hair.

Hard not to wish things were different. Zoey didn't seem like much of a threat, so maybe Lucas wasn't as bad as Andre thought. If everything just blew over, he could call the guy — have, like, a date.

Yeah, right. And then he would exfoliate four layers of skin so that Andre didn't accidentally rip his throat out.

He pulled up to the cottage and turned off the ignition. Something felt wrong. He scanned the bushes around the house, looking for anything unusual. That was when he noticed his front door was slightly ajar. Had someone been here and gone? Or were they still inside? Pedro reached into his glove compartment and pulled out his trusty pistol. Nothing would teach a guy to be ready to defend himself like school yard beatings for being *joto*.

Pedro kicked the door in and entered carefully, reaching for the light switch. Before he could hit the lights, the gun was kicked from his hand. Blow after blow landed on his torso, and he crouched down. If there had been just two or three of them, he might have had a chance. A door slammed and then the lights were turned on. The punches stopped and eight men with yellow eyes surrounded him. Pedro's gut clenched; their leader was an older version of Lucas Bennett, and he looked like one mean son of a bitch.

Fear and fury churned inside him, and he wanted to fight like a wild animal. But, he also knew there was no sense resisting them. He let them bind his hands behind him with duct tape. They covered his mouth with the same tape and then pushed him into a beat-up white delivery van.

Inside the dark van, surrounded by Hunters, Pedro's pulse raced. His mind raced with fearful images, intensifying his fear. He struggled to remain rational by planning a strategy. He had to protect Andre's plans for the wine. Should he admit he knew Andre and Kos were vampires or play dumb?

The van came to a stop and they pulled him out of its rear doors. They were at an isolated and run-down ranch house surrounded only by overgrown grass. No trees or buildings would offer hiding places, even if he could escape. Even the highway's traffic seemed sparse, with no promise of rescue by a passerby. The Hunters pushed Pedro toward a large shed in the back and locked him in.

CHAPTER 15

Zoey was tipsy and sleepy when she got back to Andre's after dinner. She planned to head upstairs, but she lingered with her foot on the bottom step to watch Susan hold Ally's hand as they went up the shadowed stairs. Sweet.

Next to her, a single light lit an oil painting on the wall and she found herself fingering the brass plate on its frame. *Maras Nekretnine.* The family estate in Croatia? A blond boy squatted in the foreground, drawing with a stick in the dirt. She could easily imagine it was Kos outside Kaštel as a boy. Whoever he was, she hoped he'd survived the ethnic wars that caused his family to flee their homeland.

"Damn it," came a deep cry from the parlor, startling Zoey.

Someone else laughed — Andre?

Then everything fell silent. The house had been so still that she hadn't noticed the parlor door ajar, a hint of golden light shining on the wooden floor of the hallway. She crept over and saw Andre, Kos, and Bel playing cards.

They all stared at their hands, not each other. Andre's jaw jutted, and Kos had his arms crossed. It was no "dogs playing poker" kind of party. There was an atmosphere of tension, and something told Zoey that it wasn't over who was winning.

Without turning his head, Andre said, "Are you coming in, Zoey?"

How had he known she was there? "I don't want to intrude."

"Not at all," he said, looking up at her. God, he was sexy in a dark pair of jeans and a green shirt that mirrored the color of his eyes. They pulled her like a magnet, drawing her into the room.

On the table sat stacks of red, white, green, and blue chips. "Poker?" she asked.

"Five card draw," Bel said.

The largest pile of chips on the table was in front of Andre, and next to his pile was a glass of wine. "You're drinking," she said. "Did you fall off the wagon?"

"He wasn't on the wagon," Kos said without looking up. He rapped his knuckles on the table, and Bel dealt more cards. They played with an easy rhythm that didn't require them to talk.

"You all must play often."

"Kos and I both suffer from insomnia—we keep each other company," Andre said. "Call."

Kos matched his bet and they threw down their hands.

"Shit," Bel said. "Drunk as a skunk and you still take all my money."

Andre smiled a crooked grin, and the gloom cleared from the room. "Things like this rarely change, Bel." He stood up and wobbled on his feet. "Hello, Zoey."

"You're drunk," she said.

"Just a little," he said. His eyes narrowed, and he reached out and drew her to him. Turning her so that her back was against his chest, he sniffed at her hair. "You're not entirely sober either."

"So what," she said. "I never said I don't drink."

He whispered in her ear. "Neither did I. You just assumed."

"Would you like to join us?" Kos asked.

"Let me get you a glass of wine," Bel said quickly, seconding Kos's invitation.

The glass was in her hand before she could refuse, so she just said, "Thank you." She took a sip of the wine. It was by far the best thing she'd tasted that day. She took a small step away from Andre to set her glass down on the table.

"Do you play poker?" Kos asked.

"I can play."

"Great. I'll deal you in," Bel said. He placed four piles of cards in a circle around the table.

Again she wasn't fast enough to refuse, even if she had wanted to. Either she was the distraction they'd been waiting for, or they wanted to torment Andre with her presence. He remained quiet as his sons drew her into their game. Did he want her there?

There were only three chairs around the table, and she wasn't sure where to sit. She swallowed a hiccup, hoping none of them heard it.

Jumping up, Kos said, "I'll get another chair."

"She'll sit with me." Andre pulled her onto his lap in one quick motion.

For the briefest second, she resisted him. He was her client. She didn't flirt. She fucked and moved on. But heat flared where their bodies touched, and melted away her misgivings.

Ethan would probably fall over if he saw her sitting on someone's lap; Andre brought out a completely different side of her. Justine had told her to have some fun, and it seemed like, for once, she might, thanks to a day of wine and an irresistibly hot client.

Zoey settled on his lap as well as she could, given her feet didn't touch the floor, and picked up her cards. Turning over her shoulder, she said, "You can see my hand."

He compared her cards to his own. "Play mine." He passed them to her, and she had to flex her toes to keep steady. He placed one of his hands on each of her hips. She wriggled a little to find her balance and felt him harden between her cheeks.

He wanted her to concentrate on playing cards with that magnificent thing underneath her? Fine. She was up to the challenge.

His hand was only marginally better than hers; he had a pair of threes. In the corner of her eye, Andre tilted his head toward his chips—an invitation to bet them freely.

"I'll raise," she said. "A green. What's this worth, anyway?"

"That one is worth one hundred dollars," Andre replied.

Zoey sputtered. "You guys don't mess around." She tapped the table with the edge of the chip reluctantly, then pressed it down onto the table with her thumb, saying, "One hundred of Andre's money it is."

Watching her with narrowed eyes, Kos said, "I fold." He swung his head to look at this brother with equal interest.

"I'll raise you two more green ones," Bel said, trilling the last words and throwing in three of his own chips. Was he mocking her?

"Call," Zoey said, quicker than she meant to. Bel's head jerked up, and his eyes also sharpened on her. Now she had his attention. Tossing in the two chips she owed, she discarded three cards and he wordlessly dealt them both more. Nothing but a jack high to go with her threes.

A muscle pulsed in Bel's jaw. He could have been Andre's identical twin, but his torn black jeans and Converse sneakers made him look younger. Still, a tell was a tell.

Holding up a chip and cocking her head, she asked, "I suppose this black one is worth five hundred?"

"It is," he replied, crossing his arms. "And it hardly matters to you, since it's Andre's money."

"Oh, it matters to me. I don't like to lose." She threw two into the pile.

Andre's breath tickled her ear when he whispered, "Are you a cardsharp?"

She shrugged and tried to keep a smile from her lips.

As Bel watched her, rubbing a thousand dollars' worth of black chips together between his fingers, Andre wrapped his large hands around her hips. He worked his thumbs up under the bottom edge of her blouse and rubbed featherlight circles on her lower back. Damn. Her heart raced, and it wasn't because of the bluff.

"Well?" she asked Bel.

"I fold."

Triumphant, she clapped her hands together and scooped up her winnings. Kos dealt another hand as Andre dipped his thumb into the gaping waistband and lightly teased the very top of the crevice between her cheeks.

She did her best to concentrate on the next game, ignoring his sexy strokes along her back. But when he twitched and grew bigger underneath her, she gave up. Between her legs, she went damp and the heavy throbbing became insistent.

Suddenly, Kos sniffed and then coughed like he couldn't clear his throat. He turned bright red.

"Kos, are you okay?" she asked, making to stand up. Andre held her in place.

Kos caught his breath just as suddenly and stood. "I'm ready to call it a night. Bel, let's go back to my place."

Bel seemed a little surprised, but when he looked at Kos he didn't argue.

Andre looked at him. "Everything's set with your—"

"I've got it under control," Bel replied.

When the door closed behind them Andre said in her ear, "Don't move."

"Is everything all right?"

The pads of his fingers pressed into her belly ever so slightly, the only sign he was worried about something. "Perfectly fine. Bel is taking care of something for me. Let's not talk about it anymore."

He lifted her hair off her neck and licked up her spine from the collar of her shirt to her hairline.

She shivered.

"Mmmm, I've been wanting to do that since you sat down. Turn around so I can see you." She stood and faced him and he reached for her again, pulling her back down to straddle him. "You smell delicious."

What did he smell? She didn't wear perfume and surely the scent of her soap and shampoo had faded over the long day. It didn't matter, really. The way he said it, all gravelly and low, was the best part of the compliment.

He cupped the back of her head and drew her into a gentle kiss. She wanted to kiss him back, but her lips simply would not open up to him.

"Zoey, about this morning—"

"Susan explained everything to me."

"What did she say?"

"She told me about your medical condition."

"Ah. What about it?"

"That Ally and several of your staff are trained to help you." When he looked irritated, Zoey hurried to defend her new friend. "She didn't violate your privacy. She wouldn't tell me more and insisted I ask you myself." His furrowed brow relaxed with relief. Some people might find his frown menacing, but not her. She smoothed the triangle between his eyes with her thumb, noticing the small lines lingering there even when he relaxed.

He brought out the strangest combination of tenderness and raw sexual desire in her. The tenderness she hadn't felt since Michael had died, the desire she was certain she had never felt so intensely. She should be scared to death about both of those, but at the moment, she just wanted to be with him.

Had she just smoothed away his worry lines? The scent of her arousal hung thick in the air; he would find her slick with wanting if he could finally get her naked. Yet she touched his face with a kindness he hadn't known since long before Mila died.

Her lips pursed into a subtle O—she'd surprised herself with the unconscious gesture.

Until that moment, he hadn't truly considered why she might have walked away from him the night they met. She must have her own reasons to remain distant. Was she fighting this attraction too?

Given how closely they sat, pressing their excited bodies together like teenagers, her resistance must be almost as weak as his.

He licked her neck again, this time from her collarbone up the length of her carotid artery. Her heartbeat was muffled, the metallic scent of her blood mixing with the delicious musk coming from between her legs. He was hungry instantly. He wanted to lick that wetness between her legs and taste it on his tongue mixing with her blood. He wanted to slip his fingers—

"Will you tell me about your condition?" she asked.

"No…"

She didn't look away.

"But I must tell you it makes it impossible for me to be with a woman."

"You've gotta be kidding me," she said, and rocked against him.

The friction sent a jolt of pleasure through him, leaving no room to doubt that he was in perfect working order. "No. That's not what I mean."

Curiosity replaced skepticism on her face.

"Because of the burden of my…condition, I decided a long time ago that I will not get involved with a woman. I tried once and it caused both of us great suffering."

Without warning, she stood and crossed to the bar. After filling a glass of water from the tap, she faced him again and took a small sip. Tilting her head, she opened her mouth, then closed it again. He scooted to the edge of his chair, trying to hear the words she wasn't saying.

Finally, she opened her mouth again to ask, "So no getting close to anyone?"

"Exactly."

She took another sip from her glass. "I have the same rule."

He had guessed as much. "That's a shame, Zoey. A beautiful, intelligent woman like you should have a husband and family. These are the things that matter in life. Without Kos and Bel, I'd have nothing."

Her lips pursed, and her eyes flicked to the door like she wanted to run. He would have chased her, but she stayed. Her chest rose and fell in unnaturally even breaths. She looked at him with her bottomless brown eyes, and he sucked in a gulp of air, wanting to know what that hurt was.

She turned her back to him and filled her already full glass. "I had those things once. They don't always last, and the pain of losing them…" Her glass clanked heavily on the stone bar. "I'm not willing to go through it again."

Her words could have been his own. Was this their mysterious connection? If so, it was the easiest way out of the dangerous temptation. Neither of them wanted to try again. He should send her to bed and be done with it: no more fantasies, no more licking.

He could not do it, though. He wanted to know too much. Moving faster than he should have, he went to her side. He leaned his back against the bar, and could see the side of her face as she stared at the wall.

"You were married?" he asked.

Angling her shoulders toward him, she rested one curvy hip against the bar and wrapped her arms around herself. "Is this a good idea? Talking about all this?"

"I sincerely doubt it." Silently, he willed her to tell him her tragedy. He had to know what had damaged her.

She replied with a squeak of a laugh. "Well, since we're being honest. Yes, I was married."

"Did you divorce?"

"No. I'm a widow." She paused, then her words spilled out all at once. "It feels weird to say that. I never tell anyone and I never use that word. I never even think it."

Wine crept back up his throat. Widow? He schooled his face, making certain that nothing about his expression showed the fear and anxiety churning inside him. Whatever was happening between them felt out his control.

Despite his best efforts to conceal his feelings, Zoey's quizzical expression told him she saw something that she wondered about. Before she could voice a question, he asked another.

"When did he die?"

"Seven years ago."

"How?"

Zoey averted her eyes and wrung her hands. He waited. Finally, she spoke. "He jumped off the Golden Gate Bridge."

"*Davo,*" Andre said. A lump the size of a grapefruit had formed in his throat. Two survivors of their spouses' suicides. It explained the recognition that had passed between them.

"Michael and I met in college and fell in love. We married after graduation. He was..."

How would he describe Mila? Even dead, she couldn't be encapsulated in a few adjectives.

Far more articulate than him, Zoey found the right words. "He was everything to me. But even before we married, he began to change. He developed schizophrenia. Turns out it ran in his family. He was paranoid, depressed. Medication helped his symptoms but made him feel terrible." She paused, as if she needed his permission to continue baring her soul.

Andre nodded and she went on.

Her face was perfectly placid, like she wore a mask. "He was miserable and not the man I'd loved." Her hands fell to her sides limply. "When he ended his life, I was relieved. I'd lost him already and I was happy that his suffering was over."

"You are very understanding," Andre said. How she managed it was beyond him. He was still furious at Mila for killing herself. "Weren't you angry?"

"I'm still angry, even though I know he wasn't in control of himself."

Her impassive face was inches from his. Where was her anger? It wasn't in her eyes, or the set of her mouth.

"He was strong and generous and he treated me like a queen. I trusted him completely. When someone you trust goes off the deep end—" She slapped her palms against her thighs.

He wished he could take away all her pain, let her love someone again. Not him, of course, but someone. "So no real connection to anyone, just sex? That's why you were in the bar that night?"

Then she peered at him and replied with a confession. "I've been sleeping with Ethan Bennett and I can't figure out how to end it."

Seconds too late, Andre tried to feign surprise.

Her eyes narrowed. "You knew. How?"

He looked away. "It was just a guess. When I hired his firm, he spoke very fondly of you."

"So do you think I'm a slut?"

"That wouldn't be fair. I've fucked thousands of women." Thousands—what was he thinking? It wasn't that many considering his age; but for a human, he would be a slut.

Her dark eyes became crescent moons when she laughed. "Strangely, that does make me feel better."

It also made it clear how alarmingly close he was to a bond that he'd sworn against—just one succulent bite away. He wanted to hold her and lick her wounds, he wanted time to explore her body with his hands, his fingers, his tongue, he wanted to make love to her slowly. And all of those were things he could not risk doing.

"So we're two of a kind." Her statement was a question. Clearly, she sensed he was holding back.

For a few beats, Andre just looked at her mouth. Then he said, "Zoey, you bring me dangerously close to feelings I want to avoid. If we take this further, we risk something neither one of us wants: an attachment."

"So I should go up to bed now, and we continue working together as if we don't want to rip each other's clothes off."

"I think that is the wisest option."

"Tell me that's what you want, and I'll leave." With her small, soft fingers she took his hand.

"I have not stopped thinking about you since the night we met." He turned to face her squarely and gripped her hand. "Now that you are here, I want you even more."

An unconscious smile played on her lips; his admission had pleased her. Her lovely, unguarded expression made what came next harder to say. "When we sat together at the bar, I imagined taking you hard and fast—a quick fuck. I do not want you to go. But if you stay, it has to be that. It has to be quick and casual. We try to get each other out of our systems."

She nibbled her lower lip. Black swirls of some emotion churned in her eyes. Finally her lips parted…

Please, say yes.

She blinked, then spoke very quietly. "Thanks for being honest. I'm going to bed." Andre's hand slid from her fingers. As she walked away, she said over her shoulder, "Can we meet in the dining room at nine in the morning? I want to show you some of my proposals."

"Certainly."

That was twice that she'd had the sense to walk away from him when he was too weak. Andre waited until her bedroom door closed before going to his own. He decided a cold shower might help relieve him. He would likely need several of those before she left on Friday, but if that kept them safely apart, so be it.

He waited until her bedroom door closed with a loud click before following her upstairs. Lena's scent laced the air, diluting Zoey's intoxicating essence. She must have been up late cooking. The smell of baking pastries often filled the house in the early morning hours, although he paid it little attention, not having eaten since before Jesus Christ was born. But tonight, it just reminded him of one more burden—dealing with his pain in the ass cook, saving the vampires, and resisting Zoey, which might be the most difficult. She kept him constantly hard, and it would be a relief to get his jeans off.

He unbuttoned them, freeing his straining cock, at the same time that he swung his bedroom door open with unnecessary force. *Davo.* Lena stood at the foot of his bed, her clothing in a pile at her feet. She wore only plain cotton underwear, her hands pulled behind her back as if she were going to unfasten her bra.

Covering his cock with his hand, he growled at her. "What on earth are you doing?"

"Let me help you with that." She tilted her head at his groin, smiling that ridiculous grin that showed all her teeth. Her eyes showed desperation, not desire, but her womanly smell was in the air. She wanted him with years of pent up sexual frustration.

He studied her. She was an ideal beauty by current standards. Her breasts were large; the rest of her figure was trim. Her wavy dark blond hair gave her a bedroom look all the time. White panties and big blue eyes added an innocence to her sensual appearance. Yet even now, with a raging hard-on, he was not interested.

"*Davo*. Not now."

"Andre, please. Let's just try. I want you. Feed from me and take me. It doesn't have to mean anything." She put her thumbs into the waist of her panties. He could smell her just as he did the day before in his office. His male instincts reacted to her feminine scent. He was already impossibly turned on. Could Lena give him some relief, help him forget about Zoey?

She stood with her knees pressed together, bowing her too lean legs awkwardly. Her breasts were bigger than Zoey's, with light areolas showing through her white bra…

No. Lena was not the one he wanted, and his erection withered. She had relieved him, all right—just not how she had meant to. Her glance flicked down to his groin and she saw that his erection had deflated.

"You asshole! What's wrong with me?" She ran up to him and pounded her fists on his chest. "I came here to serve you with my body. I'm dying for you, but you only tease me. Please!" She started to cry. "Andre, please, it's my destiny. I can't move on with my life until you give this to me." Then she dissolved in sobs.

The melodrama just annoyed Andre more. This was exactly the reason he did not fuck where he ate. For his sanity and hers, he needed her out of his house. He went to the phone next to his bed and dialed. As soon as Kos answered, he barked, "Come get Lena. She can't stay anymore."

Lena jerked her head up. "No! Don't send me away! Please."

"Quiet, damn it!"

Kos said, "What happened?"

"Come get her."

"What do you want me to do with her?"

Andre rubbed his eyelids with his thumb and forefinger. "I don't care. Keep her for yourself, or help her find a new job."

"I'm on my way," Kos said and hung up.

She had managed to get control of her tears. "A new job?"

"Yes. I am not the only vampire in the world," he called out, on his way to the bathroom.

She sniffed. "You'll help me?"

He returned with a bathrobe. "Lena. I am sorry I have disappointed you. Kos will help you find someone to serve." He bundled up her clothes and steered her down the hall.

Their loud voices must have roused Zoey. She opened her door an inch just as they passed. Lena was not quite covered by the bathrobe. Zoey's wide eyes sought out Andre. He met her gaze for a moment and kept walking. She closed the door again quickly, and he squeezed the bridge of his nose. He couldn't afford to care about what she thought of him.

CHAPTER 16

The drive to Kos's cabin at the beach usually took forty-five minutes, but he stopped in town so that Lena could pick up some groceries at the all-night supermarket. She hardly spoke. His pity welled up in the silence. She smelled like flour, wholesome. Her deep blue eyes were rimmed red, and her cheeks were still pink with the blush of humiliation. He wanted to pull the car over and pull her into his arms, to soothe away her shame.

He shifted gears, and the back of his hand brushed against her slender thigh. She jerked away, and it was a good thing too — because if she gave the slightest hint she'd let him comfort her, he would never let her go. There were about a million reasons that was a bad idea, and the first on the list was that she wanted Andre, not him.

His house came into view, illuminated by the car's headlights.

"Kos, what a beautiful home!"

He tried to see his sanctuary through her eyes. It was a modern house designed to blend into the natural environment, with a low sloping roof and cedar shingles that were the same color gray as the fog that hovered overhead most days. It was beautiful in a California way, very unlike the coastal villas on Šolta.

Glancing at her, he was pleased to see the hint of a smile on her face. "I'm glad you think so."

He carried in her two small bags and she followed him inside.

"The house only has this one main room. You'll have to build a fire in the woodstove if the nights cool off."

"Beautiful. What a cozy place."

Puzzled, he looked around. Cozy was a nice word for the way his bookshelves were crammed into every bit of wall space.

"Feel free to use the hot tub on the deck."

"Okay," she replied. Then, she noticed the basic kitchen—just a counter with a mini fridge and two-burner range—and frowned.

"Do you need something else? My kitchen's not very well equipped."

"No, no. It's just me after all. I'm not cooking for a whole household here." She said it wistfully. She must really like her job—well, the cooking part anyway.

"Lena, please make yourself at home. Take the bedroom."

"No, I couldn't. I'm already imposing on you so much. As soon as I find somewhere else—"

"Don't worry about that. I'll find you a good household. Somewhere safe and comfortable." And, somewhere far away from him, so he didn't start thinking of keeping her for himself. He had rules against that sort of thing.

"No. I was safe and comfortable with Andre. I need something more." Her cheeks reddened, and she ran her index finger along his black shiny countertop.

"Lena, I'm serious about the bedroom. I'm hardly ever here. It would be a waste of a perfectly comfortable bed for you to sleep on the couch."

She nodded too, with a bland look on her face that made Kos think she wasn't really conceding.

"I've got to go back to Kaštel," he said, "but I'll be here after sundown tomorrow to check on you. I wrote my mobile number down on the table."

He went into the bedroom to grab a change of clothes for himself. Then coming back into the living room, he found her reading titles on a bookshelf. "I'm actually glad to get you out of Kaštel. Maybe you'll be safer here. Hunters are closing in on my father and me." Her head jerked up. "You know about Hunters, don't you?"

"Yes, my grandmother told me all about them."

"So don't let anyone in. The house is alarmed, the windows are bulletproof. You'll be safe here."

"Okay." Following him to the door, she said, "Thank you. It's really too kind of you."

"Lena." He turned and faced her, taking her chin in hand to force her to look at him. He hadn't thought before he reached for her, but with her face cradled in his hand, he remembered Andre touching his mother that way. "Don't even think that. You deserve far more than my father could give you. I know how painful it was for you and I'm sorry. I will find the right vampire for you to serve."

Tears made her round blue eyes glitter and he wanted to wrap her in his arms. Instead, he pulled away and went out the front door.

CHAPTER 17

With his hipbone digging into the floor that was his bed at headquarters, Lucas lay awake, worrying over a puzzle. According to Stephen, the Hunters would watch Kaštel the following day for a chance to grab one of the household women when the sun was up. He didn't trust his father. A childhood full of unpredictable rages and deliberate cruelties had taught him that lesson. He didn't know what Stephen was up to, but it was a given that he was not party to all his father's plans. He braced himself for some kind of surprise and finally drifted off to sleep.

He awoke to commotion outside, and immediately suspected it was the surprise. He stood up, shedding the blankets he had wrapped around himself as both padding and protection from the foul brown carpet. Lucas pulled on his jeans and made it outside in time to see a muscular man, bound with duct tape, being shoved into the shed.

Seeing Pedro again like that…it stole his breath. He should have known. But still, he was frozen mid-stride, shocked and furious. Quickly, he masked those emotions. He would have to play the loyal son and Hunter.

His father and Ethan conferenced near the shed.

He swaggered toward them. "You've captured the winemaker? Excellent. I suspect he'll have more information than either of the women."

Stephen didn't bother to conceal his surprise at Lucas's reaction. "Yes, I expect so."

"What's your plan?" Lucas put his hands on his hips in case they went for Stephen's throat of their own accord.

Stephen squinted at him. "I want you to interrogate him."

He nodded. "Good cop, bad cop?"

"No, just bad cop."

Lucas kept nodding. "Okay. I like it. I'll wait until he's tired and hungry. No water or food, no bathroom breaks. Who will guard him?"

"I'll set up a rotation of initiates in pairs," Mick said.

Lucas was already walking away. So they meant to test him. How would he manage to keep both himself and Pedro alive?

CHAPTER 18

Zoey's laptop connected to a small projector, which pointed at a blank space on the wall. Like in her room, the equipment contrasted starkly with the antique table and chairs. The tiny clock on the screen's upper right corner said nine a.m. when Andre and Kos walked into the dining room. Good, she liked it when her clients were prompt.

He wore slacks and a white dress shirt with sleeves rolled up. The white looked too good on him; it emphasized his broad shoulders and showed just how white his teeth were.

Forcing a smile, she tugged on her blouse, feeling exposed. She'd told him her dark secrets, only to see a nearly naked supermodel leave his room moments later. Shit, she'd never felt more awkward, which proved her decision to keep away from him was for the best. She began to fidget with the computer. Kos poured himself some coffee and then joined them at the table.

Thankfully, as she began her presentation, her professional persona settled on her like a magical cloak. Her awkwardness vanished. She showed them some wine labels that her designer had mocked up. They were simple sketches in black and white, based on images she'd photographed around the estate. She had already sent the designer pictures of the embroidery patterns in her room and some of the motifs from the hand-carved furniture.

Andre seemed amazed by what she had accomplished. "These labels are lovely."

He stood and walked closer to the wall to look at the images. She cast Kos a sideways glance, then clicked the image, expanding it to fill the screen. Andre jumped back, and she stifled a giggle.

His broad back tapered into lean hips—he was so big. The image of him above her, all his weight on her, flashed in her mind like another picture on her screen. She squeezed her eyes shut, blanking the image.

"I'm impressed," he said. "Do you think we could see these two in full color?" he asked, sweeping his arm to gesture at the two images on the right.

"Absolutely. You have a good eye." She gestured at a third label. "While I like this one best, I think the two you selected are the most suited to your goals. They blend Kaštel's old world charm with a modern California style. I think they might get the attention of your clan."

Kos went stiff, and glanced at Andre.

"I told her about who we want to reach with the wine," Andre said. "She guessed I wasn't telling her the whole story. She was right, she needed to know." He turned to her, green eyes flashing. "Zoey, your work shows that you understood my goals very well."

The words made her tingle. Compliments like that from anyone else did not have that effect on her.

She steered the conversation to safer ground by bringing up names. Hoping to find one that would distinguish the wine, she asked them to brainstorm Croatian words. They spent an amusing half hour suggesting words, arguing with each other, laughing and translating for Zoey. She liked watching them together. They were almost boyish in their teasing.

"Perhaps I'm being insular, but words with actual vowels might work best. We want people to feel confident enough pronouncing the name to order it in a restaurant or ask for it in a wine store."

"I can't tell if she's joking," Kos said to Andre.

When Andre looked at her, his eyes practically danced with laughter.

"I'm perfectly serious," she replied in her best deadpan. "Vowels are a must."

In the lull that followed, Andre said, "Kos, where's Pedro?"

"I'm not sure. I left him a message about this meeting last night."

"It's not like him to miss a message, and he's always here by nine."
The furrow between Andre's black eyebrows deepened. He raised his
elbow, reaching around to scratch the back of his head and showing
the full breadth of his chest. His bicep caused the shirt to bunch,
and Zoey's hands unfurled in her lap. She clenched them again hard.
She didn't get to touch him.

"I'll call him again," Kos said. He dialed the phone and Zoey could
hear it ring. "It's going to voicemail," he said, then left a message.

"I don't like this at all," Andre said.

"Couldn't he have overslept?" Zoey asked. "We drank a lot of
wine last night."

"I'm sure that's all it is," Kos said, but he wasn't looking at her.
His eyes were intent on Andre.

"Yes, of course," Andre agreed. "Zoey, if you will excuse us, we
will go flush out our lazy winemaker."

"No problem. I'll go call my designer right now," she said, already
replaying their conversation about Pedro in her mind. What had
she missed?

Kos helped her with the cords as she stuffed her projector back
into its case. Then she left them alone to discuss their secrets. What
the hell were they hiding?

It amused Kos to see his father's eyes glued to Zoey's ass, which
swayed toward the door. It was a nice enough ass, but Kos found it
significantly less enthralling. Once she had closed the door behind
her, he rapped his knuckles on the table. Andre glanced at him and
then glowered at the expression on Kos's face.

"I can see you appreciate her professional expertise," Kos said,
perfectly deadpan, although it took great effort not to laugh.

Andre remained silent, his attention flicking back to her point
of exit.

"I have to admit, Father, she's not the type I would have pegged
for you. She's very…modern."

"Maybe I've finally matured enough to admire a strong woman."

"And her ass is just a bonus?"

Andre's mouth opened to object, but a fierce growl from his stomach silenced him.

"Wow. She does make you hungry. Haven't you been feeding?"

"Never mind that. We need to find Pedro."

Kos stood quickly, almost knocking his chair over. "Bel's upstairs. I'll send him to Pedro's house."

Bel could go out in the daylight; they were lucky to have him there. Still, the plan did not put Kos completely at ease.

Andre drummed his fingers on the dining room table. "*Davo.* What if the Hunters got him?"

"Let's see if Bel can find him first."

Kos darted upstairs at full speed. When he'd called last night to warn Bel that Lena would be taking up residence at the beach house, Bel had returned to Kaštel. Now, Kos looked for him in the south wing where the household lived, as far from Andre as he could get.

Kos caught his brother's not quite human scent emanating from behind a closed door and knocked. Wordlessly, Bel opened the door and sidestepped, making room for Kos to pass. What he saw surprised him — Bel had raided the linen closet and draped white sheets over the chairs and dressers.

"What the hell?"

"This place is a fucking shrine to the house on Šolta. It gives me the creeps."

Bel had been only fifteen when Hunters had driven them from their home. In the years preceding that tragedy, he'd stewed in adolescent indignation, blaming Andre for the death of his mother. The home of their childhood was probably the last place he would ever enshrine.

His phone rang. "Give me a second, Kos." Bel answered the phone. "Speak."

"Hey, we're all getting on the plane now." Kos recognized the voice of Bel's second-in-command, Vania.

"Good." Bel opened the window blinds and peered across the highway. Pointing at the bald hilltop on the other side of the two-lane road, he tilted his head at Kos in question.

Kos squinted in the bright morning light. What was he looking for? Some kind of Hunter lookout? No humans were visible on the big boulder. He shook his head and Bel nodded.

"Boss? You still there?"

Bel leaned against the sill. "I'm here. Two vans will be waiting at the airport for you. The usual set up."

"You bought vans?"

Vania had a charmingly posh British accent, and if Kos had never seen her, he would have pictured Princess Diana, not the tiny leather-clad Indonesian badass lieutenant in Bel's little band of mercenaries. He'd found the combination intriguing for five whole days on a visit to his brother's few years back.

"We'll be here for a while," Bel replied.

"Staying at your father's, are we?"

Kos could practically hear her eyebrows arching. Bel must have confided about his less than congenial fatherly relationship.

"What's the assignment?" she asked.

Bel locked gazes with Kos when he replied. "Hunters have found my father's estate."

She whistled so loudly the phone speaker crackled. "So an evacuation job?"

Bel grabbed a still-folded white sheet off the bed and covered the frame. As the sheet ghosted over the footboard, Kos recognized the pattern of carved triangles as the same one that had adorned Bel's bed frame on Šolta.

He straightened the corners of the sheet precisely. "My father and Kos need to stay here if at all possible."

Her response came through the phone so fast that Kos took a step back.

"But it's not possible. It's never possible." She paused and then continued more slowly. "Now that the Hunters have found them, they'll never stop coming. We could kill hundreds, and they'll never stop."

Kos turned away from the hopelessness on Bel's face and squinted at the hilltop again in search of his enemies.

"I know, Vania, but I'm wondering if Trys can put up some permanent protections around the estate. There's gotta be some way to supplement her power—"

Kos vaguely remembered the witch named Trys, with straw-colored hair. Bel had casually mentioned she could cast magical force fields, and when Kos scoffed, Bel insisted that magic was simply a way of controlling nature not yet understood by science. What Bel hadn't seen was the witch waving her middle finger at him from behind.

Vania's grave tone pulled Kos back into the present. "Bel, I know how hard it is when they have to give up everything to flee, and I know it's your father. But it's not his homeland. He's already a refugee. Why is it so important that he stay?"

"Just believe me, it's important. Not just to him—to all the refugees from Croatia. Maybe even all vampires."

Kos didn't understand what Bel meant, but the possibility made the back of his neck itch.

"Okay. Well, we can certainly hold them off and buy you some time, even if it's not a permanent solution. That's a start, right?"

"Right. Did you remember Trys's chocolates?"

"Of course. Five hundred quid worth." Vania's voice pitched higher. "Is Kos there?"

He froze—why was she asking about him?

Bel laughed. "He's here. Planning to rekindle an old flame?"

She and Kos had gotten pretty kinky with her pyrokinesis, and suddenly Kos wished he'd never breathed a word of it to Bel.

"Ha, ha," Vania said, her voice still flutier than normal.

"I'm serious. Should I invest in some aloe vera?"

I'm going to kill you, Kos mouthed silently to Bel.

Vania remained unaware Kos was eavesdropping. "Like vampires need aloe."

"Well, I hope you're not disappointed, but he has a new houseguest."

"Seriously?" She chuckled, her voice dropping to her normal pitch. "I'd love to meet the girl that can keep his attention."

Kos's face grew warm. Lena certainly was the girl to keep his attention, but he'd never managed to capture hers. And with that bucket of cold water dumped on his head, Kos had had enough. Pedro needed their help. He coughed and sliced his finger across his neck in the universal sign meaning, *Get off the damn phone.*

"Vania, I've got to go. See you tonight."

"Yeah. See ya."

"You're a bad sport," Bel said as soon as he ended the call.

"Gossip about my love life later. We've got a problem."

"Yes, you do."

"No. Another one. We expected Pedro at the meeting with Zoey this morning. We're worried the Hunters got him. It's not like him to be late, much less disappear."

Bel's hands slid to his side, and all ten fingers curled into fists. "Shit. I liked that bloody Spaniard. He didn't take any of Andre's bullshit."

"Don't say didn't. Maybe we can find him." Even to his own ears, Kos sounded pleading.

"You know that's unlikely. If he's still alive, there's no telling where they're keeping him. By the time we find him, they'll have given him to one of the initiates."

"We have to do something."

"I'll go to his place, see what I can find." Bel pulled on shoes. "Kos, will he break? They're highly skilled at getting information."

"I don't know. He's tougher than he looks. And, he's loyal. He loves Andre like a father."

Kos regretted the words instantly, even before Bel said, "How nice for him."

"Bel, I didn't —"

"No. I'm sorry." Bel pressed his palm to his forehead and sighed. "Andre brings out my worst. But, I'm glad to hear Pedro's tough. They'll keep him alive as long as they think he has information."

"*Krist.* But what will they do to get that information?"

Bel's look said Kos was right to worry. "I'll go now."

It was sweltering in the shed. Pedro had freed his hands by sawing the duct tape against the metal leg of an old worktable, which had allowed him to take a piss in the corner and not down his own leg. His mouth was a desert even though he was sweating heavily, which would only dry him out faster. If he stood, he felt dizzy, and it was hard to put his thoughts in a logical order.

He was startled out his delirium by the sound of the padlock being opened. The door swung wide and Lucas Bennett stormed toward him.

"I'm sorry."

Pedro saw Lucas mouth the words to him, before his fist connected with Pedro's face, cracking into his right eye.

Pedro made a misstep: he put one arm up to protect his face and therefore failed to block the second hit to his gut. He doubled over in pain, angry with himself for the poor defense. Lucas's other fist barreled into his nose and Pedro heard it crack. Blood poured out of his nostrils into his mouth and onto the ground. From his bent position, he tried to use a shoulder to throw Lucas. Pushed backward, Lucas retreated a few steps. Then Lucas planted a sharp elbow between Pedro's shoulders, taking him down. On the ground, instinct made Pedro curl up to protect his head and gut. Lucas kicked him in the back again and again.

Every time Lucas's boot made impact, it amped up his anger. He kept his mind occupied by assessing the damage; it was a tally of reasons to hate Lucas. Broken nose, likely several cracked ribs. He grunted with pain. There went another one. Bruised kidneys. He would be pissing blood for days. If he survived for days.

Lucas — *what kind of asshole says he's sorry and then whales on me like he wants to kill me?* The beating was worse than any he had experienced as a boy because there was no hope, no end in sight. When it was over, he would remain a prisoner simply waiting for the next round of abuse. All those play-yard beatings had made him promise himself he would never feel like a victim again. It made the experience of powerlessness even worse. Most of all, he hated Lucas Bennett.

"That's enough, son," Pedro heard a man say. It was the mean son of a bitch who'd broken into his house. He pulled Lucas off Pedro. "If you kill him, we can't question him."

With Pedro curled into a ball, they began the interrogation.

"How long have you worked for the vampire?"

"Vampire?" Pedro coughed and spluttered blood. "What?"

Stephen kicked him. "Don't bullshit us. You know he's a vampire."

"Who's a vampire? You're crazy. There's no such thing as vampires."

Then Lucas kicked him again and Pedro passed out. They revived him by dumping a bucket of water over him. It stung all the places his skin had split open, but it was cool.

Then Lucas shouted at him, making his battered head pound. "Tell us what you know about Maras. It will be much easier. We can do this all day and all night."

"You guys think Andre is a vampire? Are you kidding me?"

"Have you seen him eat? Does he go out during the day? Wake up asshole, he's a vampire!" This was from the father.

"He has some kind of disease. He can't go out in the sun."

"Yeah, a disease called being a vampire."

"What's the wine for? Why does it matter?" Lucas asked.

"It's a winery. We make wine. What do you mean, 'what's it for?'" Pedro had begun to sit up. Lucas knocked him back down.

"Don't be a smart ass. I'll give you some time to decide if you're going to talk or if you want another beating instead."

Then Pedro was alone again. His head was pounding. He should try to stay conscious, but he couldn't keep his eyes open. He laid his head down and passed out.

In his office, Andre stacked and restacked papers, searching for a task engrossing enough to distract him from his fear for Pedro and his hunger for Zoey until Kos strode in, slamming the door behind him.

"Bel went to look for Pedro."

"What did he say?"

Kos leaned against the doorframe looking all one hundred and eighty-three years of his age. "He wasn't hopeful. He seemed certain it was Hunters, and that they'd kill him before we could find him."

"This is my fault," Andre said. "I should have told him he was in danger long ago."

"It wouldn't have changed anything. He wouldn't have run away."

"Probably."

"For certain."

Kos went to the bookshelf, the one he always browsed when he was nervous, even though there weren't any of his kind of books on it.

"How much wine have you had?" Kos asked.

"Ten or twelve gallons."

"Is it working?"

"I am keeping it down."

"Are you stronger?"

"I do not know. I feel good. I am positively tingling with an energy that I have not felt since Croatia. But maybe it is fear for Pedro, or—" or the burning need for Zoey, or "—I'm afraid it is a delusion. I want it to work so badly."

"You look bigger, younger."

He stretched his hands over his head, pleading his muscles to answer with limber strength. "Christ, Kos, what if it works?"

Kos's finger came to rest on the spine of a narrow burgundy silk-bound book, one he had given Andre—a limited edition of Tate Adams's *Diary of a Vintage*. Andre easily brought to mind the haunting prints of winemaking in Southern Australia, the gnarled vines and pines so very like his own estate. Tate's black and white images captured something sinister that rang true for Andre as he wasted away, tending his anemic vines. How Kos had known it would be so heartrending, Andre didn't know, but its poignancy made it one of the dearest gifts Kos had ever given him.

"It's not working for me," Kos said, emotion cracking into his deep voice.

No! Andre needed this to work, he needed Kos to be well. "Are you sure?"

Kos nodded.

"Then I must be imagining it."

At the shelf, Kos turned to look at him. "I don't think you are. Look, the buttons on your shirt are straining."

Andre looked down to see his shirt pulling tight across his chest. He straightened, noticing it also felt snug in the shoulders and arms. The evidence made his stomach sink. "That doesn't make any sense. Why would it work for me and not for you? I turned you within feet of where I was turned."

"Just one more infuriating mystery of the wasting disease."

"Is the wine making you sick?"

"No."

Maybe he just needed more. "How much have you had?"

"About the same as you—at least ten gallons. On the bright side, it feels great to take a piss after so long."

Andre refused to smile at Kos's attempt to lighten the mood. He was ten times older, and yet his son felt he had to shield him from bad news. Did he still fear Andre would give up on living?

Kos pressed. "Today is the first time I've ever used a toilet. Damn handy. Shall we drink to that clever invention?"

It was useless being sullen in the face of his absurdity. "Pour me a glass."

Just as they clinked their glasses, Kos's phone signaled a message. He read it and cursed. "Bel's at Pedro's. The door was wide open, no one's there, signs of a struggle."

The stem of Andre's wineglass snapped in two. "*Davo.*" He downed the wine, and sucked his bleeding finger into his mouth. "We have to go. We'll start in Forestville, where you saw the initiates." He dropped his broken glass into the trashcan.

The phone buzzed a second time. "It's Bel again. He's going to the airport now to meet his crew, and he's going to send two of them to Pedro's to try to track him."

"So we wait?"

"I think so. For now."

Andre nodded, examining his now healed finger. "I hate waiting."

"I know. Listen, if Bel's seeing to Pedro, I need to check on Lena. She's been at my place all day alone. I'm sorry to leave."

"Of course. I appreciate you rescuing her from me."

"I don't think that's how she sees it."

"She will."

When Kos left, Andre went to the wine-red book his son had fingered; a golden quail was embossed on its cover, just like the ones that scurried around Kaštel. He found his favorite print, the slope of the hill so precisely similar that he had trouble believing it was not his own vineyard.

Ten years ago, he had stood on that hill, right at the very edge of his land. The windy, clear night carried the smell of Šolta from a neighboring vineyard. Sulfur, and soil, and sun-bleached plants, everything smelled the same. He had sat on a boulder by the spring and allowed himself to hope—if he bought that land, grew his Croatian vines, with enough time maybe a wine would contain enough of Šolta to slow the disease. A cure was too much to hope for.

For a decade, the vines produced passable fruit. But it was not his fruit. It did not make his blood sing with the power of his homeland. Pedro grumbled when he sold off the grapes, rather than making the wine at Kaštel. Privately, Andre cooed to the vines, he stroked them, he called them Ulysses and promised them their home. And then, last year, it happened. They meshed fully with the rootstock, they blossomed something fierce, and Andre supervised every moment of the bumper harvest, the press, the fermentation, and the aging.

He had been hasty to bring Zoey here before they knew for certain. For that matter, he could have hired any number of public relation firms that were not run by his ancient enemies. But she was there, she was the one he wanted, and she might very well be the best. Now, he prayed to Kos's God, and the gods of his father, and he threw in Tate Adams, divine printmaker, for good measure, please let his wine save Kos, and himself, and all his old friends, wherever they were.

CHAPTER 19

Zoey worked at the dainty antique desk in her room. Beside her sat a green glass bottle full of red wine and sealed with foil. A medallion of light shone through the neck and onto the keyboard of her computer. The bottle's label read *Kaštel Estate Old Vine Zinfandel* in blocky Roman letters. The style was perfectly fine, but nothing special. She called her designer about the labels Andre had liked.

When they hung up, she tried to read as much as she could about winemaking in Croatia, looking for references to a Maras family. No luck. Her shoulders bunched up. Wasn't there some kind of law that everything had to be on the Internet? She searched for information about ethnic conflicts in Croatia in the nineteenth century, but couldn't find anything.

Slamming her laptop shut, she lay down on the bed, closed her eyes, and pictured a rack of wine bottles. If she were from a scattered Croatian clan, would the right label leap out at her? Could their ties really be so deep, or was Andre fooling himself?

If such things were possible, she imagined she would feel it in her belly, in the comforting hollow inside her—where she felt safe, and absolutely alone. She fixated on that empty place. In the imaginary wine shop, her glance fell onto a label. It had metallic ruby lettering on ivory paper. Her heart sped up. But what were the words? Then her vision cleared, and she no longer felt hollow.

She gasped, blinking, back in the yellow room at Andre's.

I want to make that happen for him.

She wanted to make Andre's clan feel what she had just tasted. Home.

Suddenly hot, she tugged at her collar. Home was something she didn't need. But it mattered to Andre.

She closed her eyes again to recall him kneeling before her by the spring, his mouth and tongue working on her nipples. Or how he'd been hard underneath her as she sat on his lap playing poker. Her hand went between her legs to soothe her ache. It wasn't enough. She squirmed on the bed, twisting the quilt between her legs. How long could she maintain her distance in the same house with him?

Her stomach growled. Her vision may have momentarily filled the hollow in her belly, but she still needed dinner. And, God help her, something—no, someone else.

She found Susan in the kitchen, and they shared a light supper. Zoey barely tasted her food, but couldn't seem to take her eyes off her plate. She scooched the leftover spaghetti from side to side.

"You seem distracted," Susan said.

That was putting it mildly. "I'm just thinking about the project. It's quite a challenge."

"Hmm," Susan said, sipping her wine and holding Zoey's gaze.

She bristled, but looked into Susan's kind eyes and saw an invitation, not a demand. Why not? She set down her fork. "Do you happen to know what happened with Andre and Lena this morning?"

Susan laughed. "Poor girl. Apparently Lena ambushed Andre in his room, practically naked."

"Really?" How embarrassing. Poor Lena, indeed. Zoey took another bite of pasta. Suddenly, it was delicious.

"He made Kos come get her. I think he finally realized she couldn't be happy here working for him."

Zoey took a deep gulp of water.

Susan licked a drop of wine off her lip. "He's in his office, if you want him."

Zoey found herself in the cellar before she realized she'd decided. Not that she had actually decided anything. She just accepted that her desire for him was more powerful than her rational arguments to stay away.

The door to his office was ajar, and she slipped in quietly. He had obviously heard her approach, because he watched her come in. At his desk, he held a glass of bourbon. His dark brow was creased, his jaw jutting—his usual scowl. She closed the door and leaned against it. He still wore the white shirt, now with one more button undone at the neck. It revealed a wedge of his chest, olive-skinned and sparsely covered in dark hair. He looked good. Well, he always looked good—now he looked better, younger. It must have been the lighting.

She studied him for a few moments before she said, "You told me you'd fantasized about us together. The quick…way." For some reason she didn't want to say fuck now that she was really going to do it.

"Yes."

"Show me."

"Are you sure?"

She nodded.

"Come here." He didn't hesitate; in fact, he sounded relieved.

She had worried he would send her away, but she had made the decision for them, and he seemed grateful. She came to the side of his desk. He lightly gripped her shoulders and steered her to stand facing the desk, where he had been sitting. He stood behind her and stepped closer to her body, fitting his thighs against the curve of her ass. Hard already, his erection pressed into the small of her back.

Movement across the room caught her eye. There was a large mirror on the wall across from the desk. It had a thick gilt frame—another of Andre's antiques. Even though he was behind her, it afforded her a view of what Andre was doing. She could see his hands reach for her breasts and the top of his head as he bent down to put his face next to her neck.

He gently bit the tendon between her neck and shoulder. Zoey's eyes opened wide and she gasped, pushing her hips back into him. Having his teeth latched onto her neck was the most erotic thing she had ever felt, and she wanted more.

Andre was keenly aware that Zoey was breathing quickly and her heart beat nearly as fast as his own. He finally had her exactly the way he had imagined. He shuddered—the temptation to sink his fangs all the way into her was far greater than he had imagined. If only he could taste her without consequence. But no, every minute he had spent with her in the last three days had assured him that the moment he tasted her blood, he would belong to her. And then, like Mila, she could cause him unbearable pain. He wanted her desperately, but he would not be bonded, not be vulnerable again.

"Zoey, this has to be quick, like we agreed."

"I know."

He lowered her slacks and panties past her hips and pushed her shoulders down onto the desk.

"Christ, you're beautiful," he said, and dropping into his desk chair, drank in the sight of her. Her little round ass was as soft and perfect as he'd pictured it, with a pretty, faint birthmark on the left side that he hadn't imagined. She was pink and smooth, with just the tiniest patch of dark curls. His tongue slid over the roof of his mouth. In his fantasies, he had not taken the time to look at her—he was just gripping her hips and driving into her. Now that she was in front of him, on display, he wanted to admire every inch of her. Her pulse accelerated, the scent of her arousal reached him.

Did she enjoy being looked at? He grew painfully hard at the thought, unzipping his pants to free himself. She glistened, smelling so sweet—she was clearly ready for him.

They had made a deal.

But he could not bring himself to push inside her just yet. He had to touch and to taste.

He dipped a finger into her, spreading her moisture. She purred and the vibration buzzed in his fingers. He spread her open so that he could slide his tongue inside her. She tasted amazing—salty and sweet. She whimpered. He had forgotten how good it was to please a woman like this. He wanted more whimpers, and cries and shouts too, before he was done with her.

Running his tongue down her core, he found her most sensitive spot. Drawing lazy circles with his tongue, he slipped one and then two fingers inside her. She clenched around him, and he stroked her until he found what she liked.

All this foreplay was the opposite of a quick fuck, but he was learning her body so that he could please her. Even a quick fuck should satisfy a woman.

As Andre teased her with his tongue and slid his fingers in and out of her, he could feel the tension build inside Zoey. She panted and his breaths came faster in response.

"Don't make me come like this," she said. "I want you inside me."

He stopped lapping at her long enough to say, "I don't want to stop, you taste too good." It was a childish whine and she laughed at him. He did not mind her laughter, but he wanted all her focus. He slipped another finger inside to stretch her open; he would be a lot to take. She cried out then and rolled her hips, meeting his fingers in a perfect rhythm.

"Andre, quit teasing me. Now."

What a woman, bent over his desk and begging for him, but still talking like she was in charge. He stood up and finally touched his cock to her. At the first contact, a jolt of electric pleasure went through him. He rubbed up and down her, gathering her moisture. She let out a breathy sigh that made his heart race even faster.

"Oh wait. What about a condom?"

He tensed, then ground out an answer through his clenched jaw. "I'm clean, and no babies — Bel was a fluke. Can't happen again." He gritted his teeth waiting for her reply. When she didn't say anything, he feared the moment was lost. "Okay?"

"Yes. It's okay. Now!"

He entered her slowly. She was perfectly still, she even held her breath. He gauged her tightness and went only as far as she was ready. When he stilled, she exhaled and relaxed. Around him, she was wet, hot, and so damn tight.

Had he simply forgotten how good sex was?

He withdrew all the way and speared into her. She cried out and the muscles inside her quivered. No, it wasn't his long abstinence. It was because it was Zoey, and she fit him like a glove.

She pushed her hips back impatiently. He closed his eyes and imagined her lush pink flesh spreading to take more of him. His breath caught. Her purr became a groan of pleasure, and he opened his eyes to see her arching back beneath him. He thrust in and out of her slowly and strummed her clit. With every thrust, her quiet moans told him he was hitting the right place.

Careful not to lose that sweet spot, he thrust faster and faster. She matched his pace with her hips, and her muscles began to spasm. His cock jumped inside her, but he was not ready to finish. Her cries became more urgent, and he sensed she was ready.

"Come for me, Zoey. Let me feel you."

Her body responded to his command, going molten around him, hotter and tighter, until she let out one long, low sigh.

Sweaty and soft, she went limp underneath him. Her rib cage expanded with full breaths. Her pulse was fast and heavy, beckoning his hips to thrust in time with it, even though she was still and sated.

She shifted on the balls of her feet, and clenched. He was still filling her, as hard as when they had begun. She looked over her shoulder at him. "Wow."

He laughed. "We can rest."

"Hell no. Give me what you've got."

"I like it when you are bossy," he said as he began thrusting again. Finally, he was buried in her to the hilt. Gripping her hips tightly, he pulled her hard onto him over and over again. She was magnificent. Her shirt inched up her back, revealing gorgeous skin—creamy with a hint of golden honey. She gripped the front of the desk for leverage so that she could push harder against him. Her every move told him she wanted him as badly as he did her.

Her ass slammed into his hips. Eyes closed, he pretended. *She knows me, knows what I am, and still she wants me like this.* His heart swelled so big he could hardly breathe—it burned like the fatigued muscle it was.

His gums ached in warning. *Davo.*

Even with that fire in his chest, he could pound into her all night, if he were not hungry for her. But he wanted her completely—to revel in this connection, to make love to her. And all that started with a bite. One little bite with irreversible consequences.

Time to end things, and quickly, before his fangs made an unwelcome appearance.

His eyes were drawn to the tempting little pucker between the soft cheeks of her ass. Would she give him permission? He didn't give her the chance to say no. He reached down between them, finding some of her wetness to lubricate his thumb. Then, at the same time he thrust, he slipped his thumb in too.

Zoey gasped. She stopped moving against him, but didn't complain.

"All right?" he asked.

In response, she inhaled deeply and pushed back into him, taking more of his cock and his thumb inside her. "So good," she said.

Oh, Zoey, would you let me take you like this? The idea nearly sent him over the edge, even before she clenched him tighter. They moved together and he spiraled closer and closer to release, until Zoey let out a frustrated sigh.

"What is it?" he asked.

"I need you to touch me."

"Not enough hands, sweet. Show me how you touch yourself."

She hesitated, breaking their rhythm.

"Zoey, love, I want to see. I want you to have everything you need."

Love? He shouldn't have said it. Though, if there ever were a woman he could love again…

After one long second, her hand slid down to where they were joined and his thoughts gave way to primal sensation as her muscles clenched around him like a vise.

He let himself come with her, throwing his head back and shouting out just as she screamed her orgasm. As the climax relaxed his control, hunger assaulted him, and before he could stop them, his fangs descended. Quickly, he closed his lips over them and collapsed on top of her, placing a chaste kiss on her shoulder.

"You're incredible." He took in her sex-drenched scent. "I'll never forget that," he said in her ear.

"Andre?"

She sounded strange.

"Yes?"

"Stand up."

He did, and she followed. She quickly pulled up her pants and stood, turning to face him. "Open your mouth."

His mouth? *Davo.*

His eyes darted to the mirror across from his desk. She'd been watching him all along. How could he have forgotten it was there?

She would not be fooled, not his Zoey, even if his fangs had all but disappeared into his gums. He met her eye and opened his mouth, allowing them to extend again.

She touched one of his fangs with her right hand. Her fingers still carried the sweet, tangy smell of her sex. He wanted to draw that finger into his mouth and suck her juices off of it.

"Okay," she said. "Not what I expected, but it does explain some things. The night walking, the age thing. But you have a reflection?"

She sounded so normal and level-headed — too much so.

"Yes."

She took a long, deliberate breath, and exhaled slowly, as if she were annoyed that he had troubled her with such an inconvenient revelation. He wished like hell that he had not.

Then she put her hand on his chest, where his heart pounded forcefully. "Are you alive?"

He couldn't help but laugh. "Yes, completely alive." Would that reassure her?

"So..." Her voice was laced with irony, and she shrugged. "Vampires are real?"

No, she was not reassured. What could he say? "Yes. We're real. We're just..." It was very difficult to explain. "Different. I suppose you would say we are a different species." She dropped her hand from his sternum, and he missed the touch.

She brought the same hand to her neck. "Were you going to bite me?"

"No, I wouldn't allow myself to bite you."

She looked like she believed him but her pupils were large, her heart racing loud in his ears. "How old are you?"

"Very old."

"This is too much." Confusion and alarm broke into her voice, her composure slipping. She shook her head. "Too much. I have to go."

He reached out to comfort her. "Zoey —"

She sidestepped his embrace. "Andre, I need to wrap my head around this. I'm not going to call the police or anything. I just need to go."

She eyed him warily until he realized she was waiting for him to agree. He nodded and watched her rush out. He should feel relief, but a weight settled on his shoulders instead. He'd scared her to death, but he still needed her help.

CHAPTER 20

Zoey put the puzzle pieces together quickly as she walked through the dark cellar back to her room. He was biting his household staff, drinking or eating their blood or whatever. Shit—she'd just had sex with a vampire and she was pondering semantics.

She hastily tossed her belongings into her suitcase and headed straight for her car, afraid Andre, or even Susan, would try to stop her. Susan! She could have given her a little warning. To say Andre had a medical condition was the understatement of the year.

It was nine o'clock when Zoey pulled out of the Kaštel Estate driveway. Once she was on the highway, she noticed the feeling of pins and needles in her fingers, then her toes. Her throat began to close up, she gasped for air. She wanted to put more distance behind her, but had to act fast. She pulled off the road and began to forcefully slow her breathing.

It had been years since she'd felt those symptoms. The first time had been at San Francisco General Hospital with Michael, when the soft-spoken doctor had leaned over her industrial grade metal desk and said he had schizophrenia. She felt all her dreams and plans for a future slipping through her fingers, along with the man she loved. He was the sick one, but her heart exploded in her chest. She truly believed she was dying when they rushed her downstairs into the ER and told her the humiliating news that she was having a panic attack.

She'd suffered half a dozen episodes that severe before she taught herself to breathe through the panic, avoiding full-blown attacks. The skills she developed had gotten her through Michael's illness and death, and they continued to serve her well. She kept a level head with difficult clients and a cool detachment with men. Perhaps to find refuge, she had gone too far. But she felt safest when she didn't feel much at all.

Andre was a vampire—difficult not to feel something about that little revelation. Her practices came back to her quickly. She allowed her thoughts and feelings to pass right through her as her breath and heart rate slowed.

When she was certain she would not pass out, she called Ethan.

"Ethan, he's a vampire." Saying the words made her Zen fly right out the window. "Holy shit, Ethan, he's a vampire."

"Calm down, Zoey."

Oh that was helpful, she was trying to calm down. "Did you hear me? Andre Maras is a vampire!"

"Take a deep breath. Relax."

"Relax? Are you kidding me?" Why was he being so calm? That was wrong. "You knew. You knew he was a vampire and you sent me to stay at his house. What episode of the *X-Files* have I walked into?" As she ranted at Ethan, Zoey was surprised to notice she felt calmer. Things were still weird, but she wasn't losing her mind.

Ethan let out a long breath. "Zoey, I think it's time I tell you the whole story. Meet me in Forestville? There's a drive-through that's open late. A burger place right on the main street."

"Ethan, what the hell is going on?"

"Just meet me. It should take you twenty or twenty-five minutes to get there. I'll be waiting."

"Okay." Only when she hung up did she wonder why he was nearby and not at home in San Francisco.

Andre closed his eyes as soon as Zoey walked out the door and opened them to find himself in his vineyard on Šolta.

He surveyed the black, windless night. Something was strange. His connection to Mila was weak—none of her feelings or thoughts colored his mood. Perhaps she was in a deep sleep. It was a relief.

He was alone in his own skin and had a respite from the pall of her unhappiness. That made it easy to enjoy his chores.

Drizzle fell from the dark October sky. He set fire to a heap of trimmings and dry leaves. He scratched his forearms as the fire caught. When the itching became a burn, he stepped back from the heat of the flames, only to realize it was not the fire that burned him; it was a thousand, no a million, tiny rips in his flesh.

Mila.

She must be hurt. He was a league from the house. Drizzle stung his raw skin as he flew. He was there in a blink.

The smell of iron made his gut twist. A lot of blood. Please not her. He followed the scent upstairs. He prayed that he would find anyone other than her dead, but with stabs of sharp pain, his body was already telling him the truth. Then he saw it — the very blood that coursed through his veins, spilled into her bathwater. She floated, lifeless, blond hair fanning out in the pink stained liquid.

He vomited up the kitchen girl's blood.

He crawled through blood and bile to lift her head from the water. He found her wrist, gaping. His hand fumbled for a pulse at her neck instead. Nothing. Worse than just no pulse. She was too cold. She'd been dead too long to turn.

No! A howl erupted from his chest, reverberating through the house.

He was dying. A trillion hot needles bored into him; barbed wire twisted through his intestines. He had known she was unhappy. But, how had it come to this? Had he failed her? Or was he simply so unlovable?

His heart seemed to explode like a cask of gunpowder, blown into bits, and still it pumped the toxic stuff through him — her blood, dying inside him. His every cell was ripped apart as the bond broke.

Andre curled onto the floor, hoping death would come quickly. A seizure shook him, banging his skull against the floorboards.

Someone cried out. Kos. Thank God it wasn't young Bel.

Andre managed to whisper. "See to your mother."

"She's seen to herself." His words were an angry hiss. Deep in Andre's brain, relief registered — Kos did not blame him for Mila's rashness.

Kos's hand came to Andre's face. He flinched and opened his eyes to see his bloody tears streaking his son's fingers. *Please, gods of my father, let me die now.*

"Christ. What's happening to you?"

"Our bond…"

Kos pulled at Andre's shirt urgently. Andre curled tighter against the grating pain, trying to get free of Kos. Still, the boy's hands were insistently tugging his buttons.

"What can I do? What will help you?" Kos asked.

"Take my head."

"No."

"Then at dawn I will—"

"You would do that to me?"

Andre's mind was caving in on itself, but some kernel of duty remained intact. No. He would not abandon his sons.

He crawled into the cellar and suffered alone, where no one could hear him scream, wishing every second for the mercy of death.

Kos coaxed him back upstairs after two weeks by appealing to that same sense of duty. In the candlelight of the parlor, Andre saw the shock on his son's face. That was when he noticed his clothing hung loosely, his skin too. His half dead body could not begin to repair itself without a meal of blood. That meant he would have to be close to a woman, a woman who would get wet and wriggle with his bite, and who was not Mila, whom his body still craved like an opium addict. If he'd had anything in his stomach, it would have come up with the thought.

He refused to feed until Kos pricked a maid's finger for him. When he smelled her blood, his instincts took over. He pounced on her. Mindlessly, he covered her, feasting at her neck, the hot salt and iron of her blood soothing his parched gullet.

Kos's human strength wasn't enough to pull Andre off her when those same instincts demanded he take all the blood he needed. But Kos had brought two field hands with him. Together, all three men pulled Andre out of his stupor. The two laborers left with the maid and Kos sat down on the stone floor of the parlor next to Andre, their backs to the wall.

Andre cracked an eyelid and peered at Kos. He was haggard, lines of strain marring his face. Too many burdens on a young man. Andre needed to pull himself together for Kos's sake.

"Is the blood helping?"

"It is."

Kos turned, happening to brush Andre's thigh with his knee. Pain shot up Andre's femur to his spine and detonated in his brain. When the shudder came, he clenched his teeth hard. He had learned his lesson after biting the tip off his tongue, twice.

"*Krist.* Not fast enough," Kos said.

Andre focused all his energy on getting control of the shudder. Long after his tremors stopped, they sat quietly. Slowly, the maid's blood worked through him, taking the edge off his pain. Andre carefully eased his head to rest on the wall.

Kos stared at the stone floor.

"Did you know it would be like this, if she died?"

"No." If he had truly comprehended of the intensity of a blood bond, he would never have bonded to a woman he barely knew. Among his friends, the bond appeared to be pure bliss. But those bonds were shared between two vampires, not the lopsided tie he'd had with the human Mila.

She had arrived like an angel in need, with a bright and curious Kosjenic in hand. His household women had taken in the hungry and destitute pair. At twilight, he had found the inquisitive child under a grapevine examining fruit almost ready for harvest.

"Sir, how do you know when they are ready?"

"I know by their smell. But look here. When you squeeze them, if the pits come free of the flesh, you know they are ripe."

The boy's small hand brushed Andre's to take the little globe of fruit, and a lifeless place inside him flooded with tenderness. In nearly two thousand years, he had never passed more than a few words with a child. This small boy was a miracle of sentience and vitality—perhaps all children were.

Coming upon Mila in the kitchen later that evening, full behind bent over a basket of potatoes, he had desired her instantly. When she stood and greeted him with a curtsy, the hunger he felt was something new and astonishing. He felt more alive than he had in years. And Kos—the son he had not known he wanted—had made her irresistible. No, he could not tell Kos that part of the story.

"There are many things about the bond I did not understand. If you still want me to turn you, I will explain them all to the best of my ability."

Kos cleared his throat, and Andre saw the gloss of grief over his gray eyes. "Do you know why she did it?"

Andre had barely strung together a rational thought since he found her dead. But he had pondered that question in every lucid moment, and he would damn well never tell Kos that his desire to have him as a son had tempted him into a bad match. The boy would feel responsible.

"She did not want to turn."

She hadn't wanted to from the start, but she had wanted the security Andre could provide. They had gotten along well enough, and she seemed to desire him. In truth, she had feared going hungry again, so she hid her unease about his vampire nature. The moment he bonded to her, he felt her deceit like a shadow inside him. It poisoned his affection for her, which, in hindsight had not been nearly enough. Infatuated with the idea of a family in need of a father, he had acted hastily.

Now a man of nearly twenty, and still everything Andre could ask for in a son, Kos stood up suddenly and went to the hearth, throwing a log onto the fire. "She could have grown old."

"She felt my longing for her to turn too keenly. She found it stifling."

For years he held out hope that she would come to accept him. If she turned, a shared bond between them could restore their affection. But a one-sided bond with a human…he knew her every emotion, and she hardly knew him at all. She offered him her long white neck and her lush body without knowing he could sense revulsion intermingling with her desire. It ate at him, but by then he was bonded and what she offered was his lifeblood, so he pretended along with her.

When he begged her to turn, she put him off with the promise of another child, and conspired with Uta on that secret magic. When Bel was born, she ran out of excuses.

"Did you threaten to turn her?"

"*Davo*. Kos…" Andre's eyes burned. Double *davo*, he wanted to rub them. But if he started he wouldn't stop. He would rub them raw and bleeding, and it would be a day before he could see again. He had found that out the hard way too. "Do you really have to ask?"

Kos didn't answer.

A terrible thought dawned him. "Is that what Bel thinks?"

Still, Kos remained silent, no doubt protecting him from that grim truth; just as he sought to protect Kos from any sense of responsibility for the decision to marry Mila more than a dozen years ago.

Bel. Andre squeezed his hands into fists so hard that his fingernails sliced into his paper-like skin. Opening his palms, eight crimson half-moons healed slower than they should. He wanted to turn Bel over his knee, and then enfold the little devil in his arms. But then, that was how things had always been between them in the eleven years since he was born. He was too much Andre's son.

"Will you live?" Kos asked.

He wiped his thumb across his palm — smooth. "I will live, and by the gods of my father, I will walk into the sun before I ever bond to a woman again."

Kos sped to his house. The drive normally took about forty-five minutes, but he made it in little more than half an hour. He didn't have Lena's cell phone number, and she hadn't answered the phone at his house. He couldn't help but worry, given Pedro's abduction.

When he arrived, he found her curled up on the couch asleep under a blanket. Her soft curls framed her face and her cheeks were pink with the warmth of sleep. She was even drooling a little onto the couch cushion. Adorable —

He shook his head. There could be no adoring Lena. She was the kind of woman who could tempt a man to break a vow. And he was the kind of man who kept his vows.

A volume of poems by Rumi lay open and face down next to her — the one that had been next to his bed. So, she'd done a little snooping. He'd expected that, but hadn't worried — he didn't have anything to hide from her.

Not wanting to wake her, he left a note saying he'd dropped by and asking her to call with her phone number.

He hopped back into his Mercedes, stopped in Forestville to slake his thirst for Lena on his friend Maria, and gunned the engine all the way to the Santa Rosa Airport, where Bel waited with his newly acquired sun-proof vans. He arrived just in time, as Bel's jet landed and then taxied on the runway.

"How's your girl?" his insolent brother asked while they watched the plane slow.

"She's not my girl. She's a householder who's been severely disappointed by our callous father, and I'm going to find her a new job as quickly as possible."

"If you say so."

The plane came to a stop and Vania deplaned first, then two vampires Kos had met in London — the surly Henry, who needled the massive Omar with his elbow.

"Damn it's good to see those mofos," Bel said, laughing.

Kos chuckled too.

The rest of the crew piled-up behind them, everyone dressed for a fight in what Kos thought of as their uniforms — as yet unsoiled leathers or fatigues. He hung back as Bel greeted the crew with a series of high-fives, punches to upper arms, and one sideways hug for Vania. Then he was down to business.

He directed two of his vampires to Pedro's house, slapping Kos's back. "They're skilled trackers and they've succeeded on missions more hopeless than this."

Kos didn't appreciate being reminded of its hopelessness. He rolled his shoulders, which grew tenser and tenser with every hour of silence from Pedro.

"I'm serious, bro. If anyone can, they'll track him."

In his dark blue Mercedes, Kos led the caravan back to Kaštel, pausing with his left turn signal on to let a silver Audi screech out of the drive. Zoey's car, if he wasn't mistaken. What had Andre done to chase her off?

Vania hopped out of the van and sidled up to him. She extended her hand, wearing an unreadable expression. "Hiya, Kos."

"Hello, Vania. Welcome to Kaštel."

"Who was the bat out of hell?" She nodded toward the drive.

"I think my dad just got dumped."

"Zoey, was it?" Bel strode toward them, grinning.

Kos shook his head — Bel still delighted in Andre's defeats, after all these years. But that wasn't the whole story; he was here after all, and with his crew. When it mattered, he was loyal to their father.

The ragtag band of mercenaries unloaded duffel bags and the cases of guns. Only, they weren't really ragtag anymore, not like they'd been when Bel had assembled them years ago. Old and powerful vampires, witches like Trys, and whatever the hell Vania was with her magic firepower. They were an impressive force.

Andre opened the door as the last of the crew approached the house. He peered around them, apparently looking for Zoey. Kos's father looked younger, which meant the wine was working, but its youthful effect was counteracted by the scowl on Andre's face.

Kos pitied him instantly. "She's gone. Did you bite her?"

"No. But she found out." Andre clenched his teeth so tightly he barely let the terse sentence out of his mouth. "For the best. Needed her gone."

"If you say so." Kos crossed his arms over his chest.

"Bel. Introduce me to your crew."

Bel made the introductions, first naming the six vampires and four humans he employed. In the back of the crowd, Ani and Vania were bickering about bringing in some sort of machine from the van. The others made room for them in the semi-circle they'd formed around the front door.

"Ah, let me guess. Vania? Kos has told me you can do amazing things with fire."

"Fire likes me." Vania shrugged, turning pink.

Kos wanted to kick his ass into a bright afternoon. It had been a major mistake to confide in either his father or his brother about that kinky little affair.

Krist, was Vania batting her eyes? Kos's head fell forward, and a bug flew into his gaping mouth. Spitting, he glanced at his brother to find a dark scowl. Bel would not take well to Andre charming his best friend.

"I'm Ani," said a young woman, stepping toward Andre.

Andre studied her. In Ukrainian, he asked, "Short for Anastasia?"

"Of course," she replied, beaming at him.

Some of the pity Kos felt for Andre spilled over onto poor Bel. His badass mercenary chicks were practically eating out of Andre's hand.

The oldest vampire on Bel's crew, Omar, inhaled through his nose. "Not a trace of Hunter in the air."

"Let's hope our arrival remains under their radar." Bel pushed Andre aside to enter the house, effectively seizing control. Over his shoulder, he called out, "Henry, Trys, pull the vans behind the house into the workroom. Then meet us inside."

Andre opened his mouth, and Kos braced his hand against the stucco wall for an alpha showdown. But his father bit back the words and silently followed Bel into the house.

As Andre drew up to the dining room table, Zoey's presentation seemed like a long lifetime ago. *Davo.* He was a live wire—anxious for Pedro, traumatized by the memory of Mila's death, and relieved Zoey was gone. Yes. Relief was the best word for the emptiness her absence left.

He had to keep his household and his vines safe, he had to cure Kos and save the other refugees. He had no right to mope. More importantly, he had no right to assert control. Bel was a man, and he'd built this army; he was their leader, and Andre respected that. His crew gathered around the table and Andre gave them all his focus.

He could sense a lot of power coming off Omar—probably the oldest of the vampires that worked for Bel. Omar was even taller than him, with onyx-black skin and intelligent eyes. Underneath his British accent was the slightest West African rhythm, and he cut straight to the point.

"Vania says you want to secure this entire property, including all the vineyards. Assuming for the moment that's possible, I'd like to know why."

Bel started to answer Omar's question, but Andre spoke first. "Bel, if it's all right with you, I'll answer. I assume that I can speak freely?"

Bel blinked, then nodded, seeming to appreciate the deference. "Yes, I trust them with my life."

"In short, I believe the wine we are making can cure our wasting disease."

Omar looked closely at Andre. "How long have you been in exile?"

"A century and a half, give or take." Omar's mouth opened in surprise and Andre took some pride in his newly youthful appearance.

"Keep talking," said the big male.

"In our homeland, I made wine that we could drink."

Two other vampires murmured a sound of disbelief. Omar hissed at them, showing a little more predator than Andre thought polite in mixed company. "Let him speak."

"Tell them from the beginning, Andre, or else they won't believe you."

"I was a soldier in the Roman Empire in the first century. According to Roman custom, I was given land for my service, in Illyricum — Croatia, now."

Omar nodded and the movement caught Andre's eye. He scanned the others to make sure they were following. "On my tours of duty, I had seen the vineyards in Italy and Gaul. I was fascinated by them and learned as much as I could. I was determined that, if I survived my service, I would plant a vineyard and make wine."

"Let me guess…" said Vania, tapping her neck with two fingers. Apparently she had heard stories like this before.

"You're right. Just as I settled on my land and began to plant vines, I awoke with that splitting not-quite-a-headache, hungry for blood." Andre saw several of the vampires shield their eyes or cover their ears, remembering the sensory overload that debilitated every new vampire. "I'd been set upon by a vampire as I slept and turned against my will. Only instinct told me to seek shelter before dawn, or I would have burned right up."

"I'm grateful those days are over," Omar said. He rubbed his neck and Andre silently agreed. To turn someone against his or her will had become a punishable offense.

"Enough already. Get on with the story," Bel said.

"I despaired that my dream was lost until I realized that, with my night vision and my sense of smell, I could still make wine. Over the centuries, my wine got better and better. I bred a grape that became popular all over Dalmatia. I brought it with me when we fled. It has been called Zinfandel."

Omar huffed, letting Andre know he was getting impatient. "But what on earth made you drink it?"

"The smell. One day, I was drawn to an open vat of wine as if it were blood. I sat on the floor next to it and tried to sniff out what was calling to me in the wine. It was something elemental. I don't know how to describe it…" He scratched his scalp. "I could smell the minerals in it and my body wanted them. Like a woman I knew in the village who ate dirt every time she was pregnant."

"So you tried it?"

"I had only the smallest sip. But when I put it in my mouth, it felt right, with a velvety texture like blood. When I kept down the sip, I drank a glass. I did not need to feed for a week. The more I drank, the less blood I needed. I would still get hungry for blood, but less often."

"And when Hunters came for you, you were able to bring some of the vines?"

Andre nodded.

"How did you keep them alive?"

He recalled their travel through the Mediterranean and across the Atlantic in the hold of a ship. He and Kos had been able to dig up six root balls while the household staff packed a cart of their most precious objects. They wrapped the roots in sackcloth and loaded them onto the top of the heavily-laden cart. Kos pulled the cart to the harbor faster than a team of horses, while Andre flew the household staff two at a time. He was not fast enough, and the last four women were killed in the fire set by the Hunters. He still especially missed Magda; she had grown old in his service and he regretted he could not give her a proper burial.

The members of his household who survived the fire were terribly seasick on the crossing. One poor maid died of dehydration unable even to drink water. Andre offered to turn her into a vampire, but she said she would rather die than live for eternity pursued by the evil Hunters.

In the hold of the ship, the vines had no sunlight and precious little water. He hoped they would go dormant as they did in winter, but eventually the roots started to rot and the sack-cloths showed mold. For the entire journey, he troubled over them — they were all he had left of his homeland.

"Only three of the vines survived the journey. I coddled them for decades when we first came here, but they didn't produce wine I could drink until recently. I found a vineyard with soil just like home. Our first vintage of the wine from that vineyard was barreled last year. Kos and I can both drink the wine. It is making me stronger, but not Kos."

Saying so aloud made Andre grim. They hadn't told Bel that news yet. He tucked his chin in acknowledgment.

"I'd like to try it," Omar said.

"Of course," Andre said, defaulting to hospitality. "But, my friend, you're not Croatian. I don't know if you will even be able to keep it down."

"I know."

"Let me bring some up." Andre went down to the cellars to fill a decanter and when he returned, Kos entered the house and walked with him into the dining room.

"Any news of Pedro?" he asked Bel.

"No, we just got here and my trackers haven't checked back in."

"So, boss," Henry said, "Am I getting this right? You want us to protect your dad's vineyards into eternity, and meanwhile, we're sitting ducks for the Hunters."

"Don't be so dramatic," Vania said. "Trys can work up a protection spell for the whole estate, right?" She turned to the other woman.

"Yes," Trys replied. "I can certainly make it more difficult for them to get to the house. It won't be impenetrable, but I wouldn't call us sitting ducks." She tucked a lock of her fine blond hair behind her ears and swallowed once before she went on. "The vines, though — that's a lot of area to cover. If I stretch the shield that big, it won't be strong enough. I'll shield the house, you guys patrol the vines."

Andre didn't like her answer. Bel, Vania, and two human men were all the muscle of use during the daylight. His vines would be wide open.

Henry's words indicated he was equally displeased. "The spell won't last forever and the Hunters will keep coming forever. Andre, you'll never be ready to leave now that you've found your panacea — it would mean exile all over again. We should just evacuate you now."

Henry was right, but Andre couldn't bring himself to agree. He sensed Bel's eyes on him and glanced at his son.

Bel dropped his chin in a clipped nod meant only for Andre — a show of support. "You're right, Henry," he said. "There is no permanent solution. But between Trys's spell and all of your skills, we can buy some time for my father and for my research."

Bel's loyalty was unexpected, and it gave Andre a thread of hope to hang onto.

CHAPTER 21

When Zoey arrived, Ethan's car was the only one at the drive-in burger place. She parked in the spot next to him and got into his car.

"Are you okay?" he asked. "You're not hurt? He didn't bite you?"

"I'm fine."

He handed her a Coke and an order of fries. It was thoughtful of him, and yet she would have preferred a burger and a milk shake. With strenuous focus on steadying her nerves all the way to Forestville, she had succeeded in staying calm, but she was not above feeding her feelings. She considered placing an order and looked up to see a young man turn off the lights and begin to lock up. Zoey resigned herself to the fries. At least they were still warm.

Ethan remained quiet until she spoke again, demonstrating more knowledge of her preferences than his order of food had. Or perhaps he guessed at her state of mind—he had never seen her lose her cool.

She took a long sip from her Coke. "You may as well start from the beginning."

He angled to face her in the cramped driver's seat. "I knew Maras was a vampire. Lucas and I have been looking for him for years. It's why we came to California. We're vampire Hunters."

"So vampires are real and you are both vampire slayers? I thought there was only one in every generation."

"What?" His fair brow furrowed.

"You know, like *Buffy the Vampire Slayer*."

"That old TV show? I never saw it." He shook his head dismissively.

How like Ethan that he was an actual vampire slayer and he'd never bothered to watch a show about them. "So vampires are real, and you hunt them?"

"Yes."

Zoey had control of her breath, but she could still feel her heart pounding as his words sank in. "Andre Maras bites people and drinks their blood?" It was still so hard to believe, she needed Ethan to confirm what she already knew.

"Yes."

"All those women that work for him — they're like cattle?"

"Exactly. He keeps them for food and likely for sex too." He was oddly enthusiastic.

"They let him bite them?" The idea of someone sucking her blood out of her body was frightening and disgusting. *Breathe.*

"They're enthralled by him. He's seduced them and they no longer think for themselves. They won't leave him, regardless of what he does to them."

She undid her ponytail and slid the hair band onto her wrist. "I'm having a hard time wrapping my head around this. They didn't seem enthralled, except maybe that bitchy cook." Flick. The sting of the hair band must mean she wasn't dreaming.

"They don't realize they've lost their free will."

She stared out over the dash before turning to Ethan. "Do vampires kill people?" *Does Andre kill people?* That was the question she really cared about. Light-headed, she realized she was holding her breath, rather than regulating it.

"Yes, vampires have slaughtered entire villages."

"Villages? When?"

"In the past. Vampires are smarter now; they try to stay out of the news. When they kill people, no one knows vampires did it."

"But they don't kill people when they drink their blood. I mean, I saw one of the women leaving his room, presumably after feeding. She looked perfectly healthy."

"No, Maras wouldn't kill his household women."

"So when you sent me to stay with a vampire, you didn't think he'd kill me?"

Ethan looked surprised by her question. Idiot. He should know it wouldn't slip her notice that he had sent her into danger blind, no matter how shocked she was.

"No, I knew he wouldn't kill you. I assumed he'd try to seduce you and I had every confidence he'd fail. You'd never let someone use you the way he uses women."

Zoey's eyes prickled with shame. She was thankful it was dark so that Ethan couldn't see her face redden. Andre hadn't failed; he was such a skilled seducer that every step of the way she had thought that she was in control.

Had she been used? It hadn't felt that way. In the mirror, she had seen the look on his face as he had moved inside her. His intent expression had stirred her numb heart. It wasn't seduction if he didn't know she was watching. She still wanted that look to be real, even if it was what had cracked her open, leaving her vulnerable to a flood of emotions she had thought lost.

As soon as she admitted it to herself, the tightness in her chest eased and she could take deeper breaths. It was a shock to learn he was a vampire, but she wasn't afraid of him. Finally her heart rate slowed and curiosity replaced her fear.

"Why did you send me to work for him, Ethan?"

"We hoped you could get some information for us. We knew it was a long shot, but we felt we had to try."

Ethan placed his hand on the emergency brake between them, and she crossed her leg to avoid touching him. "Go on."

"Years ago, Maras — Marasović he called himself then — was discovered living on a small island off the coast of Croatia. He managed to escape. Croatia was a vampire enclave and somehow they received advance warning." The tendons of Ethan's hand came into relief as he gripped the lever of the brake tightly. "Far too many of the Croatian parasites eluded the Hunters. When we found him, we hoped Maras would lead us to them. Lucas thinks the wine is the key, but we can't figure out what he's up to. So we sent you to work with him, in case he revealed something to you about the wine."

What had she learned? She closed her eyes and thought through their conversations. "He wants to use it to reach them."

"What?"

She looked into Ethan's yellow eyes and explained. "He thinks the right branding will get their attention and perhaps they can be reunited. He doesn't have another way to reach them."

"He told you that?" He touched the hair at Zoey's temple, and guiltily, she tried not to flinch. He didn't deserve such cool treatment. She was just overwhelmed.

"Yeah. I could tell he wasn't giving me the whole story, so I just kept asking him questions until he explained his real goals for hiring the firm."

"You're amazing. I knew my instincts were right about sending you in there." He reached over to embrace her, and she shivered.

"Ethan, I'm tired."

"Right, I should have realized how late it is. I got us a room in the motel down the street. You should get some rest."

"I want to go home."

He must have finally picked up on her signals because he said, "Don't worry, I asked for separate beds. But you shouldn't be alone right now."

He was right. She was in no shape to drive back to San Francisco and she didn't want to be alone. Ethan was a friend and she trusted him. Although, she lamented, she didn't trust him as much as she had hours ago, before she had learned that neither he nor Andre was who he appeared to be.

"All right."

"I'll get your bag from your trunk and we can take my car."

"Thanks."

Andre jumped when a knock shook the front door, and Kos went to open it. Seconds later, he led Bel's trackers into the dining room.

"Are you the ones searching for Pedro?" Andre asked.

"Yeah."

Andre's concern must have showed—the other vampire's tone became more solemn. "No luck. There were easily a dozen Hunters in his house, probably about twenty-four hours ago. We couldn't follow the scent past a few miles from the house. They must have taken precautions to minimize their trail."

Andre's gut sank, taking his thread of hope with it. "*Davo.* He's been gone that long? What are the chances he's still alive?"

"Not good," Bel said. "But we won't give up." He had spread out large satellite images of Kaštel Estate. Kos drew lines around the most important vineyards. Andre poured a glass for himself, Kos, and Omar.

"To the homeland," Kos said, raising his glass.

"The homeland," Omar and Andre replied in unison.

Omar sniffed the ruby liquid in the glass. "Mmmm, smells good." He hesitated briefly, then took a small sip and set his glass down. "I'll take my time with that, I think."

"Wise," Andre agreed.

"Where's Zoey?" Kos asked. "I didn't see her car out front."

The respite Bel's arriving crew had brought him was suddenly over, and Andre tried to grind away the pressure in his jaw. He could sense Bel trying to warn Kos off the subject.

"Bel, since you do not have a preternatural sense of hearing," Andre said, "you might be surprised to know I can actually hear the rapid shaking of your head."

He had not meant it to be funny, but the others in the room laughed.

"Don't tell him all our secrets, man!" Omar said.

In spite of their mirth, Andre felt stony.

"With Zoey gone, I think we should expect the Hunters as soon as tomorrow," Bel said. "Andre, Kos, I need some time with my crew to plan. Make yourselves scarce."

"Leave the wine, though," Omar demanded.

Andre stood and Kos followed. As he passed Bel on the way to the door, he put an appreciative hand on his son's shoulder. To his relief, Bel didn't shrink from it.

On their way to his office, he asked Kos, "Lena's settled at your house?"

"She's not settled. Her stay is temporary. But she seems comfortable for the time being."

Kos's tone was defensive, and Andre couldn't resist the chance to taunt him.

"Vania is extraordinary. You never said she was so beautiful when you described her...special talents."

Kos was usually tight lipped about his lovers. He had probably assumed Andre would never meet Vania, because he had told him more than he normally would about their affair. Apparently, fire flew from Vania's fingertips. With a wink, Kos had said it was the hottest sex of his life.

"All right, that's enough. I shouldn't have told you about that."

"Relax, Kos. You're always a perfect gentlemen, something I've never aspired to be. What you forget is that women gossip too. Vania likely told her girlfriends everything about you." Andre held up his hands a scant several inches apart to illustrate his point.

Kos scowled. "Bait me all you like, but I'm still going to ask about Zoey."

"I don't want to talk about it."

"Yeah, well, if she weren't running back into the arms of her Hunter, that might be an option."

Andre growled as if Bennett were in the cellar with them. *Davo.* He could not afford to feel possessive about her. She was gone and no longer a threat to his self-control. Andre opened the door to his office and then followed Kos through it. He took one of the big chairs in the sitting area, and Kos sat opposite.

"Besides," Kos said, "if we're staying for a while, we need to find a new PR person." He picked up a deck of cards from the coffee table.

Just the sight of their well-used deck soothed Andre. Thankfully Kos's Uno phase was over. His good-natured son believed their urge to play kept them amused over a very long lifetime. Andre did not quibble with him, but in all his centuries, he had never felt bored. It was clear that vampires needed constant competition to satisfy their inner predator and remain civilized. But the reason did not really matter. What did matter was that Andre and Kos had a way to spend every sleepless night.

Kos began to shuffle the deck. "Why did she leave?"

"She saw my teeth."

"And why did you let that happen?" Kos shuffled again.

He glanced at the mirror that betrayed him. "Believe me, it wasn't on purpose. I lost control for a moment."

"Did you fuck her?"

Andre flinched at the word. It sounded crude, especially coming from Kos. It also did not suit what had happened between him and Zoey, despite their intention to do just that. Still, he said, "Yes."

Kos put down the deck of cards to look at him closely. "What was it about her that got to you?"

"I don't know. It feels as if I know her. She makes me feel alive. And then she told me about her husband—"

"She's married?"

"He jumped off the Golden Gate Bridge. He was a suicide."

Kos froze and Andre dealt the cards.

Finally, Kos spoke. "Did you tell her about Mother?"

"No." He was not fool enough to tell Zoey about Mila. So what if the spark between them was not merely sexual chemistry? That didn't change anything. He would not be bonded to a woman again. "I could not risk that much intimacy."

"So you decided to have sex instead?"

Not this again. Kos's jab was boringly predictable. His noble son only took lovers he cared about, even if he often had more than one at a time. He had judged Andre's forays into San Francisco for anonymous sex cold and empty. Which was precisely the point.

"We agreed to keep it casual."

"How'd that work for you?" Kos provoked further.

"What do you want me to say? 'You're right, son. Sex is beautiful and it should mean something when you do it, and because the only woman I've ever loved in two thousand years decided she would slit her wrists rather than be with me, I just won't do it anymore.'" Andre stood, leaning over the coffee table toward Kos, his volume rising to a yell. "Even though I am a red-blooded male who feeds from aroused women and who can't—" *What did the boys say?* "—jack off!"

He could not remember the last time he had yelled. Was it when Mila had killed herself, or a few years later when the Hunters came? Now he had revealed to Kos just how much Zoey had gotten under his skin.

Kos held his hands up in surrender. "Okay, fair enough. I was being an ass. But clearly, with Zoey it did mean some—"

"Kos, she's gone. I do not want to talk about her anymore. We'll assume she is safely returned to her Ethan Bennett."

"What if he learns she had sex with you? Will she be safe?"

Davo. "I had not considered that they might treat her like a member of my household." The wine in his gut sloshed as his stomach flip flopped. "You don't think she'd tell him, do you?"

"For her sake, I hope not."

CHAPTER 22

Pedro didn't know what time it was. He could no longer see the sun through the cracks around the shed's door, but it was still very hot in his makeshift cell. He figured it had been about twenty-four hours since he'd been kidnapped. Longest day of his life. When would they be back to continue the interrogation?

What he couldn't guess was how long he had been unconscious. When he awoke there was a tin cup of water on the floor next to him and another cup with something that looked like instant oatmeal in it. The gluey cinnamon-spiced mush revived him a little. It was good to get the taste of his own blood out of his mouth.

His ribs ached when he breathed. One eye was swollen shut. He managed to limp to the corner of the shed to relieve himself. As he had expected, he pissed blood—from a bruised kidney or something worse, he didn't know. It was by far the worst beating of his life. But one calculated to keep him alive for questioning.

God damn. How did he end up here? He tested his jaw, stiff from the punch Lucas had landed on his face when Pedro was still trying to read his lips. Then he flashed all the way back to their hungry mouths joining in the office of the tasting room. He'd wanted more, had thought often of that kiss. But now the image of that yellow-eyed bastard made his whole body throb with anger. He would kill Bennett if he had the chance.

He had not revealed anything to the Hunters. Did they suspect he was withholding, or did they believe him to be ignorant? He didn't know. Neither option was good: torture or death. Pedro's mind went to the horrible things they could do to extract information from him. He could withstand another round of beating, but he feared other kinds of pain. His heart began to race with frightened anticipation. *Keep it together,* he told himself. *What can you do? What choices do you have?*

Pedro looked around the shed. Besides the work table pushed against one wall, there wasn't much. There was definitely no way out, and no potential weapons. Well, there was one way out. There was an exposed metal beam supporting the roof of the shed, which crossed over the worktable. His belt around that beam, then around his neck, a step off the table...that was the only exit Pedro could think of. He wasn't ready yet, but if they resorted to other kinds of torture...

Anything was better than being a powerless victim of those sickos. Strangely, he felt better having that option. He was ultimately in control of his life, even if his control lay in ending it.

CHAPTER 23

In the fluorescent light of the rustic motel bathroom, Zoey took a shower. Her composure had returned, but after her brush with panic, she was exhausted.

As she rinsed off the remnants of sex with Andre, she tried to process everything Ethan had told her about vampires. Blood-drinking predators disguised as humans frightened her, but Andre did not. Images of vampires she had seen in movies played in her mind—pale, with slicked back hair, wearing black capes lined with red satin. In spite of her shock, the idea of Andre in a cape made her want to laugh. His olive skin, his warm body so clearly not dead—whatever he was, it didn't fit with her image of a vampire.

She remembered his eyes bright with tenderness in the mirror across from his desk. After she had seen his fangs and told him she was leaving, another expression had formed on his face. She would have missed it if she hadn't been alert for evidence he was a vampire. The look was grief. It was the look of someone who had lost something that mattered more than life itself and it wasn't for her; he didn't know her well enough to feel that way. Yet her departure reminded him of something. What had he lost to leave him so sad? Her heart ached for him, in spite of her confusion.

Once she dried off, she changed into the pajamas she hadn't worn at Kaštel.

Ethan sat on his bed, flipping channels on the TV. She turned down the bedclothes on the other bed and climbed in. He turned off the television and the light. "I'll let you get some sleep."

In the darkness, Zoey realized she had too many questions to sleep. "Ethan, I thought of something in the shower."

He yawned. "What's that?"

"Why were you looking for Andre—for Maras, I mean?" she asked, hoping he wouldn't make anything of the intimacy.

"I told you, our people have been hunting him for years."

"But, I mean, what will you do now that you've found him?"

"Don't worry, Zoey. You're safe. My father has three dozen Hunters planning an attack right now."

"You're going to attack him? At the Estate?"

"Probably. He's unlikely to leave."

Zoey needed to see Ethan's face, needed to see his expression as he answered her questions. She pushed up on her elbows and turned on the light. "How did your family wind up in the business of vampire hunting?"

Ethan sat up too, swinging his legs off the bed so he could face her. He was just wearing his boxers, and it made her feel surprisingly awkward, given she'd been naked with him three days ago.

"It's really more than a family business. We're members of a larger family. I guess you could call us a clan. We're all related, spread out all over the world, Hunting vampires."

"A clan?" Andre had used the word to describe his own kind. He'd implied they were an ethnic minority or something, but all along, he'd meant vampires.

"Yes. We marry within the clan and pass on its traditions. The Hunters are very old."

"How old?" Zoey brushed a stray lock of hair off her brow.

"Prehistoric."

She dropped her feet off the bed and leaned toward him. "No way."

"It's true. We have ancient artifacts proving Hunters slew vampires before humans invented writing."

A memory came to mind—the burdened curve of Andre's shoulders hunched over a bar. "But why hunt them?"

"It's an ancient battle against vampires. They're powerful and seductive. We can't allow them to take over the world and turn us into cattle, as you put it. Someone has to pass on the knowledge of their evil and protect humans. Hunters like me have been trying to exterminate them from the beginning of time." Ethan said the words so calmly, he could have been talking about the weather, his tone a bizarre mismatch to the meaning of the words. Zoey had to think twice before she understood.

"Like vampire genocide?"

"They aren't people."

The story finally clicked — it was Andre's description of an ethnic conflict, but from the other side. She had thought he was paranoid. Instead, he had every reason to fear for the safety of his fellow vampires.

"So when you capture him, will you take him to some kind of vampire prison?"

Ethan huffed. "We won't capture him. We'll kill him. That's what Hunting means, Zoey."

"Oh."

"I know it's hard to understand because you saw him masquerading as a human. But he is a bloodthirsty predator. His kind is an ever-present danger to humans. They must be killed."

Genocide of any kind didn't sit right with her, but Zoey sensed it was a bad idea to disagree with him. She didn't like this creepy side of Ethan at all, and she would get away from him first thing in the morning.

"What about the humans that live with him? Pedro and all the women? How will you get them out before you attack?"

"I'm not used to seeing this sensitive side of you. Can't you see that they've been seduced by Marasović? They betrayed humanity and allowed themselves to be brainwashed. There's nothing we can do for them. They have to die."

If Ethan thought it would be evident to Zoey that they had to be killed, he was truly insane. What if he knew she'd had sex with Andre? Would he want to kill her too? For the first time, she began to feel frightened. She stifled a little cry.

Too quickly, he was next to her, holding her and offering comfort. He smoothed her hair and shushed her. "I know this is a lot to take. You're safe now. Don't worry."

Inside Zoey recoiled from his touch, but she didn't let him feel her reaction. It might well be dangerous for him to know how much her feelings had changed.

"Thank you, Ethan. I'm okay. Let's try to get some sleep." She pulled away from him to make it clear that she wasn't inviting him into her bed.

He stood up and returned to his own. Soon his breathing settled into the steady pace of sleep.

There was no chance she'd sleep. Her mind raced with pictures of Andre and his beautiful home under attack. The fries in her stomach turned to rocks. And there was Kos and Pedro—she liked them. Oh God, and all the women who worked for him—Susan and Ally and the others. She was going to throw up. Sitting up, she inhaled for a count of three and exhaled just as long. By the time her nausea eased, she had a plan.

After hours of lying awake and nervous in the dark, she gave up on sleep, yet somehow it came. When she actually awoke she was surprised to discover she'd dozed.

Ethan was gone from the dark hotel room. A note rested on his bed; it said he would be back with breakfast by eight a.m. According to Zoey's watch, it was seven-fifteen.

She pulled on jeans and a light sweater, the last clean top in her suitcase. Quickly, she brushed her teeth and pulled her hair into a ponytail. Jitters made her nauseous and sped up all her movements. After scrawling a note to Ethan saying she had gone home, she jogged down the main street, dragging her rolling suitcase behind her. She drove away from Forestville fifteen minutes later and hoped that, wherever Ethan was, she wouldn't pass him on the road.

CHAPTER 24

Andre and Kos tossed down cards in silence. After his outburst, the tension had diminished to a simmer between them. Andre let his mind wander and rest, while some place in the back of his brain attended to the card game. Footsteps in the cellar roused him from the nearly hypnotic state.

Seconds later, the door flung open so hard the knob hit the brick wall. Andre winced, expecting bad news, but Bel had just kicked the door open because his hands were full. In an even tone, he said, "The vampires are patrolling the perimeter."

"Find anything?" Andre asked.

"Not so far."

What would the Hunters do? With Zoey gone, an attack seemed likely.

"I'm going to run some experiments with the wine." Bel bounced a metal case. Presumably his supplies were inside. "Can I have a vial of blood from each of you?"

Andre unbuttoned his cuff in a silent agreement.

Bel went to Kos first. "Do either of you need sleep?" he asked, as he tied a tourniquet around Kos's arm and drew the blood.

"No, we don't sleep," Kos replied.

Thankfully their wasting disease had not progressed that far.

"What about you? Do you sleep these days?" Andre asked as Bel drew near.

Bel palpated a vein in the crook of his arm. "About an hour a day. It helps clear my mind. Any more makes me lethargic." Bel placed the needle square in the vein so fast he could have been a vampire.

The vial filled with his deep red blood. "That's less than you used to need."

"Much less. I learned to focus better. My brain doesn't get so cluttered." He removed the needle from Andre's arm, and the small puncture closed immediately. Andre licked his thumb and wiped off the droplet of clotted blood. "Perhaps I'll find something useful from these." Bel placed different colored caps on each of the vials.

Andre rolled down his sleeve and buttoned his cuff as Bel made for the door.

"Good night," he said as he stepped out.

Wordlessly, Kos dealt another hand and they played game after game.

Hours later, tires screeched to a halt in the driveway.

"Who the hell is that?" Kos asked.

Pedro? Hope surged up in Andre. Then someone knocked urgently on the front door. Pedro wouldn't knock unless he was without his keys.

"Hurry!" Andre said. They sped through the cellar and up the stairs. With his new strength, Andre beat Kos to the door by a full quarter of a minute and opened it. Careful to stay in the shadows created by the narrow overhang, no sunlight reached him directly. But a radiant heat made his skin tingle. Or maybe it was just her.

Zoey stood on the other side, nervously biting her lower lip. When she released it, it was deep pink and a little swollen. He wanted to catch it between his own teeth.

"Fuck," he said.

"Nice to see you, too."

"Go home, Zoey."

"Andre, they're coming after you."

He couldn't believe she was here. His gums were aching where his fangs wanted to extend; his breath was getting shallower. He had to have her. If she didn't leave, he would have her and he would regret it for the rest of his immortal life.

"We know, Zoey. Go home." He tried to keep his voice calm.

"You already know?"

"We knew weeks ago, and we knew you were with them."

"But I didn't—" She shook her head. "Never mind. Listen, he said they have three dozen men," Zoey persisted.

"Zoey. Get. The hell. Out of here."

"I told them about the wine."

"What?" Kos roared as he spun toward Andre. "What did you tell her?"

What had he told her? His fangs and his cock refused to let him remember. "I don't know. Bring her inside. Figure out what she told them. Then, get rid of her. I'm going back to my office."

He didn't make it to the office. He sat down on the bottom step in the cellar. In the sanctuary of the cool darkness, he breathed slowly until he managed to calm his raging desires. He wanted her gone and he wanted her to still want him after seeing his fangs. The conflicting desires pulled his muscles into knots that wine and cards with Kos had done little to relax.

The floorboards muffled Kos's and Zoey's voices, and he had to concentrate to hear. He leaned his head against the wall and listened.

Stunned, Zoey glared at Andre's back. Kos took her by the elbow and began walking. Even though it was a gentle touch, he was too close to be friendly, his shoulders were pulled back in an alert posture, his eyes darted quickly around the entryway. Everything about the way he moved commanded her to walk with him. It erased her last trace of doubt—there was definitely a predator inside him. Her spine went rigid, and she remained on alert as she walked alongside. But nothing about his actions triggered her panic. Then he did something so civilized it put her completely at ease.

"Would you like some coffee?"

"Thank you. I do need a cup. Guess I can have the whole pot to myself?"

"Sometimes I like to smell a little." He shouted down to the kitchen, "Susan, can you send up a pot of coffee in the dumbwaiter?" Then he steered her into the sunny parlor.

"What's wrong with Andre?"

"I need to know about the Hunters first, Zoey."

Fair enough. It was a life or death situation for them. Her confusion about how Andre had greeted her was minor in comparison, but his greeting certainly stung. Last night he had fucked her like he loved her—she hadn't even known that was possible. And this morning he told her to get out of his house and go home. She wanted to warn him, to help him remain safe, but they had agreed to keep things casual. Did he think she'd come back here to cozy up to him and play house? Arrogant jerk.

Kos sat her on a sofa facing the wide swath of French doors and took an armchair for himself.

"What did my father tell you about the wine?"

Her empty stomach clenched. Had she ruined everything for them? She gulped. Press on, tell the truth, remain confident.

"Remember when you learned I knew about the Croatian refugees?"

"Yes."

"That's what he told me. That your, uh, people fled Croatia in an ethnic conflict and that you dispersed and changed your names in order to hide from your enemies. I thought he sounded so paranoid at the time."

"I bet."

"Anyway, I realized there was something he wasn't telling me about why you hired me. When I pushed him, he admitted he hoped for a way to reestablish contact with the others. These are the other vampires that fled when Ethan's psychotic ancestors tried to kill them all, right?"

"Bennett told you that?"

"Well, psychotic is my word." Kos seemed to be waiting for her to continue. "He told me that the Hunters...is that what they're called?"

"Yes, in English they call themselves Hunters."

"He told me the Hunters want to kill all vampires. I'm not saying you don't freak me out, Kos. I'm freaked. But exterminating a whole race, or species, or whatever. That's genocide. That's about hate, not about helping humanity."

She couldn't read his reaction from his neutral expression. After a moment, he asked, "Did you tell Bennett you feel that way?"

"I pushed back at first, but he just got more zealous. So I shut up. Honestly, I was a little scared of what he'd do with me if he knew I was sympathetic to you all."

"That was wise. How did you get away?"

"I slipped out when he went to get breakfast."

"You spent the night with him?"

"In separate beds." Why did Kos looked relieved? Oh. "Did Andre tell you about me and him?"

"Zoey, this will sound weird. We could smell it on you when you arrived."

"Smell what?"

"That you'd had sex with a Hunter. We assumed it was Ethan Bennett because we know Lucas is gay. Hunters reek."

Zoey rubbed her arms. It made her feel dirty that they smelled him on her. Even worse, he had made her stink.

"Kos, I didn't know anything about this when I came here. They were using me."

"We knew that."

"Then why did Andre tell me about the wine?"

"Hell, I think he'd tell you anything you asked him."

What did that mean? She wanted to ask, but Kos needed her to focus on Ethan instead. "I'm sorry, Kos. I didn't know."

The dumbwaiter squeaked to a stop. She stood to get some coffee while she asked, "Do you all have a plan to defend yourselves or will you have to run again?"

"We desperately hope not to run, but it's nearly impossible to fight them off. They will keep coming from all over the world to kill us, now that our location is known."

Her coffee turned bitter in her mouth. They might have to abandon everything they'd built. What would happen to Ally and Susan if Andre and Kos had to flee?

Should she ask Kos about Andre's rude dismissal? No, she'd already done what she came to do and might as well leave. She didn't need to get more involved in their situation, and Andre clearly wanted her gone. She would go home, send Ethan her resignation, and start looking for a new job.

"Kos, I wish you the best of luck. I hope you're able to stay." She set down her mug, ready to leave. "I wish I could have finished the project for you. That would have been a great fuck-you to Ethan, and I was enjoying the work. But clearly it's time to go."

"You're a real spitfire, huh? Maybe that's why Andre likes you."

"Yeah. He likes me a lot." She brushed her perfectly clean hands off on her thighs. It was time to put Andre behind her.

"Well, do you want the bad news or the worse news, then?"

She froze. "What do you mean?"

"Let's start with the bad. What Andre didn't realize when he ordered you to go home is that you are no longer safe there. Hunters are undoubtedly watching this place, and there's a good chance Ethan will know you came here. To them, you are now a part of this household and you must be killed. You're stuck here for a while."

Her jaw went slack with the shock. *Shit.* She had placed herself in the middle of a battle that would not end, only to relay useless information to Andre. She would have to go on the run.

Wait. Kos had said there was more bad news to come. She looked up.

"Ready for the worse news?"

"No."

"Too bad. My father was angry to see you because he is at least halfway in love with you."

Did she hear that right? "No, he's not."

"Yes, he is. And, Zoey, he'd rather die than be married again."

"Who the hell says I want to get married?"

"You don't understand, Zoey. He wants you, but he won't let himself get close to you."

"I understand perfectly."

"No, Zoey, you don't." Kos bunched up his shoulders and then released them.

"Then tell me."

"It's because of my mother, Mila, that Andre won't get close to a woman again."

She was hooked. In spite of herself, she did want to know about Andre's past. Only because she had revealed her own past to him and it was fair she also know his. Not because she was impossibly curious.

"Was she a vampire?" Zoey picked up her mug again and took another sip.

"She was not. She refused to let Andre turn her. When they married, she promised him she would go through with it, but then refused year after year. She was aging, and Andre feared for her health. I believe she loved him, but in the end she couldn't choose to become like him."

"So she grew old and died?"

"No." Kos looked away from Zoey, gazing out the window.

Was that all she was going to get?

He turned back to her suddenly, opened his mouth and closed it once, then spoke. "Zoey, he found her dead in the bath. She'd slit her wrists."

Stunned, Zoey couldn't lift a finger, couldn't take a breath. Her mind raced. So that was it — the spark, the connection between them. How disappointing. If only it could have been cataclysmic sexual chemistry or some kinky vampire thing. Instead, they were the walking wounded, two people totally damaged.

The look on his face was expectant.

"I take it Andre told you my husband also committed suicide?"

He nodded.

"I understand this is a very strange coincidence, but it hardly makes us soul mates. In fact, it makes it clear why neither of us wants a relationship. I decided a long time ago that it was best for me to be alone."

"But, Zoey, it's not that simple."

"Why not? It sounds like we're on the same page. When he saw me at the door, he thought I was getting clingy, right? Don't worry, I'm not the kind of girl that thinks a good fuck is a marriage proposal."

"Zoey, you don't understand. You can't leave, but he can't be around you. He can't control himself. Your being here is a train wreck."

"What do you mean he can't control himself? He's certainly not going to force himself on me. He's a little domineering, but he wouldn't hurt me."

"Of course not. But, Zoey, I'm not talking about sex. He —"

"Enough, Kos." Andre was in the door. Kos didn't look particularly surprised he was there.

Again she took in his beauty. Broad forehead, dark brow, and high cheekbones. His cheeks were hollow, his face purely masculine. He still wore the white shirt he'd had on yesterday, now rumpled. Zoey remembered a flash of sadness in the shower when she'd washed him off her. Was that why he hadn't bathed?

"Listen boys, I'm leaving. I'll figure out how to walk away from my life. I'm sure I can find instructions on the Internet. Train wreck averted."

He was next to her inhumanly fast. "While I admire your courage, Zoey, I can't let you leave."

"Andre, you just told me to go home, and not nicely."

"Kos is right. I wasn't thinking clearly when you arrived. I can't guarantee your safety if you leave, even if you don't go home. You came back here to protect me and I owe you protection in return."

She wasn't feeling all that brave about walking away from her home and identity. She had a lonely but comfortable existence. She would probably pull over a safe distance from Kaštel and melt down in the car where no one would see. But she was ready to start doing whatever she would have to — better to act than to think about it.

"What do you mean? You don't think I'd be safe in hiding?"

"I mean, they may tail you from here and get you the first place you stop. I don't know how sophisticated the Hunters have become. Perhaps they can even track your credit cards. You have to stay here for the time being. You'll be safe from them, and I promise you'll be safe from me."

Why was he a threat to her?

All at once, the floor started to shake underneath them. Her pulse skyrocketed, but surely it was just a little tremor. They happened all the time in wine country.

Then something exploded.

CHAPTER 25

Ethan returned to an empty hotel room to find Zoey's note. She must have been more spooked than he thought if she left without waiting for him to bring breakfast and say goodbye. His cell phone rang.

"Hello."

"Your Zoey just pulled back into Kaštel Estate and went inside." It was one of the Hunters on surveillance.

"Are you sure?"

"Silver Audi, dark hair, nice ass."

So she'd gone back. That was disappointing. "Yes, that's her."

"We're preparing to firebomb the house."

What was this cold feeling in his chest?

"Do it."

As he hung up his phone, the feeling spread into his bones. Was he grieving Zoey? She was rather special. Something inside her was broken, a mirror of the iciness he hid within himself.

Still, the feeling itself was astonishing. Had he ever been so attached to another person? Perhaps if she hadn't run away, she would have seen him for what he was; perhaps she would have wanted him, darkness and all.

Another feeling seized him, spiking his pulse and making his cell phone creak under the pressure of his grip. *Call back, call off the attack. Get her.*

No. That was not an option. He hated to lose her, but if she went back there, she was already lost. And this hysteria did not suit him.

Ethan gathered what few items he had in the room and sped back to Hunter headquarters. Mick was leading the mission at Kaštel, but his father and Lucas were in the back room. The crumbling plaster walls and sloppy table made the label "command center" a touch too ironic. It probably pained his father to be there instead of at Kaštel, but they couldn't trust Lucas alone with Pedro, in spite of the punishment he had dealt out to the winemaker.

Lucas was surprised to see Ethan. He must have heard that Zoey went back to Kaštel and so came straight to HQ.

"I want a go at Pedro. Let's see if we can get anything of value to use against Maras."

Lucas had no choice but to agree. He walked with Stephen to the shed as Ethan went to his car, and pulled out a small black leather bag. It looked like the kind doctors used to carry for house calls.

Lucas eyed it warily. "What's in there?"

"Just some tools I brought along in case Pedro needed persuading."

At the door to the shed, Ethan ordered the initiates standing guard to restrain Pedro on the worktable inside. Even in his battered state, he resisted the young men, but together they managed to pin him down. Then one of them wrapped duct tape around his wrists, ankles, and hips, securing him firmly to the table.

Ethan barked at the initiates. "Get out."

He squatted down and laid out his tools on a cloth he had inside the leather kit, pulling out razor blades, pliers, a vise, and his sun dagger before Lucas turned his head away, struck with fear for Pedro.

Pedro seemed to realize this was his last chance, and he didn't want to go out quietly. He cursed them in Spanish, which only Lucas understood. Damn, Pedro knew some nasty expressions.

In English he said, "You think they are evil predators. Look in the mirror, you dogs, you're the animals — filthy, sick animals. He's only ever been kind to me. He takes good care of the women. You make your children kill innocents and you call the vampires cruel." He spat on Lucas, who stood closest to him.

"Whom do you mean, Pedro? Do you mean the vampires that don't exist?" Ethan's voice was so cold that he no longer sounded familiar. He barely sounded human.

Pedro's face fell for a moment when he realized he'd given up his strategy of denial. Then he shored himself up. "I don't know anything. Just kill me; send one of your yellow-eyed little boys in here to do me off."

"But how can we trust you, Pedro? After all, you lied to us about knowing what Maras was. I think we will have to extract information from you in a different way. Take off his shoes." Again he barked the order, that time to Lucas.

Ethan took the pliers in hand. "I am going to pull out your toenails one by one. You can stop this any time by telling me what you know."

"Fuck you!"

"You must be confusing me with my brother."

Lucas's head jerked toward Ethan in astonishment. But he clicked his teeth together before he was caught, mouth agape. Ethan had just shown one more card—this brutality was all about Lucas, which meant he was to blame for dragging Pedro into it.

As Ethan started in on Pedro's first toe, Pedro began sobbing and cursing, but he never lost his will to fight. After a while, he was only crying out in Spanish. Lucas wanted to ignore him, wanted to stop his brain from translating into English. But he owed it to Pedro to listen. Eventually, his cries became pleas for Lucas to help.

He had to think carefully about some of the words. He wasn't fluent, but he could make out the message. "Friend, just kill me, please. Don't let him do this to me…" Pedro was careful. As he spoke to Lucas, he didn't change his tone from the cursing and exclamations of pain. "Just get them out of here for a minute and get me free. I'll hang myself from the rafter with my belt."

Lucas wished he could let Pedro know his plans, but the foreign words wouldn't come to him. Every second of Pedro's agony was seared into his soul, but he had to wait for the best opportunity.

Ethan had removed three of Pedro's toenails. His feet were a bloody mess, the toes swollen beyond recognition. He removed the duct tape at Pedro's ankles as he explained that next he would peel the skin off his legs, beginning at the ankle and moving up.

Lucas was sick and panicked inside. Perhaps saving Pedro was no longer possible. Would it be most merciful to create a distraction and kill him somehow?

At the sound of the explosion, Zoey asked, "What is that?"

Andre and Kos sped out of the room. Were they running? They moved so fast she couldn't make out the action of their bodies. Zoey followed them to the door and saw them in the entryway.

A swarm of people Zoey hadn't known were in the house began to appear: six huge men that Zoey somehow knew were vampires, Andre's other son Bel, a dark-skinned woman, a red-headed girl, and four other people she couldn't see clearly were behind them on the stairs.

"It's the Hunters," Bel said. "We're under attack."

There was no damage visible, but Zoey smelled smoke.

Someone called out. "What happened?"

As Bel opened the door, Andre, Kos, and Zoey all shouted, "No!"

The pretty woman with dark hair said, "It's all right."

"The shield is holding," Bel said when he looked outside. He held the door open wide enough that Zoey could see. There were men advancing on the house, throwing bottles with flaming wicks. The bottles were breaking against some kind of invisible barrier, creating walls of fire as the fuel in them spread against the barrier and ignited. The fuel ran down the invisible wall forming a ring of fire that burned out quickly on the cement drive of the house. Zoey's mind couldn't make sense of what she was seeing.

Kos stood in the doorway to the parlor, looking out through the wall of French doors. "They've surrounded us, but the shield is holding on this side too. The flames are catching the lawn on fire back here." The dark-haired woman ran past him into the parlor and Kos followed.

"What exploded?" Andre asked Bel.

He looked to the right out of the door. "I think it was Zoey's car. Sorry, Zoey, you arrived after she shielded the house, or Trys would have protected your car."

Now she was really stuck. She glanced at Andre only to find him watching her. "I guess I'm staying."

Suddenly he was next to her, and he said into her ear, "It's for the best — they attacked now because they knew you were here. You wouldn't be safe anywhere else." Concern rumbled in his voice; his offer of protection wasn't simply a repayment for her attempt to protect him. Damn it if it didn't melt her. He might want her gone, but he also wanted her safe.

"I still don't understand what caused that earthquake," the redhead said in accented English.

The huge black-skinned guy answered her from where he looked out a window. "There is someone on that hill with a rocket launcher — they must have tried to rip a hole in the front of the house to get their Molotov cocktails inside. But the rocket bounced off the shield. Damn, Trys. This is the best one you've made. Remember that time in Finland when my thigh was torn open by the RPG that got through your barrier?"

"How could I forget, with you constantly reminding me, Omar?" said a twiggy blonde with something smudged on her face — it looked like chocolate. The woman continued. "But you always leave out the part where my spell stopped your bleeding and we got you out before the place went up in smoke."

The smack talk was clearly a familiar script between them.

"Who are they?" she whispered to Andre.

"They're Bel's crew. Vampire mercenaries he brought to protect us from the Hunters."

"We're not all vampires!" the redhead said. "I'm going to check the police scanner."

"Wow. You have a police scanner now?" Kos asked.

"I never leave home without it," she replied.

"Not since Vania and I spent the night in jail in Mumbai," Bel said, stepping into the center of the entryway. He took charge. "They're retreating now. Arden, Vania, come with me. We'll tail the Hunters. Trys, brilliant work with the shield. Do whatever it takes to keep that up. Kos, be ready to handle the police if they show up. Say it was an engine backfire."

"Yeah," Kos said. "That will explain everything."

"Well, think of something. Just take care of it."

"Will do. But, Bel, remember they have Pedro. Please attempt a rescue before Vania burns them all down."

The news that Pedro had been kidnapped made Zoey's stomach drop.

Bel nodded in agreement. The gathering dispersed quickly and she was left alone with Andre.

"The Hunters have Pedro?" she asked.

His eyes drooped with worry, and he said, "I'm afraid so. We think they picked him up after dinner with you on Tuesday night."

"Oh." It was chilling to consider what Ethan and Lucas might be capable of. Her skin crawled and her face felt heavy with the same expression of concern on Andre's.

"Bel's men have been trying to track him, but if he's still alive, maybe they'll find him."

Zoey closed her eyes and imagined Pedro's handsome laughing face. Lucas had seemed to like him, but nothing was what it seemed anymore. "Andre, I'm so sorry. Is this somehow my fault? Could I have saved him?"

"I've been asking myself the same thing." The muscles of his jaw bulged.

After a moment, she asked, "Is that shield outside…magic?"

Andre swiped his hand over his short black hair, and scratched the back of his head. "Apparently so. I do not know much about magic. Bel says magicians are simply people who know how to control things we do not. And that witches require a lot of chocolate."

That explained the smear on Trys's face. Then she shook her head. That didn't explain anything. Magic, witches, chocolate?

"Shit." Astonished, she leaned her head closer to him. "When are you going to stop blowing my mind? I can't take much more of this."

Andre's green eyes glinted with an almost-laugh, and the tension between them eased, if not her fears about Pedro.

"I am sorry, Zoey, I truly am. That they involved you in this and that I did not protect you better."

"It's not your job to protect me, and I'm sorry I came back. Sounds like I've screwed things up royally…" She glanced away, focusing on a crease in the shoulder of his rumpled shirt. "I ruined my own life and made yours difficult in ways that I don't understand."

"I may as well explain, then…" He rubbed the back of his neck.

Was he serious? She met his eye again, and felt that space of deep knowing open up between them. All the willpower she possessed couldn't have budged her gaze. "That would help me," she said.

"Perhaps it will make things easier on both of us." His nostrils flared and his pupils dilated at the same time. "But, first I need to… eat."

Her stomach sank as a confusing progression of emotions passed through her—fear, revulsion, and finally curiosity. Andre watched her closely as she roller coastered through them. He seemed relieved by what he saw in the end.

"Can I watch?" she asked.

CHAPTER 26

Lucas's eyes tried to clamp shut, but he forced them open. He owed it to Pedro to watch. A razor thin line of blood seeped from the incision Ethan cut into his leg, then he pulled Pedro's skin away from his raw flesh. Lucas went cold. Pedro screamed and thrashed on the table, no longer bothering to beg. His wild eyes told Lucas he was even more afraid of what might come next, which meant Ethan's technique was excellent. Sick bastard. When had he learned to torture? That little black bag confirmed his worst fears about his brother.

Stephen's phone rang. "Bennett."

He listened for a moment and Lucas assumed it was Mick.

"What? A shield, around the whole house? Is it an electro-magnet? Can't the cocktails go through even if the grenades bounce off?" Stephen was silent again. "Shit." He hung up. "They're retreating. There's some kind of shield around the whole house. None of the weapons can get through."

Ethan turned his concentration from Pedro. "A shield? That doesn't make sense." He examined his blood slick blade. "Let's ask our little friend." Pedro was unconscious, so Ethan slapped him. "How are they shielding the house?"

"What?" Pedro's eyes were shut tight, and his head rocked back and forth.

"There's a shield around the house. How's he doing that?"

The rock became a shake. "Don't know!"

Lucas could hear the first Hunters arriving at the compound. They must have left well before Mick called Stephen. His father went out to meet them.

"Maybe this will help you remember." Ethan made a vertical slice into the skin on Pedro's calf, intersecting the one circumscribing his ankle. Then he used the razor blade to get under a corner of the incision and begin to peel away the skin.

Pedro's throaty scream vibrated in Lucas's bones, tipping him to the point of decision. He picked up Ethan's sun dagger and pummeled his brother in the head. Stunned, Ethan turned toward him, but Lucas acted fast. He brought the hilt of the dagger down hard on his brother's head again. Then he landed a punch to his face and a knee to his gut. Ethan went down. Would he be out long enough for Lucas to get Pedro out? He taped Ethan's mouth closed, then both hands and ankles together. He landed one last hard kick to his brother's head, knocking him over and unconscious.

Pedro was also unconscious. Lucas used Ethan's sun dagger to cut him off the table. Then he put it in his back pocket and lifted Pedro into his arms. His keys were in his pocket and the plan in his head only got him as far as his car.

Outside, it sounded like all the Hunters had returned. There was a lot of shouting—utter chaos and confusion. Maybe that would give him a chance to escape. He kicked open the door of the shed and ran toward his Land Cruiser as fast as he could with Pedro's dead weight. When he was almost to his car, he looked up to see two men and a woman blocking his way. Who the hell were they?

"Give him to me, Hunter, and I'll kill you fast," the big one with dark hair said.

"Back off, he's hurt. I'm getting him out of here."

"You're not going anywhere," said the chick. She was decked out in black leather like Catwoman. Too weird.

"He needs help."

"He's not your problem now—we are."

Behind them, Lucas saw tall flames dancing around the side of the house and catching the grass on fire. A window shattered on the back exterior wall, where black smoke climbed into the sky. Stephen barked orders at the initiates to try to save his family tapestries. Two men collided while trying to get the weapons through the front door.

One of the kids apparently noticed him carrying Pedro. Pointing, he shouted, "Hey, Mick, what's he doing with the prisoner?"

Lucas extended Pedro's heavy, limp body to the big man. "Just take him—make sure he's safe." A shot rang out and too late Lucas saw his father aiming a gun at him. The bullet missed him and slammed into Pedro's side as he hung between him and the other man. The force knocked Lucas back, but he held onto Pedro.

The man helped Lucas right himself. Pedro groaned loudly. The bald stranger took out his gun and provided cover, aiming at Stephen Bennett and the other Hunters.

"You've been shot," said the dark-haired man. "I'm taking you to Andre. He can help."

Pedro eyes weren't focusing, but he turned his head to the man, then to Lucas. His face contorted with the effort it took to speak, and his voice was raw from screaming. "Bel...he comes with us... they'll kill him...for freeing me."

"Oh, hell no, Pedro. He's a Hunter."

Lucas could feel wet blood trickle down his hand where he gripped Pedro's side. A lot of blood.

Pedro shook his head. "No...a coward maybe...not a Hunter anymore."

The one he called Bel asked Lucas, "Well?"

"He's right. I'm not...anymore."

"Shit." Bel took Pedro from Lucas without much effort and tilted his head in the direction of escape.

"Not that way. Let's take my truck so we don't have to carry him." Lucas's car chirped when he unlocked it. Once they got Pedro inside, the woman and the one called Bel climbed in quickly. The bald one kept the door ajar and his gun trained at the group of Hunters amassing by the front door of the house. Lucas gunned the engine and skidded onto the highway.

Thirty yards down, the woman said, "Stop here." Lucas slammed on his brakes. She and the gunman got into their van, and he raced behind her as quickly as possible toward the Kaštel Estate.

In the rear view mirror, Lucas watched Bel in the backseat applying pressure to Pedro's wound. He took a deep breath and tried to sound calm for Pedro's sake. "That's a lot of blood."

"Clean exit though, that's good. Pedro, buddy. You still with me?"

"Yeah. Yeah." After a minute Pedro said, "Lucas?"

"I'm here."

"Fuck you." It was the least he deserved for his failure to rescue Pedro sooner. But the words made the situation clear—he had betrayed his family for someone who would hate him.

Bel laughed. "Man, I like you more and more." Then his voice became calm and matter-of-fact, like somebody used to being in the line of fire. "Listen, Pedro, you're losing a lot of blood…"

"It's okay…made my peace." He paused for a few breaths. "But I'm glad…" He coughed and Lucas saw a spray of blood splatter Bel's face. "Glad you got me out…wanted it on my terms…not theirs."

"Pedro, you have a choice."

"What choice?" he rasped.

"We can't get you to the E.R., but we can get you to Andre. He'll turn you, if you want him to."

"You mean…into a vampire?"

It was probably the only way to save Pedro, for him to become what Lucas hated most.

"Only if you want. Or you can die in peace. Both are good choices, my friend. If it makes a difference, Andre and Kos have been worried sick about you. They would miss you if you decided to go. And they'd be happy for you to join their card games."

"Hell no. I'm not playing Uno with them. If I don't have to sleep…I'm going clubbing."

Chuckling, Bel asked, "Is that a yes?"

"Yeah, man. Let him do it." Pedro closed his eyes.

"Faster, Bennett. If he dies in this car, there's nothing Andre can do."

Lucas pushed the gas pedal down and approached the bumper of the van ahead. It sped up in turn. Hatred or not, he wanted Pedro to survive.

CHAPTER 27

Andre sucked in a breath. Zoey wanted to watch him feed. Mila had never seen him bite someone else. It had made her nervous just to think of it. What would it be like to have Zoey's eyes on him? The idea intrigued him, as evidenced by his growing erection. But what if she was repulsed? Well, then she would stay away from him and his problem would be solved.

He did the math in his head. He had fed from Susan on Monday, it would be safe to take a small amount more blood from her. With all the wine he had been drinking he only needed a little to keep his blood lust for Zoey at bay.

"Let me find Susan."

Zoey followed him to the south wing of the house where Susan and Ally shared a room. He rapped his knuckles on their door, and when it opened, his entire household was inside.

"Is everything all right?" Ally asked him.

"So far. The house is secure."

"When we felt the earthquake, Bel shouted down the hall for us all to gather in here," Susan said.

"Was it an earthquake?" Ally asked.

"No, it was a rocket bouncing off a magical shield surrounding us." Zoey said it so matter-of-factly that his women weren't sure whether she was joking. Damn, he liked her wry sense of humor.

"Really?" Susan asked.

"Yes. It is true," he replied. Everyone was stunned into silence. "The Hunters are gone for the time being. But I expect they will be back in the next few days. Next time you hear anything, I want you all to head into the cellars. You know where the emergency exit is?"

"You mean that creepy tunnel opening out on the hillside in the north vineyard?" Ally asked.

"Yes. If it comes to that, you may need to evacuate. Take flashlights with you, and your wallets."

"Where do we go from there?"

"If it seems safe, walk to the Farmhouse Inn. You know the one?"

"Yep, I know it," Susan said. "Your friend Sam owns it."

"Exactly. Just tell him you need his help and that I'll be along shortly." The women nodded that they understood his instructions. When he was satisfied, he turned to Susan. "If you don't mind, I need you."

She gave him a puzzled look until she realized what he meant. "Sure. Where?"

Andre looked around at the room that she shared with Ally. It would be a violation of their space to feed there. But, with Zoey in his room—

Zoey must have guessed the problem because she said, "Let's go to my room."

Susan's brows came together. "All three of us?"

"If it's all right with you, he said I could watch."

Susan's smile was sly. "You two are getting kinky."

"No, we're not," Andre said. "But Zoey is stuck here with us, against her will, and it seems fair to me to give her all the information she wants."

"Whatever you say."

The three arrived in Zoey's disheveled room. When she gathered her things to flee the night before, she must have been more frightened than he had thought. Yet here she was half a day later, asking to watch him feed. She showed no signs of Mila's reluctance, only curiosity and a firm determination.

"Where do you want me?" Susan asked them both. It made him nervous, the way she was being deliberately provocative.

He looked at Zoey and she shrugged, as if wanting to appear at ease. "Do your thing."

Andre's heart pounded. He shouldn't care so much what her reaction would be. Should he sit Susan next to him in their usual arrangement, or sit her on his lap? That was the easiest position for feeding. Did he want her to see how sexually arousing his bite could be? Yes, but—

"Sit down, Andre," Susan said gesturing at the bed. When he planted himself, she sat on his lap. She was so much smaller than him that she had to straddle one of his large thighs to find her balance. "You owe me for this," she whispered so quietly that only his ears would hear.

Zoey backed herself against the wall, her jaw open in fascination. Their eyes locked for a moment, but then he turned his attention to Susan. Her chin-length hair left her neck exposed to him.

"Ready?"

"Yeah."

He placed one hand on each of Susan's upper arms and licked her neck in the spot where he would soon bite. Zoey released the breath she was holding. Did she remember him licking her like that? His cock certainly remembered.

"Behave." Susan whispered another barely audible word when he hardened underneath her.

Andre opened his mouth wide and let his fangs extend fully so they were visible to Zoey. With his head angled to the side, he looked at her again. Her lips had changed shape, forming an O, while her eyes remained wide. In this moment, before a bite, Andre felt fully in possession of his prey. He felt powerful.

He caught Zoey's attention, and was surprised when she did not shy away from his display of dominance. Instead, she met his gaze and licked her lips, as if she were anticipating her own meal. The gesture was automatic and natural; there was nothing coquettish about it. God, she was perfect.

Susan dug her fingernails into his thighs on both sides; she was losing patience. He let his teeth sink into her flesh before his mouth closed over her neck so that Zoey had a complete view. Then he took a deep draw from Susan's vein. Susan let out a low moan; he had never heard her make that sound before.

Zoey's eyes moved from his to Susan's, and her expression went cold as she observed Susan's reaction to the pleasure. Zoey inched forward, gaze glued on the other woman.

Davo, were Susan's hips rolling? In the subtlest of movements, she was rocking along his thigh back and forth. He just needed one or two more swallows and then he could stop. Susan let out another moan, and as the sound abated another noise replaced it, very quietly. It came from Zoey. She was growling? Her possessiveness shouldn't feel so damn good. Shame on him.

He opened his mouth and his fangs retracted. Feeling Susan shiver, he lapped up the blood seeping from the puncture wounds and they healed instantly. He moved his hands from Susan's arms to her hips to give her a boost off his lap. She stood and turned to him, winking. "See you two later." She was out the door faster than most humans moved.

Zoey stayed where she was and looked at him. He grew nervous again waiting for her to speak. Looking around, he remembered that on Šolta all the rooms had been yellow, simulating the sun. But since he installed the tinted windows, Kos had all the walls at Kaštel painted different colors. He missed the yellow, or maybe it was Zoey making him feel so warm.

Finally, she said, "Is biting always like that?"

"Like what?"

"So hot?"

Andre laughed. "It was hot because you were watching."

"Your erection says otherwise."

He shook his head. "That never happens with Susan. I promise it is you."

With her palms, she pushed off the wall and took a step toward him. "Last night, did you want to bite me?"

"Yes, but I would not have."

She stood just inches from where he sat on the bed. "Why not? If you knew it would give me so much pleasure?"

"Didn't I give you enough pleasure?" He couldn't help but show her all his teeth when he remembered her passionate response.

She did not smile back. "You know you did. Answer the question."

"If I tasted your blood, Zoey, there would be no going back."

"What would change?"

"It is difficult to explain." He had promised her answers, but instinct told him to evade the question.

"Start from the beginning, then." Zoey lowered herself into an armchair facing him on the bed.

"For vampires, an emotional tie has power. Any desire that goes beyond lust—if a vampire feeds from a person he or she truly desires, a blood bond is formed." He looked down at his hand, where he had worn a wedding ring for just a sliver of the years in his long life. "It is like a marriage, but more intense. It is biological. It ties two people together in every cell."

"You think that would happen if you bit me?"

"Yes. I knew it from the moment I saw you on Monday. And I know neither of us wants such a bond."

"You shared one with your wife, Mila?"

"Not shared, no. I was bonded to her, but because she was not a vampire she was not bonded to me."

"That's what you're afraid of? Being bonded to someone who can't reciprocate?"

"Do not make it sound trite, Zoey. The bond is primal, physical. To share it with a human is a terrible burden."

"I don't understand." Zoey tilted her head slightly, intent.

"Before she killed herself, I lived in constant fear that Mila would die and leave me suffering. When she did, it was even worse than I feared." He scrubbed his hands down his face. "It felt like I was being ripped apart cell by cell. The pain is both bodily and psychic. It persists still…as a dull ache. More than a hundred years later, I feel something like phantom limb syndrome—she is always missing."

With his thumb and forefinger, he rubbed his eyes through closed lids. When he opened them, her chocolate brown ones drew him in with their compassion. She came to stand in front of him.

"Did she understand what it would do to you when she killed herself?"

Of course she would ask that. Andre relaxed under her focus; she understood. "I do not think so…not really. I tried not to pressure her to turn, so I did not fully explain. The only thing worse than losing a bonded mate would be an eternal bond with someone angry at you for turning them."

"Why did you bond in the first place? Was it an accident?"

"No." She was already looking at him, but he reached up to where she stood and gently held her chin in place. "I am old, Zoey. Very old. She was the first woman in nearly two thousand years that I desired. I had grown bored. When she appeared with little Kos in hand, both of them so vibrant and alive, I could not resist them."

"Two thousand years? No wonder you wouldn't tell me your age." She dropped to a squat and rested her elbows on his knees with her legs slightly parted. "If it was so unusual for you to feel that way, why do you think you'd bond with me? You can't think we're soul mates." Her front teeth rested on her full lower lip.

"I can smell that you want me."

"What?"

"I can smell that you're sweet and wet between your legs, Zoey. When Susan moaned, it poured out of you." He grinned. "She was really hamming it up for you."

Pink faced, Zoey stood up and took a step back. "Okay, setting aside how weird it is that you can smell me, why does that matter? The night we met, lots of other women in that bar wanted you."

"You growled at Susan when you saw how much she was enjoying my bite." He couldn't help it; a little pride crept into his voice.

"I did not." Her ponytail wagged as she shook her head.

"Yes, you did. You watching me feed was already…arousing, but when you growled—"

"You're saying I'm jealous?" She started pacing. Probably the same path she had trod when he had listened to her footsteps the day she arrived.

"Yes. I was jealous too when you went back to Ethan Bennett."

She turned to him. "I like you; I like being with you. You make me feel…"

He waited, longing to know what he made her feel.

"Just feel. You make me feel."

A thousand times better and worse than if she had named an actual feeling. "It's the same for me."

"What do we do?"

"Simple. We keep away from each other. The only reason you are not underneath me on this bed with my fangs in your neck is

Susan's blood. I am guessing it will keep me satisfied for another hour." Another wave of her sweet scent assaulted him. Apparently that had not scared her the way he'd meant it to.

"You need to feed that often?"

"No, I am not hungry, Zoey. I am craving you."

Her delicate throat rippled with a swallow.

"If I am near you, I will bite you. And it will be decided. Regardless of what either of us wants, you will be mine." He stood and stepped close to her. It was always handy to have such an intimidating stature. "If that happened, I could not let you leave. You would have to stay with me, forever. Do you understand?" He put his palms flat against the wall on either side of her head, caging her. "I won't go through that again. If we bond, I'll turn you whether you like it or not."

Davo. No quickening pulse. No sour odor. Zoey did not reveal a trace of fear. Instead, her eyes were soft and her mouth sad.

"I like you, Andre. But I don't want to be a vampire, and I don't want to hurt you the way Mila did. I know something about what that was like. So, I'll keep to myself."

He went back to the bed and sat in silence while she looked out the window.

Eventually, she said, "Andre, what will I do when it's safe to leave?"

"Kos has prepared for us to escape. There is cash and more than a dozen new identities. You'll have one of those, whether my household stays or goes."

She came to sit next to him. "I don't have many friends, my family's all dead, and I don't have a pet. I don't even have a job anymore. But still, I don't want to walk away from my life."

He wrapped his arm around her waist and she put her head on his shoulder. "I know, sweet."

"Andre?"

"Mmhmm." He smelled her: her hair, her skin, her breath.

"Is it safe enough for you to hold me for a while?"

"Not entirely," he said. "But enough, I think." He picked her up and laid her on the bed; she turned on her side and he curled around her. She nestled back into him, creating as much contact between their bodies as possible. Again, her round cheeks cradled his erection in a way he was getting accustomed to. "By the gods, Zoey, do you know I have thought about your luscious little ass every day since I first set eyes on it?"

"Funny, I've been imagining giving it to you for just as long."

It would have been pure torture to stay like that with her, so hard against her curves, if she hadn't fallen asleep almost instantly. He stroked her hair and the soft skin of her inner arm. His fingers grazed over the bluish veins visible under the thin skin there. Her blood pulsed under his fingertips, and he admitted the inevitable truth to himself—if she would turn for him, he would bond with her, no matter the risk. She was worth it.

Chapter 28

Andre only enjoyed a few minutes curled around Zoey before two cars screeched to a halt in his drive. What on earth?

When he stood, Zoey stirred. "What is it?"

"I don't know. I need to go downstairs and investigate."

Below, the front door opened and Bel shouted. "We've got Pedro, Father!"

Andre dashed out the door.

"He's in bad shape. Andre! Get down here. He wants you to turn him." Andre was standing next to Pedro by the time Bel finished calling out. Kos was already there too.

Pedro's feet looked like ground beef. "*Davo*. Fuck and *davo*."

Bel uncovered the seeping gunshot wound. "This is the real damage." Andre sucked down a breath; Bel had gotten Pedro to him just in time.

The reek of Hunter grew stronger, and Kos growled. He turned toward the open door, bared his fangs, and hissed at the Hunter who stood there.

"That's Lucas Bennett. He freed Pedro. He was trying to save him when we showed up. Pedro wanted us to protect him from his family." Bel spoke quickly, before Kos pounced. "Deal with him later. Pedro's pulse is weak. You have to act fast."

"I'll do it," Kos said.

Andre put his hand on Kos's arm. "Kos, please. He is already like a son to me. Will you have him as your brother instead?"

"Of course." Andre had asked kindly, but it wasn't really a request. Kos owed Andre obedience in matters such as these.

"Who will feed him when the blood hunger comes on?" Andre looked around for a volunteer. In a vampire household, it was an honor to feed a newly made vampire. But his household wasn't present. The only humans there were Bel's crew, Lucas, and Zoey watching from the bottom of the stairs. He looked at Vania.

"No way," Vania said. "We have a no biting rule on the crew. Keeps things less complicated for all of us."

"But it is life or death, his heartbeat is fading—" He was beginning to panic and it came through in his voice.

"I'll do it," Zoey said.

"No, you won't."

She looked surprised. He didn't have time to explain the extent of his possessiveness.

"Me. It should be me. I couldn't protect him. It's the least I can do." It was Lucas.

Andre would have rejected him too, but they were out of time. "Come here."

Bel applied pressure to Pedro's bullet wound. Soon more blood would be in his veins, and they needed it to stay there. Andre sliced his left wrist open with his fang and began to bleed into Pedro's open mouth. Kos handed him a sharp blade to keep the wound from closing.

Zoey was mesmerized by the dark ruby liquid dripping from Andre's wrist into Pedro's mouth. The entire scene was beautiful. Andre's fatherly care moved her, stirring a longing to belong somewhere, to have a family like his. He gave something of his own life to this man, whom he already considered a son.

It was like a birth. She'd never been squeamish about blood, but certainly it was meant to stay inside one's body. Yet, a warm feeling crept from her stomach up her throat, reassuring her—there was nothing wrong with Pedro drinking the blood. It was only nourishing him.

What the blood did to Pedro was astonishing. First his color returned, then the swelling in his face and feet eased. The wounds on his legs and toes closed and new skin formed. In a matter of moments, he looked as good as new, minus toenails.

"Get ready," Andre said to Lucas. With his right hand, he lifted Pedro's upper lip to look at his teeth. Then he tilted Pedro's head back so he could open his jaw. Using the knife Kos had given him, he sliced Lucas's wrist open and placed it under Pedro's nose. The smell of the blood caused his new fangs to descend. He still seemed unconscious to Zoey, but when Andre brought Lucas's wrist to Pedro's mouth, he clamped down on it hungrily. The movement of his Adam's apple showed how quickly he was sucking down the blood. Lucas let out a cry of surprised pleasure.

Andre mocked him. "They never told you about that part?"

Wide-eyed but tight-lipped, Lucas shook his head. Suddenly, Pedro released his wrist and threw him down, rolling on top of him so he could bite Lucas's neck.

"Damn," Bel said. "I'd say your blood is as strong as ever, Andre."

"No kidding," Kos said. "Should we worry he's taking too much?"

"I'm inclined to let him drink him dry," Andre replied. Lucas was watching the men discuss his fate, but it was obvious that Pedro's bite was demanding most of his focus.

"That's not what Pedro wanted."

"Fine. You tend to Bennett, I will get Pedro off him." Andre bent down next to Pedro and whispered in his ear. "You've had enough, Pedro. Let him go. There will be more blood, plenty of blood for you. We'll find you some pretty boys for dinner." He rubbed Pedro's back up and down his spine soothingly. Finally, Pedro released Lucas's neck and lifted his head.

A gaping tear marred Lucas's neck, so unlike the clean punctures Andre had pierced in Susan's neck. Kos spit on his palm and pressed it to the wound. Under his splayed fingers, the torn flesh repaired instantly, smooth and caked with clotted blood.

"Kos, call some of your women over here," Andre said. "He will need more blood soon."

"Of course."

Andre helped Pedro to his feet. Disoriented, the new vampire toppled over Andre's outstretched arm and stumbled into the wall, knocking a framed photo askew. He was like a newborn animal, and Zoey wanted to coddle him. Kos crushed Pedro to him in a bear hug, and Pedro let out a grunt that turned into a sigh of comfort. In Kos's arms, his spine straightened. With his back to Zoey, Andre waited for his turn to embrace his offspring.

When Pedro opened his eyes, Andre said, "What the hell?"

Once a gorgeous aquamarine, his eyes had gone the yellow-gold of a Hunter.

Zoey gasped in time with several others in the room. Everyone turned to stare at Pedro. The silence was thick until it became clear their stares were frightening him. He hadn't spoken yet, but his hands were moving over his face, trying to feel what everyone was looking at. He caught his fang with a thumb.

"What?" he croaked, sounding like he had just woken from a long sleep. "What is it?"

Lucas stepped forward. "It's your eyes."

"What about them?"

"They look like mine."

Pedro returned Lucas's stare. Finally he said, "I owe you a debt. I will ask Andre to protect you. But, Lucas, I do not forgive you. You gave me no choice. I hate you." On confident feet, Pedro stepped toward the stairway. Kos strode to catch up, proffering an unneeded arm. Pedro gently pushed it away and climbed the stairs.

The beauty of the scene lingered with Zoey, even as the emotional currents in the room set her teeth on edge. Poor Pedro. Poor Lucas.

Chest high, Andre looked like a proud papa, grinning as he traced Pedro's slow, stiff progress up the stairs. When Pedro and Kos moved out of sight, Andre pulled her into the parlor.

His green eyes shone feverishly, manic with joy and something else. Bending toward her ear, he whispered. "I am sorry my one chance to hold you was interrupted." Instead of meeting her eye, he looked down to where he traced a circle on the inside of her wrist with his thumb.

The touch sent sparks up her arm. It might be the last time he would touch her.

"I am also sorry you had to see that all that horrific scene."

Did he mean turning Pedro? "Horrific? It was beautiful. It was like the time I saw a foal born. He was gangly and awkward, then suddenly graceful…" The image replayed in her mind, wonder stealing her breath.

"Beautiful?" His eyebrows drew together and his lips parted.

"Don't you think so?"

"I have seen many vampires made and it has always seemed gruesome to me. Death is so near." He wiped at his mouth, tugging the lines of his face out of shape so that he looked haunted. "It is traumatizing to both the sire and offspring. If there had been time to keep the old customs, to seek the comfort of the prayers…" He shook his head. "But I have not observed those traditions since I turned Kos. They are no longer meaningful to me."

The emotions that played across his face fascinated Zoey. Inside him was an entirely new world, with rules and beliefs and feelings she couldn't begin to comprehend. God, she wanted to peer in there, to understand him. But his strange world wasn't only internal—it was real, and it had ruined her life and swallowed up Pedro too.

She glanced over her shoulder, to where the new vampire had vanished into the hall.

When her attention returned to Andre, he was staring at her with that same manic expression. "In a few minutes, I need you to go to your room and lock me out."

It was intoxicating to be wanted like that—and a little frightening, in a good way. "Can't you can break down a door?"

"Yes, but it is likely to slow me down enough to think straight."

He deserved a kiss for being both honorable and honest. She stood on her toes to brush her lips against his warm cheek. He gripped the back of her head to deepen the contact, and she wanted to melt, to surrender to him.

"Andre, please don't test my resolve."

For a moment, he looked ready to insist, but then he squeezed both her arms gently and let her go.

CHAPTER 29

Lucas contemplated Pedro's walk up the stairs alongside the blond vampire. He closed his eyes and pictured documents from the Hunters' dossier on Marasović. Kos must be Kosjenic, Andre's son. Pedro held himself upright, but his shoulders leaned slightly toward Kos. They seemed close, brotherly, even.

By contrast, he was utterly alone and a sharp feeling of loss stabbed him. He had betrayed his brother. But the version of Ethan he was close to hadn't been real, even if he had pretended to be Lucas's protector and friend.

With hushed conversations echoing in the foyer, the group of vampires and humans disbanded. Alone and with nowhere to go, he dropped into a straight-backed chair. After a few minutes, Zoey came out of a sunny doorway down the hall. When she saw him, she headed his way.

"Come down to the kitchen with me. I'll fix us a pot of coffee. Then you can keep me company."

He followed her wordlessly. When the coffee was brewed, she let him carry the tray, probably just to give him something to do. Zoey held the door to her room open for him and then locked it behind him.

"You lock your door?"

"Andre asked me to."

"Why?" Sliding knickknacks across the dresser to make room, he set the coffee tray down.

"So he doesn't try to come in."

"I don't understand." He poured Zoey's coffee. She took it black with sugar. Mugs clinked together in his trembling hands.

Taking her mug, she put a palm over his hand to still it. "It's complicated."

"Yeah, well, I suddenly find myself with a lot of time if you want to explain."

"Damn it, Lucas. I want to be angry with you for getting me into this, but you seem to be in worse shape than me."

He looked down; Pedro's blood stained his clothes. On both hands, his knuckles were split open and swollen.

"I'm fine. This is Pedro's blood." He took a sip from his too hot mug.

Holding her mug steady, she inched back the bed and sat cross-legged. "You look like you're in shock. You haven't blinked since you walked in the room."

"Really? Well, my father tried to kill me and I watched Pedro get turned into a vampire. It's been a shocking day."

"But you knew that they would kill him, right?"

"Zoey, they planned the kidnapping without me. It was a test of my loyalty. I failed." Zoey blew on her coffee and looked at him expectantly. "I watched and waited for a moment I could rescue him. They guarded him non-stop. It finally came, but it wasn't a clean exit."

"Does Pedro know that?"

"I tried to tell him I was sorry without giving myself away to Ethan. But I'm not sure it matters."

Zoey bit her fingertip while her eyes bored into him. Her scrutiny made his face burn. Finally, she said, "Lucas, Ethan's nuts — he's like a psychopath, or something."

"Not like. I've been worried he's exactly that for a long time. I'd hoped his feelings for you meant I was wrong. But when I saw him torture Pedro I was sure."

"He tortured Pedro?"

"Yep, right out of a manual from the Inquisition or something." He spared her the details.

"Jesus. I'd never have thought he could do something like that. He's good at pretending he cares."

The words hit him harder than they should have. Ethan had been pretending to care since they were kids, and he had taken every bone Ethan had thrown him. Zoey watched intently. Could she guess what he was feeling?

"What are you going to do, Lucas?"

"Run. They'll be hunting me now. I have some savings and I can get a new identity. I'll be fine, I think." Even to his own ears, he sounded tired, lonely, and unpersuasive.

"I guess that's what's in store for me too."

"You're not going stay with Andre?"

"I don't want to be a vampire, Lucas. And besides, he hasn't asked me to stay."

"And if he asked?"

"He hasn't." In other words, end of discussion.

"We can stick together for a while, if you want." God, he sounded desperate, like he was asking her on a date.

"Lucas, I —"

"Zoey, you don't have to —"

"How can I trust you? I mean, you're not who I thought you were."

"Well, If It makes a difference, I'm not who I thought I was either."

Kos perched on a wooden stool next to where Pedro lay on the bed. It was uncomfortable. Pedro used it to pile clothes; he'd probably never sat on the damn thing.

The new vampire was awake, but quiet. Physically, he looked great. Kos had seen a number of turnings in his life, but it was always surprising to see a person's youth restored. He hadn't even noticed the signs of aging that Pedro had acquired in ten years, until becoming a vampire had erased them.

"How do you feel?"

"My body feels amazing. Better than new. My head's...more messed up."

That was to be expected, so Kos waited. Pedro needed to go at his own pace. The young vampire squeezed his eyes shut and covered his ears. Kos listened for the new sounds Pedro would hear. His own pulse and breath would be loudest, aside from the occasional roar of an empty stomach. The sounds of the house would be deafening too. For the first week of Kos's vampire life, every time a door slammed he dropped to the floor and took cover, like a battle-scarred veteran, which he was not. Kos stood up and turned off the light.

"Thanks, man…"

Pedro had begun to tremble on the bed.

"Pedro, are you messed up about being a vampire, or messed up about being kidnapped?"

"Fuck, I don't know. Both." His shakes were getting worse. "I feel like a shiny new sports car with a frazzled motherboard."

"Turning will definitely fry your motherboard. All your wires will be crossed for a while."

"And torture…what does that do to your motherboard?" Pedro whispered. In his newly sensitive ears, it probably sounded like he was shouting.

"Christ, Pedro. I'm so sorry we—"

"Can this not be about you feeling guilty?"

Ouch. "Yes. Whatever you need. I'll listen, if you want. Or I'll just sit."

It was a slow five minutes before Pedro said, "I thought I was going to die, but now I'm sitting here looking at eternal life. And all I can think about is what that asshole would have done to me next."

Kos had no words of wisdom. He endured more silence with all the patience he owed his new brother.

Pedro seemed to get his shakes under control. Then, he continued. "I was going to hang myself in the shed, but I missed my chance."

Kos's gut twisted. It was their fault that Pedro had to make a choice like that, but he kept his guilt to himself. "I'm glad you missed it."

"Yeah." The response came too quick.

"Pedro, it will get better."

He let Pedro have more of the silence he seemed to need. Then he looked at his watch; the warning was due. "Listen, any minute now the blood hunger is going to take you over. It's frightening. Not as bad as the shit you went through today, but bad." He looked into

Pedro's alarmingly gold eyes, and saw his pupils twitch. "I promise you'll get through it. I'll make sure you get enough blood."

Pedro nodded. Then there was more silence.

"Kos, I didn't tell them anything about the wine."

"I know. I didn't have to ask." The line of Pedro's mouth softened, showing Kos how much his trust meant. "How are you feeling? Cold? Weak? Empty? Thirsty?" It was impossible to describe what the hunger would be like, but he needed to know if Pedro was beginning to sense it.

"No, man, I'm good."

"Nothing? Skin tight? Eyes dry?"

"Kos, if I could turn my brain off, I could run a frickin' marathon. My body feels that good."

"That's weird."

CHAPTER 30

Andre sought out the peace and quiet of his office. Leaving the lights off, he walked straight to his desk and put his feet up. Once again, Zoey had been the stronger and more disciplined one. He had nearly declared himself, but thought better of it just in time. She was certain she did not want to be a vampire and it was a dangerous business to try to sway her—Mila had taught him that lesson well.

Thank the gods that Pedro was safe. But soon, terrifying and painful blood lust would overtake him, and he would fear losing himself to the craving entirely. And his escape would only inflame the Hunters. What would they try next to escalate their attack?

Andre tried to breathe deeply and be in the present moment, but he wasn't good at all that New Age claptrap. He needed Kos and a deck of cards. However, at that moment, Pedro needed Kos far more than he did.

A glass of wine…now that might help. All the wine glasses in his wet bar were dirty; he filled a pint glass and drank the wine in two long swallows.

The sound of footsteps caught his attention—fast and heavier than Kos's. That meant it must be Bel. His son opened the door and strode in, already speaking. "Perimeter's clear. It seems like the shield really threw them; they're completely gone."

"That is good. At the very least, Kos's friends will arrive unseen when they come to feed Pedro." The Hunters would regroup and return. They always did.

"True," Bel said. "About the shield—Trys says she can extend it around the vineyards too, but it will be weaker."

The vines had to remain safe. His jaw locked and forcing it open took all his concentration. "Surely it will hold?"

Bel poured himself a bourbon from the decanter on the bar and drank it down as smoothly as Andre had the wine. "We had the element of surprise. And it blocked their weapons, but Trys thinks they could walk right through unarmed."

"Why?"

"Because Zoey did."

"Right." And damn it if he wasn't glad she had. He licked his teeth. "How does it work, Bel?"

"Honestly, I don't know. She refuses to explain it to me."

Andre squinted at Bel. He had been inquisitive as a boy, had wanted to grasp how everything worked. But since Mila's death, he grown obsessed with learning how his mother had done the impossible—conceived a vampire's child.

He couldn't imagine Bel putting up with all the cobwebs and arcana of witchcraft. "Does she cast spells and make potions?"

"No. Somehow she unleashes and manipulates the natural energy in the air and the earth."

A hint of peevishness tinged Bel's scientific explanation. Clearly, he resented that he didn't understand. He had become such an angry boy, and Andre wished once again that he could wipe away the decades of misunderstanding between them. But some secrets had to remain hidden and some magic was far too danger—

"By the way, Trys has already gone through gobs and gobs of chocolate to fuel the shield. We're almost out, and she's very particular."

"You must be joking."

"I'm afraid not. She requires an enormous caloric intake to maintain her shields. That's how I know it's some kind of natural, rather than supernatural, process at work. Technically, she could eat anything, but she likes chocolate. The good stuff. Where can I get some?"

"Have Kos ask Lena."

"Right. Also, I want to question Lucas about what the Hunters know," Bel said, refilling his glass. "Kos said Zoey didn't tell them anything new about the wine. If they aren't suspicious, then Trys can focus on shielding the house, and the rest of the crew can patrol the vineyards."

"Do you think Lucas will cooperate? Or by question do you mean the way they questioned Pedro?"

"I'm not sure. If it comes to torture, you're in charge—you have way more experience."

Could he even remember how? He hadn't tortured anyone since his days in the Roman army. "I'm out of practice."

"It's probably moot. In spite of how Pedro feels about Lucas, he wouldn't condone us torturing him. He offered Lucas protection, and he has more honor than that."

Bel's admiring tone pleased Andre. "You like him?"

"I do. He's got balls. And he was cracking jokes when we both thought it was over for him."

Laughter erupted from Andre's chest, surprising him. It had not been over for Pedro, after all. "I would have him be a true brother to both of you."

Bel lifted his glass—it was an acceptance of Pedro into the family and it brought out more of Andre's fatherly feelings. *Davo,* he was turning soft.

In the silence that followed, a knock sounded on the oak front door. "Someone's at the door. Likely Kos's girls."

And just in time, too. Pedro must be losing his mind to blood hunger.

Andre remained in the shadows behind Bel, who stood in a bright shaft of sunlight when he opened the front door to find two women waiting. Andre took an involuntary step back—they weren't what he was expecting.

How odd. He rarely, or rather, never met Kos's girlfriends. But surely his son did not fancy hippies. Their very long hair hung down over flowing sundresses. They were both pretty enough in a plain way, but neither appeared to shave her legs or armpits. Zoey's classic, tailored clothes and impeccable grooming put them to shame.

"Hi. We're Kos's friends," said the one with light brown hair.

"He called because his brother needs...help," said the other.

At a loss, Andre resorted to hospitality. Stepping to the sharp edge of the shadow, he said, "Thank you for coming, ladies."

They pivoted to face Andre, and behind them, Bel shrugged, palms up. His shaking head told Andre he found the girls as surprising as Andre did. The women shuffled around, waiting for Bel to introduce himself.

He bowed his head politely, in a flash of old world manners that made Andre proud. "Yes, thank you. I'm Kos's other brother, Bel."

Andre crossed to the bottom of the stairs. "I'll take you to them."

The women followed, and Bel trailed behind. Andre knocked on Pedro's doorframe and then strode in without waiting for an invitation. Kos rose to greet his friends.

"How are you? Hungry?" Andre asked Pedro.

"I don't think so."

That was odd. Unease blew across Andre's skin, and his gut tensed.

"Let's try this," he said, nudging one of the women toward Pedro.

The new vampire showed no signs of hunger in response.

Andre lifted her hand to his mouth. "May I?"

"Sure."

Pricking her finger with his fang, he held it under Pedro's nose. Pedro didn't respond. His breath should have quickened, his eyes should have dilated.

"I don't understand," Kos said. "He should be starving by now."

"Ladies, Pedro's not ready for you. If you don't mind waiting, I'll take you down to my parlor and pour you a glass of wine." Andre took the taller girl's arm.

"Thanks, that would be nice," said the brunette.

In the hallway, Zoey's smell reached him from behind her closed door. The tension in his gut melted away, and his stomach growled out its desire for her.

"Sounds like somebody's hungry," the woman said, squeezing his arm.

"Indeed. But I am not the one you came for."

She halted mid-step and faced Andre, putting slim hands on his chest. "But he doesn't need us. And we would be very disappointed to come all this way and be unable to help." Lifting and tilting her chin, she exposed soft tan skin and a fluttering pulse. *Davo.* They were lusty hippies, which perhaps explained his son's interest. Kos did not desire them anymore than Andre did Lena, but blood was blood and the one whom he desired he could not have.

"I would be very grateful for your assistance," Andre said without taking his eyes from her neck.

Behind him, the other women cleared her throat, and Andre sprang into action. He wrapped his arms around each of their waists and lifted them, hurtling down the stairs. The scent of Zoey teased him, even as their hot blood poured down his throat, one woman at a time—their taste was flat compared to the promise of hers.

In case Pedro needed their blood soon, Andre took only sips from both of them, dulling the sharp edge of his craving. Tactfully, he extricated himself from their lithe arms. The women seemed content to drink wine and giggle on a sofa in the parlor, waiting to be needed again.

Pedro's room was silent when Andre returned. Had no one spoken in the minutes he was gone? The same uneasy tension returned to dance up his spine. Pedro looked too good—something was most certainly wrong. But Andre did not want to voice the fear, so he simply contributed to the ominous silence.

Finally, Bel spoke. "Kos. What is up with your girls?"

"They're cute enough." Kos's smile was sheepish and it erased more than a century of wasting from his suddenly youthful face. But only for a moment.

"Yeah, cute in a Woodstock kind of way. Have you bought them a pack of razors? They're hairy enough for Pedro."

"Not by a long shot," Pedro said.

Kos blushed. "Leave them alone. They're very sweet."

It had never been his own way, but Andre admired Kos's chivalry. And the girls were indeed agreeable, more so than Andre preferred.

"Sweet's not my style," Bel said, echoing Andre's thoughts.

Bel leaned over Pedro, placing a finger under one eye and tugging the lower lid down. Andre was unfamiliar with the significance of this eyeball examination, but Bel was the expert.

"So, buddy, not hungry?" Bel asked.

It happened so quickly, even to Andre's eye. A door closed across the hall, Bel was thrown to the floor, something crashed, something else shattered. Kos rushed from the room, and Andre followed. In the hall, Pedro was on top of Lucas again. He pinned him with his hips while pulling Lucas's head over by the hair to lengthen his exposed neck. Pedro hadn't bitten him, but his face pressed against Lucas's skin and he took deep breaths. Lucas went pale and held himself very still, as if afraid movement would provoke Pedro.

"Why does he smell so good?" Pedro asked. "Do I want him instead of the girls because he's a guy?"

"No," Andre said. "Blood is blood. Perhaps you will prefer to feed from men, but when you are hungry it will not matter."

Kos knelt down next to the pair. "You've already taken a lot of his blood, Pedro. He probably can't afford any more."

"I won't. I don't feel hungry. But I could smell him and my body took me here."

Lucas sank into the floor, apparently relieved. Andre felt no such thing. What the hell did Pedro mean?

Bel's frown reflected Andre's thoughts. "Is that what you feel like when you smell blood?"

"Not unless I'm very hungry." Kos shook his head. "Then I can hear blood pounding and smell it. It's hard to focus on anything else."

"Is that what you feel, Pedro?"

Pedro sniffed deeply, running his nose along Lucas's neck. The Hunter appeared to be listening carefully. With his head cocked at an odd angle, he strained to keep Pedro in the corner of his eye.

"I can hear his blood…but it's something else. Smelling him makes the blood in my veins buzz. Like I drank one hundred espressos at once."

"I've never felt that," Kos said.

"Nor I," Andre agreed.

"So there's something different about Lucas's blood. It's the only explanation." Zoey spoke from her doorway, near where Andre leaned against the wall. Startled, he sidestepped away from her.

"Great, I'm vampire crack." In spite of the bitterness in his tone, Lucas's words were laughable, cutting the tension.

Bel chuckled. "So it would seem. Bennett, you're not going anywhere for the time being."

Lucas nodded.

Zoey stepped into the hall, circling Andre with her dark brows raised. She wasn't focused on his face, but his chest. He looked down. *Davo.* A red droplet of blood marred his rumpled white shirt.

Stupidly, her jealousy thrilled him. He pointed at her, hoping she would realize it was for her safety that he kept his hunger at bay. "I think it is time we tell Pedro about the conditions of his new life," he said, hoping to distract her.

Pedro grimaced, struggling to pull away from Lucas. "Yes. I need to know the rules."

Kos reached down to help pull him to his feet.

Andre pointed again, straight into Zoey's room. "Not you, Hunter. I do not want any information getting back to your kind."

"He can't ever contact them again," Bel said.

"Do you want him in on this, Pedro?"

Pedro didn't spare Lucas a look. "I couldn't care less."

"Then you're out. Back in Zoey's room. Now."

"Andre," Zoey said his name in barely more than a whisper.

Before he thought better of it, he was at her side in a flash.

"Can I listen? Maybe I'm safer if I don't know anything. But it seems I'm not safe from the Hunters regardless."

Andre wanted nothing more than to hold her and protect her forever. The feeling was not chivalry. It was a need for her alone.

"Fair enough," he replied, then wiped his hand over his forehead and down the back of his head, lingering over his knotted neck.

Lucas closed himself in Zoey's room while the others went into Pedro's. He headed to the window, where the afternoon sun dipped behind the hills and glared into the already bright room.

Something unique about Hunter blood? Didn't that make all kinds of sense.

All the old stories came back to him. No wonder Hunters were absolutely forbidden to give their blood to a vampire. And no wonder he didn't know vampires' bites were better than blowjobs. Either that information had been suppressed by Hunters long ago and lost to the modern clan, or no one had told Lucas.

Maybe his father's book was true. After showing it to Ethan, Stephen's attempt to hide it from Lucas had been a failure. He had broken into his father's desk and flipped through the ancient tome, astonished by images of vampires and Hunters living together in peace. Under a flat yellow sun, male and female vampires with golden eyes companionably held the hands of human Hunters. The final illustration showed a bloody battle, with many dead on both sides.

He closed his eyes and brought the illustrations to mind. Would Pedro be able to tolerate sun?

He'd like to get his hands on that book now, to learn what he could about Pedro's new status as a golden-eyed vampire.

Marasović's home seemed safe enough, for a while. But he wasn't ready to ally himself with the vampires and reveal his theories—let Pedro believe he was a regular vampire for now.

Pedro is a vampire.

He had been raised to hate vampires; revulsion had been drilled into him every day of his life. Yes, he'd felt like an outsider. Yes, he'd questioned the Hunters' tactics against humans. Still, he had always hated vampires.

But he did not hate Pedro. When Pedro fed from him, he was terrified, sure his throat would be torn out even as waves of pleasure assaulted him. The unexpected bliss had confused him.

He had done all the club drugs. He liked ecstasy best, but the sensual euphoria of that little pill had nothing on Pedro's bite. The arousal came from the inside out. First a gentle relaxation bloomed throughout his body. Then his skin tingled and burned for contact. He'd sucked his lower lip into his mouth because he'd longed to feel something between his teeth and against his tongue: a finger, another tongue, a nipple, anything. Every part of his body became an erotic receptor, yearning for stimulation.

The second time Pedro was on top of him, there was less fear—he was too aware of Pedro's newly powerful body covering him and radiating anger while his cock hardened between them. Had Pedro noticed Lucas's own hard-on? What a mess.

He couldn't blame Pedro for his anger. It wouldn't be easy for him to shake the memories from the shed either: Pedro's screams, his terror and his request that Lucas kill him—they would haunt him for a long time.

CHAPTER 31

Zoey was cramped in Pedro's room with four big men circling, so she climbed onto the bed and sat cross-legged, leaning against the headboard. Everyone followed her cue. Kos winced when he sat on an unfriendly looking stool. Pedro sat on the other side of the bed with one foot on the ground. Now there was enough room to breathe.

Her gaze kept going to the crimson spot on Andre's shirt. It made her angry. She didn't like those friends of Kos—especially whichever one had fed Andre. She shook her head, trying to clear it of jealousy. *He isn't mine. He won't ever be. He needs to eat, and from someone other than me. Let it go—*

"Where should we start?" Kos asked Andre.

"With the most important thing: the ways we die."

"Right," Kos said. "There are three ways a vampire dies. Fire, de-capitation, and the wasting disease we told you about already."

Wasting disease? She glanced at Andre, but he wouldn't meet her eyes. Apparently she wasn't going to learn any more about that tonight.

Andre jumped in. "Fire includes the sun. Any exposure to direct sunlight and you'll burn right up."

"What about all the windows in the house?" she asked.

"Treated to block the damaging rays," Kos explained.

"I wouldn't want to be the vampire who had to test which rays were the bad ones," she said.

Bel snorted.

"Indeed," said Andre.

"What about a stake through the heart?" Pedro asked.

"A convenient misinformation campaign our kind started in the middle ages," Andre replied.

"Seriously?" she asked.

"Yes."

"That's good PR work."

Amusement showed in his handsome smile. Her heart thudded in reaction. His brow creased a tiny bit. Could he hear her heart from across the room? It was hard for a girl to have her secrets around vampires.

Andre turned back to Pedro. "At first you will find it disorienting that you no longer need to sleep."

Pedro's Adam's apple bobbed in a silent gulp. Zoey understood why—never sleeping again sounded miserable.

"You'll need to let your mind rest, probably in a dark, quiet room, which will allow your brain to process things it currently does in sleep. Over time, your brain will adjust and you'll need less and less quiet."

"Pedro informed me that while you two are lamely amusing yourselves playing cards, he'll be in San Francisco cruising," Bel said.

"I meant dancing, asshole."

"Whatever," Bel replied.

For some reason it made Zoey happy that they were already acting like brothers.

"Enjoy it now," Andre said. "You'll find that bars, like everything, get rather boring after several decades."

He said it playfully, but sadness colored his words. That was why he'd found Mila and Kos so full of life when he met them. Clearly Andre tolerated boredom, because he preferred it to risking his heart again. But with the way he'd described his broken blood bond—more than his heart was at risk.

"You haven't told him the worst part yet," Bel said.

"What part?" Kos asked.

"You know, that thing you told me the other night when Zoey was upstairs…" Bel looked at her like he had put his foot in his mouth.

What was he talking about? "I'll tell him later," Kos said, trying to smooth things over.

"I don't think so," Zoey said. "I want to know."

"Zoey, sweet, I don't think you do," Andre said.

"Out with it."

"Fine," Bel said. "Vampires can't—" he searched for the word "—masturbate."

Zoey felt herself turn crimson. "What? Jesus Christ, there is no privacy around here. You all can hear everything."

"And smell it," Pedro added.

Andre said he could smell her when—suddenly she realized what Pedro meant and turned so quickly to look at Andre that her ponytail slapped her face.

He nodded, confirming that anything he had smelled, Kos had too. Every time she had gotten hot and bothered for Andre…

"Oh for fuck's sake," she said. "What about you, Bel? Do you have super hearing and smell too?"

"Nope. Not me," he answered easily. "Quite a mouth on her, Dad. Part of her charm?"

"Definitely," Andre replied. "I told you that you did not want to know." His smile was almost apologetic.

"So anyway," Kos said. "For whatever reason, vampires are unable to bring themselves to orgasm." In spite of her embarrassment, Kos's formality was almost funny.

Pedro raised his voice. "You think that's the worst part, Bel? Worse than never seeing the sun?"

"Kind of."

"That's pathetic. You guys are so pussy whipped. Let me tell you, a man never says, 'not tonight, honey, I have a headache.'"

Kos turned as pink as Zoey felt.

Pedro noticed too because he asked, "What's bothering you, ugly?"

Kos shot him a bird in reply.

"Can we talk about something important now, like how much blood I will need?" Pedro asked. He seemed suddenly anxious to continue his tutorial.

The Maras men—or vampires, or whatever—exchanged glances.

"That's tricky," Kos said. "For whatever reason, you're not experiencing the blood hunger. We think it's got something to do with Lucas's blood."

Andre shifted his weight. He seemed a little anxious too. "I've seen hundreds, if not thousands of vampires made. I've never seen anyone's eyes change color. There's something odd happening to you that we don't understand."

Pedro's hand trembled as he smoothed the hair on his forehead. "Great, that's just great. You guys really know how to comfort a baby vampire."

"I'm sorry, Pedro," Andre said. "If I'd known that would happen, I would have had someone else feed you."

Bel stepped closer to Pedro. "I've been doing some tests with Andre's blood and Kos's, and the wine. I'd like some of yours too. And I'll get some of Lucas's, whether he likes it or not."

The wine? Questions were queuing up on Zoey's tongue when a phone rang.

Kos answered his. "Lena? What's wrong?…A fire? Are you okay?" His face went gray, and he looked out the window at the setting sun.

Strange—he seemed to care deeply for the bitchy woman who'd tried to seduce his father only the day before. Maybe vampires had different rules about these things.

Kos glanced back and forth between Andre and Bel, repeating details from Lena. "Two Hunters, chased off by the highway patrol. She's unhurt."

Sweat beaded on his high forehead and he wiped it with the back of his hand. His obvious worry stirred Zoey's sympathy—if not for Lena, at least for Kos.

"I'll be there as soon as I can. Lena…" He turned his back, and Zoey could only imagine the emotions he was hiding from the family gathering. His voice was a whisper. "I'm sorry. I thought you'd be safe."

He hung up. "They tried to set fire to my house with her inside. She called the cops and they showed up before the fire caught. Chased off the Hunters."

"Damn," Bel said.

"You'll have to bring her back here, of course," Andre said. "So she's safe."

All of a sudden, Andre and Kos spun to face Zoey, and she realized she was growling. Again.

Kos's jaw hinged open in disbelief.

Andre winked one sparkling hazel-green eye at her.

Shit, she couldn't even keep her jealousy a secret. Without a word, she turned from them and went to sulk.

CHAPTER 32

"So, Mr. Wizard, can I watch your experiment?" Pedro asked, startling Bel, who jumped, barely managing to keep the contents of his graduated cylinder from spilling.

He added its contents to a beaker of solution.

Pedro took stock of the makeshift lab, erected in the warehouse-like room where he and Andre made wine. The sink and large work surface made it a good space for Bel's little project, and his supplies covered one of the long stainless steel counters in the facility.

When Bel squinted at him, Pedro felt strangely self-conscious.

"What? Spinach on my fangs?"

Bel shook his head, returning his focus to mixing the solution. "Dude. You should rest. You've been to hell and back twice today."

"Right, so you can understand if I don't want to sit by my lonesome and think about it."

Bel stared into the solution, and a muscle in his jaw twitched. If he was anything like Andre, which he clearly was, that meant he was stressed about something.

Finally, Bel shrugged. "Watch if you want. It promises to be boring."

"Suddenly, I have all the time in the world. Is that a chromatograph?"

"Yeah."

Bel's answer was really a question, but Pedro didn't bother answering it. Instead, he leaned over the portable unit, smaller than the type he was familiar with. It looked more like a disc player than a piece of lab equipment, except that in the place of speaker cables were tiny tubes that would pump precise amounts of fluid into the machine.

"Where did it come from?"

"Vania brought it from London."

"So you're going to run the blood samples and the wine to test for chemical composition?"

Bel cocked his head, and Pedro felt smug. Bel wasn't the only one who knew about chemistry.

"Just a few elements, actually. How did you know?"

"I used one all the time at university. But mine was bigger than yours."

"Piss off," Bel said, chuckling. "Did you study chemistry?"

"No, viticulture and winemaking. But I—"

"Viticulture? That a fancy word for growing grape vines?"

"Exactly. Why use a normal word when you can use a fancy one?" Pedro flashed his teeth. In a bar, that smile usually made guys cross the room, but Bel went back to work, oblivious to his charm. The silence made Pedro itch, so he continued to talk. "When I was in school, it was trendy to use trace elements to identify the provenance of wines. The soil where a plant grows has its own signature of elements—tiny amounts of those elements get into the plant."

"So you can test for those elements in wine and know where the vine was grown?"

"Yes. Cool, but rarely useful since you can just read the label." Pedro picked up an opaque black plastic bottle. "What elements are you going to look for in the blood?"

"Iron and copper."

Pedro glanced over the bottles spread across the table. From the look of things, Bel still had a lot of mixing to go—for each element he wanted to trace, he would need a different solvent. He pointed at a bottle, which happened to be closer to Pedro. Handing it over, Pedro said, "I'm guessing iron from hemoglobin. But why copper?"

Bel poured a measure of solvent into his solution. "In human blood, the iron in hemoglobin binds with oxygen to transport it through the body. Vampires' blood has a different protein—it uses copper to carry oxygen."

"No shit?"

"It's true. I isolated it a few years ago and named it *Hemocuprum*. Not that it matters, since I'm the only one on the whole planet doing scientific research on vampire blood."

"I guess you can't exactly submit your results for publication." Pedro laughed at his own joke as he read the label on another one of the bottles. When he looked up, Bel was not amused. "So vampire blood is completely different from human blood?"

"Completely different. Animals like clams and snails also have copper in their blood, but they don't have the vampire protein, *Hemocuprum*. That bad boy is a super protein — it delivers four times more oxygen to the cells of a vampire than hemoglobin for humans."

Pedro opened an unlabeled bottle and noxious acetone fumes burned his sinuses and tightened his throat. Maybe being a vampire made his nose more sensitive. Coughing, he resealed the bottle.

Bel finished mixing the iron solvent and set the beaker down. "Time for the copper," he said, pointing at another bottle.

"And that oxygen makes them...us...stronger?"

Reaching for a clean beaker, Bel said, "Yes, and your brain processes faster. Have you noticed?"

Pedro squeezed his eyes shut and then opened them. "Seriously? I thought I was just on overload."

"Nope. Your brain is assimilating everything much faster than it's used to."

"Is that why I have all this pressure in my head? It doesn't hurt, but it's intense."

"Totally normal. Your brain will feel really full for a while. Especially since you won't sleep. Now that you're a vampire, you will have twenty-four hours' worth of data running through your noggin super-fast. Before you're used to it, you'll probably feel like you're about to explode. Or so I've been told."

Pedro leaned heavily against a wall. Closing his eyes, he tipped his head backward. Everything Bel said made sense. His thoughts came faster and clearer. Too fast, and far too clear.

He couldn't say how, but with one of his new vampire senses, he knew that Bel was watching him. Then the meaning of Bel's words registered. He opened his eyes and the fluorescent lights stung.

"You've been told? You were telling the truth then—you're really not a vampire?"

"No. Although I age like one. I'm eight years younger than Kos—one-hundred and seventy…" he looked at the ceiling while he did the math "…nine. One hundred and seventy-nine. I stopped looking older in my early thirties. All vampires do."

"But you don't—"

"Nope. Meat and taters sort of guy—rare and bloody, but no actual blood. I'm not especially strong. No super hearing or vision, or, thank God, smell—that sounds nasty, or around a pretty girl, distracting. Kos must be thinking about sex constantly."

"Maybe, but he's too polite to tell us."

Bel laughed.

And, yeah—they had the same doofus sense of humor. Years ago, Kos had become the brother Pedro never had. Bel very well might be another.

But it was still confusing. What the hell was Bel, if he wasn't a vampire? Pedro had to ask. "So if I—God forbid—had sex with a woman and knocked her up, would that make little Bel-style half-vampires?"

Bel gasped, stepping back as if Pedro had punched him. "No. Vampires can't make babies. They're infertile."

Pedro ran his gaze up and down Bel's form—a body as tall and ripped as his father, same black hair, same green eyes. Bel wasn't the apple fallen near the tree, he was a frickin' clone. "Don't bullshit me—"

"I don't know how it happened. Andre says he doesn't either. It's bullshit, obviously. He did it—he has to know."

"Maybe he's not really shooting blanks."

"Pedro, he's two thousand years old. If that were true, I'd literally be one in a million."

He had a point there; Pedro nodded.

"My mother wanted a baby. She learned of some trick to make it happen—begged him to go through with it. He told me that much, but says that he doesn't know the trick."

"So you're, like, the only one of you?"

"Yes. I'm the only one."

"Do you have hemoglobin or *Hemocuprum* in your blood?"

"Really? That's your question?"

Pedro nodded again, and his head felt like an overfilled water balloon.

"Both. I have both—fifty-fifty."

Pedro took a step toward the counter and lifted the flasks containing the two solvents that Bel had just made. Then he set them down, captivated by what he saw in the stainless steel surface—his reflection. His shocking yellow eyes glowed back at him, the unsettling reminder of all that he had lost. He wiped the countertop, but they were no less vivid. And, all at once, he knew.

"We need to look for another element."

"What's that?"

"Gold."

CHAPTER 33

Andre found Zoey watching the television in the living room shared by the household women. Her bare feet were up on the coffee table, and he observed her unnoticed. It was hard to sense her mood, but seeing her do something so mundane stirred his possessiveness. Suddenly, a comfortable, domestic life with Zoey was almost as tempting as her blood.

The doorframe bit into his shoulder blade, and he shifted. She turned to look at him, her expression unreadable. Muting the television, she said, "Hey."

"I just wanted to check on you after all those...revelations. Make sure you aren't upset." He couldn't keep the amusement out of his voice.

She crossed her arms and leaned against the arm of the couch. "Oh really? You were worried my embarrassment might turn fatal, and had to come check on me?"

Fair enough. So they both knew it was a pretense. He grinned.

"Do you want to sit down?" Making room, she scooted to the far side of the sofa.

He shouldn't. He did.

Sitting as far away from her as he could on the sofa, he looked at the television. "What are you watching?"

"A travel show about Rome."

"May I?" He held up the remote for permission to turn the sound on again.

"Sure."

They watched the host sample from a plate of olives.

"Have you ever been there?" he asked her.

"I have. I did the grand tour in college. Me on a train with an oversized backpack. I spent almost a week there—longer than I'd planned. I really liked it."

"It is an incredible place. I have not seen it years…" In truth, it had been centuries, but he did not need to say that.

"When did you go?"

"The last time was before Mila died. But I was born nearby."

"You're Italian? I thought you were Croatian."

She switched off the television and turned her breasts toward him. Her whole body, really, but he noticed her full, firm breasts first.

With effort, he looked at her eyes. "Roman, really. But I consider myself Croatian. I lived there so much longer, and that is where I became a vampire. So I am bound there forever."

"Bound, like the blood bond?"

"Similar, but not the same. We become ill when we leave our native soil."

It was charming the way she bit her lip when she was thinking. "This is the wasting disease you mentioned?"

He nodded.

The corners of her mouth turned down. "Are you sick?"

The worry in her voice pierced him. "I was getting weaker," he said instinctively. "But I'm getting better now."

"Is that why you look younger than you did on Monday?"

Nothing got past her. It made him proud, as if she was his to be proud of. "Yes. It is the wine. It cures the disease. At least I think it does."

Understanding lit up her face, making her even lovelier.

"That's why you want to find the other vampires? You want to give them the wine!" Her voice rose higher than its normal alto with excitement.

"Yes." It was the last secret between them and her guess had made him an honest vampire. The unexpected lightness of relief came over him.

She sunk into the couch, becoming thoughtful. Finally, she asked, "How did you wind up in Croatia?"

"My parents had a small farm outside of Rome. I joined the legion to escape their meager existence."

"The Roman legion?" She tilted her head and leaned in. "Did you wear a bronze pointy helmet?"

Interesting—she knew some Roman history. His chest puffed up. "I was a centurion. My helmet had the red-feathered crest."

"A centurion. Of course you were. I should have guessed. Did you wear one of those skirty-things?"

"It was a tunic, not a skirt, thank you. We all wore them." He plucked a loose thread from the couch cushion. When he looked up, there was laughter in her eyes. "I much prefer a pair of jeans, though."

"Yeah?" Her eyes roamed over him brazenly.

That one word did dangerous things to him. But her cocoa-colored eyes still held a playful glint. He could be a good boy too. He rerouted the conversation.

"I served in southern France. I was fascinated by the vineyards there. I began to dream of my own land, my own vines. It must have been in my blood."

"So to speak." She winked.

Was she testing him? *Davo,* he would prove he was as willful as her. Nonchalantly, he went on with his story. "When my term of service ended, I received land in Illyricum. Rome was sending retired soldiers in an attempt to civilize the savage place. It was not called Croatia until the Slavs moved in six hundred years later, but it has almost always been home."

"What's it like?"

"Šolta, where I lived, is stunning. The Adriatic is so blue, the vine-covered hills drop right into the water, and villas like this one sit on the hillsides. I wish I could show you."

"Me too." Her eyes dropped to the cushion between them.

"And we could go to Rome." It was a flight of fancy, said to cheer her up. They both knew it could never happen.

"You'd hardly recognize it with all the cars."

Cars? All things considered, he had adjusted remarkably well to the countless changes he had seen in his lifetime. But sometimes they were too damn jarring. The idea of Rome full of cars—that was wrong. "I have to see that."

They both reached for the remote control to turn the television back on. When her hand brushed against his, she pulled it back. He pushed the power button and set the remote back down. Then, he took her hand inside his and rested them on the couch in the distance between them. Holding hands, they watched the television host explore Rome in its ancient, modern glory.

He did not mind the tiny Italian cars zooming past the Coliseum nearly as much as he expected to.

When upbeat accordion music began to play and the travel show rolled its credits, Zoey turned off the television.

"If I'm stuck here for a while, I'm going to need something to do."

"What do you mean?" Andre asked.

"I mean, I'm a workaholic. I don't take vacations, I don't relax, and I don't sit behind magical shields and twiddle my thumbs." God knew, if she sat on the couch and watched TV with Andre much longer, she'd be in his lap, halfway to being a vampire in a matter of minutes.

"I see. Do you have something in mind, or shall I put you to work in the kitchen?"

"I dare you to try." She raised her eyebrows in challenge, but her lips quirked of their own accord, betraying her delight. The way he teased her wiped away her worries and made her giddy, like he was her first crush. "I assure you, the other humans would revolt with one taste of my cooking."

She drew her knees up to her chest and leaned against the arm of the couch. "So instead of playing chef, why don't I keep working on your project."

He sat up, suddenly serious. "You understand that it may be a waste of time?"

"I have time to waste. And maybe I can accomplish something, now that I know the truth. Tell me about the vampires you want to reach. How many are there?"

"There were almost four hundred of us living in Dalmatia. We all fled to the United States. I assume they fare as well as Kos and I with the wasting disease. So, unless Hunters have found them, they live, though they are weak." Where his brow had been newly smooth, the old furrow reappeared.

"Will they die, if they don't get the wine?"

He bent forward and placed his chin in his hands. The angle of his back was the same tragic line she'd first seen when they met in the bar. She'd wondered what could burden a man like him. Now she knew.

"They may die regardless. As yet, the wine seems to be making me stronger, but not Kos."

His jaw muscles bulged and ground. Her fingers reached to caress them. *Oh, right.* She pulled back. He was a fortress. He didn't need her. Still, she wanted to take away his burdens.

"You don't know why?" she asked.

"I have no ideas. My only hope is that it is affecting him more slowly, simply because he is younger and less powerful than me…"

His fear for Kos made the air heavy. She waited for him to continue. When he didn't, she knelt on the couch and placed her palm on his back, rubbing small, soothing circles. Some of his tension eased under her hand. His back rose and fell with a deep breath.

"He saved me when Mila died, and now I cannot save him."

She pulled him up to see his face, and cupped his handsome jaw in her hand. His nostrils flared and his fangs glinted behind parted lips, but the pain in his downturned eyes kept her close. He was no threat.

"Andre, you don't know for sure. And believe me, it does no good to despair. Tell me this. Why are the vampires in hiding?"

"We went into hiding to protect each other, so that if one of us was found, he or she could not lead the Hunters to the others. This plan was my suggestion, and a poor one, since, as you know, it means I have no way to reach them." He had said as much before, on their nighttime walk to the spring.

He closed his eyes, resting his head in her hand. Did her touch comfort him? Her heart was full, imagining she could give him any peace. She had to swallow to choke back the emotions coming up her throat. Her voice came out thick with them. "I see. Were you their leader?"

"Not formally, although I was nearly the oldest. Among vampires that affords me authority. And it is why I feel so responsible for their fate."

"Do you think so? I suspect you could be only as old as Pedro and still feel responsible."

Eyes still closed, his smile was sad when he said, "Perhaps you are right."

Suddenly, she couldn't bear the intimacy. She dropped her hand from his face and tucked it behind her. In response, he picked up the end of her ponytail and a gentle tug made her scalp tingle as he rubbed her hair between his fingers. She wanted him to pull it so that she fell into his arms. She wanted to hold him and promise that Kos and all his old friends would be okay. But what right did she have to make promises like that?

She was a chicken, and he was a hero. He had suffered a loss at least as painful as hers. But, while she had retreated into a lonely existence, he embraced his family, took responsibility for his friends, and insisted on making a home for everyone he loved. What would it be like if he loved her? Could she have a home again? Did she want one?

"Tell me about your life in Croatia. Did you live in fear? Did you hide in the cellars all day?"

"No, we were not afraid. It was idyllic, until the end. Life has a way of moving slowly when it lasts for centuries. I watched the seasons change, I played cards with my friends, I cultivated my vines. When I married Mila, I took great pleasure in watching the boys grow."

"But you never played catch with them in the sunlight?"

His eyes darted from her ponytail to her face, and he examined her closely. His green eyes went dark, and she felt her skin heat with a blush. He had told her he could hear her heart and smell her every reaction to him. But he'd never confessed to mind reading. Still, he knew what she was really asking.

"The longing for the sun never goes away, Zoey. We simply accept it as a condition of our existence, the way you accept you cannot fly, or breathe under water."

"But I've never done those things. Once, you did feel the sun on your skin." Something in her was desperate to understand what that life would be like, if...

"As I said, it never goes away, but it does not pain me. Many things you do in daylight can be done at night. In Croatia, each year, everyone gathered at my home for the Night Harvest. It was our great festival. We picked the grapes and crushed them, we drank and danced all night…there can be joy without the sun."

As he spoke, she could see his white teeth between his moist lips. She couldn't take her eyes off them. Long after he stopped speaking, she continued to stare. He licked his lower lip, just a hint browner than his olive skin.

"Zoey?"

Her blood pounded in her ears. "Yes?"

"I am going to kiss you."

"Please," she breathed.

His body crushed her into the couch, and his mouth opened onto hers. She was ready to be devoured. Lips, fangs—whatever. Everything. A mindless surrender.

His tongue filled her mouth, softly stroking her own. She groaned around it and arched her body up to press into him. He slowed the kiss and pulled back, brushing his lips against both her cheeks, then her eyelids. She opened them to find his eyes right above hers.

"Sweet, I have nothing to offer you. Do you understand? My home is under attack. At any moment I may be driven away, to die slowly all over again. All I have…" He put his hand over her sternum, where her heart raced.

When she understood what he meant, it beat even faster, thudding so hard it hurt. He was offering her his heart? She gasped, couldn't catch a breath.

His eyes went wide, and he was on his feet in an instant.

"*Davo*. I am sorry, Zoey. I do not know what came over me. For a moment…"

Air. The oxygen rushed in, clearing her mind.

He wiped his hand over his forehead. "But, you have made it very clear you do not want—"

"Don't apologize. You have also been clear we are playing with fire. I'm sure I was giving you all the wrong signals. It's my fault. I'll go back to my room."

"That would be best."

At the door, Zoey's hand came to rest on the doorframe and she fell back into her vision of the wine shop. That ivory label with red metallic letters came suddenly into focus.

"Andre?"

"Yes, sweet?"

"Let's call it Blood Vine."

"Blood. Vine." When he said it, his accent thickened to its most exotic.

She shivered, gripping the doorframe.

"Yes. That's it. By the gods, Zoey. You've done it."

Her face felt tight as she cast him a smile over her shoulder. She couldn't shake the feeling she was walking away from the only home she would ever know.

Together, Pedro and Bel made short work of the third solvent, but then Pedro lost his wind. He pulled a stool up to the counter and collapsed, resting his head on his folded arms.

Bel powered up the chromatograph, which whirred so softly only vampire ears could hear it. Then his vampire crew blew into the workroom. "Sundown already?"

"Just now," one of the men said.

Pedro kept his head down, not caring who spoke.

"Did you get your satellite feed working, Ani?"

"*Da.* All clear. No sign the Hunters are interested in the vineyards."

"Good. Then same protocol as last night—patrol the perimeter without giving the Hunters any sign you're there. If they see you in the vineyards, they get clued into the importance of the wine."

"Can't have that," Omar said in a baritone that vibrated Pedro's bones and made his eardrums itch.

He shuddered. His senses, his body, weren't his own anymore.

Bel's working-class London accent was easier on Pedro's ears. "Anybody hungry? You all can slip into town one at a time."

The group murmured enthusiastically.

"I do need two escorts for Kos's friends. If you're charming, they might even be up for a little feeding and fun. Pedro's not hungry and they have to go to work in the morning."

"Not hungry?" Omar asked.

Pedro cringed from either the mention of his freakish vampire abnormality, or the sound of Omar's voice—he didn't know. He simply pressed his face into the crook of his arm and willed the world to go still and silent around him.

Two vampires volunteered as escorts, then the crew trod out of the workroom in a cacophony of jokes, laughter, and earth-pounding footsteps. When the door closed behind them with a soft thud, he inhaled deeply.

Bel's hand came to rest on his shoulder, stinging like a burn without heat. "Man, you need to get some rest. I can finish this on my own."

"How do I rest if I can't sleep?" Pedro straightened, shrugging off Bel's palm.

Bel rounded the table, and Pedro screwed up his eyes to make them focus. It sort of worked, revealing a concerned-looking Bel resting his elbows on the stainless steel surface.

"Sit in a dark room. Turn some static on your radio to block out sounds."

Pedro snorted. "Maybe I should try whale noises and a lavender eye pillow. Or should I just book a day at the spa?"

"Go to hell. I'm only trying to help. You need white noise and as little light as possible."

Pedro stumbled toward the door and then thought twice. With a grace that surprised him, he spun to offer his hand to Bel.

His new brother stared at the proffered hand for only a moment before taking it. "Welcome to the family."

For the briefest moment, Pedro's achingly tense face eased into a smile. Then the lights went out.

"Shit," Bel said.

It was pitch black in the huge space, but Pedro knew the workroom like he knew his own cock, which was to say, better than the back of his hand.

"Shit," Bel said again.

Pedro's eyes adjusted, and the ambient light from a glowing red switch on a surge protector illuminated the room like a warm harvest moon.

"Wow. I can see."

"Yeah. Only time I ever wish I'm a vampire is for the night vision."

The darkness ended the onslaught against Pedro's newly sensitive eyes. It was a desperately needed reprieve. "Take my hand, I'll lead you upstairs."

"Aw, dude. I didn't know you cared."

Pedro smiled, the little jab assuring him Bel had none of Kos's old homophobic hang-ups.

Hand in hand, they emerged near the kitchen hallway. Down the hall, a closet door hung open and someone rustled around inside.

"Hello?" Bel called out.

"Help me with these boxes," Andre said.

With Bel in tow, Pedro arrived at the closet where Andre stood surrounded by precisely labeled boxes. He clicked on a flashlight and handed it to Bel, who shone the light like a nightclub beacon, skimming the hand-written labels.

"Good old Kos. Always prepared."

Andre grinned, shuffling a box out of his way. "I must bring flashlights and batteries upstairs."

Pedro and Bel followed him to find Vania, Susan, Ally, and Zoey lighting candles. As soon as Andre set down his load, the women started to distribute the flashlights.

"You think the Hunters cut the power?" Pedro asked.

"No doubt about it. It would be easy to do, since the line is above ground. I should have had it buried."

"Upsetting the household is part of their usual bag of tricks," Bel said.

That was news to Pedro, and it made his torture less personal. Perhaps they would have treated anyone that way. Then he remembered Lucas's knuckles crashing into his cheeks and the taste of his own blood. How could that not be personal?

"This isn't scary," Ally said. "It's like a camp out."

"Or like living before electricity—it's kind of romantic," Susan said.

"We should be scared." Vania jumped in, spoiling their play. "With no power, all the food will go bad. It will be damn hard to bring in supplies and there are a lot of mouths to feed here that don't have fangs."

Everyone was silent; Pedro decided Vania wasn't much fun.

"It's not so bad," Andre finally said, attempting a reassuring tone. "During the day, the solar panels will power the estate. During the dark hours, the generator can run the refrigerator."

"You have a generator and solar panels?" Vania asked.

"This is a working vineyard. The generator comes in handy all the time. And of course I have solar power. Vampires are concerned about global warming. We are the ones who will live to see it. I would not be surprised if we were behind all the major renewable power initia—"

"Go get the generator, already," Bel said.

Pedro snickered at the familiar sentiment. When Andre talked like that, he never knew if the crusty old vampire was bullshitting or taking himself too seriously.

Susan pointed her flashlight under her chin, casting a spooky illumination on her face. Zoey laughed, and Ally jumped, squealing with delighted fear. Bel drew up to Vania and began discussing the estate's defenses. All the while, flashlight beams jiggled and flared. The din swelled, and so did Pedro's newly altered brain. Before he knew it, his knees folded, and he was ass-to-the-ground at Bel's feet.

A giant olive-skinned paw was in his face instantly, offering a boost. "Okay, bro. Off to bed with you. Can I trust you to rest, or do I have to send in Omar to give you the spa treatment?"

"Screw you. I'll rest." He couldn't bring himself to say thank you, but he squeezed Bel's hand, hoping his gratitude didn't go unnoticed.

His feet carried him to his room without complaint, and he un-plugged every glowing device, turned on static and threw a blanket over his stereo. *Dios mio, if you listen to the prayers of vampires, please turn off all the juice running into my brain and let me find some peace and quiet.*

Kos squatted across the coffee table from where Lena sat, surpris-ingly calm and composed, on his couch.

"Come on, we've got to go."

"I'm not going."

Had he known she was this stubborn? "You're not safe."

"Kos, I feel better than I have in years. Thirty-six hours away from there, and I feel like my old self. I won't go back. I have friends I can stay within the city. Take me to Santa Rosa and I'll get a bus."

"Lena, if they know your name, they can find you anywhere. It's possible they'll even tail us from here."

"I won't go." She shook her head and crossed her arms. If it weren't so infuriating, it would have been cute.

Kos set his jaw *à la* Andre and put on his most determined expression. "You will."

Although she looked surprised at his forcefulness, she still said, "No."

He rolled his shoulders. Reason wasn't working, neither was coercion. He had one more option. "Lena, do it for me. I'd never forgive myself if something happened to you." It wasn't strictly manipulation if it was true.

"What do you mean?"

He put his knees down and leaned over the coffee table. "In Croatia we lost four members of the household. I promised I'd never let that happen again. Please don't put yourself at risk and put me through that again."

She inched toward him, but her arms were still crossed over her chest.

"Please?"

Finally she said, "Okay. I'll go if I can borrow one of your books?"

"I have tons of books at Kaštel too. You're welcome to them."

"But I'm enjoying this one." She touched the cover of *A New Selected Poems* by Galway Kinnell.

"You are?"

"I like the one about the footsteps." She blushed, keeping her eyes on the book.

That poem was one Kos's favorites too, about how Kinnell's son appeared every time his parents finished making love, to climb in between them in the bed where he was conceived.

"It got me thinking I might not want to do this anymore, the household thing. Maybe it's time for me to have a normal life." Lena thumbed the pages of the book where it lay on the table. She still wasn't looking at him.

"I understand that feeling, but it's a decision that will have to wait. I'll help you with whatever you want, but first we need to keep you safe."

"Why is Kaštel safer?"

"Magic."

"What?"

"I'll explain on the way."

He drove slowly, describing how Bel's crew was protecting the house. After Lena asked a few questions and he answered to the best of his ability, she fell silent. As they approached Kaštel, she fiddled in her purse, closely examined her fingernails, became a bundle of anxiety. He pitied her, and for the first time he was angry with Andre for the way he had neglected her.

He called ahead and got Bel on the phone in case they had any trouble getting through the shield, which snugly hugged the house and the back building where they made wine. He turned off the highway into the drive.

Just as the rank smell of Hunter wafted out of the air conditioner vent, something burst loudly and the steering wheel jerked—one of the front tires was blown. They were under attack.

"Lena, listen to me. Hunters are shooting at us. When I say go, I want you to get out of the car and meet me in the front. I will carry you to the house."

"I don't want to weigh you down. I'll run myself."

"Lena, your weight is nothing to me and I'm ten times faster than you. I will pull you across the seat and out my own damn door, unless you do what I say. Okay?"

She nodded curtly.

"Now."

She opened her door and hopped out, but two Hunters were there waiting for her. Shit, he'd let his guard down to argue with her and hadn't seen them. He froze in place as two of them pulled her backward off the drive into the bushes, pointing a gun to her head. His heart pounded in his chest.

Six yards to one Hunter, eight to the one with Lena. Rage boiled up inside him that they dared to threaten her. He could break both their necks and have her safe before they could shoot her. Toes twitching in his shoes, he gave himself a countdown. Three…two…one. Another shot rang out and a bullet grazed his side.

He was on the ground again behind the Hunters before he realized he hadn't sprinted, but flown. Bullets were still raining down where he had stood seconds earlier.

"Hell yeah!" he said, both shocked and thrilled by his first flight.

Both Hunters turned. He went for the bigger one first, snapping his neck in a quick motion. The other one yanked Lena and tried to hold her in front of himself. She fought him, throwing an elbow to his gut and a heavy stomp to his foot. He pushed her down and she landed hard.

"Lena?"

Kos froze, and the sharp shooter had time to aim. A bullet tore through his shoulder, burning through flesh and bone before exiting the other side.

It didn't matter. Was Lena hurt? Her slender rib cage rose and fell rapidly where she lay on the asphalt. The Hunter stood over her, his frightened eyes glued to Kos. In one fast step, Kos closed the distance between them and snapped his neck too.

Hunters approached on all sides. He went to Lena and saw a line of blood trickling from her hairline. He bent and, banding his arm around her ribs, said, "Hold on." His shredded shoulder was on fire, but it was already knitting back together. What hurt him most was to see Lena, clutching his book of poems in her hand as if it were her lifeline. He launched them into the air, fueled by the need to protect her.

"Oh my God," Lena whispered. "You're flying. Kos, you're flying."

Her child-like excitement broke through the fear she must have been feeling. He landed at the front door more gracefully than he expected. Bel promptly opened the door.

"Son of a bitch. You flew!" he said, as he dragged Lena inside. "Shit, Kos, you're soaked in blood. How bad are you hurt?"

"Fine. Healed already." With the door closed and the shield keeping the armed Hunters out, Kos shooed Bel away and focused on Lena. She was shaking with fear but holding herself together.

"Kos, you're bleeding," she touched his shirt and her hand came away red.

"Not anymore. Look." She would worry until he proved he was fine. He undid two buttons on his ruined shirt and bared his chest to show her the wound was closed.

"Oh, wow." Dazed, she looked from her hand to his chest and back.

"Lena, where are you hurt?"

"I'm fine."

"You have a head wound. Anything else?"

She paused for a second to touch her head where she was bleeding, then said, "My wrist." He looked down to see it beginning to swell. He manipulated her hand and she flinched a little, but her range of motion was good. "I don't think it's broken. Just a sprain. But let's get some ice on it."

"Why is it dark in here?" she asked.

Kos panicked. Was she blacking out? Then he noticed the lights were out.

"Hunters cut the power," Bel replied. He tried to hand Lena a flashlight, but she refused to put the book down and her other hand was clearly causing her pain.

Kos took it for her. "Bel, two dead Hunters out front need to be taken care of."

"Sure thing. Chances are their friends have taken care of them already. They're as committed to leaving no trace as we are."

"Lena, come down to the kitchen for an ice pack." Walking slowly, he stayed next to her so she could see the ghostly sphere illuminated by the flashlight. He sat her down on a stool at the counter, scooped a handful of ice into a plastic baggie and wrapped it in a kitchen towel. While she placed it on her wrist, Kos cleaned the blood off her head.

He'd never been so close to her, aside from their quick flight to the front door. Her hair was soft under his fingers, and she smelled like the salty ocean air at his house.

"Lena, this is already bruising. How hard did you hit the ground?"

"I don't remember." Her forehead creased with the effort.

"That's not a good sign."

"I guess not." She wiped her brow with the back of her hand.

"Are you feeling tired?"

"Very."

"Also not a good sign."

"Oh…you think I have a concussion? I don't think I hit that hard."

"Lena, you just said you don't remember."

Her lopsided smile was an admission that she'd been caught in an inconsistency.

He filled a glass of water for her at the sink and slid it across the counter. "Listen, I want you to stay in my room so I can watch for any signs of a concussion while you sleep. I'll wake you up every few hours."

"There's no need for that. I'll sleep in my room. I can set an alarm and wake myself up."

"Sleep wherever you're most comfortable. But I'll be keeping watch either way."

"Really?"

He nodded.

"Then I'd prefer your room. Mine will bring back all the unhappy memories of living here."

"No problem. Let's get you settled."

As they stood, Andre walked in carrying the generator. He gave Lena a cursory glance and then focused on Kos. "What happened?"

"Hunters att —"

"Andre, Kos flew!" Lena said.

As the news sunk in, Andre's face lit up with surprised eyes and a huge smile. The corners of Kos's mouth pulled to mirror it. The way Andre was looking at him reminded him of feeling Andre's pride as a little boy.

"*Davo,* Kos. That's good news." He set down the generator and embraced Kos.

"I don't know whether I'm happier to fly, or to know the damn wine works."

"It works." Andre shook his head, still smiling. "Blood Vine. It is called Blood Vine."

"Is it? Did Zoey come up with that?"

Andre nodded absently. So Kos was sharing Andre's pride with Zoey. He didn't mind. There seemed to be enough to go around.

Andre's smile faltered, and he spared attention for Lena. "You're all right?"

"I'm fine."

"Good. I need to know how many days' worth of food you have. We have so many humans here, I am concerned we'll run out."

"Days? Are you kidding? Didn't you check the pantry?"

"Pantry?"

With only a flicker of hesitation, she surrendered the book she was holding to Kos in exchange for the flashlight. "I'll show you." She led them into the back of the kitchen where a door opened into a hallway. The final door on the right opened into a huge pantry, stocked from floor to ceiling with dry goods and non-perishable items.

"Whoa," Kos said.

"My grandmother taught me that a vampire household always needs to be prepared for a siege. I've been building up this stockpile since you hired me. There's more in the still room."

"Why didn't Susan tell us all this is here?" Andre asked.

"Honestly, she probably didn't know. I did most of this work at night. I should have mentioned it when I left with Kos, but I was distracted—"

"I knew the women appreciated your cooking, but I had no idea you were preparing us for an emergency." Andre looked from side to side as if there were a tennis match in the pantry.

Lena smiled, revealing her satisfaction with the preparations she'd made.

Kos had rarely seen her smile genuinely. It was lovely. But something made her even sexier than that heartfelt smile. Her orderly pantry was so much like the way he stockpiled supplies, hid money in offshore accounts and prepared new identities. That obsessive part of him had a raging hard on for Lena. Not just a pretty face, but a planner—could she be more perfect?

"Andre?" Zoey called out from the kitchen. Kos could see the beam of her flashlight moving across the doorway.

"Down here."

She followed his voice down the hallway. "Hey, I was just coming to see if you got the generator set up. I'm hungry—" She stepped into Lena's little utopia and scanned up and down the shelves with her flashlight. "Wow. I guess we don't have to worry about running out of food after all."

Kos noticed Andre's posture relax immediately. He hadn't looked so at ease since Kos was a child.

"Kos, would you help me with the generator?"

"Sure."

The two men walked away, and Zoey found herself standing alone with Lena.

"He's different around you," Lena said with a shy smile.

A gooey, warm feeling radiated outward from Zoey's heart, as if Lena had passed her a note across the sixth-grade classroom, promising that Andre like-liked her.

Yep, she was different around him too, which was a problem.

She changed the subject. "You've been preparing for some kind of emergency?"

"Yes. Just in case."

"This is really impressive. I bet you could feed all of us for two months with this much food."

"I was hoping to have enough for six."

"You don't think we'll be here that long, do you?" Zoey asked.

"I sure hope not. I don't want to be here at all. But it's possible. Hunters never give up."

That was the consensus. They never gave up, and they were after her. She could strike out on her own, or stay here until Andre deemed it safe and helped her with a new identity. That could take months. Still, given those two choices, Kaštel was preferable, as long as she could avoid getting too close to Andre.

"Are you hungry?" Zoey asked. "I came to get myself dinner. Everyone else ate already."

"Now that you mention it, I am."

Zoey noticed Lena's icepack. "You don't look like you're in any shape to cook, but I can follow instructions well."

"That's a deal."

Andre and Kos had just finished running a long extension cord from the generator into the kitchen. It astonished her to see Kos lift and shift the fridge back against the wall like he was moving an empty cardboard box. The meaning of super strength sunk in.

"We're going to check on Pedro," Andre said. "Will you two be all right?"

"Yes, Zoey's going to cook us dinner."

Andre cast Zoey an inquiring look, and she nodded in reply, touched he thought she might need his protection. But Lena was no longer giving Zoey the cold shoulder. She could handle being alone with the woman.

At Lena's suggestion, they decided on grilled cheese sandwiches.

"I promise this Gruyere is to die for." Lena held up a wedge of cheese.

"I'd settle for good enough," Zoey replied. "Suddenly, I prefer my cheese with lower stakes." She sliced thick slices from what might be the last loaf of bread in the house.

"Yeah, I imagine a whole new world and an ancient war could come as a shock."

Lena was pretty nonchalant about the whole vampires and Hunters thing. "How long have you worked here?" Zoey asked, thinking it was a harmless question.

Apparently not. Lena's glum pout revealed that she'd steered them into dangerous territory. Lena held a spatula in her good hand with a death grip.

"Hey, I'm sorry if you don't want to talk about it."

Lena relaxed her grip, and got control of herself slowly. Then she plopped onto a kitchen stool.

Finally, she lifted her face. "It's okay. I've been here a few years, but it wasn't a good situation for me. I guess I had unreasonable expectations…"

Whatever that meant sounded personal, and it became obvious that Lena was lost in thought. Zoey kept quiet and finished grilling the sandwiches. When they were done she said, "Hey, Lena, I don't know about you, but I need a drink. What do you have down here?"

"Not much. There's a wine rack in the parlor upstairs, and we have a wet bar in the householder's living room. Down here I just have some sherry and brandy for cooking."

"Brandy, huh? Like all the heroines in Victorian novels drink to recover their nerves?"

"Exactly." Lena laughed. "Sounds perfect for the occasion. But don't tell Kos. He's worried I have a concussion." She hopped off the stool and went to a cabinet.

"Is it just for cooking or is it the good stuff?"

"I only cook with the good stuff," Lena replied in a darn good Julia Childs impersonation.

She sat next to Lena at the counter. After only a few sips of brandy, she felt it. Phew. Strong stuff—no wonder they used it "medicinally." Her face flushed and she was almost happy to be sitting in a vampire's kitchen under lockdown eating grilled cheese with a woman who hated her, or at least had hated her yesterday.

With her tongue loosened by her mini-euphoria, she asked, "Are you in love with Andre?"

Lena snorted and brandy actually came out of her nose. "Oww! That burns!"

A fit of laughter seized Zoey and then Lena started too. They both had tears streaming down their faces by the time their giggles finally waned.

"No, I'm not in love with him," Lena said, reminding Zoey of what had set off their laughter. "He wasn't very nice to me."

"He was mean?"

"Cruelly polite."

"Is that like killing someone with kindness?"

"Sort of. But it's more of a vampire thing. Imagine being sweet talked, fed from, and curtly dismissed every week or so for years. You know about the feeding, right? How sexy it is?"

"Yeah, I know." Zoey's memories of watching Andre feed made her voice sound husky.

"Well, a lot of vampires choose women for their household to be both their lovers and their blood supply. It's a natural combination and it's what I expected."

"Oh." Zoey tried to take in all the new information. It was a whole new world, with rules and customs she didn't understand.

"But Andre doesn't 'fuck where he eats'—those are his words, by the way, not mine." Then Lena gave Zoey a knowing look. "Not usually, anyway."

"Oh, he's not eating me." Then she blushed and shook her head. Damn brandy. "You know what I mean. He hasn't bitten me."

"Why not? Are you nervous? I promise you'd like it."

"No, it's not that. He's worried about some kind of blood bond."

Lena's blue eyes grew wider. "He thinks he'd bond with you? Zoey, you should do it, let him turn you! How wonderful for you!" Lena surprised her with an awkward hug, banging the ice pack into her head.

"Lena, that's not it. He doesn't want to bond with me." She drained her glass. "And I don't really want to be a vampire anyway, so I'm fine with that." Why did she sound so defensive? She had her own four-year-old promise never to get close to anyone.

"Oh, I'm sorry. I shouldn't have assumed—"

"Don't apologize. There's a lot I don't understand about this weird vampire world, but it sounds like your assumptions were perfectly logical."

Lena rubbed her eyes with the heels of her hands and smiled weakly. "Thanks for saying so, but I probably should have kept my mouth shut."

Zoey patted her arm. "Brandy's making me sleepy. Want to walk upstairs together?"

"Good idea. I'm tired too. But, Zoey, I'm glad we had a chance to hang out."

"Me too."

As they stood, Zoey saw Lena touch the cover of a book on the counter, then tuck it under her injured arm. Zoey led them upstairs with her flashlight. Kos must have heard them on the stairs, because he was waiting for Lena outside Pedro's room.

"Everything okay?"

"Great," Zoey replied.

"Yep, great," said Lena and followed Kos down the hall to his room.

Zoey reached for the knob on her own door, but it swung open to reveal Lucas. She jumped. "Oh, I didn't know you were in here."

"Sorry. I didn't know where else to go."

Pushing past him, she said, "Right. I could ask Andre—"

He remained firmly planted in the doorway, his golden eyes large like a lost puppy instead of a fierce wildcat. "No, don't bother. Get some rest. You look beat."

She smoothed her hair. "Thanks. You look great too, Lucas."

He opened his mouth, and she braced herself for a battle of wit. But then he snapped his jaw shut as if he were too tired to bother with a retort.

Pedro called from his room. "Hunter."

Lucas flinched, even as his body straightened with new purpose. Zoey didn't envy him. An invitation from someone who'd publically declared his hatred of you hardly counted for a comfortable place to spend the night.

The impatient voice called out again. "I'm not asking, Hunter."

She raised her eyebrows at Lucas, and he shrugged at her before obeying Pedro's command.

Closing the door behind him, she leaned against it and closed her eyes. For the first time since returning to Kaštel that morning, she was truly alone. She lay down in the cozy yellow room. In this bed, she'd fantasized about Andre three nights ago and watched him drink blood from Susan that morning. It had been a hell of a week, and her life would never return to normal.

When she closed her eyes, Andre's magnetic smile appeared, just like it had her first night at Kaštel. Suddenly hot, she kicked off the bedspread. Cool air on her legs was a reality check.

She glided her hand up her belly and let it rest between her breasts.

He had put his hand on her heart and offered — or almost of-fered — her his love. But he'd withdrawn the unwanted offer just as quickly. That was for the best. It spared her any temptation.

Still, what harm was there in closing her eyes again and imagin-ing a life with him?

CHAPTER 34

It astonished Andre that the crowded house was so completely silent. He had visited Bel in the workroom already, but his son was a bore when he was focused on chemistry. Tonight he was especially grumpy he would have to wait until dawn for the solar panels to light up and power his graph-o-whatever machine.

It would be nice to have a card partner to distract him, but Kos had decided to watch over that fool girl Lena. Hmm. Considering her pantry, maybe she wasn't as foolish as he had thought. But she was no Zoey...

With a whole night alone, there would be no distraction from her, sleeping a few doors down. If he concentrated, he could make out which of the breathing patterns was hers. The breaths confirmed she was out cold, and even snoring a little. Charming. Did she know she did that?

A strange, warm feeling encased his heart. He looked down to see if there was some physical explanation other than the one breathing down the hall.

He was filthy, with a spot of blood on his shirt, even. He hated that, as he was generally a fastidious eater. When was the last time he'd had a shower and a change of clothes? It was Wednesday evening when he and Zoey had — right, that was why he had not showered. He could still faintly smell her on his body, like she had marked him as hers. He hated to lose her mark, but it was definitely time to clean up. It would have to be a cold shower, given how his body was reacting to the memory of her.

In the shower, rivulets of cold water stung his skin. It kept his cock heeled, but his mind replayed memories of Zoey throughout the day. Twenty-four hours ago, he had ripped the rug out from underneath her reality and all day long she had coped with curiosity, humor, and not a little jealousy.

God, was there ever a sexier sound than when she growled?

She had been probing with her questions about sunlight. Was she open to turning? He feared asking her. He believed in his bones what he had told her about Mila: the only thing worse than the death of a bonded mate was to turn that mate and have them regret it. He never pressured Mila, and after her death, even during the worst pain, he did not second guess that decision. She would have regretted turning and they would have had an eternity of bitterness to share.

But Zoey was not Mila.

She was strong, and she was not only concerned about herself. She had tried to protect him only hours after learning what he was.

When she had described Pedro's turning as a beautiful rebirth, it had resonated in his bones. He would keep that image forever, with her to thank. Somehow, it soothed the wound of Mila's rejection.

Andre turned off the shower and dried himself. His muscles no longer ached with fatigue. He flexed them in the mirror — definitely bigger. He squeezed his bicep. Harder too. Briefly, he smiled at his reflection, feeling fitter than he had in years.

He had guzzled wine all day in addition to the extra blood he had consumed to resist Zoey. But strong as he was, his brain was overloaded like a young vampire's. Obeying the urge to sit in a dark room, he turned off the lights in his bedroom and lay down.

The thoughts would not stop coming. Images of Zoey flashed inside his head: an embarrassed flush, a finger touching his fang, her perfect ass bent over a box of flashlights. Aroused and fixated, anxious energy started in his groin and spread throughout his body. Flopping from side to side, he understood what humans meant by the expression tossing and turning. His sheets were scratchy and his mattress too hard. He didn't remember the last time he had actually used his big, empty bed.

It was the emptiness that tipped him over the edge. He pulled on his favorite jeans and a soft flannel shirt before he walked down the hall.

As quietly as possible, he opened the door to Zoey's room and gently eased himself onto the bed beside her. He did not want to wake her. Maybe she would never know he had been there. But he wanted to be next to her as he tried to calm his mind. It worked. He could look at her and listen to her breathe. With Zoey next to him in the flesh, he stopped searching for her in his mind and found peace.

Zoey's dream had a blurry-edged quality. Time sped up and slowed down in the dreamy way. She was on the lawn behind Kaštel Estate. Tables were set up with white cloths, twinkling lights hung from the fruit trees, and paper lanterns were strung up over the tables. A fiddler was tuning his instrument. It was night.

Men and women started coming out of the vineyards. Then Zoey noticed they all appeared to be the same age, thirty or thirty-five. So they weren't men and women, they were vampires. They wore work clothes. Some of them looked dusty and disheveled, but they all seemed happy.

Lena carried a case of Mason jars out of the kitchen door. She looked different. Her pretty face was fuller and luminous with satisfaction. She placed the jars on a table next to a big wooden barrel with a tap on it. Someone handed Zoey a Mason jar full of wine. She took a sip and knew it was Andre's special vintage. The fiddler began to play music, and a lanky redhead began singing in a language that could only be Croatian.

Zoey had the feeling it was the beginning of a party that would last until dawn. The festivities gathered steam, and several people looked to be on the verge of dancing. The joyful atmosphere was contagious, and Zoey's heart soared with the music.

Then he was next to her, bending low to speak in her ear. "Hello, love."

"Andre, what is all this?"

"It is the Night Harvest. Are you having fun?"

"I'm just watching."

"Good, then come with me." He put his arms around her waist, and suddenly they were flying through the air. In less than a minute they were on the ground outside of the little stand of trees surrounding the hot spring. Dream Andre was sentimental—he'd brought her to the site of their first kiss.

"What are we doing here?"

"Finishing what we started."

He took her hand and led her into the trees. He lifted her onto the same rock she had stood on to kiss him.

It was a dream. He wasn't real. It was safe to kiss, because he couldn't bond to her in a dream. She reached for him, wrapping her arms around his neck. His face shone down on her, bright with that gorgeous smile that made her heart thud. On his face, there was none of the intensity and concentration she'd grown used to. He wasn't fighting the attraction, or the blood hunger. Instead, he was relaxed and at ease.

A cruel thought interrupted her appreciation of him: *This happy ending is only in my subconscious.* Her joy ebbed.

"What's wrong?"

"This isn't real. I don't get happy endings."

"Zoey, it is real. This time you do."

He kissed her before she could argue. He skipped the gentle kisses he had led with before. He gripped the back of her head and coaxed her lips open with his tongue. She let him explore her mouth, running his tongue along her teeth and then stroking her own. He took his hand from behind her head and gripped both her shoulders, while pulling her lower lip between his teeth.

"I want to see you, Zoey. I am going to take this off."

She looked down to see what she was wearing. Her linen dress and a wrap to keep the cool night air off her bare arms.

Andre stepped back from her and tugged the wrap off, letting it fall to the ground. He hooked a thumb under each strap of the dress and slid them off her shoulders. His thumbs caressed her inner arms as he lowered the dress down past her breasts, her waist, and finally her hips, letting it pool at her feet.

She checked for panties. Of course not, who wears panties in an erotic dream?

Any self-consciousness she might have felt about standing before him naked was erased by the hungry and adoring look on his face. It was a look she had seen there before, and the memory made her instantly wet for him.

He opened his mouth like he wanted to say something but Zoey cut him off.

"Sshh. Come here."

In response, he flashed his sexy smile again. "You're the boss." He closed the distance between them.

"I want to see you, too." She reached for the top button of his shirt, but it slipped out of her fingers. She grasped for it, but he faded away and she couldn't get a hold of him. "Andre, what's happening?" His body became translucent. Panic tightened her chest. She tried to grab empty space. "Andre?" He was gone. She screamed. "Andre!"

Some part of Zoey's brain reminded her that it was just a dream, but panic won. Her limbs went rigid. Blackness took over her field of vision. She was alone. No one knew her. No one cared about her. She couldn't breathe. She was dying. All alone and dying. She tried to scream but had no air. Her words were a harsh whisper. "Andre! Come back!" He had left her alone. Just like Michael. She sobbed. "Andre, please come back."

She was shaking, her body being rocked unmercifully.

"Zoey, Zoey. Wake up, sweet. It's just a dream."

There were hands, two big, warm hands jostling her from the dream-turned-nightmare. When she opened her eyes, Andre's face was bent over hers. He smoothed her hair off her forehead.

She reached up and grabbed his wrist. "You're here."

I'm not alone. I'm not dying.

She could breathe, and she did, inhaling deeply. She locked her eyes on him and tried not to blink for fear he would disappear again.

"I'm here. I've been here the whole time. I'm not going anywhere." He smoothed her hair off her forehead again. "Christ, that was some roller coaster of a dream," he said, looking worried.

Zoey still didn't speak, just stared at him.

"You were smiling, you were turned on, and then suddenly you were screaming at the top of your lungs."

"You disappeared, right before we could…finish what we'd started…" She repeated his words from the dream. He raised an eyebrow.

"Well, I can understand being disappointed by that, love, but screaming bloody murder is a bit much." He teased her, but her mood wouldn't lighten.

"Andre, you dematerialized or something." A thousand images raced through her mind. Her dead goldfish, her parents' gravestones,

Michael dead on a stainless steel table, their empty apartment, his wedding ring in the palm of her hand. All she could say was, "It scared me."

A quiet rapping sounded at the door.

"Zoey?" It was Kos.

"Are you okay?" Lucas chimed in.

Andre watched her, and she nodded.

"She is all right," Andre replied.

"I want to hear from her," Lucas demanded.

"I'm fine," she called out toward the door. "I had a nightmare. Really guys, I'm fine. Sorry for the drama." She was glad they couldn't hear her shaking.

Andre pulled a trembling Zoey into his arms and rocked her back and forth the way he had rocked young Kos and Bel after their bad dreams. Finally, the tension in her shoulders and neck gave way. She leaned into him.

"What are you doing here?"

"I needed to be close to you. So I tanked up on wine, slipped in here and planned to slip out before dawn. But then you began to dream and—"

"Is it dangerous?"

"I should be able to resist my hunger for you, for a while, so we are safe. Somewhat, at least."

"Exactly how safe? I need to know."

Her stare remained intense; she didn't take her eyes off him. He realized what she was asking and his cock twitched. To have her again…he would do anything. But it was risky.

"Well…if we are careful. Possibly safe enough…"

"That's not very reassuring."

"No, it is not."

"How about a safe word? Like if I say 'spatula' then you remember not to bite me."

"'Spatula'? Why on earth would that work?"

"I don't know. Can't you tell I'm desperate? You disappeared in my arms. I need to feel you."

She needed him? *Davo*, that felt good.

"Zoey..." He could remind her it would only make it harder if she decided to leave, but he did not want her to leave. He would make love to her. He would offer her his heart again. It was a way to ask her for forever.

"Please."

He would give her everything, pour out his soul all over her peachy, soft skin. "I'm all yours."

Zoey swung her legs off the bed, and hesitated to undress, but her heart told her dream-Andre's response was true. She stood.

He came to her with hands outstretched. He surrounded her, cupping her ass and a breast at the same time, pulling her close. When she reached for his shirt, the dream threatened to swallow her up again, but she bit down on her lip and made short work of his buttons. He shrugged out of it.

He had the big body of a man who worked hard and ate well. He must have been a fearsome sight in Roman armor. There was a dusting of dark hair across his broad chest and down his belly.

He pulled her panties and top off, and began to kiss her neck and caress her thighs.

"Andre, I already dreamt the foreplay. You know what I need."

She expected him to make a joke, maybe call her bossy as he had in the dream. Instead, he tilted her chin up so he could see her face fully.

"Zoey, love, I want to give you what you need. But you are very shaken. Are you sure it will help?"

"It will help get me through."

After a curt nod, he tossed her onto the bed.

In one motion he lifted and spread her legs while sinking into her all the way. She grunted as her muscles clenched, resisting and welcoming him at the same time. Then she relaxed and bent her knees to open wider, cradling his hips between her own.

Somehow he knew to stay still. He pressed her into the bed with his weight. That was what she needed—to feel he was real, he was there. A part of her wanted to close her eyes and lose herself to the sensation of him filling her. But she needed every sense focused on his presence to keep her fear at bay. She looked at his lips and they were on hers in a second. His eyes were closed for the kiss.

All the while, he didn't move inside her.

His big hand went to her breast and squeezed it hard, harder. Perfect. He read her perfectly, sensing just what she needed. No gentle caresses. Panic still lingered deep in her muscles and bones, but the firmness of his touch distracted her. Their kisses were so deep their teeth clacked together. Still his eyes were closed. He ground into her: pubic bone against her sensitive spot. Zoey moaned. But still he didn't thrust. She gasped, exhilarated by sex or fear of letting go, she wasn't sure.

Finally, he began to move inside her. He found the angle she liked immediately, like they'd been lovers all their lives. She rocked her hips to meet his thrusts, never taking her eyes off him.

He looked over her body. "Seeing you like this…moving like this, sweating with sex…*davo*, you are beautiful."

He bit her nipple, hard. Then he licked away the ache. She clenched around him at the pleasure. When it subsided, he attacked her other breast, causing her to pulse around him again. "You feel so good around me," he said. Her fear began to give way to pleasure.

Starting between her breasts, he licked over her breastbone, into the hollow at the base of her neck and finally up under her chin. It made her shiver and clench again. He laughed. She loved that laugh, that smile. It pushed the fear out of her mind.

As if he knew exactly what she needed, Andre became even more intent on pounding into her, fast and deep. He held her arms above her head, tilting her hips to receive all of him. He was there, solid, real, filling her. Every time he stroked her the right way, she grew less afraid, like he was tamping down her fear as he drove into her.

"Were you made for me, sweet?" He reached down between them and found where she most liked to be touched. Like his bites to her breasts, he pinched her clit between his fingers, hard. Then he stroked her and thrust into her in time. At once, the pressure began to build inside Zoey and she bore down on him. "So tight," he whispered. He pulled all the way out of her and came back in fast, sending her over the edge.

When Andre felt her coming, he locked his jaw closed for fear of his fangs. Then he exploded inside her with a force he had not felt…in a long time? Ever? He did not know.

He rolled them so that she was above him and she sat up with him still inside her.

She smiled a satisfied smile. But it was wrong. It was one of those that did not touch her eyes. Where had she gone? His gut twisted with worry.

He put his hands on her hips. "Zoey?"

"That was great. I feel so much better. God, you know how to fuck. Thank you."

Her words were like a slap. "Zoey, that was not a fuck and you know it."

"You're right. I had a bad dream. You comforted me. It was sweet. Nice job not biting, by the way." She climbed off him, and pulled the sheet around herself.

A chill went up his spine. "I ought to bite you now. Do not pull away from me after that."

"Pulling away?" she said. "I thought we were both staying away."

"I was wrong. We should not stay away. I want you. I want you forever. I want you to stay. I want your blood in my body." He could not stop himself, and the words came out all at once. It was a mistake. Maybe if he had given her space, she would have warmed up again.

"Andre, you don't want that. It's the blood hunger talking. Neither one of us wants that."

"I am not hungry. I'm in love with you."

She looked away from him.

His fierce, beautiful Zoey looked away.

His mouth went bitter where he still tasted her kisses. She had used him and rejected him. If he tasted her blood, the acrid shadow of revulsion would surely linger in it, just like it had Mila's, for all those years.

He had offered her his heart, poured out his soul, but thank the gods of his father, he had not tasted her blood.

With his clothes in hand, he walked out and down the hall, naked, miserable, and unloved.

CHAPTER 35

"Maybe a fertilizer bomb would dismantle the shield." Atop the stack of wooden pallets, thick fingers slid a pack of matches next to an upside down coffee mug, sans handle, representing the Kaštel Estate.

Ethan's lips pulled into a sneer of their own accord, and he covered his mouth. Too bad they didn't have any little plastic soldiers for their war play. After wiping away his expression, he said, "Mick, with that shield in place, getting into Kaštel is no longer a matter of force. We'll have to outsmart them, or lure them from the estate."

"Let's hear Mick out," his father said. "Are you thinking a truck bomb, like Oklahoma City?"

"And if that fails, will you subject your bombers to the same discipline as your fake Highway Patrolmen?" Not that he pitied them; they'd earned the beating their comrades had delivered. "Too many failed attempts, and the men will blame their leaders, not each other. Especially after you let Lucas get away."

Stephen hurled the coffee mug at the wall. It bounced, denting plaster but landing unharmed on the carpet. His father was a child, Ethan thought.

What a shame that he had to teach strategy to these amateurs. When he was young, he'd admired them so much. Had he simply grown up and learned to do things better, or had the Hunters become more incompetent? It hardly mattered. In the end it was simply true — they were failures and he never failed. He would have to take things into his own hands soon, and his plan was foolproof.

"What's your proposal then?" His father's tone was challenging, but sullen.

Ethan examined his father, who inched backward under the inspection. Was he ready to pass on the mantle, hoping Ethan could succeed where he was failing?

"I'd like more information. How is it possible the younger Marasović can fly? By all reports he's lived in exile all but a few years of his life."

"The only way to get answers is to capture a vampire or someone in the household," Mick said. "Unless you want to call up your Porter woman and see if she'll spill the beans on her new lover."

Inexplicably, Ethan felt his pulse quicken. He'd given up on Zoey when he'd ordered the attack on Kaštel. But maybe she wasn't lost. How deep was Zoey in? Had Marasović seduced her? Or had she returned out of sensitivity? She'd never seemed like the type to adopt a puppy from the animal shelter, but…

"It's worth a try," he said, rising from the crate where he sat to step outside and place the call.

He got voicemail. "Zoey, listen. I'm worried about you. I'm sorry about the attack. I wish they hadn't done that and I want to get you out of there. I don't know what Maras has told you, but you can't believe a word he says. Charm and seduction are how he survives, but at heart, he's a predator. Call me, and I'll find a way to rescue you."

Normally, he took pride in his ability to predict people's actions several steps ahead. But Zoey had always been unpredictable. He hung up, utterly uncertain whether she would call him back. But his still-racing heart confirmed he was not entirely indifferent to the outcome. She'd chosen a vampire over him, and still, he wanted her for his own.

Shielding his eyes from the morning light, he tilted the screen of his phone until there was no glare and checked his email. A message from Dr. William Oliver topped the list. It said he was available around lunchtime that day to go over the translation. Ethan agreed to the meeting, suggesting a time and place.

Pedro was dizzy, and his head felt like it was going to explode. It was the worst headache he'd ever had. Only it didn't hurt—it just felt like it should. Even without pain, it was seriously unpleasant. Bel was right, thoughts raced through his brain much faster than before. He would have thought that was cool. It wasn't. He wished he could turn it off. But sleep was no longer an option.

He grunted, squeezing his eyes against nonexistent light in his pitch-black room. Rolling over, he buried his face in his pillow. The smell of goose was so ripe he may as well have stuck his nose up the bird's ass. He threw it across the room and heard something fall over at impact. He didn't care what it was; he crammed his face in the crook of his arm. Thank God his mattress was synthetic.

His head demanded he lie perfectly still. He closed his eyes and found himself in Ethan Bennett's hands again. His lids flew open. Cold sweat formed all over him. The remembered pain was only a shadow, but it sliced across his skin and sent ice up his bones. He drew his knees up underneath him like a child.

He had told Kos he was glad he hadn't hanged himself, but that was only true about ten percent of the time. The other ninety percent, he wished he was dead. He would give anything to erase the memories of the shed, and Ethan's sick little tool kit. He trusted that feeling would pass, if for no other reason than he was likely to live long enough to get over it. But he'd be stuck with it for a good long while.

A chair creaked as Lucas shifted in it.

Lucas—the witness to his humiliation, worse even than the pain. He had been unable to protect himself, in spite of all his precautions. Lucas had beaten him to a pulp and seen him cry like a baby. Even if that Hunter piece of shit had been trying to save him all along, he couldn't forgive Lucas for seeing him humiliated. Maybe it was unfair, but all his anger at the Hunters was concentrated on Lucas.

Yep, he'd been hot for Lucas, and now he was even hotter for his blood.

Shame, anger, lust, and blood. And to top off that perfect cocktail of fucked-up, desperate not to be alone, Pedro had ordered Lucas to sit with him. What could possibly go wrong?

He rolled over and looked through barely opened eyelids. With his new vision, the shadows cast shadows in a pitch-black room. Lucas sat, tipped back in his chair with his head leaning against the wall. His breathing was regular, his eyes closed. The son of a bitch was sleeping, an escape no longer available to Pedro.

Could Andre send Lucas away, somewhere safe and far? And if so, could Pedro do without the blood in Lucas's veins?

The lines of Lucas's face were long and handsome, his features fine and his nose narrow. Pedro remembered them twisted in cruelty as he had beaten him. He recoiled, and must have made a sound because Lucas's eyes slid open.

"Does it hurt? Your head, I mean."

The words were a mallet on his eardrums, thundering. "Shut up."

Lucas was silent, but Pedro could see he was wide awake. They stared at each other for the better part of an hour, although he wasn't certain Lucas could see him.

"When I was a teenager I got migraines. A hot shower helped."

"Are you trying to piss me off? I may be a baby vampire, but I feel strong. I'm almost certain I could snap you in half."

"Fine." He could tell Lucas wasn't the least bit frightened and that infuriated him. Did he doubt his anger? Did Lucas think he owed him something for saving him? Screw that.

He moved fast so Lucas wouldn't know what was coming. In a matter of seconds, he had him by the neck. Pedro stepped onto the chair to gain the height he needed to dangle him in a chokehold. It seemed fair, to strangle Lucas in the manner he'd planned for his own suicide. Lucas didn't struggle, but Pedro could smell a tart human stink, and his new instinct told him was fear. The *ba-boom* of the man's heart was a frickin' bass drum in his ear.

That was better. He had control; Lucas knew he was in charge. The power was intoxicating.

He threw Lucas down onto the bed face first. With newfound lightness, he dropped down. The ball of one foot glanced off the floor and he and pounced on Lucas. He sat astride the lean torso, wrapping his hands around his long throat.

His head was miraculously cleared by the action. The choice became clear: *Which will make you feel better, his submission or his death?*

"Do you realize I could do anything I want to you?" The threat was meant to be violent. Only after he said it did the other, sexual threat, occur to him. A flash flood of blood went to his cock. This was a new side of himself. Teeth pressed together, he felt like a wolf when he smiled into the dark. He would dominate Lucas in every way he wanted to, make Lucas feel the kind of fear he had felt.

Lucas turned his face to the side so he could speak. "I understand why you want to scare me."

"No. You don't."

"I'm not saying I've been there. I'm saying it makes sense to me." Lucas tried to push up and face him.

"I don't care." He spread his fingers around Lucas's skull and forced it back down and pressed his knees into Lucas's side.

Muffled by the mattress, Lucas said, "It probably makes no difference to you, but I'm sorry. I wish I could have saved you from the whole thing."

Hearing Lucas say it made all the difference, as much as Pedro wished it didn't. It was a drop of water in an ocean of hate, but it made all the difference.

"Go to hell," he said, standing and going into the bathroom to splash water on his face. When he came back, Lucas was gone.

CHAPTER 36

How long had she been in the shower? Zoey didn't know. Her skin was pink from the long exposure to heat. God only knew how red her eyes were from the gallons of tears she'd shed. She assumed the water would eventually turn cold, but somehow steaming warmth rained down on her until she'd had enough.

Now it was time to leave.

It was just like that old saying about moths and flames. She'd been so sure she wasn't a moth, but apparently, she was wrong. She certainly felt singed around the edges. Her panic was barely under control. Some part of her had claimed Andre, had fallen for him hard, and that rebellious portion was fighting to keep her at Kaštel. But the other part knew she had to leave and that part would win. It had to.

Yesterday's coffee tray still sat on the dresser, and next to it, a pair of jeans and a couple shirts. Susan had brought them by when Zoey mentioned all her clothes had been blown up with her car. Her hot, too-clean skin slipped into the soft denim, one leg at a time. The jeans were tight in the thigh, loose in the waist, but good enough. A black T-shirt that spelled out *Wine Slut* with sequins glittered on the dresser. Too true. She picked the one underneath it: safely striped with pink and gray. It was a little tight across her breasts, but it had to do. Her thin-soled sandals would be trashed after this hike.

From the window, a cloudless sky suggested another day just as hot as the one before. Good. She didn't need a jacket. She slid her wallet into her pocket and glanced at her cell phone — battery nearly dead and charger a pile of ash in Andre's front lawn. Suddenly, the phone blinked with a new message from Ethan. Yeah, right. She hit delete.

She couldn't leave from one of the exits off the main house, but Andre had mentioned a tunnel from the cellars leading north into a vineyard. That would put her beyond the shield and presumably beyond the Hunters' watching eyes. He'd told his household staff that there was an inn within walking distance. She would call Justine to pick her up when she was out of the tunnel. A phone call could be too easily overheard in the house. Then, she'd walk to the inn. She'd go home, pack her things, and then go on the run.

When it was time to leave, the panic rose up in her and she almost faltered. But she could not really reconsider. If she stayed, eventually he would slip through her fingers, just like in the dream. He would forget he was a vampire and walk into the sun. He would grow bored of her. He would be killed by Hunters. Better to lose him now than to get closer, to think she had her happy ending, and then lose him.

With resolve, she said goodbye to her cheerful yellow room, grabbed her flashlight, and made for the stairs to the cellar.

The cellars were lit with the murky blue of exposed compact-fluorescent bulbs. The solar panels must have been powering the estate. The cold air raised sharp bumps on her overheated skin. She rubbed her arms and headed away from Andre's office, in case he was there. She got lucky — the entrance was at the far end of the cellar. The door was locked from the inside. She wriggled the big bolt until it slid back, then yanked on the door. It creaked open. The tunnel on the other side was dark and she was glad for her flashlight. She slipped in and closed the door softly behind her.

Two steps into the pitch black tunnel she stubbed her toe. It throbbed, and she raised her knees higher with each step to protect her nearly bare feet. Her progress was slow and fumbling in the dark passage. Finding her footing was hard work. It was cathartic. She imagined she was going backward in time. She peeled off layers of memory, shedding Andre like a skin. No more sexy smiles, no more igniting looks. She banished him from her mind. Next came Ethan. It wasn't hard to scrape him off, he'd only ever been skin deep. A few faceless men she'd fucked in the past. She didn't remember them, but she remembered the blessed heat their bodies had lent her when she was desperate to feel something. That made them closer to her heart than Ethan, and she had to pull out the memories one by one and release them into the dark, damp air.

And then she was in that deep, raw place of memories long buried. Her husband's handsome face, the one she hadn't let herself see for years, was finally there. His eyes sparkled flirtatiously, then turned dull with medication. She slowed her already plodding pace and dropped onto the ground. Every joy and contentment of their early years welled up inside her.

They were at the beach, he was proposing to her—he had no ring, he didn't get onto his knee. "So, I was thinking, baby, let's get married." The sun was setting and they huddled together against a cool breeze. They'd been talking about getting married for months, but this time he sounded different.

"Are you asking?"

"Uh huh." He turned his head and kissed her, deep and long. It was a promise of forever. God, they were so young. They had no idea what kind of shit life could hand you.

She broke the kiss to say, "Yes." And then he changed before her eyes; growing thin and wild eyed, then thick and sluggish from his pills. They never made love, they never talked. She fretted over him, he gave up on life, and eventually, she gave up hope. She had no more tears for her young self, she just let the memories dissolve away. As they faded into the darkness, she felt completely new. It was time to move on. Ahead, a rectangular rim of light revealed the end of the tunnel.

Blinking in the glaring brightness, she emerged from the tunnel reborn, a clean slate. Surely, she'd traveled only about a quarter of a mile, but it had taken at least an hour. After her eyes adjusted to the afternoon sun, she took out her cell phone to call Justine. It would not turn on. She would have to call her from the inn.

She could see the busy highway just down the steep slope of the hill. Her flat-bottomed sandals slipped across dusty dirt and dried-out grass. She clung to the thick trunks of old vines to keep upright, careful not to dislodge any of the precious fruit along the trellis. At the bottom of the hill, she kept back from the road out of sight, following it in the direction of the inn.

It was hot. Burrs and gravel sifted into her sandals. Blisters gave her something to focus on. She was a professional, an independent woman. She could take care of herself. She had rebuilt her life once, and she could do it again. *No, don't think about that, only think about the future.*

Her watch said it was nearly five p.m. by the time she arrived at the Farmhouse Inn, but a sign said they didn't start serving dinner until six. She walked in the front door and a young woman looked startled to see her. At the unfriendly look, Zoey realized she would have to say his name. The panic roiled in her veins and her gut. Her lungs deflated in a rush and she gasped for air. *Put it in the box,* just one more memory crammed into the dark cold closet where she hid her grief. There was plenty of room in there, if she just emptied it out.

"Can I help you?"

She licked her teeth to lubricate her forced smile and stepped forward. "Hi, I'm a friend of Andre Maras over at the Kaštel Estate Winery. He mentioned the owner, Sam, was a friend."

Before the adolescent gatekeeper could shoo her off, a man's voice came from the kitchen. "Cary, who is it?"

"Someone to see you."

He exited the kitchen in the clean white shirt of a chef, wiping his hands on a towel. "Hi, do I know you?"

"No, hi. I'm Zoey Porter, a friend of Andre Maras. He speaks kindly of you, and I thought I might ask you for a favor?"

He scratched his head and waiting for her to continue.

"Could I possibly use your telephone and then wait for a ride to arrive from San Francisco?"

"Sure. That's no trouble. Would you rather wait at Andre's? I can have someone take you there."

Her lungs tried to revolt, but she showed them who was boss by letting her breath out slowly. "Thanks, that's kind of you. But there's no need. I'd just as soon wait here."

Zoey lifted the phone in Sam's office to her ear, but her fingers hovered over the buttons. Could she really trust Justine? She called to mind the overly friendly airhead, trying to recall the color of her eyes. Behind those funky reading glasses, they were clear blue. Zoey dialed.

Justine picked up on the first ring. "Hey, Zoey. What's up?"

It was good to hear her voice. "I need a ride. I'm still in Sonoma, at a place called the Farmhouse Inn. Can you come get me?"

"Totally. Everything okay?"

Zoey eased, settling into the desk chair. Justine was way too much of a ditz to be in cahoots with Ethan — he hated airheads.

"I'm fine. It's a long story."

"I'll leave right now."

Good old Justine. "I'll be eternally grateful."

Ethan stopped for gas in Healdsburg and saw the dollar store. He couldn't resist. Inside, the odor of strawberry-scented candles and industrial floor cleaner mingled, becoming something toxic. He coughed. The wall to his right was covered in toys — probably made of lead. Sure enough, they were there. Ninety-nine cents for a bag of those green soldiers. *May as well buy two.*

He tossed them in the passenger seat.

As his car crawled down the Interstate, he mused over his good fortune to be born a Hunter. And he would have an army of plastic soldiers with yellow eyes at his disposal, if all went well.

In a more vanilla American family, his lack of human emotion and his fascination with violence might have caused him problems. Instead, it was easy to blend in, and to learn. The important lessons weren't about how to kill vampires or blow up buildings. Instead, he observed that, motivated by deep hatred, Hunters went against their own self-interest for the cause. They were poorly educated, didn't move up in society, and they bankrupted themselves financing missions. How easy would it be to harness that hate into his very own army of fanatics?

He had the charisma and intelligence to lead. Professor William Oliver was going to give him a secret weapon that would ensure his success. If he could unlock the secrets of the Hunters' past, the entire clan would be his to command.

He was almost to Berkeley when his phone rang. The number told him someone from the office was calling.

"Hello?"

"It's Justine."

"Yes?"

"Zoey just called me. She's at a place called The Farmhouse Inn, down the road from the winery several miles."

"You're kidding?" Ethan sucked in a breath. This was better news than Oliver's translation.

"She's waiting there for me to pick her up."

"Perfect. I'll send her a driver straight away. Nice job."

"Just doing my duty, for the cause."

He pictured her behind the desk at his office, a female green plastic soldier wearing hideous pink-striped glasses. "Your dedication is honorable," he said before ending the call and dialing his father. "Zoey is at someplace called the Farmhouse Inn. Go get her."

He expected some resistance as he assumed a tone of command, but his father simply agreed. "I'll be there as fast as I can."

"Do not take her to headquarters. That's the first place Marasović will look." He hung up the phone.

What was she thinking leaving the Kaštel Estate like that? Perhaps she had received his message. Perhaps she would come back to him willingly. His heart beat absurdly fast.

Then, in a wide-open intersection, he slammed on his brakes. His father and Mick would think Zoey was fair game for any kind of sport. They might even hand her over to the initiates since she was defiled by vampires. He didn't care if she was pure, he didn't care if Andre Marasović had fucked her every way but Sunday. He wanted her back.

Frozen in the crosshairs of the streetlight, it changed to red. He pressed the gas, screeching into motion, and veered to the side of the road, where he scraped his hubcap on the curb. He fumbled with his phone to call his father and demand no one harm her. But when he pictured Zoey hurt, he finally knew his own mind—he wanted her that way.

All along, he had thought he found her confidence alluring, when what he really wanted was to break her of it. No more assertive, demanding Zoey. And whatever the initiates would do to her would be a perfect start. Cutting off the call, he pocketed his phone and began to drive.

After another few minutes, he pulled into a parking garage near the Berkeley campus. The History Department receptionist pointed him to Oliver's office. He had taken care to disguise his appearance.

He wore contacts, eyeglasses several years out of date, and a false mustache made to match his blond hair perfectly.

The door to Oliver's office was open in expectation of his arrival. The academic stood when Ethan approached.

"Ah, welcome. Have a seat." He gestured at a chair across from the desk.

"Thank you. You have the translation?"

"Yes, I have my best guess at the meaning of the text. As I said, it's most unusual. Completely atypical of Celtic mythology. It describes a conflict between a group who worshipped the sun god and one who worshiped a god of darkness or night. The text was written by the sun god's followers, and depicts the night god's people as evil."

"What was the nature of the conflict?"

"Some of the sun god's people fell under the influence of the night god's people. An older group of sun worshipers killed them all. A Noah and the Flood type myth about starting over with a clean slate. Only this one has a twist. The new, pure generation was given a mandate to destroy everyone who worshipped the night god, total extermination."

"I see. What a curious story. Does the text suggest why the sun worshippers hated the night worshippers so much?"

"Good question. The middle portion seems to address the reasons, but I am having trouble translating it. It's clear that the sun worshippers associated the night worshippers with death, and saw them as unclean. Here—" Oliver pointed at the paper where he had transcribed the text "—I think this says 'they drank death.' And this phrase seems to be saying something about 'eyes of the sun.' But I don't know what that means—perhaps that the sun god is watching."

"Fascinating. Professor Oliver, do you have any ideas who might be able to complete this translation?"

"As a matter of fact, I've given copies to a couple of colleagues for help."

"Which colleagues?"

Oliver told him the names of two other professors.

"I can't thank you enough for your help with this," he said while he pulled out a gun with a silencer. The discrepancy between the gun and his words clearly confused Oliver. He shot him quickly to spare him further confusion. Taking the scrawled translation from Oliver's hand, he folded it into his pocket. The codex itself was safely ensconced in its hard-sided case on Oliver's desk. He grabbed it as well and walked casually out of the office.

After Andre was ejected from Zoey's room, he retreated as far as possible from the seductive scent that tempted him to march right back to her, begging and pleading. He took refuge in his office. Over in the workroom, Bel paced and clanged around, signaling his impatient need for electricity to power his experiment.

Andre preferred solitude to Bel in a foul mood, so he played a stiflingly boring game of solitaire. Then he set about reading an equally stifling textbook called *Scientific Principles in Winemaking*. Perhaps the explanations behind practices he had long employed would have been interesting, if he were not so miserably heartbroken. *Davo.* His self-pity was pathetic, but he could not shake it. Fate had tricked him into loving again, only to bring him another razor-sharp rejection.

When the solar panels lit up at dawn, Bel went silent, and Andre assumed he was putting his own scientific principles into action.

The letters on the page of Andre's book ran together. Every word spelled Zoey. He didn't know what time it was. Her scent reached him all the way from the house and her pull finally became so forceful that he could no longer stand to be alone. He slammed the book shut and sought out Bel. Just as he expected, his son was hunched over that strange machine.

"Solve any mysteries?" he asked, hoping to sound casual. He was careful not to meet Bel's gaze, or his son would see right through him.

In the silence that followed, Andre sensed Bel's scrutiny. Or perhaps he inferred it; it was always so easy to read Bel. Sometimes he was more twin brother than he was son. Andre concentrated on hiding his tells by softening his features and relaxing his jaw.

Bel chortled. "Nice try. What did she do to make you so—?"

Andre held up his palm to silence him. "Just tell me what you have learned."

"Nothing yet. I just ran the last sample. You're welcome to look at the results with me." He indicated the jagged line on one of the thin slips of paper. "This peak indicates iron is present in the sample. It's what I was expecting. Only Lucas's blood has a significant amount of iron, since he's human."

The zigzag of data on the paper was meaningless to Andre. Only, it did look a little like the letter Z—

He shook his head, handing it back to Bel. "What about Pedro? Does he still have iron in his blood?"

"He has only trace levels. He had so little blood in his body when you gave him yours, it's almost all been replaced by vampire blood now."

As if on cue, Pedro entered the large room via the dimly lit cellar and flinched in the bright light. Andre shuddered in sympathy. It would be days before the new vampire's senses adjusted to their heightened sensitivity. But he looked otherwise well—young and fit—if strained around the eyes and with tightly pressed lips.

Bel leaned against the countertop and bumped a glass beaker, sending it sliding into another one with a clang. "Man, you do not look better. Were you able to rest?"

"Oh yeah. Like a baby. The whale sounds really helped—thanks."

Bel flashed his middle finger at Pedro.

"What are you talking about?" Andre asked.

"Pedro's a little—"

"I'm fine." Pedro rubbed his eyes, then wiped a hand over his face, which was ashen under his bronze skin. Andre tried to remember. Did all baby vampires go pale from the shock?

"Tell me the results," Pedro said.

"We are just reading them now." Andre pointed at the other three printouts. "Is this what you expected?"

Bel arranged them side-by-side on the countertop, trailing his finger along the slips where each one spiked high. "Yes, loads of copper in your blood—that's the *Hemocuprum.*"

Andre recognized the word; Kos kept him apprised of Bel's research. He pressed his finger onto another pile of slips. "What do these say?"

"Yes, these are the unexpected results."

Pedro took two stiff steps closer. "Are those the tests for—?"

"Gold. Yep."

"Gold?" Andre repeated.

"It was Pedro's idea—and a damn good hunch. I'll admit I ran them twice, I was so shocked to get a hit." Bel leaned over the print-outs, and both vampires drew near to study the data. "It looks like the highest concentration of gold is in Lucas's blood."

"Is gold normally in human blood?" Andre asked.

"No." Bel's tone left no room for doubt. "Perhaps it's a Hunter thing."

"Whose blood is this?" Pedro asked, holding up another slip.

"Sample C—that's you," Bel replied.

If Andre was reading it right, it showed a high concentration of gold. "Perhaps this is an ignorant question," he said, "but is gold normally in vampire blood?"

"No. I did broad-spectrum analysis on the components of vampire blood when I began my research. No gold, not a trace."

"So Kos and Andre have small concentrations, and I'm practically made of gold," Pedro said, looking at the printouts side by side. "Mine must have come from Lucas, but where did yours come from?" He frowned up at Andre.

Andre's gaze flew to the expert in the room.

"It's the wine." Bel crossed his arms over his chest, clearly prepared to defend his hypothesis.

"What?" Andre said at the same time Pedro did.

"Think about it. Lucas's blood satisfied your blood hunger in record time. Whatever potent mojo he's got, what if it's in the wine too?" A hint of uncertainty tinged his voice, but Andre observed his determination—Bel was convinced he was on to something.

"Damn," Pedro said.

"*Davo.* Do I understand you correctly? You believe that whatever cures the wasting disease is the same…" Andre could not recall the technical word, although surely he had read it moments ago, in that tiresome textbook. He repeated Bel's term. "Mojo present in Lucas's blood?"

"If my hypothesis is correct, then yes."

Andre asked the next logical question. "Why is it in my wine?"

"Good chance there is gold in the soil of your new vineyard," Pedro replied.

"Exactly. Maybe there is some organic compound—like the hemoglobin or *Hemocuprum* that contains gold instead of the other metals. I don't know. That's just an idea."

All three were silent, and Andre's mind raced. Somehow, Hunters, gold, and his wine were tied together. For a blessed few moments, there was no room for Zoey in the lightning storm of thoughts firing in his brain.

Bouncing on his toes, Bel broke the silence, barely able contain his excitement. "I have a friend down at UCLA who has the right equipment. Maybe we can find the compound."

To Andre, he looked impossibly young. "Bel. There is a bigger dilemma here. Why would something so important to the health of vampires exist in the blood of Hunters?"

"Could it be a coincidence?" Pedro dragged a stool from under the countertop and fell onto it, approximating the correct way to sit on a stool, even if he was sagging under the weight of becoming a vampire and why it had been necessary in the first place.

Davo. Andre's household was becoming an asylum for the broken and miserable. He was a well-suited warden of such a place. "I don't believe in coincidences," he replied, attempting to mash out the muscles in his neck with his fingers.

"That reminds me—I've been wondering about something since Lucas got here. What do Hunters smell like?"

"What do you mean? They smell like Hunter. The sky is blue."

"How do you feel when you smell it? Is it bad, like a skunk, or rotten food?"

"No. It is not…repulsive, exactly."

"That's for damn sure," Pedro confirmed.

Astonished, Andre jerked to look at his new son, and under his stare, the baby vampire shrugged. "He smells amazing. I want to eat him alive."

"Interesting…" Bel said. "You haven't learned to be wary. You're not conditioned to fear the smell."

The lightning storm went off in Andre's head again, as he grasped Bel's theory. "We can smell it! The mojo. By the gods, Bel, you are a genius."

Bel's face transformed under the praise, and for a flash of a second, they were a father and his boy, back on Šolta. Andre wanted to fold him into his arms and tell him he was proud of him every single second of the day, not only once in a century, when he managed to say so.

But instead, a woman's voice called from the cellar. "Andre?"

"In here."

Lena appeared in the doorway. "Hey, where's Zoey? I made her dinner."

"She is in her room."

"No, she's not there. I just checked."

"*Davo.*" The lightning started up again, jolting through his brain and stealing all reason. Even as he wondered where she was, he already knew she was gone.

Zoey thumbed through a restaurant supply catalog. Each item received her full attention — ramekins, baking sheets, and giant rolls of parchment paper. It would have been much easier to focus her attention on the catalog if she ever actually cooked anything.

The oh-so-friendly hostess rapped her knuckles on the door. "Hello?"

"Yeah?"

"Your ride just called. Justine is waiting outside for you."

"Oh, thanks." That was fast. Justine must have good traffic karma. Soon she would be back in San Francisco, ready to begin a new life.

When she opened the front door of the inn, she was surprised that it was already twilight. She didn't see Justine's car, so she took another step outside. A hand wrapped around her mouth and something sharp poked into her ribs.

"Hello, Ms. Porter, we're so happy to see you."

CHAPTER 37

With his palm on glass, Andre watched an excruciatingly slow sunset from his dining room window. He could have handled her rejection, but he could not stand for anything to happen to her. How could she be so stupid? Was his love so terrible?

"We know where their headquarters is. If they take her there, we can find them," Kos said.

"That is why they will not take her there. Maybe she went to her apartment. Fuck, I don't know her address."

"Maybe Ani can find it." Kos took off to find Bel's computer whiz.

Ten agonizing minutes passed. Five more. The sun was finally dipping into the horizon. Soon he could go out to look for her, but where should he go?

Kos returned, placing a scrap of paper in his hand. "Ani hacked the Department of Motor Vehicles database. The address was entered a year ago, so hopefully it's current."

His jaw was clenched so tightly, he couldn't have spoken. Stepping through the front door, he turned to looked at Kos before he launched. All his anger and fear must have been painted on his face, because his son said, "Go easy on her. I'll organize Bel's crew to provide cover when you bring her back."

Thirty anxious minutes later, he walked up something called Russian Hill, scanning buildings for their street numbers. He found the building. Her flat had its own entrance, and he pulled the door open as quietly as possible, which wasn't quiet at all since the deadbolt was in place. Even from down the stairs, he could smell her scent as if she was next to him, but the apartment was empty. *Davo.* Where was she? He walked upstairs to see if she had been there. Clearly not.

The apartment was full of classic looking furniture and pleasing colors, but it was right out of a catalog. It had no soul. Not a single item was personal. Except...

There was a green envelope on the table. He opened it. A greeting card, some white dog on a red doghouse. Inside, it said, "Best wishes on your birthday, Aunt Pearl." He checked the postmark as the off key notes of a birthday lullaby drifted through his memory. *Davo.* It had been her birthday. The realization, coupled with the impersonal apartment, made him sad for her.

When he peeked in her bedroom — which held no Ethan scent, thank God — an idea occurred to him. Kos had carried Lena's dresser up to his room. Zoey would need clothes too. Because, damn it, once he found her she was not leaving Kaštel again until he could ensure her safety, no matter how bad she wanted away from him. Coming back here would not be an option for her.

Andre found two large suitcases under her bed, each marked with orange ribbons on their handles. He crammed as many of the clothes from her drawers as would fit into one, but hesitated over her underwear. Finally, he threw a handful of pink, nude and black panties on the top. They landed like fallen leaves. At the closet, he filled the second case. Before he zipped it, he realized she would need shoes. Turning back to choose from the pairs on the floor of the closet, he noticed a newly exposed felt hatbox, which had been hidden behind the clothing.

He couldn't resist opening it: a wedding album, rings, some stray photos, a death certificate. She had been a gorgeous young bride, married far younger than most career women those days. Her husband was handsome and impossibly youthful — tall, thin, and smiling. The man's image made Andre feel a million years old. Every snapshot of them showed a friendly intimacy few lovers ever held for long. The contents of the box made him ache for her and for himself.

It shocked him that she'd kept the box. He had burned everything of Mila's; there was only Kos to remind him of her appearance. How did Zoey manage to keep her detachment with all her grief tucked away in the closet?

More importantly, what should he do with the damn thing? Since she could never come back to the apartment, it would be lost to her. That wasn't his decision to make. He found a belt and strapped the box to the smaller suitcase. No other items of sentimental value leaped out at him, so he went out to the street. When it was clear of pedestrians, he bent his knees to launch himself. But his phone rang in his pocket.

"Andre?"

"Who is this?"

"It's Sam Carr, from the Inn."

Andre had a bad feeling. "Sam. What is it?"

"It's your friend, Zoey. She just left here. Something wasn't right."

"Where is she now?"

"I don't know. She asked if she could use the phone to call for a ride. She waited in my office. Just now, two men showed up. She walked with them to the car and got in, but it didn't look right."

Fuck. Ethan and Stephen? He would rip them apart with his fangs. "What did the car look like?"

"Black sedan, heading north."

Away from their headquarters. *Davo.* Where were they taking her?

"Thanks, Sam. Really. Thank you."

Gripping her suitcases, he flew into the air, praying she would survive to wear her clothes again.

Zoey sat in the back seat of the car, her chest so tight that her lungs had no room to expand. Short on oxygen, her brain was a jumble of fears. She was going to die. She would be tortured first.

Then a whisper broke through. If she could think straight, maybe she could save herself. She focused on her breath, slowly bringing down her heart rate. Her body calmed, and ideas formed.

Stephen Bennett had Ethan's build; he was large and fit. She had no chance of overpowering him directly. His weird gold knife pointed at her, but limply. Clearly, he didn't see her as a threat. Maybe she could gain the upper hand.

It was a dangerous move, but anything was better than what they had done to Pedro. If she succeeded in disabling Stephen in the back seat, the driver would have to pull over and she could run for it. The driver was on the downhill side of middle aged and pudgy. She had a fighting chance to outrun him.

Three. Two. One. With her left hand, she grabbed at his knife, while she went for his eyes with her right. He was caught completely off guard. The knife fell to the floor. Her thumb poked into his eye, and he cried out in pain. Hopefully she'd done serious damage.

Her success was empowering, but short lived. As she went for the other eye, he threw her down onto the seat and dug his knee into her belly. He punched her in the side of her head and her ears rang.

"Bitch." Another punch landed, to her jaw that time. "Vampire whore."

Her words rushed out before she could stop them. "Can you blame me? There's no choice at all between Andre and Ethan." It felt good to piss him off, even if it would earn her another blow.

Instead of striking her, Stephen grabbed her breast. "We know what to do with whores, don't we, Mick?" His threat stole her boldness. She imagined herself restrained by the one called Mick, Bennett straining and grunting over her, and it made her stomach twist. She would fight with everything she had not to be used like that.

She flailed her fists but couldn't land a blow against the big man. Her squirms and kicks had no effect. Stephen's eye was red and swelling, but it didn't stop him.

"She's a pretty one, Mick. The boys will have fun with her when we're through."

"Won't Ethan be pissed if we turn her over to the initiates?"

She froze mid-flail. Would Ethan protect her?

Stephen probably sensed her hope; he looked her dead in the eye and said, "Ethan? Now that she's turned vampire whore, he'll enjoy watching."

Like a popped balloon, the fight rushed out of her and she fell back on the seat.

"Is he on his way?"

"Yes, but he said he would be another hour. In the meantime, we'll check into the Motel 6."

"Better gag her. I'll bet she's a screamer. No doubt she's got some fight left in her."

That was good to hear, since it sure didn't feel like she had any left.

"I can think of much better things to do with her pretty mouth." She turned her head, but he gripped her chin roughly, forcing her to see his cruel leer.

If she could stay calm, surely an opportunity would present itself. Could she bargain? Reason? Would they let down their guard again? Unlikely. They pulled off the road into a lot. With Bennett holding her down, she could see the roof of the motel.

As soon as Mick got out of the driver's door, Stephen slithered over her. "Alone at last. Tell me, did you like the way Ethan fucked you?"

She didn't respond, and kept her face bland so she didn't provoke him. Her pride refused to let him see the fear he wanted.

"Maybe you'll like me better, and then Mick, and then me again." He pressed his pelvis against her, unmistakably erect. Minty, antiseptic breath blew across her face. "And if we're not enough for you, then all the kids will surely satisfy."

There must be something she could say to shut him up.

Mick tapped on the window and barked. "Come on."

Stephen hit her again. "You scream and we'll leave you bleeding in that motel room faster than you know what hit you."

Obediently, she walked with them toward the motel. Mick had secured a remote room across the lot from a self-storage place. The other rooms were dark and the parking lot was empty. No one would hear a call for help. Once inside the room, they shoved her in the bathroom and closed the door. It was a relief to be alone.

"Weren't we going to have some fun?" Mick asked, his voice only slightly muffled through the door.

"Ethan will be here soon. I don't want him walking in on us."

It took all of her concentration to just keep breathing.

The television came on loudly. Voices were cut off one after another as someone changed the channel. Finally, one was permitted to continue, the droning anchorman of a news show.

Andre had no news from Bel's crew. It was too damn hard to track a Hunter in a car. That was what it came down to.

"I can't stand waiting. I'm going to fly, look for the car."

"I'll go too," Kos said. "We can cover more ground. And I'll suggest the same thing to Omar. He's been anxious to test his wings."

Over the phone, Omar said he would take the eastern side of the county, sweeping from north to south, because he was already near Santa Rosa in one of the vans. Kos offered to take the coastal side, leaving him the central stretch, in which Kaštel was located. He wasn't hopeful, but he was grateful for something to do. They went their separate ways.

When he left Kaštel, he imagined looking for a black sedan in a haystack. But as he scanned the rush hour traffic from the air, it was so much worse — every twelfth car fit the description.

Twenty miles or so north of Kaštel, a shiny new four-door Toyota was carelessly parked on the side of the highway, its nose protruding into thick brush. He inhaled, trying to catch a hint of Zoey's scent. All he smelled was acrid burning plastic, which alerted him to the smoke curling up from under the hood. To be certain, he landed in a shadow, thudding into the soft earth. A rotund gray-haired man spoke into his cell phone, calmly describing his location. Fury boiled up in Andre and he wanted to rip the door off the car and shake the man for not being Zoey and not being a Hunter. The only thing that stopped him was the decision to reserve the fury for his enemy.

Above an isolated farmhouse, the scent of garlic and butter and Zoey wafted into the sky. But through the kitchen window he spied a woman nothing like his love stirring a pot on the stove. Closer, her smell was similar, but not quite Zoey's natural essence, and his ears told him no one else was in the house. His fury redoubled, and he shrouded himself in a dark shadow before launching himself into the sky once more.

He was almost to the northernmost city of Cloverdale, chilled to the bone, pissed as hell, and scared to death, when his phone rang. Descending abruptly, he hit the ground too hard and jarred his knees. *Please let it be good news.*

"Not sure — faint scent." *Huff, puff.* Omar was out of breath.

Andre gasped for air too. "Where?"

"North side of Santa Rosa —" *huff, puff* "— I'm flying —" *huff* "— Both vans are circling —" *puff* "— We're homing in on something. Hurry. I'll call Kos."

Zoey had to get out before Ethan showed up. Her toes curled at the memory of Pedro's mangled feet. And her captors had threatened far worse.

There was no room on the floor of the cramped motel bathroom. At least it was clean. She stepped into the empty tub, sat down, and tried to make a plan.

She could still hear the television through the door. Each time panic choked her, the blare of the twenty-four hour news cycle was a comforting drone that anchored her in reality—she was okay, for the moment.

She pulled her hair back into a ponytail. Think. How could she get past Bennett and Mick to freedom?

Suddenly the door to the bathroom opened and Mick came in, unbuttoning his pants. Oh, God. This was it. Blood pounded in her ears and she gagged.

He came to stand at the toilet, facing the wall where she leaned. "Relax, bitch. I'm just taking a piss, but, you'll get your turn. Look all you want." She squeezed her eyes closed, likely the reaction he wanted. He laughed and shuffled closer to her as he urinated. As the stream of urine thinned, he darted his hand out and crushed her breast in his thick fingers. When he shook himself dry, he gave her breast another painful squeeze and let go. She refused to cry out, but her eyes teared.

He left. The television still blared. She was still okay.

It was her stupidity that had gotten her kidnapped; only her brains would get her free. If she could get out, there would be help. A motel receptionist or something.

A phone rang and someone turned off the television.

"How long now?"

It had to be Ethan.

"Shit. What should we do with her?"

He must be delayed.

"Let me take her to headquarters. We have defenses there."

Didn't he know Ethan hated to be second-guessed? Stephen wouldn't get anywhere by sniveling.

"I don't like it at all. I feel like I'm trawling with live bait. I don't want to catch sharks."

Did that mean he expected Andre?

Mick said, "Ask him if we can—"

"Shut up. Ethan, hurry. This was a bad idea. As soon as you get here, we've got to leave."

No one spoke again and the television remained quiet. The silence got terrifying fast.

She didn't let herself tremble in the bathtub for long. This was her chance, before Ethan arrived.

She studied the bathroom door. It was standard motel issue: wide, laminated plywood with a levered handle. There was a full half-inch between the beige-on-beige tile and the bottom of the door. If she pressed that lever slowly, the door would probably swing silently over the low pile of the carpet and into the entryway of the room. She would be near the exit, but would have to sneak all the way around the bathroom door to get out.

What would she find on the other side—an escape route or Mick and Stephen ready to pounce? She tiptoed over the tile and gripped the lever as lightly as possible. Pressing down only a millimeter, she listened for squeaks and clicks in the mechanism of the door latch, or for reactions on the other side. Nothing.

The handle went all the way down just as silently. She inhaled with relief, then held the breath for her next task. It was time to crack the door and take a peek.

A mauve bedside lamp filled the room with a jaundiced glow. Mick was nowhere to be seen. Stephen sat on the bed, legs extended and leaning against the headboard. He was cleaning under his fingernails with that bizarre gold-handled dagger, which was way too big for a manicure. The chances were, even in the shadows, if she opened the door wider, he would catch the movement. If she moved very gradually, maybe…

Her pulse hammered. She counted every centimeter. It was just like counting her breaths to ward off a panic attack. Twelve whole inches opened up before her—plenty of room to slip through.

Goose bumps rose up on her arms. Stephen was still engrossed in his nails. She moved her body along the wall slowly. Stephen had hardly budged. Was he too intent on his personal hygiene?

Her best route was clear. She closed the bathroom door. Pressing against the wall, she glided at a snail's past toward the exit. She was almost free—

Something whistled past her head. The dagger, now stuck in the exit door. Deep, chilling laughter rang out and Stephen clapped slowly. "God, that was fun. You looked exultant. I don't know what Marasović told you, but fucking a vampire doesn't make you invisible."

Her eyes flicked to the door. Should she run for it?

"Don't bother. Mick's out there chain smoking with his left hand so he can pull a trigger with his right."

Her hope of escape vanished. She reached for the bathroom door again, to return to the sanctuary of the tub.

Her hand stalled on the handle when Stephen said, "Come here."

"Fuck you."

"If I have to come get you, I'll drag you back to this bed by your pretty hair."

The courage to defy him came easy. Her dusty sandals remained firmly in place. In three long strides, he had his blade in his belt and his hands around her neck. She spat in his face. He didn't bother to wipe the spittle off, but with a shove, he forced her onto the bed and pointed his knife into her chest as if she were a butterfly about to be pinned.

The sharp point bit into her skin and pressed into her sternum. Wet blood spread hot on her shirt.

"Take off your pants," he said.

She looked him in the eye. "Don't you need Ethan's permission?"

He smiled, letting her know the attempt to provoke him had merely glanced off his cruel intentions. "Don't worry. Ethan won't mind sharing. Take off your pants."

"No."

He struggled to hold the dagger and open the button on her jeans, but it was no comfort. Even if she could get away, Mick was right outside and would be happy to provide an extra set of hands. She jerked under Stephen, resisting with her last bit of fight.

Then something changed. First the room cooled. Mick must have come back in. She looked at the door. The Hunter came flying through it and thudded onto the carpet. Behind him, a big scary vampire took up the whole doorway—Omar.

"Let her go," he said.

"I don't think so," Stephen said. "She's all I've got to bargain with."

Andre pushed past Omar, baring his teeth. Expressions of fury and relief warred on his face. "Get the fuck off her."

Stephen kept his dagger poised at her heart while he yanked her to sitting.

"Hunter, you have no options."

"Who do you think taught Ethan to cut? I can have her entire heart in the palm of my hand in ten seconds. And you can't turn her then."

"You may nick a big artery," Andre replied, "but I'll have your entire head in the palm of my hand in five seconds. Then I'll turn her."

"No!" she shouted.

Andre's head jerked to her. His jaw hung loose, and his eyes blazed with some awful emotion. "You would rather die than—"

"Omar, you do it. I mean, if I'm going to die…" She wouldn't have him stuck with her forever in order to save her life.

Andre's face twisted, and she shied away from its raw emotion.

She was in Omar's arms in the next second, and she whipped her head around to find Andre again. He had Stephen and Mick by the scruffs of their neck.

"All right?" Omar stood her on her feet.

"Yeah, I'm all right," she said, but the simultaneous sobs betrayed her bravado. "That was way less than five seconds."

"He was bluffing, to distract them," Omar explained. "They'd never have been able to hurt you."

Andre didn't speak.

"What are you going to do with them?" she asked.

"We have to kill them," Omar replied. "It's the only choice."

In this world, she had to be willing to protect herself. "Let me do it," she said.

"No." Andre took a menacing step toward her.

"What do you mean, no?" she shouted. "You saw—he was going to rape me. They said they'd give me to the other Hunters." Her voice trembled.

The stare between them stretched out. He was deciding something, but she didn't know what. Was he checking for injuries? From the feel of things, her face showed the worst of them. Everywhere his gaze hit her body, she burned with shame. She was a fool.

Abruptly, he severed the stare and dropped Mick. His hands were around Stephen's neck before she saw him move, squeezing the life out of him. As he avenged her, something primal thrilled at the display. And envied it. If she were strong like him, she could protect herself. Would she feel queasy regret to remember this moment later? Maybe.

Omar slung Mick over his shoulder. The fat Hunter's head hung at an unnatural angle.

Andre didn't say anything else. The set of his jaw kept adrenaline pumping, even though she was safe. How angry was he?

"I'll clean up," Omar said. "Kos will be here any second. We'll get rid of the bodies."

A phone rang in Stephen Bennett's pocket. "It has to be Ethan," Zoey said. "If you don't answer, he'll know something's happened."

"I wager he'll know either way," Omar replied. He took the phone out and crushed it under his foot. "But, I'll wait here in case he shows."

Andre stepped closer, crowding her.

"What are you doing?" she asked.

Without answering, he hooked one arm below her bruised breasts and carried her outside, where he pushed off into the air.

"Shit. Andre, put me down." Again, he didn't respond. She closed her eyes so she didn't have to look at the ground. Pressed against him, she could feel the anger coming off him in waves that made her teeth vibrate and her skin itch. His spine was as rigid as a pylon. Worst of all, there was no affection in the way he gripped her.

All she wanted was him curled around her, big arms wrapping her in reassuring warmth. But she wasn't going to get it, because nothing had really changed between them. What right did she have to his comfort, if she wouldn't accept his love?

CHAPTER 38

Andre tried to imagine he was a rocket with steel casing, piercing the midnight blue sky with precision. Or maybe a comet, a ball of ice plummeting through space. Anything other than what he was—a warm-blooded male holding the trembling woman he loved, but who did not want him.

Holding her close, feeling the shudders wracking her body and the tears blown off her face on his, only worsened the sting of her rejection. He wanted to cradle her and promise to protect her forever. But the last time he mentioned forever, she had made it clear she wanted nothing to do with him.

His fangs had not gotten the message, though. It took all his concentration to fly when he could smell her blood and hear it pumping through her veins.

Circling above his house, he located the Hunters' lookouts. But no one moved to attack them as he descended with Zoey and set down lightly in the back of the house.

He could not look at her. Roughly, he dragged her inside by the wrist, the one he had been stroking yesterday when he realized he wanted her stay. *Davo*. He had to get away from her.

Lena rushed to the kitchen door.

"Oh my God. Is she okay?"

"Get a first aid kit and come upstairs to tend to her."

"I'm fine," Zoey said. "I'm not hurt beyond a few bruises."

He ignored her. Picking her up, he carried her like a child.

"Andre, I'm fine. I can walk." She pushed against his chest in protest. Her hands lingered, like she would wrap them around his neck. Then she quickly pulled back and clutched them to her chest instead.

He ground his molars so hard he thought they might actually crack. Useful habit when trying not to bite her.

In her room, he dropped her on her bed and left.

"Incompetent idiots! Do I have to do everything?" Ethan threw his phone onto the dashboard. For a split second, he marveled at his reaction. No woman had ever caused him to lose his temper. Few things did.

Something had gone wrong, and Zoey had slipped from his grasp again.

He clenched the steering wheel. His father had not been paranoid to think she was such tempting bait. Marasović must have a serious hard on for her, and Ethan could not blame him. His mind overflowed with fantasies of breaking his little ice queen until she begged him for mercy, until she submitted to him body and soul. But that would have to wait.

He called the Hunters back to headquarters.

After trying to reach his father for several hours more, Ethan followed Hunter custom—he assumed his father was dead.

In the ramshackle house, he took command of the mission. Dutiful son was a role he'd played easily, but he did not grieve the death of his father. Still, he cast his eyes downward as the Hunters and initiates crowded into the living area.

"Today has been the worst of many unsuccessful days in this difficult operation against Marasović." He tinged his words with false emotion and the compassionate faces around him showed that it rang true. *Perfect.* Could he strike the right tone with the next statement? "My father was a courageous and skilled Hunter, but he called you here against my advice. I knew we weren't ready to attack."

He focused on one face at a time, making sure to touch everyone with his eyes. "None of us expected a shield in place to ward us off Kaštel Estate. Even more unexpected was that two long-exiled vampires retain the ability to fly. There are mysteries that must be solved before we strike at them again."

"You're calling off the operation?" asked one of the initiates, shoulders slumped.

He needed to be his most persuasive, or these kids might start a feeding frenzy. Hunters did not like to go home without a kill. "I'm suspending the operation until I've gathered the knowledge we need to prevail against our enemy. You all are a fine fighting force and I — "

He looked at his shoes, then back up to one eager face. "I hesitate to speak this way about my father, but I attribute the need to retreat to his hasty decisions. You all are not to blame." With the sweep of his hand, he absolved all of them of responsibility.

"I will find a way through that shield and I will discover why Marasović remains powerful enough to fly. With those answers, I have every confidence that we can exterminate him and his household. Those of you who long to earn your daggers will have your chance."

One of the younger initiates whooped at Ethan's promise and several of them began cheering. Their enthusiasm was a drug. He was unstoppable.

"How long will you need?" A question cut into his euphoria. The skeptic was a full-fledged Hunter who looked to be slightly younger than Ethan.

"Derek, right?" The man nodded yes. "I'm not entirely sure, perhaps a month or six weeks. But I won't rush. We need to be prepared to face him next time."

"How do you hope to gain an advantage and solve the mysteries you mentioned?" Derek asked.

Still riding the initiates' excitement, he drew on their energy. He had carefully planned what to reveal — just enough to cause a stir. He wanted their trust. But more than that, he wanted them to spread the word about his research.

"I think the answer to Marasović's persistent power might lie in our past. I've been researching the history of our people and I've uncovered clues about our origins that I plan to explore." He stepped back and dropped his volume. "Now, I'd like some time alone."

Dismissed, the Hunters began to gather their things and plan to depart. An excitement buzzed among the gathering, and again Ethan knew his suspicions were right. The Hunters wanted to know where they came from and if their myths were true. If he could unlock those secrets it would earn him the right to lead them.

More importantly, he needed to know what happened when vampires and Hunters mixed. Because Lucas living in Andre Marasović's household could be a serious problem. He had not expected him to seek protection there. Now there were two people in that house that Ethan needed: Lucas to kill, Zoey to keep. Eventually, he would have to find a way inside. But first, he needed to know the secrets of the codex.

The Hunter Derek approached Ethan. "I'm still curious about the other vampires. I heard the wine contains some kind of message to them. I can follow that trail with Marasović's distributor, if you'd like." It was a logical lead. Ethan needed time with Oliver's translation and the images in the codex. Plus, two other academics knew of the book and he would have to take care of them. Should he delegate the task? A clever face and intelligent golden eyes stared back at him, waiting for an answer.

"Yes. I could use the help." He extended his hand.

Zoey got dumped onto the bed without any ceremony. She didn't want to see Andre's angry back, so she rolled away and curled her knees to her chest. He slammed the door. She shivered, already longing for him to return, even if it had been his fury keeping her warm.

She stood to climb under the covers, and saw two black suitcases on the floor. Each had an orange ribbon tied on the handle. Someone had gone to her apartment—Andre.

A brown felt box captured her attention and she clenched the quilt in her hands. She hadn't seen it in years.

She fell to her knees and unstrapped it from the suitcase. It was heavier than she remembered. When she stood, she teetered forward and the box spilled before she could consider the wisdom of opening it. Her wedding band and Michael's were the last things to fall out. They thumped onto the quilt and she felt it in her chest.

Steeling herself, she flipped a photo over. They sat in crowded booth on her twenty-first birthday, and he was kissing her cheek. Underneath it was a picture from a gray day at the Eiffel Tower. What a sweet boy-turned-man he'd been.

Closing her eyes, she waited for the panic. Surely deep despair was only seconds away. But it never came. She didn't even want to erase him from her memory. In the cold, empty recesses of heart, warmth seeped in.

Lena burst into her room. "Okay, let's get you fixed up."

Zoey jumped. "Lena. Thanks, but it's not necessary. I'm fine."

"You have a huge bruise turning purple across the left side of your face and your lip is split open." Lena held up her first aid kit and a basin. Then, her eyes flicked to the items scattered on the bed. "Zoey, is that your husband?"

Zoey studied her; Lena was about the same age she'd been when Michael died. Her forehead was lined with concern and Zoey softened. "Yeah, that's him. Want to see?"

"Really? Yes, I would love to see."

Zoey put everything back in the box, straightened the quilt, and climbed onto the bed. Then she hesitated. Did she want this? To share?

Lena leaned forward, interested. Her blue eyes were sad, and Zoey trusted them with her past. She patted the spot next to her and laid the wedding album on her lap. "We got married at this funky community center in L.A.," she said, pointing at the first picture.

"How did you meet?"

"In college. Our freshman year."

"You were so young."

She rubbed her thumb over a too bright image of her youthful self. "A lot of people said that."

"Kos told me what happened. I'm so sorry."

"Me too. He was the best man I've ever met." That was fair, right? Since Andre technically wasn't a man.

"Do you miss him?"

"Honestly, I haven't let myself think about him in years. I do miss him, now that I see these pictures. But…"

Gently, Lena touched the corner of the album and the right words came to Zoey. "Really, I miss the optimism I had — that nothing bad could possibly happen."

It would have been perfectly natural for Lena's mouth to pull into one of those forced half-smiles of reassurance. It didn't, and Zoey liked her all the better for it.

"When Michael got sick, it became hard to trust people, to believe they were what they seemed."

"It must have been quite a shock to find out Andre was a vampire."

In the photo, Michael's eyes gleamed, and he stood straight in his tuxedo.

"That was weird for sure, but Andre didn't really change. Not like Michael did."

"Zoey, are you really okay?" Lena asked. "We were all so worried."

"I'll survive," she replied on a sigh. "The whole time, I was hoping Andre would save me, and was pissed off I needed him to."

"Well, it's kind of his fault they're after you."

"Do you think so? I think it's just their fault for being so crazy and evil."

Lena touched her arm. "Let me clean you up, okay?"

Zoey tensed. It had been a long time since anyone had mended her scrapes and bruises. Lena gave her arm a gentle squeeze, and Zoey went soft. God, it might actually feel good to let someone take care of her.

"Yeah, okay."

While Lena filled the basin in the bathroom, Zoey stood and peered into the mirror. Dark circles under her eyes, a puffy lip, and a deep blue bruise that swelled even as she watched — it was worse than she expected. Lena came back with warm, lavender-scented water and Zoey flopped down on the bed.

"Andre is really mad at me," she said.

"Seems like it," Lena said into the side of Zoey's head.

"Does he stay mad for a long time?"

"I don't know. I've never seen him mad before."

Zoey tried to fit that detail into her picture of impulsive Andre.

"Did he really ask you to turn and stay with him?"

Her words were delivered with perfect neutrality and Zoey gave her credit for trying not to pry. "He did."

"Do you love him?"

She squeezed her eyes shut and pictured Michael. "I think so."

"Why did you run away, then?"

As Lena rubbed some kind of salve into her wounds, Zoey kept her eyes closed and pictured that innocent bride. "Because I'm not that girl anymore."

Lena was quiet. She must have heard the question in Zoey's answer. Zoey felt her dab ointment on her lip. Then she lay down next to her and took her hand.

What an odd sensation, not to be alone. Odd and nice. She let emotions swirl through her body, into the long dead places. Every time she felt afraid, she squeezed Lena's hand, and the pressure was returned. Zoey didn't know how much time had passed. It felt like an eternity before she finally decided to talk to him.

She sat up, and Lena rolled onto her side. She said, "I'm going to leave Kaštel. Kos is going to find me a job in another household. But promise me we'll still be friends after I leave. Whether you stay or go."

"I don't have a lot of friends. I'd be very happy to count you among them."

"Good."

"But, do you have to leave? Kos seems to really like you."

"Oh, he's like that with everyone. And this place is toxic to me. I've got to go."

"I hope you find what you're looking for." Zoey had the surprising urge to kiss Lena's cheek. She did, and then climbed off the bed.

She knocked on the golden oak door to his room but there was no answer. Trying the handle, she found it unlocked, and she paused. What would she say? She wanted to make peace with him, to apologize. She wanted him to hold her and coo to her and tell her everything would be okay. But the price of receiving his comfort was eternity.

She closed her eyes and tried to imagine a future with him, but her vision was blank. Without knowing her mind, she went in.

The bedroom was empty and the shower was running. She stepped into the bathroom, enveloped by steam. His huge form was barely visible through the fogged shower stall. Heavy, moist air filled her lungs, suffocating her. Her pulse pounded as loudly as the water rained down. She wanted to run away. But she'd already tried that once and it was no use.

Just being in the room with him stirred in her a riot of longing, and tenderness, and need. She opened her lungs to the thick, hot air, surrendering to it, and the feelings. Neither killed her.

Instead, she felt heavy, her bare feet anchored to the tile floor.

She squinted through the clouded stall, and he came into view. Against the wall, his face was buried in the crook of his arm. Rivulets of water poured down his back.

The small room was suddenly way too hot.

It was a beautiful back, broad and muscled across his shoulders. His powerful ass was a perfectly cut masterpiece. She wanted to touch it, him, so she stepped closer. He was lost in thought, or he would have heard her.

"You found my box of photos," she said.

He turned off the water and reached a long arm around the shower door to grab a black towel. When it was tied around his waist, he came out. Green eyes blazed with fury. Tendons in his neck were raised. His shoulders bunched as if he would pounce on her.

"*Davo,* Zoey. What the hell were you thinking?" He spit the words with quiet fury, and his fangs appeared behind tense lips.

She should have been scared of his hunger, but she only felt the sting of his anger. Shame over her foolishness burned hot on her face. "It was stupid," she whispered. "I know that now. I came to apologize." Then her words spilled out fast, and her voice grew louder. "You have every right to be angry with me. I'm sorry I put you through—"

"Why did you go?"

He deserved the truth. "I was scared."

"Am I that scary?"

She stepped toward him. "Andre, you're not—"

He backed up. "Then you told Omar to turn you. *Omar.* By the gods, Zoey. Why not fuck Ethan Bennett right in front of me?"

"I told him to do it so you wouldn't be stuck with me." She took another step, and he backed against the tile wall.

"Stuck?" His fists flexed into the wall. Two black square tiles cracked into spider webs.

The shatter echoed in the small room and caused her to flinch, but she kept her feet planted on the floor. It was starting to feel like they belonged there.

"*Davo!*" His jaw muscles ground and he wiped his hand across his wet head. "I asked you to bond with me. How could I—"

"I wanted you to have the choice." She reached her hand toward him, and he somehow retreated further, into nonexistent space.

"Zoey, I already chose." He spoke slowly and clearly, as if she was an idiot. "I told you I loved you and you ran away."

Just like Mila. The unspoken words ghosted through her mind.

God, she was an idiot. She'd rubbed salt into his old wound, and now she'd backed him into a corner, or a shower stall, at least, tempting and rejecting him at the same time. She stepped back.

The thick ropes of his shoulders dropped the barest half-inch.

"Do you want to know why I was scared?"

He nodded.

She gulped down another mouthful of heavy air. A shallow wave of grief came first, and then her arms ached for Andre. "Did you look in my box of photos?" she asked.

His eyes seemed so sad. For her or himself? "Yes, I looked."

"I hadn't looked in years."

"I assumed as much. You can't go back to your apartment. I didn't want the box to be lost."

Was it her imagination, or did he come a tiny bit closer?

"I'm not that girl anymore."

"No, you're not. I don't think I would have loved that girl."

The love in his eyes was ancient, sadder, and darker than anything Michael had felt for her. Her knees gave way. He reached for her arm, digging his fingers into flesh to steady her. He grabbed her just like the night they met, when she walked away. Maybe she didn't have to walk away again.

"I shouldn't have left like that. It was stupid."

He dropped his arms, and his anger flared again — bright fireworks in his eyes. "I thought I made it very clear. If you did not want me, I would have left you alone."

"I wasn't running from you. It was the box, the memories…" She was shaking, and light-headed with fatigue, or something. But she wasn't scared. "You saw me after that nightmare, falling apart over the idea of losing you. That's why I left."

There, she'd said it. She let her knees collapse, dropping into an exhausted, cross-legged heap on the floor. She looked up at him, repentant and pathetic. Turning away, he walked to the sink and splashed water on his face. He punched the wall next to the sink again, but not hard enough to crack the tile. He paced the length of the room twice like a pent up lion. He was all anger and power and beauty and pain, and she couldn't take her eyes off him.

He stopped on the far side of the room and faced her. "It has been a century and a half since Mila died, and yesterday I decided I could love again. It would be unreasonable to expect you to do so after only a few years." He blinked at her, with that same ancient longing. "Truly, I understand. But you cannot stay here. Tomorrow, you have to go. Kos will see to it."

She looked at the floor in front of her. A black rug, damp from Andre's wet pacing. "I looked inside the box, at the pictures."

He sighed. "I know, sweet."

It must have been hard for him to be kind, frustrated and hungry as he was. A patient effort expended on her behalf, because he loved her, even if he didn't want to.

"It didn't kill me to look," she said.

"No, love, even humans aren't that fragile. Broken hearts heal." She looked up to see his sad eyes crinkled with kindness. "Yours will, in time." He headed for the door. "I'm going to get dressed. Lena or Kos will see to anything you need."

"If I lost you, it would kill me."

In the door, he came to an abrupt stop and spun to face her, his stare pinning her to the floor.

"I'm very hard to kill."

She stood, pointing at him. "Don't bullshit me. They're Hunting you, and me. If they don't blow us up, you'll still have to run and you'll get sick with the wasting disease."

"All of that is true." In spite of the fateful admission, a quiet hope rang in his words.

She dropped her accusing finger and tugged on her ponytail. "So I'm just saying, if I lose you, it will kill me."

He was rapt, but she wasn't trying to torment him. The words just wouldn't come out whole.

"Zoey. Do not toy—"

The bittersweet hope in his voice squeezed her heart too tight, forcing the words out. "Yes! If you will still have me. Yes."

"You're sure?" His eyes raked her up and down, as if suddenly unsure she was real.

"Yes."

Like a knot of string, his body unwound before her eyes.

Still, his question was tentative. "You understand this is forever?"

"It's all or nothing for me too, baby."

He arched a dark brow. "Baby? It's been millennia since anyone called me that."

She raised both of hers in a challenge. "I think it suits you."

"Do you?" God, his smile melted her, every time. He stepped forward and tucked a strand of her hair behind her ear. "Say it again, Zoey. I need to hear you say the words."

"Bite me, turn me, keep me. All of it. Biting first, please."

He pressed his finger over her mouth, shushing her. "How about you let me be in charge for once?"

Before she could reply he replaced his finger with his lips. He tugged at her shirt and she lifted her arms. Where Bennett had drawn blood, the shirt was stuck to her skin. It pulled off like a Band-Aid and she began to bleed. He licked his thumb and wiped it over her wound. For the briefest second, her skin stung, then knit together.

He reached around her and unhooked her bra. She stood up and slid her jeans and panties off. He lifted her onto the counter and dropped down between her legs.

"Andre, no."

"No?" He nuzzled her inner thigh. "I can't be in charge?"

"No." The heat of a blush crept up her neck. "I mean, don't do that…"

He stood up with a question on his face. Instead of answering she dropped to the ground in front of him.

"My turn."

"Zoey, you don't have to —"

"I want to taste you."

He growled; she was still in charge after all.

Drops of water from the shower still clung to him. Running her tongue along his stomach, she licked them off. She tongued his solar plexus all the way down to his hard length. She licked him from base to tip and he moaned.

A drop of fluid beaded on him and a question formed on her lips. "Andre, if I become a vampire can I have a baby?"

His fingers stilled in her hair. "No, love. Vampires are infertile."

"What about Bel?"

"It was something Mila worked out. I don't know how she did it. But, Zoey, she wasn't a vampire. That's why she could have a baby." He tugged her up to standing. "Do you want to be a mother?"

She flattened her hands on his chest and looked him in the eye. "Not really. When Michael got sick, I stopped wanting that."

He put his palm against the side of her face and stroked her cheek with this thumb. "Because if you do, we could wait. There is someone I can ask." She let him cradle her head, and he brushed his thumb on her lower lip. "It is possible I could give you a ba—"

"No. Let's do it now." Then she remembered crimson blood flowing from his wrist. "Maybe someday I'll be a mother the way you're Pedro's father. But I want you to turn me right away."

"Thank you." He leaned in to kiss her mouth, but she turned her head and whispered into his ear.

"Now stop interrupting me."

She kissed down his chest and stomach again while gripping him. Then she took him in her mouth as far as she could.

He groaned, and his knees buckled into her chest. She opened her eyes to see him gripping the counter. His reaction was thrilling, but when she looked up to see his fangs descending she could hardly wait. Soon, she would find out just what those babies could do.

"Zoey." His "Z" sounded funny, with his tongue against his extended canines. "We need to move this to my bed."

"I want to make you come."

"No. It's time for biting."

Her body hummed at his words. He was in charge again. For the moment.

Andre didn't wait for Zoey to agree. He picked her up and carried her to the bed. Tossing her on it, he dropped to all fours above her and kissed her. Her tongue explored his fangs without hesitation.

Still, he worried. Did she understand that this was his forever, not human forever? He dominated her lips and her tongue, licked every surface inside her mouth. She groaned into his throat and, for once, lay back submissive. It seemed too good to be true.

Her dark hair was a halo on the pillow. He smoothed it off her brow and touched her neck. There was still a smear of dried blood on her sternum. Its smell made his pulse race with his hunger for only her.

"When I bite you, love, there's no going back. You will belong to me. You will become a part of my every cell. I will never let you go. Tell me you understand."

He watched her mouth, waiting for her response. It didn't come. Until her breasts tightened, and her back arched a little. Damn. She licked her lips.

Saliva flooded his mouth, and he swallowed. She looked sure. But he wanted her to say it. He raised his eyebrows, beckoning her.

She rolled her hips against him and tilted her head, exposing a long neck the color of honey and cream. She smelled even better, like musk and metal and Zoey. Her finger trailed from her jaw to her collarbone a little too slowly. His little vixen was teasing him.

"*Davo.* Zoey, answer me."

She laughed and arched up to plant a kiss on his lips. "Andre, I understand."

A word came to him. Whole. With her love, he wasn't broken anymore.

With his face against the soft skin of her neck, the scent of her fear lingered. If he had his way, she would never be afraid again. The instinct to protect her opened his jaw, and he slid his fangs into her tender flesh.

Once her artery was pierced, he withdrew his fangs and hot blood filled his mouth. She released a long sigh, and already threads of the bond formed, allowing him to sense her pleasure in his mind. Her bright, rich flavor made him come on her belly.

"Andre?"

He pulled away from her neck only long enough to say, "Yes, you taste that good."

She giggled. What a sweet, girlish sound. He wouldn't have thought she had it in her.

He took several long pulls on her neck and his brain tingled as a spider web of connections formed, linking their every cell in the eternal bond. She went limp beneath him from the bite's relaxing effect. The nascent bond meant that he felt it too, deep in his core. Wet and hot, her tongue was suddenly in his ear — the oral urges had hit. An instant later, the urges echoed in his mouth and he circled the punctures on her neck with his tongue.

"Damn, Andre, I feel amazing."

Every square inch of his skin thrummed with her pleasure. Amazing was right, and hearing her say so made it even better. He cupped her chin and slipped a finger in her mouth. She sucked on it hard, making him remember her mouth on him.

Her nipples pearled against his chest and his own skin blazed with sensitivity as he sensed her response to the bite.

He caressed her belly, and the muscles of his abdomen quivered. He stroked her breasts, and his nipples tightened. He rubbed her thighs, and his knees went weak, each caress resounding in him because of the bond. And her love burned like a hot coal inside him. His cock strained, his balls tightened, but mostly his heart thundered out his joy.

He teased over the sensitive flesh between her legs with feather-light strokes and she spread herself, wrapping her hand around his length. He shuddered, feeling his own rigid erection through her excited reaction.

"You never get tired, huh?" she asked.

Latched onto her neck, his lips tried to smile. He didn't want to take too much of her blood, so he licked her wounds closed, and giving his lips free rein, he looked down into her face. "I have yet to find the limit of my stamina."

Her dark eyebrows rose adorably. "Is that a challenge?" she asked.

"A promise."

Suddenly, her desire hit him full force. When she guided him into her, he couldn't have resisted if Hunters barged in the room. The tether of the bond put them in perfect rhythm, and they came together quickly. Her last delicious spasm finished, and he settled his weight on her. It was another promise. He was not going anywhere.

CHAPTER 39

Zoey closed her eyes and let Lena tug her arms up. The bodice of the dress drew tight around her bruised breasts. She tried to imagine Andre waiting in his room, with Kos, Bel, Susan, and Ally to keep him company. Lucas was there too. He was a friend from her old life, and so she'd insisted, even if he didn't believe he was welcome.

"I'm so glad we're keeping to the old customs," Lena said.

Zoey opened her eyes and peeked at her reflection. "You promised they would comfort Andre," she replied. The dress Lena had found was too big and too white. Pedro stepped forward and shooed Lena away, gathering extra fabric in his hands.

"Is this supposed to be like a wedding dress?" Zoey asked.

"Yes, and a shroud," Lena replied.

"That's not very comforting."

Pedro went gray, but didn't speak. Apparently he didn't have any words of comfort either.

"Then go with the wedding idea. It's a purity thing. Starting a new life with a clean slate."

"A rebirth," Zoey said, just like when she emerged from the tunnel, free from her saddest memories.

"Exactly. And you have to die first for one of those." Lena's eyes found Zoey's in the mirror. Again, she didn't offer treacly reassurance, but a firm nod.

Suddenly, all white teeth and glittering gold eyes, Pedro said, "Ladies, let's focus on the important things. You'll never get old and you get to have super-hot bitey sex all the time." He'd learned about the perks of his new life from Kos.

"I know. It's totally unfair. I've been waiting for super-hot bitey sex my whole life," Lena said, playfully shoving Zoey's shoulder.

She couldn't quite laugh, though she was grateful for their jokes. She needed the distraction. Her stomach roiled, and she wanted to pace, but her case of the nerves was nothing like her anxiety attacks. Normal, pre-vampire-turning jitters, she assumed, but she had no idea how to handle them since she couldn't numb out the way she used to. It was time to say goodbye to Zen Zoey. Probably a good thing, although she wouldn't mind a little bit of the old calm at the moment.

Pedro snapped and pointed at a pincushion, Lena handed it to him. Expertly, he began pinning the dress. Zoey's waist suddenly appeared in the mirror.

"Pedro, where did you learn to alter a dress?" she asked.

"Drag bar in Buenos Aires."

"Really?" Lena's eyes went wide.

"No." He shook his head with a smile, keeping his eyes trained on the dress. "My mother taught me."

"What do you think you'll miss the most, Zoey?" Lena asked. "The sun?"

"Yes. And bourbon. And coffee," Zoey replied.

"What about food? Pedro, do you miss it?"

"Not that much. Although sometimes, like when I smell your scones baking." He stood behind Zoey, and shortened her straps. "I know what you'll miss most, Zoey." He looked at her in the mirror and wiggled his eyebrows.

It took her a moment to get it. The jerk was teasing her about when the vampires overheard her masturbating. "Oh shut up!" She swatted at him to cover her embarrassment and a strap came un-pinned. "Andre assures me I won't need to do that anymore. So now you're the one who's not getting laid." She stuck her tongue out at him.

"I'm afraid this is as good as it gets," Pedro said, stepping back to look at Zoey.

It wasn't bad at all, she had to admit.

"You look lovely." Lena's smile was genuine as she pulled Zoey's hair back over her shoulders.

"She's all yours," Pedro said to Lena, who offered Zoey her arm and led her out of the yellow room.

Her bare feet pattered on the wooden floor. She was about to become a vampire, to give up food and sun and isolation for an eternity with Andre. And there was no second guessing. It seemed her subconscious had made peace with her happy ending after all.

"You okay? Getting cold feet?" Pedro asked.

Zoey had started this adventure almost a week ago in Ethan's apartment with cold feet. "Nope."

"Who's going to feed you?" he said in a whisper, as they neared Andre's room.

"Lena volunteered, but I think she needs a break from being food for a while." She squeezed the younger woman's arm, and Lena placed her hand over Zoey's.

"Susan offered," Lena said. "For a householder, it's a great honor."

And then they were at the bedroom door, looming in the shadows at the end of the hallway.

Lena knocked and raised her voice. "I bring Zoey Porter, bonded of Andre Maras, for her turning."

Zoey watched Lena say the strangely formal words, then glanced at Pedro, who rolled his eyes. She almost managed a smile. The door swung open, and Andre's room was bathed in light.

When she walked in, wearing a dress that didn't quite fit, his heart leaped. Lena told her to lie down on the bed.

In Croatian, Kos said the traditional words for turning a human into a vampire. Andre had forgotten how beautiful they were.

Bel translated for Zoey. "It's a bunch of nonsense about rebirth."

"Be quiet, Bel," Kos said. "Zoey, it's a blessing for the turn. It means that we will be with you as you end one life and begin another, we promise to help you, and we welcome you."

With the words in mind, Andre rallied his courage. The morbid ritual was downright frightening when you loved the person you were turning. He would have to remove almost all of Zoey's blood in order for her body to accept his. The memory of the pleasure they had shared last night brought him comfort; his bite would subdue her body as it was drained of blood. And through their new bond, her pleasure would soothe him too.

Andre laid himself down on the bed next to her. She smiled a nervous smile for him. "You're really sure?"

"Stop asking me. I'm all yours."

When it was time to bite her, the act seemed newly intimate and he wished they were alone.

Zoey must have sensed it. "It's okay. Pretend they aren't here," she said. The words were meant to calm him, but she seemed more at ease herself, once she said them.

He licked her neck where her pulse fluttered. Biting her warm skin, he immediately began taking long draws of her blood. He wanted the whole thing over as quickly as possible.

She responded to the bite even more intensely than the night before. Body limp. Skin on fire. Tongue searching. Wet between her legs. Her arousal soothed them both until she was unconscious and he was in a stupor caused by her blood and her pleasure pulsing through him.

"Now, Father!" Kos roused him.

Kos took Andre's wrist and sliced it open with a small wide blade, made to stay in his flesh and keep the wound bleeding. Andre let his blood flow into her mouth, which was held open by Kos. The sight disturbed him until he remembered she'd found it beautiful. He tried to see it through Zoey's eyes as he watched her color return and the fine lines around her lips and eyes smooth away. He would miss them; they were a reminder that she was a woman, not the girl who had married Michael all those years ago. A small scar on her forehead disappeared and he worried that pretty birthmark on her ass might too.

Her breath was coming evenly now, and her eyes fluttered open. Zoey was reborn a vampire. He inhaled deeply. As an immense wave of relief washed over him, his joints loosened and his muscles melted. His heart buzzed with an unfamiliar feeling—joy? Perhaps even ecstasy. His loneliness was over; he belonged to her, and she to him.

"Okay?" he asked, though he could see she was.

"I feel incredible."

He wanted her to himself, but Lena offered Zoey a hand and pulled her to standing. One by one, everyone hugged her and congratulated him. Susan sat next to Zoey on the bed and offered her neck. Guided by her new instincts, she fed easily.

Susan kept her laughing eyes on Andre the whole time. Her smirk said she wanted him to know how much she enjoyed being his mate's first meal. When Zoey licked her wounds closed, he helped Susan to her feet and whispered, "Don't get any ideas."

She winked and led Ally out of the room.

They were finally alone, and Zoey sank into the bed, glad for the quiet and its softness.

"I have something for you." Andre sounded pleased with himself as he pulled a silk pouch from behind the pillow. "A birthday present, of sorts, though it is yours by right."

"Birthday? How did you—?"

"I saw the card from your Aunt Pearl. It made me sad not to have known." He touched her cheek with the pad of his finger before he tipped the contents of the small bag into her hand.

A plain brass key tumbled out, and her heart stuttered.

"Is this...?"

"The front door. Absurdly small for such a big door, don't you think?"

She couldn't breathe, couldn't speak. With awe, she held the key between her finger and thumb and examined the stripes on both sides while her pulse slowed to normal. She let the silence go on too long, and Andre tensed beside her on the bed.

"*Davo.* It's not enough. There will be a ring, jewels, anything you want. But, there was no time. I just thought—"

"Andre, you thought right. It's the best gift I've ever received."

The relief on his face was adorable, and she cupped his chin and smiled up at him.

He pulled her to sit between his legs, and she leaned against him.

"Will it feel the same, if we bite each other now?"

"Better, I have been told. But I do not know firsthand. No one has bitten me since I was turned."

"So I get to pop your vampire cherry?"

He laughed and hugged her against him tighter. "I suppose you could say that."

"I have another question."

"Go ahead."

"Remember our first night together in your office?"

"Every single second."

"Can we try more of that naughty stuff?"

"I was hoping you would ask. But first, let's —"

She was already on her knees facing him. She parted her lips and kissed him gently. He slipped his tongue in her mouth and examined her new teeth.

Pulling back, he said, "Zoey, love, these are very sexy."

"Good. I know just what to do with them." She licked his neck because she wanted to taste and feel his skin; he didn't need help healing. Then she slowly slid her fangs into his neck. He gasped and she pressed her body up against him. With the first swallow of his blood, a jolt of sensation overwhelmed her brain. Lightning went off behind her eyes. His feelings and desires were inside her as if they were her own.

Seconds passed as she grew accustomed to the bond. And then, his blood in her mouth was like a liquid orgasm pouring down her throat.

When he latched on to her neck, drawing down swallows of her blood at the same time, Zoey felt him inside her as pure pleasure. He was inside her every cell. His mind in her mind. His heart in her heart. And he would never slip through her fingers again.

EPILOGUE

Two Weeks Later

Zoey straightened the tablecloth on the banquet sized dining room table, pleased to finish the final touch. Her arrangements for the launch party were complete. She took her ponytail down and shook her hair out. Her whirlwind PR project was over, and after two weeks, it was time to celebrate the new brand.

She found Andre next door in the parlor. Excitement skittered across her skin. His green eyes drank in her appearance, and she could feel his hunger for her in her own belly. He broke the gaze, and she shook off his pull. They'd gotten stuck looking at each other for hours the day before, and right now they had a party to host.

Looking at his lapel, he said, "I cannot believe so many people said they'd come. You're a miracle worker." He picked a piece of non-existent lint of his jacket.

"Nervous?"

"I haven't been around this many people since I left Croatia."

Kos strolled in and said, "Guests arriving in thirty minutes. I need a glass of wine."

"Me too," Zoey said.

Andre poured three glasses and passed them out.

"To the homeland," Kos said.

"To Blood Vine," Andre replied. His voice deepened with pride — he liked her name for his wine. From toes to scalp, her body heated.

She raised her glass to them.

After he took a sip, Kos turned on the stereo. With Lena's help, he had imposed a song on the happy couple: George Gershwin's "Our Love is Here to Stay." Andre wasn't a fan, but Zoey didn't mind, especially when Kos played Ella Fitzgerald's rendition. As Ella's voice filled the room, Andre surprised her by wrapping his arms around her and shuffling her in a little dance step.

"You're dancing?"

"Any excuse to touch you." He nuzzled her neck, sending shivers of anticipatory pleasure down her spine.

"Why do you need an excuse?"

The doorbell rang, and Kos left the parlor to answer it with Andre and Zoey trailing behind. A delivery person held an enormous flower arrangement.

Andre came to a sudden halt. "Did you order those?"

"No."

"They're Dalmatian Irises. They only grow in Croatia," he said.

"That's right. We had them flown in this morning," the delivery woman said.

Zoey signed for the flowers as Andre opened the envelope. Inside were a card and a folded piece of paper.

He read it aloud: "Congratulations on Blood Vine. Very good news for all of us. We need to talk. I'll be there soon, Uta. P.S. Say hello to the halfling for me."

"Who's Uta?" Zoey asked.

"She's the oldest vampire I know. An old friend, I guess you could say," Andre replied.

"Friend is perhaps an overstatement," Kos said.

Bel walked into the room. "Did you say Uta? What does she want?"

"So, who's the halfling?" Zoey asked at the same time.

"Did she call me that?" Bel snatched the card out of Andre's hand and snarled. "What a bitch."

Kos looked intently at the paper Uta had sent. "Holy shit."

Zoey jerked her head to look at him. His fair complexion went white, and he handed the paper to Andre. Andre's teeth clacked shut, and his molars rubbed together loudly.

"What is it?" Bel and Zoey asked at the same time.

"It's a color photo of an ancient Greek text, with illustrations," Kos said.

"What does it say?"

"I don't know. My Greek is pretty rusty. It's the illustration that's got my attention." He handed it to Zoey to examine. Behind her, Bel stepped close so he could look over his shoulder.

On the page was a gruesome illustration of a battle. Men were fighting with heavy swords. All the men had yellow-gold eyes. Half also had fangs, exaggerated in length by the rudimentary drawing. It was a battle between Hunters and golden-eyed vampires, and they fought under a bright yellow sun.

Acknowledgments

I have been blessed with an amazing cadre of encouraging, helpful friends during the process of writing *Blood Vine*. My first fantasies of being published included the chance to thank them from the depths of my heart, so here goes. Sincerest thanks to my very first writing partner Jim Ludwig; to beta reader extraordinaire Emily Mellott; consultant on all things m/m Will Hocker; "chemistry" consultant Salying Wong; and the two best writing friends a girl could have—Jess Russell and Celia Breslin. Most importantly, I thank my husband, who helped me squeeze time out of stone so that I could follow my heart into writing this novel.

ABOUT THE AUTHOR

Amber Belldene grew up on the Florida panhandle, swimming with alligators, climbing oak trees and diving for scallops…when she could pull herself away from a book. As a child, she hid her Nancy Drew novels inside the church bulletin and read mysteries during sermons — an irony that is not lost on her when she preaches these days.

With a B.A. in comparative religion and an M.A. in theology, Amber is a Christian minister and student of religion. She believes stories are the best way to explore human truths. Some people think it is strange for a minister to write romance, but it is perfectly natural to Amber. She believes the human desire for love is at the heart of every romance novel and God made people with that desire.

Amber is addicted to vampire stories, but loves to read all kinds of romance and literature. Her favorite books examine history and cultural origins, like Neal Stephenson's *Baroque Cycle*, Anita Diamant's *The Red Tent*, or Salman Rushdie's *The Satanic Verses*. And, yes, she was named after that Amber, of the classic romance novel *Forever Amber*.

From the wine country of Sonoma County to the foggy neighborhoods of San Francisco, all of Amber's fiction is set in Northern California, where she lives with her husband and two children.

→Young Adult←

Shades of Atlantis and *The Ember Series: Ember* and *Iridescent* by Carol Oates
Breaking Point by Jess Bowen
Life, Liberty, and Pursuit by Susan Kaye Quinn
Embrace by Cherie Colyer
Destiny's Fire by Trisha Wolfe
Streamline by Jennifer Lane
Reaping Me Softly by Kate Evangelista

→Historical Romance←

Cat O' Nine Tails by Patricia Leever
Burning Embers by Hannah Fielding

→Erotic Romance←

Becoming sage by Kasi Alexander
Saving sunni by Kasi & Reggie Alexander
The Winemaker's Dinner: Appetizers and *Entreé*
by Dr. Ivan Rusilko & Everly Drummond

→Anthologies and Singles←

A Valentine Anthology including short stories by Alice Clayton, Jennifer DeLucy,
Nicki Elson, Jessica McQuinn, Victoria Michaels, and Alison Oburia

It's Only Kinky the First Time by Kasi Alexander
Learning the Ropes by Kasi & Reggie Alexander
The Winemaker's Dinner: RSVP by Dr. Ivan Rusilko
The Winemaker's Dinner: No Reservations by Everly Drummond
Big Guns by Jessica McQuinn
Concessions by Robin DeJarnett
Starstruck by Lisa Sanchez
New Flame by BJ Thornton
Shackled by Debra Anastasia
Swim Recruit by Jennifer Lane
Sway by Nicki Elson
Full Speed Ahead by Susan Kaye Quinn
The Second Sunrise by Hannah Downing
The Summer Prince by Carol Oates
Whatever it Takes by Sarah M. Glover
Clarity by Patricia Leever
Glimpse of Light by Jennifer DeLucy

www.ingramcontent.com/pod-product-compliance
Lightning Source LLC
Chambersburg PA
CBHW020353120726
47904CB00002B/543